"Do not come closer, MacTavish!"

He scowled, baffled, and who could blame him? Her own emotions felt raw. "What is this then, Megs?" he asked.

"This . . ." She raised the blade slightly. ". . . I am told, is a dagger."

"Tell me the truth, lass. Tell me who you are."

"My name—"

"Spare me *that* tale."

" 'Tis not a tale!"

"Nay, 'tis a lie straight out, lass, and I tire of it."

She said nothing. Indeed, she was certain she could not, for his chest was bare and so hopelessly alluring that she felt lost in feral feelings. Suddenly he was there, inches in front of her, with an arm around her back and a fist wrapped around her knife hand. In a moment she was disarmed. Her head fell back unnoticed. Her breath came hard. He kissed her once, took the knife, and left the room.

She stood dazed. Good Lord, what was wrong with her? One thing, and one thing only, was clear.

She had to escape and it had to be soon. . . .

Other **AVON ROMANCES**

CHEROKEE WARRIORS: THE LONER *by Genell Dellin*
THE CRIMSON LADY *by Mary Reed McCall*
KISS ME QUICK *by Margaret Moore*
ONCE HE LOVES *by Sara Bennett*
A SCANDALOUS LADY *by Rachelle Morgan*
SOARING EAGLE'S EMBRACE *by Karen Kay*
TO MARRY THE DUKE *by Julianne MacLean*

Coming Soon

ALL MEN ARE ROGUES *by Sari Robins*
ONCE A SCOUNDREL *by Candice Hern*

And Don't Miss These
ROMANTIC TREASURES
from Avon Books

LONDON'S PERFECT SCOUNDREL *by Suzanne Enoch*
LOVE WITH A SCANDALOUS LORD *by Lorraine Heath*
STEALING THE BRIDE *by Elizabeth Boyle*

ATTENTION: ORGANIZATIONS AND CORPORATIONS
Most Avon Books paperbacks are available at special quantity discounts for bulk purchases for sales promotions, premiums, or fund-raising. For information, please call or write:

Special Markets Department, HarperCollins Publishers, Inc., 10 East 53rd Street, New York, N.Y. 10022–5299.
Telephone: (212) 207-7528. Fax: (212) 207-7222.

LOIS GREIMAN

THE PRINCESS AND HER PIRATE

AVON BOOKS
An Imprint of HarperCollinsPublishers

AVON BOOKS
An Imprint of HarperCollins*Publishers*
10 East 53rd Street
New York, New York 10022-5299

Copyright © 2003 by Lois Greiman
ISBN: 0-06-050282-7
www.avonromance.com

First Avon Books paperback printing: July 2003

Avon Trademark Reg. U.S. Pat. Off. and in Other Countries, Marca Registrada, Hecho en U.S.A.
HarperCollins® is a registered trademark of HarperCollins Publishers Inc.

Printed in the U.S.A.

10 9 8 7 6 5 4 3 2 1

To Beverly Greiman,
the most elegant woman I have ever known.
Thanks for everything you've given me.

Chapter 1

Portshaven, Teleere
In the year of our Lord 1817

"**L**ook there. Ain't that the biggest ass you ever seen?" Ralph asked, and pointed gleefully over the heads of his shipmates.

Not daring to glance right or left lest her stomach spew forth its dubious contents, Tatiana Octavia Linnet Rocheneau, crown princess of Sedonia, kept her eyes strictly on the balding head of the passenger ahead of her. She could not help but wonder, however, if some Teleerian maid should be mightily offended or if, perchance, there was a prize-winning donkey upon the blessed terra firma they had almost reached. 'Twas impossible to guess with the giant called Ralph. Indeed, hiring him was near the pinnacle of folly. But boarding this leaky tub was surely the worst mistake of all. She hated the sea. When she returned to Sedonia, she would ride astride for a week and never board a ship again.

The waves slapped hard against the ship's weathered

sides. Beneath her feet, the *Melody* heaved and groaned. Tatiana's stomach did the same.

"Ahh." Ralph sighed and shook his oversized head, apparently oblivious to the sickening roll of the ship. "Makes me 'appy just to think of the things I could do with an ass like that."

Behind her, a plump woman with two whining children jostled her. The mother smelled of garlic, the children of things Tatiana dared not consider. Her stomach heaved again, but she controlled it as she controlled all things, with a stiffened backbone and dogged determination. They would be disembarking in a moment, leaving the wretched vessel behind forever. She focused on that thought and that thought alone. Not the gilded gifts hidden in her deceptively worn leather bag, not the milling docks of Portshaven, and not the man she had traveled nearly two hundred leagues to meet. Just now all she needed was to reach a place of privacy before her stomach betrayed her, plummeting her to the level of her strong-smelling shipmates.

The *Melody* bucked. Tatiana swallowed hard and closed her eyes against the roiling misery.

"Aye, she was the finest ass I ever 'ad, she was." Ralph sighed, and Tatiana realized somewhat belatedly that her hired bodyguard may well have been waxing nostalgic about his long-lost burro for quite some time, but in that moment he noticed her expression. "You unwell, missus?" he asked. He'd called her that from the first, though she'd ordered him more than once to refer to her as Mrs. Mulgrave, or Widow Mulgrave. Or even Linnet, if he must. But Ralph was something like an upset boulder. Once he was set on a path it was difficult to change his course. Still, "missus" was better than some things he might call her if he knew the truth. If he knew she was a crown princess incognito, with a paid impostor on the throne.

"Yer lookin' a mite green about the gills there, missus. If'n yer gonna vomit, 'twould be best if you made yer way to the rail."

She gritted her teeth. "I am not about to—" She paused to swallow and squeeze her eyes closed again.

" 'Tis naught to be ashamed of, missus, and you'd feel the better for it."

She didn't respond. Didn't dare.

Ralph elbowed her with a chuckle. She bounced off his arm, ricocheting into a stout man holding a speckled chicken. It squawked its offense and fluttered wildly while its owner cuddled it to his chest and glared at her from beneath his frayed cloth cap.

"Yer a tough little acorn despite yer wee size, ain't you, missus?" Ralph asked.

She suppressed a groan and reminded herself that while Viscount Nicol might be one of the few advisors she trusted without question, he had not chosen this particular guard for either his wit or his charm. Ralph had fists the size of draught-horse shoes and shoulders like battering rams. He'd been hired to stave off trouble, but thus far he'd not managed to do a thing about the battle that roiled like a summer storm between her breast and her pelvis.

"I am not"—she gritted her teeth and swallowed again— "little."

The deck of the *Melody* shifted wildly. She focused on the horizon, but not a soothing blade of grass could be seen. Indeed, nothing but lumbering crowds and tilting buildings met her gaze.

" 'Ey," he exclaimed. "There's that ass again. I can see 'er ears." He laughed happily. "P'raps I could 'ire 'er so as you could ride in style to yonder abbey." He sighed. "I bet she'd give you a 'ell of a fine . . ." he began, but at that moment the man ahead of her stepped onto the plank, leaving a bit of space between them and drawing all her attention to a lovely wisp of air that feathered with blessed gentleness across her face. She gulped it in, but in a second it was gone, stifled by the host of bodies jostling toward shore.

"Me uncle Toddle 'ad 'im an ass once, though 'e weren't near so big as that lady's—"

"Cease!" she gritted. "Cease talking about the lady's ass." Perhaps her words were a bit louder than necessary, but Ralph's expression was as placidly mild as ever. She sensed the other passengers turning toward her, however, and felt certain their hideous odors increased with their misplaced attention. Remembering her intention of remaining unnoticed, she forced a smile and lowered her voice. "Please."

"Poor little missus," Ralph said, and chuckled to the crowd that pressed in on them like so much spoiled barley. "Not her usual jolly self, she ain't."

Perhaps he was mocking her, for she was not inclined toward jolliness even on her best of days. And perhaps Nicol was correct, she might not be as patient with others as she should be. But she tried to be fair, even to those who stank like rank hounds, which every passenger on this leaking tub surely did.

The thought made her feel light-headed.

"Have you got my trunk?" she asked, changing the subject as she pushed her thoughts from the odors and risked dire consequences to turn toward the giant.

"Got it right 'ere." He hoisted the leather-bound receptacle onto his shoulder like another might lift a lute, then nodded toward the solid earth beyond. "Way's clear."

She glanced ahead and found with breathless relief that he was correct. She stumbled onto the plank, shambled down the dock, and blessedly, miraculously, reached the firm soil of Teleere. Her head swam at the sudden cessation of movement. Her stomach boiled, but she straightened her back and glanced about. There was little to see, for bodies milled around her like living eels, pushing and shoving and cutting off any hope of a better view. She tried to lever her way through, but it was impossible. She was surrounded in a sea of reeking peasantry.

"We're to make our way to the abbey," Ralph said, above the ebb and flow of the din.

She knew he was right, but she was mired in humanity and could see nothing but bobbing bosoms and lumbering backs.

Behind her, Ralph shuffled his gargantuan feet. "This ain't no good place for a lady, missus," he said. "Best not to be dawdling 'ere."

She tried to shoulder her way between two sailors, but they were drunk and loud and tipped her off-balance, leaving her unsteady in their wake. The movement did nothing to still the turmoil in her stomach.

"'Ere then, let Ralph 'ave a go," he said, and, stepping around her, thrust the crowd aside like so many grains of sand. For a moment a draft of almost fresh air washed over her. She gloried in it, feeling her knees weaken. "You'd best keep up," Ralph rumbled, and she tightened her grip on her valise and hurried after him.

He waded through the mob. She tried to stay close, but the scent of hot apple tarts melded sickeningly with body odor and rotting mackerel. Her stomach knotted, bending her double.

"Missus." Ralph appeared before her again. Or rather, his stained knee breeches appeared. "We'd best be off."

She gritted her teeth. She was not about to vomit in front of a servant. She was not! But at that moment, her throat filled up. "Go away!" she snarled.

"What's that, missus?"

She swallowed hard, shivered at the bitter effects, and straightened as best she could. "Go find the abbey."

He shook his great head as if baffled and unhappy in equal measures. "I was told strict not to leave you, missus. And I follows me orders."

She straightened her back with a jolt. Her stomach twisted up like a sailor's knot, but she ignored it. "And I am ordering you otherwise. Do you understand me? This is a roy—" She almost lost control. But she didn't. "I've no time for delays. You will find the shortest route to the abbey and you will return for me posthaste."

"But missus—"

"Now!" she commanded.

He nodded with obvious uncertainty and turned away.

Tatiana closed her eyes and willed her stomach to last a few seconds longer. Her upper lip was moist, and her head was swimming with the effort. But a tavern stood just a few yards away. It was a shabby place to be sure, but it would afford her some privacy—a place to deposit the contemptible contents of her stomach. She stumbled toward the tilted door of the ramshackle inn. But the earth shifted beneath her feet, seeming to throw her off-balance. She careened toward the corner and laid a hand upon the rough wattle and daub. It felt cool beneath her palm. She leaned into it, pressing her cheek against the solid surface. Behind her, a man made a disparaging remark about her condition. His companion chuckled. She longed to confront them with the truth, but she dared not turn, dared not challenge her fragile system, for she was better here, her stomach somewhat settled, her face cooled against the coarse siding.

She sighed, and in that instant of relaxation, her valise was wrenched from her hand. The force of the motion spun her about like a child's top—yanking her off-balance and onto her knees. She cried out in shock, but her bag was already gone, whisked through the crowd by a ragged, darting figure.

"No," she muttered in disbelief. No one tried to help. She scrambled to her feet. "Stop him! I command you to stop him!" Not a soul turned to comply, but the crowd was as thick as London fog, barring the small thief's way. He clawed at their backs, fighting to get through, and in that moment she saw her chance. Snatching up her drab skirts, she lurched after him. He turned in a panic, his face soiled, his eyes wide, and she almost had him, but at the last instant, the crowd murmured and broke. He skimmed between two elderly men, darting into the mob.

There was nothing she could do but give chase, past the laughing maid with the goat, over the drunken sod. A dappled horse reared, thrashing huge hooves above the thief's head. He cowered away, and she took that opportunity to lunge at him. But her equilibrium was still unsteady, and she tottered sideways, careening into a man with a cane. He cursed and swung at her, striking her on the shins. She leapt away. A hound snapped at her heels, latching on to her billowing skirts. She pivoted about, grasping her gown in both hands and swinging the mutt off its feet. It let go with a whine, and she swiveled toward the thief. He was some rods ahead now, but still slowed by the crowd. So she bolted after him, rapidly covering the distance where the mob was thinner.

Her lungs ached in her chest, but in a moment she was upon the narrow robber. Her fingers skimmed his ragged tunic. But suddenly the crowds opened and he dashed through. She stumbled after him, tumbling into a solidly built man and tottering backward. He caught her, his hands tight upon her upper arms.

"Careful there or you'll—" he began, then stopped short as his grip tightened around her biceps.

"The devil!" he hissed.

She jerked back, startled as much by the intensity in his deep blue eyes as by his daring to touch her. "Unhand me!"

But he didn't. Indeed, his grip tightened and with that a smile lifted his lips. "So my luck holds," he said and laughed. "Another thief caught."

She glared up at him, trying to catch her breath, her wits, to decipher this turn of events. "You've apprehended him?" she asked.

He canted his head slightly. His hair was fair, a bit longer than fashion deemed proper, his face clean-shaven. "You know Wheaton, do you?"

"Wheaton?"

His lips lifted a little at the corners, as if he laughed at her. Perhaps, if he were not so young and foolish, she would be truly offended. As it was, she would allow him to live.

"Yonder thief," he explained, and turned her slightly. "Do you know him?"

She jerked at her arms again. But it was a futile effort. "Of course I do not know him," she said. "He snatched my bag and fled. Might you believe I asked his name beforehand?"

He stared at her for a moment longer, then laughed. "I knew you were a clever lass, but I admit, I'm impressed."

She straightened her back and glared. " 'Tis easier to impress some than others," she said. "Where is your lord?"

"My lord?" He was still smiling, looming over her like an overdressed barbarian. His cravat was nearly as white as his ridiculous smile, though it had come undone and hung askew.

"Yes, your master, whomever you answer to. The lord of this isle, preferably."

"You want to speak to Laird MacTavish do you?"

"Yes."

"Laird Cairn MacTavish?"

"Yes!" She yanked away, and he finally released her, so that she stumbled slightly with the sudden change, but the crowd was tight and silent behind her, and she had nowhere to go. That much she could tell without turning. "I will have a word with him," she said, and lifted her chin. "And when I tell him of your treatment of the prin—" But she stopped, remembering all. She dare not spill the truth. Not here. Not in front of this self-important cretin, for she had traveled far and risked much. She pursed her lips. The crowd seemed ungodly quiet behind her, and the scent of rotting fish and too potent perfumes were dripping relentlessly into her consciousness once again, twisting her stomach. Perhaps Lord Paqual had been right. Teleere was not a place she should visit. But how could she determine a man's quality if she had never met that man? And it was too late for a turnabout now. She had set her course and she would see it through, despite all. She glanced around, trying to find a more suitable man with whom to settle her disputes, but at that moment her stomach lurched.

Fifty strides away, above the heads of the packed crowd, a gallows stood against the gay blue of the sky. And upon those gallows a body swung with slow deliberation, like a grotesque pendulum.

She gasped, crossing herself as she did so.

"A friend of yours?" asked the cretin. "Or is it Wheaton you favor?"

She tried to shift backward, away from the staring corpse, but there was no room. "What did he do?" she rasped.

"Rethinking your sins, wee one?"

"Cut that man down." Her voice was impressively strong considering the turmoil in her stomach. The corpse's eyes were open wide and staring. "Does your lord know of this . . . this . . ." She faltered, realizing with belated nausea that there was another man awaiting execution—a dark, handsome fellow with black rakish hair and a pale expression. He could not have yet reached his twenty-fifth year. Her stomach roiled.

"Does your lord know of these proceedings?" she demanded.

"Aye, he does." He watched her like a hunting falcon and stood too close. "In fact he is enjoying the . . . proceedings . . . even now."

Dear God! So the stories about Teleere's rogue ruler were true. She'd been entirely wrong to come, but she lifted her chin, unbowed. At least she knew the truth now, could return to Sedonia and choose another to share her throne. "Then I will see him at once."

"MacTavish?" There was laughter in his voice. Laughter at her, laughter at this situation, with the corpse swinging grotesquely and the pretty lad silently awaiting his horrible fate. "Will you now?"

Rage shook her. Aye, she was young, and some called her haughty, but she did not seek entertainment in others' misery. She ruled her people as best she could. "Laugh at me, and you will wish you shared the fate of that hapless corpse," she vowed. "Take me to MacTavish."

He gave her a mock bow. "Tell me what game we play, little midge, so I may know the rules."

"You think this a game?" She gestured toward the gallows. The corpse was jerking now, as if, even in death, he were fighting for life. The smell of feces fouled the air. She refrained from covering her nose and barely kept from gagging. "Take me to your pirate lord."

He grabbed her by the arm, startling her breathless and leaning in close. "I *am* the pirate lord, as you well know, and you have played your last trick." His fingers cut into her flesh.

She reared back in shock. "Let me go!"

"Go?" He laughed and pulled her closer. "I think not. In fact . . ." He nodded toward the gallows. "There seems to be an extra rope for you, my wee thief. Do you suppose you will soil yourself, too?"

"My lord," said a soldier from behind. "The hour grows late. Are you ready for Wheaton?"

He didn't turn toward the soldier, and in that insane moment Tatiana wondered if he had told the truth. Was he really Lord MacTavish—the man she'd hoped to wed to fulfill her uncle's requirements and become queen regnant in her own right? If he was indeed the man she sought, then she'd been foolish. It was clear that he was the devil himself. Panic burned like bile in her stomach.

"What say you?" he asked, his grin still crooked on his boyish face. "Are you ready to see your friend die, or would you prefer to test the rope first?"

She tugged frantically at her arm.

He tightened his grip until she nearly cried out in pain. "Of course with your light weight it would hardly be a test atall. You might hang there for hours without effect."

"You're mad." The entire world had gone insane. Surely this was a nightmare.

"And you're a thief," he gritted "But I'm not above a bit of thievery. Murder, on the other hand—"

"Murder!" Her heart was battering at her ribs, threatening to burst from her chest.

"Aye, murder," he gritted and shook her. "But perhaps you didn't know that about him aye? Perhaps you only warmed his bed. Or did you share in his plans?"

"What are you talking about?"

"I tire of games, wee one," he gritted. "Spill the truth or share his fate."

She didn't speak. Indeed, she could not. He grabbed her

chin and turned her toward the gallows. The corpse's eyes bugged from his head, his tongue was a grayish purple, and still he twitched.

She jerked her chin free, but too late. Her stomach revolted. She tried to control it, but there was no hope. Half-digested food spewed forth, striking MacTavish full in the chest, plastering his blue cutaway and dripping from his double row of brass buttons.

The crowd gasped and drew back. A soldier hissed something unintelligible. From the gallows there was a scrape of metal. A woman screamed.

MacTavish jerked away with a curse. "Daniel! No! Peters! Stop him!"

A pistol fired. Then another. Tatiana watched in disbelief as the man called Wheaton raced toward a galloping horse. A gun fired again, but he had already grabbed the rider's waist and launched himself behind the saddle. The steed reared, bearing both men high. The crowd screamed and milled, trying to escape, and into that opening path, the riders raced, knocking down pedestrians as they ran.

Soldiers yelled and swore, but MacTavish turned back to her with a deadly silence.

She backed away, realizing belatedly that she should have run, should have escaped while she could. But nothing in her life had prepared her for this.

"Well." The single word was articulate and low, accompanied by a smile that was still strangely boyish. "It seems you have accomplished your goal, my little harlot. But you forgot one thing."

She didn't speak, didn't move. Couldn't, for the hatred in his eyes held her entranced, like a field mouse before a striking adder.

"We are not biased here on Teleere. We hang women just as well as men."

She tried to voice the truth. To back away. But she could do no more than stare at the vomit that hung suspended from the black piping of his lapel. It swung gently back and forth. She watched its cadenced movement for a moment, and then, like a broken marionette, she fainted.

Chapter 2

❦❦

"You swoon very well."

Tatiana awoke blearily.

"Have you been practicing?" MacTavish asked, and crossed the floor toward her.

She sat up with an effort, wincing as she did so. Her head was swimming, and her throat ached, as if it had been scrubbed with sea salt and left to dry, but her stomach felt somewhat restored. One glance at MacTavish assured her he was rid of his soiled jacket. In fact, he had changed his entire ensemble and now wore a simple tunic of soft brown. It was open at the neck and belted over a short, plaid skirt of sorts. His knees were bare and his wool stockings gartered over lean-muscled calves.

She stared, blinked, then pushed back a few dark tendrils of hair that had come loose from her sensible coiffure. Back home she wore it intricately coiled and oft as not embellished with jewels. But of course that would have been inappropriate and foolish here. No, the valise was all she had brought to the isle of Teleere that would attest to her wealth and station.

But it was gone now, and her looming interrogator seemed deluded enough to think they had met before. Nevertheless, she would keep her head, literally and figuratively, and would find her way out of this mess. There was naught to do now but find the escort that waited at the abbey and return home posthaste.

She calmed her nerves with an effort and raised a slow, imperial gaze to his. "Where am I?" she asked. Her voice sounded cool and aloof, befitting a queen. Or a hastily crowned princess.

He said nothing, but seated himself on the edge of her bed and poured wine from a bottle into a silver goblet. Yes, she was sitting on a bed. It was wide, huge really, and draped in velvet curtains that boasted an intricate pattern of bright gold and deep green swirled in a background of rich burgundy. Beyond that, the room seemed to go on forever, but instead of the barren, clean-swept expanse of her own chambers, the place was packed with an odd assortment of every imaginable item. A huge, textured globe stood on clawed, walnut feet. A Grecian statuette stood in feminine grace beside an immense, cluttered desk. Draped over the statue's bare, ivory shoulders was a silken scarf of sapphire blue, and scattered about the room were scores of other articles she could not begin to identify or consider.

She smelled the contents of the goblet and tasted the wine. It was dry and robust. She emptied the glass and handed it back.

MacTavish raised his brows, glanced into the goblet, and returned his attention to her. "Who is he to you?"

She turned slowly toward him, shifting her attention from the strangely organized clutter of the room. Her mind was clearer now, as was her eyesight, but still she could barely believe her senses, for she would never have imagined the pirate lord to look like this. Nay, though she had made it a point to learn a good deal about him, she had not inquired about his physical appearance. Why would she? She had intended to marry the man, not paint his portrait.

He was the lord of Teleere, shrewd, cunning, and powerful enough to gain control of the island's unruly people. She had assumed his physical attributes would agree with his nature. He would surely not be young and fair-haired. And he would certainly not have a crooked, gleaming smile that spoke more of boyish pranks than of an empire conquered and ruled. Everything was entirely wrong here.

She stared at him, suspicion growing in her mind. "Is this some sort of intricate deception?"

His brows rose slightly. They were only slightly darker than the wheat-toned hue of his hair. But it was his eyes that held her interest, for they were a blue so vivid it seemed beyond the realm of possibility. "Deception?" he asked.

The way he said the word only raised her suspicions, for his tone seemed too happy, too even-tempered and light-hearted to possibly suit this horrid situation. And suddenly she was certain she was right. "Nicol coerced you into this." She said it as a statement of truth rather than a question, for she had learned long ago that uncertainty bred chaos. Always be assured. Always think things through. Never rush in.

"I don't know a Nicol," he said.

She ignored his words and raised her gaze to glance about the room, half-expecting the handsome viscount to step out from behind some bulky, unidentified article. "Is he here?"

Her captor's smile had faded a bit, but that fact did nothing to diminish his beauty. It was ridiculous, really, how pretty he was. Golden and gleaming and perfect. And that fact, more than any other, assured her she was right. Nicol had planned an intricate prank. Nicol, who had found the girl, Birgit, to take her place on the throne. Nicol, who forever believed she could not understand her people unless she lived like them for a time. Well, this certainly would satisfy his desires, wouldn't it?

"Where is he?" she asked, anger burning through her.

He canted his head as if uncertain of her meaning, but amused just the same. "Maybe that's not the question you should be asking just now, midge."

"My name is not midge," she said and, pulling her knees up, prepared to swing her feet from the mattress, but at that precise instant she realized the truth. She was naked. Completely and utterly naked.

Snatching the blankets back up to her chest, she pursed her lips and caught her breath. "What have you done with my clothes?"

He smiled again. Slowly, leisurely, like a golden cat that had cornered its prey and chose to toy with it before dining. "Ahh, now there's the question," he said and, placing a palm upon the mattress, leaned back slightly and drew up a knee. His woolen plaid, crafted of dark blues and bright reds, slipped languidly away from his thigh as he settled more comfortably onto the bed. His legs were hard with muscle, tight with sinew, and all but naked.

She scowled, her mind whirring. True, Nicol could be inappropriately capricious at times, but even he would not have gone so far as to put her in such a compromising position. Yes, he had often said she was too stiff, too cool, too removed from the common man, but he cared for her as few others did. Of that she was certain. Something had gone wrong here. Terribly wrong. But she was not sure just what it was. So she raised her chin slightly and looked her captor directly in the eye. "Who are you, sir? Truly."

He watched her in silence for a moment, then nodded once. "Very well then, midge, I shall play your game if you like," he said, and executed a truncated bow from his seated position. "I am Cairn MacTavish, pirate lord, as you called me, and bastard son of the late laird of Teleere." He paused. His lips tilted lyrically. "And pray, midge, who are you?"

He was keeping with his story then. Whoever had put him up to this had bid him be convincing. But if they meant to fool her, they should have found a more believable pirate. "You lie," she said simply.

Something flashed in his eyes, but he smiled. "Do I?" he asked, and rose abruptly to his feet. Pacing to the dark, over-sized desk, he placed the goblet atop it and turned back toward her. "I suppose you should know a liar when you meet one, aye, Megs?"

There was a sudden intensity about him that belied his grin. An intensity that did nothing to soothe her own unease. She tightened her grip on the bedsheets and watched him carefully. "My name is not Megs."

"Isn't it?" Pacing back, he sat again, closer still, so close, in fact, that she could smell the wine on his breath, could feel the warmth of his body against her arm. "Then who are you?"

She sat absolutely still, her mind storming in her head. Who was *he*? Perhaps he was MacTavish as he said. Who else would have access to such lavish rooms but the lord of the isle? And who else would dare treat the princess of Sedonia with such casual disrespect? But then, he didn't know she was royalty, did he? No, for she had planned carefully, had put a well-tutored impostor in her place.

"Her name is Birgit," Nicol said.

"And where did you find her?" Tatiana asked.

"In Teleere. Just to the west of Portshaven is a village called Thornborough. There is a tavern not far from there. She is the spitting image of you, Anna, except that you are a princess and she is a . . . well." His crooked mouth had shifted into a smile. "A barmaid I suppose."

"A barmaid!"

"Aye," he said. "A commoner. And who else? She is young, and she is hungry. There is no other class in the world so easily manipulated."

"I have no wish to manipulate anyone," she countered.

"Don't you? Think on it, Anna. You need someone to take your place without spilling your secret. Even if she told the truth, there is none who would believe her, since she is naught but a commoner."

Tatiana scowled. "If she is so common, what makes you think she can succeed in this ruse?"

"Because common is not the same as slow-witted. Neither is it the equivalent of worthless—no matter what your noble counselors think. She is clever, Anna. Maybe as clever as you."

Nicol had told her the tale of his journey to the tavern many times. Had told her of his meeting with Birgit, and from those tales, they had secretly laid their plans. The girl would sit on her throne for a few short days while Tatiana traveled to Teleere. Yes, she had planned to meet with Lord MacTavish, and if he was the man she judged him to be, she would offer an alliance. Indeed, she would offer a royal marriage, for that was the only way for her to fullfill Sedonia's requirements for her. She must marry and marry soon. But her decision would be a quick one. She would return to her homeland long before Midsummer's Eve, for she had no wish for another to make the annual sojourn to Bartham to choose Sedonia's finest steed. It was a tradition begun countless years ago and one that she would not abandon. Her uncle, the old king, had raised the price of the horse chosen, thereby improving Sedonia's stables as well as elevating public morale.

Yes, she had planned to make a quick trip to Teleere and find herself a suitable husband.

But she no longer had such plans, for she had witnessed

the pirate lord's true nature, had seen the light in his eyes at the execution. She would not bind herself to such a man no matter how dire Sedonia's straits, no matter how unsteady its government. She would find another way to solve her country's problems. Her advisors had been right. She must marry and marry wisely. But MacTavish would not be her groom. Even Lord Paqual's assessment had been correct. MacTavish was a scoundrel and a barbarian, hardly above the rumored murder of his young wife.

Tatiana had misjudged him completely, had hung her hopes on a dream. Despite MacTavish's ability to rule a country, he was nothing like her dead uncle, the old king. She'd played a bet and lost, but it was not too late. He did not know her true identity. He could not spill the truth to her advisors or cause any harm to befall the young woman who sat upon her throne.

"It should not take you so long to think of your name, lass."

She stared at him, her mind buzzing. He was toying with her. But why? What did he hope to accomplish? Might he know her true identity? Might he be planning to hold her hostage? Despite her country's diminutive size, it was a wealthy empire—rich in spices and diamonds and a dozen other gemstones. Did he hope to gain a ransom for her return?

"Unless the bump on your head has addled your thoughts." Reaching out, he touched the side of her skull. She winced, surprised by the pain, but in a moment, he left the wound and trailed his fingertips along the curve of her ear. The caress was gentle and strangely unnerving. She shivered at its descent. "Have you lost your memory, lass?"

She said nothing, but watched him closely. He had an odd lilt to his voice, as though he had been carefully schooled, but had not quite smoothed out all the rough edges.

"I admit that you are bonnier than I recall," he said, and skimmed his knuckles down her cheek to her throat. She shivered, for the sensations were disturbingly erotic, but she found her tongue and spoke coolly.

"We have not met before."

He grinned. His teeth were ungodly white, his smile tilted like a satyr's. "Aye, we have, lass. Surely you remember. I was just about to board the *Skian Dubh* with my first mate when you caused a distraction and stole my brooch."

She started in surprise, and he pulled his hand away with a chuckle.

"Neither did I think you so fine an actress."

She gave him an imperial stare, though her heart was thumping hard against her ribs. "You are deluded!" she said. "I am neither an actress nor a thief."

"Oh but you are," he said and stroked her fingers where they clung to the blankets. "You are called Megs, and you stole me mother's brooch from off me very chest. 'Twas quite a bold move." He smiled. "But you are a bold lass, are you not?" His knuckles skimmed along her forearm and up to her shoulder.

"I am not who you think I am!" She said the words in a rush. It was not like her at all, for she'd been taught from infancy to take her time, think things through. She was royalty. The world would wait.

"Truly?" His fingers stopped for a moment. "Then who are you?"

"Who are *you*?" Her words were breathy and he laughed.

"I believe we have covered that ground already, lass."

"You are not MacTavish."

"And all the while I thought I was," he said, and let his fingers drift southward.

"Don't touch me," she warned, her voice steady again. "Unless you wish to pay a heavy price."

He raised his brows. "You are daring—for a liar and a thief who has been caught dead to rights."

"As I have said—"

"You are not Megs," he finished for her. "Then who are you? Her twin sister perhaps?"

"I know no one named Megs."

"Lucky for you, since she tends to steal from those nearest her. Then again . . ." He paused and let his gaze slip down from her face. "I almost think it might be worth the loss now that I see you like this."

She pulled the blankets higher.

"Men have died for less insolence."

"Are you threatening me, lass?"

Yes, she was, but she would be a fool to admit it, for she could not tell him the truth. Could not admit her true identity, for though she was uncertain of his name, she knew he could not be trusted.

"I have not stolen from you," she said evenly, "or any other."

"No?"

"No."

"Then what is your attachment to Sir Wheaton?"

"Wheaton." Her mind was still spinning, but she tried to steady it, to be smart. "The man that was to be executed."

"The man that escaped!" His smile was gone and his words growled. He jerked to his feet and paced the room, limping slightly. "How did he get the knife, Megs?"

"I don't know what you're talking about."

"The knife," he said, and strode back to loom over her. His perfect teeth were gritted, his golden face intense. "The knife with which he killed Daniel while you stood there watched."

She felt herself pale, for the implications were painfully clear. He had lost a friend and believed she was to blame. "I don't know Wheaton," she said, and though she had hoped for defiance, she barely managed audibility. Still, he drew back, straightening on a long exhalation.

Silence fell hastily into the room.

"Tell me where he is, lass."

She blinked, searching for sanity. "I do not know Wheaton," she repeated.

"So you cannot tell me."

" 'Tis obvious—"

She never saw him move, but suddenly the blankets were whipped out of her hands and she was left unclothed and uncovered.

"Then I shall have to seek my revenge with you," he said, and reached for her.

Terror consumed her like a hungry wave. She leapt to her feet on the bed just as his fingers skimmed her arm. She squawked at the contact, almost falling onto the floor, but finding her feet and spinning about to face him. They watched each other like cornered badgers.

"Come now, lass," he crooned, and stepped easily onto the mattress. "It will not be so bad as all that. Surely if you can tolerate Wheaton's touch, you can bear anything."

"I know no one named Wheaton," she breathed, backing away, "and if you touch me again, I shall see you hanged before dawn."

"Hanged!" He laughed and leapt.

She darted away. He was after her in an instant. She heard his feet strike the floor long before she'd reached the door. Fingers tangled in her hair, snatching her to a halt. She whirled about, slapping wildly, but he was already pulling her up against his chest, muffling her protests, stilling her movements with the strength of his arms around her naked torso.

She struggled, but there was no hope. Despite his silly

good looks, he was strong and determined. She stilled, conserving her strength, engaging her mind.

The sound of their breathing was all that could be heard. His grip eased up a mite. She didn't move. At least here, pressed against his body, he could not see her nakedness.

Keeping one arm wrapped about her, he stroked his fingers through her hair, and she realized suddenly that it was completely undone and hung in heavy waves down the length of her back. How had that happened? How long had she been unconscious? Where were her clothes? And Ralph? Panic threatened to drown her, but she swallowed it back.

"You're damned poor at defending yourself," he murmured. She still didn't move. "For a thief and a murderer."

"Murderer!" She reared back, but he eased her against his chest again.

"Perhaps just his accomplice, aye?" he said and skimmed his fingers down her spine to the crease of her buttocks.

She quivered in spite of herself. "Cease!"

"Tell me where he is, Megs," he said, and, leaning back, stared into her eyes. Perhaps there was anger there, but another emotion burned brighter, something far more frightening.

"I told you—" she began, but he leaned forward and kissed her.

For a moment she remained frozen in shock, then she shoved with all her might, managing to break free and stumble backward. "How dare you!"

He smiled and stepped forward. "I dare much, lass. And this is but the beginning unless you cooperate."

She backed away, breathing hard and fighting to control her emotions, to think, to plan. "We do not deal with brigands such as you."

He stopped abruptly. "We?"

She scowled, but continued on. "You'll get no ransom for me. So you'd just as well let me go."

"Ransom?" His eyes were narrowed. "Wheaton would pay for your return?"

She shook her head. Was he merely trying to trick her into admitting who she was, or did he truly think her a thief? Was her life in danger or just her pride?

"So you're important to him," he said.

She continued to retreat, but her thighs struck something cold. She stopped with a gasp, but dared not glance back. Instead, she thrust her hand behind her, feeling the smooth edge of a desk. "I don't know what you're talking about."

"I'm talking about life, Megs," he said, and took a step closer. "Your life. I'm offering it to you in exchange for a small piece of information."

"I don't know what you want." Behind her, her fingers skimmed the surface of the desk. She felt smooth, unseen objects beneath her hand.

"I want to know where to find him." His voice was soft, but the words were gritted. "And that you know." He nodded as if to himself. "Wheaton would not waste a prize like you. You're clever. You care about him. And . . ." His gaze raked her nakedness. The light in his eyes sparked brighter. "And you are bonny."

Something cool and hard met her fingertips. She inched breathlessly along an edge.

"No." His tone was thoughtful, his eyes narrowed. "He will use you again. Believe me, Meggie mine, 'tis what he will do. He will use you and leave you to hang."

She merely stared, her mind racing along the edge of the unseen object, trying to conjure an image in her head.

"He has abandoned you already."

She said nothing, and perhaps he took her reticence for disagreement, for he continued on.

"Is he here now then? Bent on saving you?"

The object was strangely shaped. Triangular almost. But not too large, and—Her breath stopped as her thumb brushed the point. It was narrow and deadly sharp.

"Were he in your spot, he would give you up in an instant," MacTavish said. "Believe me, lass. I know 'tis true."

She didn't answer. Didn't breathe.

"He will sacrifice you to save himself." He shook his head and stepped closer still. "Tell me where he has fled."

She remained breathlessly silent, then shook her head. "I do not know what you speak of."

He reached for her with a curse, and in that instant she struck, snatching the instrument blindly from the desk behind her and stabbing it into his chest.

Chapter 3

~~~⟨⟩~~~

Pain sliced MacTavish's chest. He swore at his own stupidity and reached for the brass compass, but she had already snatched it out and dropped it like a writhing adder to the floor. Her gasp was one of utter horror—as if it were she who had been stabbed, and her eyes were tremendously wide, green as a mossy bay and filled with terror.

Behind him, the door slammed open and footsteps thundered into the room. That would be Lieutenant Peters and his entourage, nosy as aging schoolmistresses and too bored to keep to themselves.

She obviously noticed their arrival, too, for she was staring past his shoulder, her eyes wider than ever, her plump lips parted, and he realized without looking that his men had come armed and ready. He turned slowly, careful to step directly in front of her, covering her nudity.

Five men stood in an arc before him. Peters was the closest. His saber was drawn, and in his right hand he held a pistol. The others were armed in similar fashion. Triton's balls! You would think the girl was a gorging tiger shark instead of

27

a slip of a thing that barely reached his chest—which ached, by the way.

"My lord!" Peters's tone was breathless, his expression tense. "You are wounded."

Cairn glanced down at his chest. There was a hole some five inches below his left shoulder. Blood had seeped into the soft fabric of his tunic. There were things he missed about being a sailor; the coarse material of a seaman's clothing was not one of them. "Aye," he said, and scowled at the wound with some fascination. He hadn't considered using a compass as a weapon before. Intriguing. "So I am."

"By her hand," added Peters.

"True." Reaching toward the Grecian statuette, Cairn pulled the silken scarf from its shoulders and handed it to the girl behind him. "Cover yourself," he ordered.

The sheer fabric shook as she took it, and he almost smiled. So she was finally scared, but was it because of his too diligent bodyguards or because of the blood that he'd inadvertently smeared across the silken fabric? Perhaps she thought he was about to keel over from the wound she'd inflicted upon him and dreaded the consequences. He supposed even Peters's freckled countenance could look pretty imposing in the right light.

"My lord," said Peters again, "if you will step aside, I will see to her punishment."

He should step aside of course. She was a thief, a liar, and most probably a murderer's accomplice if not a murderer herself, but even now it seemed he could see her eyes—green as a mossy inlet with her hair wild and unbound about her splendid breasts. Of course, it was neither her breasts nor her terrified eyes that kept her from punishment. A bastard had no time for foolish sentiment. It was merely that he was certain he could convince her to reveal her lover's whereabouts.

She was young, scared, and alone. Surely Wheaton's charms were not so enthralling that she would keep silent in the face of such formidable odds. He tightened one fist, but remained otherwise unmoved, reminding himself that eventually she would weaken, and he would learn the truth.

"Go to supper, Peters," he ordered, his mind elsewhere. "I have use of the girl here."

"My lord—"

"And take your men with you."

"But—"

"What's afoot?" Burroun appeared in the doorway like a looming bad omen. One gargantuan hand was wrapped around a leg of mutton, and a bit of grease shone in the left braid of his golden beard. Cairn scowled. The giant had certainly heard the commotion sometime ago, for he had the senses of a mischievous wildcat, but, as usual, he had chosen his own leisurely course in getting there. Strange, perhaps, for a laird's bodyguard. But then, Burr had been strange for as long as he could remember. He had the build of his ancestral Vikings, the brogue of his homeland, and the frightful strength of a seasoned smithy.

"Good of you to join us," said Cairn to his hirsute friend. "The lads were just about to take their supper."

Burr nodded, wiped his mouth on the back of his hand, and belched softly. Some might find it difficult to believe he had the fencing skills of a master and the mind of a scholar. Or that he had managed to find time between meals to save Cairn's life on more than one occasion.

"She stab you?" he asked.

"Aye," Cairn answered.

Burroun nodded again, his expression something between admiration and boredom before he turned to the guards. "Well, lads," he said, his tone jovial as he slapped the nearest shoulder with convivial heartiness. The soldier called Cormick held up commendably under the assault. "There's a fine bit of lamb to table. What say we test it afore it's gone."

"My lord—" Peters began again, but Cairn quieted him with a glare. Why was it that he couldn't find a guard with a temperament somewhere between the lieutenant's obsessive worry and Burr's sporadic disregard.

"All is well, Peters," Cairn assured him. "You needn't worry."

"She's dangerous, my lord."

"Aye," he agreed amiably. "It could be you're right there."

"Let me—"

"What you thinking lad!" Burr rumbled, and glared at Peters as if he were a recalcitrant hound. The Norseman wore an unbuttoned vest made of some unidentified fur and no tunic of any sort. A plaid kilt was belted tight around his girth, and despite the fact that he ate like a starved white shark, not an ounce of fat showed in the muscles that bulged like sheep's bladders from every limb. "You gonna chew his food, too?"

The lieutenant drew himself up, affront written on his fair features. " 'Tis my job to protect the lord of this isle. And protect him I will."

"Aye, aye," rumbled Burr. "But if the lad can't save himself from wee woodsprite yonder"—he jerked his head toward the girl—"I'll kill him meself and have done with it. Now get your arse gone before I take a spanking to you."

For a moment Cairn thought Peters might actually venture a second objection, but apparently he wasn't completely daft, because he finally left, his back painfully straight and his expression disapproving.

The room was nearly empty in a moment. Only Burr's huge form marred the landscape.

"Stabbed you," he said and, chuckling, shambled toward the door. "Good for her."

They were alone in a moment. Cairn turned slowly toward the girl. The numbing shock had worn off and his chest was beginning to throb rhythmically, but one glance at the diminutive thief drove all thoughts of pain from his mind. In truth, it drove thoughts of any kind from his mind, sending all his blood pumping down to lower regions.

She stood as perfectly still as the Grecian statuette, her golden body unmoving, and draped down the midsection, like a sultan's gossamer curtain, was the silken scarf. He hadn't realized what an erotic picture she would make, and wondered suddenly if the sight of her might not have had something to do with Peters's laggardly exodus. Perhaps he should not place so much stock in the man's loyalty to himself as to the girl's . . . well . . . He stared at her and felt his blood pressure rise with his cock. If he didn't detest the very thought of anything that belonged to Wheaton, he might well be tempted to bed her. Then again, since when did affection have to foreshadow sex?

Perhaps his thoughts showed in his eyes, because she bunched the cloth more tightly between her breasts and backed up a step. But if she hoped for modesty, she would have been sorely disappointed, for though the scarf managed to shield her midline from view, the sheer fabric seemed to do little more than magnify her bounteous charms.

Beneath his kilt, he hardened and grew. Sometimes Hoary, as Cairn called his favorite nether part, forgot the greater good, preferring to embark on his own endeavors. Cairn stared at her in silence, taking in the wide verdant eyes, the rigid shoulders, the firm bulges beside her arms, which were pressed in an inverted v against her chest.

Hoary stirred restlessly. Cairn's gaze flickered downward,

then up. His cock waited in taut anticipation for her reaction, but if he'd hoped for unbridled desire, he, too, would be sadly disappointed, because she did nothing but raise her chin and tighten her grip on the scarf.

"So you truly are Lord MacTavish," she said. Her voice was low and quiet, perhaps from spending too much time in smoky taverns, waiting for her victims to drop in alcohol-induced unconsciousness.

"Aye," he agreed amicably. 'Twas so simple to be amicable when one had the upper hand. When cornered and tortured, he tended to be more cantankerous. Luckily, she'd only had a cartographer's tool close to hand, he thought, and smiled a little, wondering what would have happened if his interests ran toward weaponry instead of maps.

Her eyes had the slightest slant to them, but her nose was as straight as a whaler's harpoon. Had she not been a thief and a liar, she would have made a fine lady—aristocratic, superior, cold. Aye, she might be many things, but at least she was not nobility. She stole honestly. He took a step toward her and thought it unfortunate that he hadn't given her a handkerchief instead of a scarf, for while the silk teased and suggested, it also hid some of her more intriguing features, falling just to the middle of her thighs.

"I am MacTavish," he said and bowed slightly. Sir Albert—Bert, as Burr called him in an ever successful attempt to peeve the narrow baron, had taught Cairn some of the accoutrements of nobility. Bowing was one of Cairn's more successful endeavors. Language was not. "And who are you?"

She licked her lips. Hoary took note of the quick dart of her tongue, and despite that appendage's distraction, Cairn managed to notice that she hesitated yet again. But finally she spoke.

"My name is Mrs. Mulgrave."

He felt his brows rise. He hadn't expected her to tell the truth at this late juncture of course, but somehow he hadn't thought she would portray herself as someone's wife. Perhaps because she looked so very young. Hoary tightened hard against his belly, so maybe his reasons tended to run more toward wishful thinking.

"Mrs. Mulgrave," he said.

"Yes."

"And your husband?"

She raised her chin again as if challenging the devil himself, which wasn't a bad comparison. "He is dead."

"Really?" Cairn said. "Did you kill him?"

"What! No! How—" she began, but he gestured toward the hole in his chest. It was seeping sedately into the fine fabric of his favorite tunic, widening a pinkish stain on the French linen. "Of course I did not kill him." Her fingers tightened perceptibly in the scarf. They were slim and smooth and long for her small size. "And I would not have stabbed you if you had ceased—"

Her words stopped. Her gaze remained frozen on his chest.

"What are you doing?" she demanded.

"I've known you less than a full day and already you've ruined more garments than I did during my entire voyage to Patagonia, including the capture of the *Maiden*."

She swallowed and he scowled as he tugged his shirttail from beneath his belted tartan. Strange how nervous she seemed around him. True, she was naked, and he had threatened to have her hanged, but from what he had heard of Magical Megs, she had been in tighter spots. It was said she once had the hangman's noose tight around her neck and had still managed to escape without a trace. Like a shadow. Like a cloud of dust. Like magic. But she would not be so fortunate this time. Nay, Cairn the bastard had a tendency to get what he wanted, and this would be no different. Tossing the spent shirt onto his desk, he scowled down at his latest wound. It was small, but Bert had assured him that a sovereign laird should be able to go a full week without losing blood. Thus far, that theory had yet to be proven.

"How then?" he asked, glancing up.

She ripped her gaze from his torso to his face. Was it his chest that fascinated her or the wound? It was really Hoary that wanted to know. He had an insatiable curiosity.

"What?" she asked.

"Your husband," he said, and, crossing his arms against his chest, settled himself upon the edge of the desk. "How'd he die?"

"Oh. He drowned."

"Drowned."

"Yes."

"What was his name?"

"William."

"When did it happen?"

"Last May. He was boating on the Thames."

"Tragic."

"Quite."

"What was his occupation?"

"He was a tailor."

Cairn smiled. Damn, she was good. "And where did you and your beloved live, Mrs. Mulgrave?"

"In London."

Clever. London. A sea voyage and a long journey afoot unless one were foolish enough to challenge one of those damnable carriages—not somewhere accessible where he might travel easily and thereby prove her lies.

"Where in London?"

"On Craven Road, just across from the gardens."

He paused for a moment, and she pursed her lips with regal disdain. "Might I have my clothes back now?"

"No." He said it without thinking. True, there had been no weapons hidden in her garments. Neither had there been any stashed away in that dark bundle of hair she'd had piled atop her head, but it had been a good excuse to see her unclothed.

"Whyever not?"

"Because . . ." He thought for a moment and realized that he needed no reason. "You're my prisoner. I am the laird of Teleere. You'll have your clothes when I see fit—Miss Megs."

"I am not Megs." She could state the denial with absolutely no inflection of her voice.

He bowed again. Old Bert had endeavored to teach him a host of things—from judging wines to tying a cravat, but bowing was what he excelled at. God knew, Cairn was never meant to be a laird. But his mother had been young and bonny, and the king had taken a shine to her. The old wick had no way of knowing that his only remaining heir would turn out to be a ragged-assed Scot with no decent name but the one garnered from the pile of rocks where he'd been found.

"My apologies, Mrs. Mulgrave," he corrected and shushed the old bitterness. What did he have to be bitter about, anyway? He was the acknowledged laird of the isle of Teleere. So what if he'd spent a few years amidst a bevy of sailors who were as likely to slit his throat as look at him? It had taught him the art of sleeping light. "But you see, I have a problem."

She stared at him for a full five seconds before speaking. "The lowest of men can change his temperament if he so wishes."

It took a moment for him to understand her meaning, and when he did he didn't try to contain his grin. Little Megs had a smart mouth—*and mind-numbing lips*, Hoary added with a nod. Great, now he was starting a dialogue.

"You think my temperament a problem?" he asked, and circled her slightly. His intention was to reach the caneback chair that accompanied his desk, but he would not mind a view of her in profile—or from the rear if that opportunity presented itself.

"You did threaten to hang me," she reminded him.

"And, of course, you don't deserve to be hanged." He admitted that he said the words with some sarcasm as he placed a hand on the top of the chair. She kept her chin up and turned to face him. It denied him a view of her profile. But full frontal gave him nothing to complain about.

"Nay, I most certainly do not," she said.

"And, of course, neither did Wheaton." He tried to continue with his causal tone, but the very thought of Wheaton twisted his stomach. Months ago he had vowed to obtain revenge. He was laird of this isle. How hard could it be to execute one man? One brigand! One murderer!

"As I have told you—"

"Aye. You told me," he growled, and, lifting the chair in one fist, slammed it back down against the hardwood floor beneath.

Her gasp spilled into the room. He gritted his teeth and watched her, calming his nerves, easing his tension.

"Tell me the truth, Megs, or I swear your bonny looks will not save you from the consequences."

"My name is not Megs." Her words were no more than a whisper.

"You lie." Easing his hand from the chair, he approached her slowly. "But damned if you don't do it well."

He watched her swallow. Watched her lift her chin so as to keep her gaze on his face as he neared her.

" 'Tis not gentlemanly to accuse a lady of untruth," she said.

"Gentlemanly," he said, and laughed. "I could almost believe you are from abroad," he said. "With such foolish talk. Except that you speak the Gaelic so perfectly."

She stared at him with eyes as wide as the heavens, or as infinite as hell.

"No one has ever accused me of being a gentleman," he said, and touched her cheek. The skin was as soft as the heather blossoms of his homeland. "Tell me where to find him."

She shook her head, her gaze never leaving his face.

"What has he done to gain such loyalty?" he mused, then thought of a new idea. "Or is it fear? Do you think he will harm you if you spill the truth, lass? Is that it?"

She opened her mouth to speak, but he slipped his fingers over the plump rise of her lips, shushing her. They were ungodly soft and unusually full. Hoary stirred, and he scowled, remembering to concentrate.

"Don't speak," he ordered. "But listen. Wheaton is dangerous. I don't know what he's told you—what he's promised you, but you can't trust him. Tell me where he is, and I will make certain he never harms you."

They stared into each other's eyes. She shook her head.

"I cannot."

He stopped the curse before it reached his lips. "Then I have little choice but to imprison you, lass."

"For refusing to say what I cannot?" Her voice was hushed, but he discerned no desperation, no panic.

He forced a smile. "For withholding information from your sovereign laird."

"I told you, I do not know where he is. I am not this Megs you speak of. I am Lady Linnet Mulgrave of—"

"Of London, on Craven Road, where you made your home with your dearly departed husband, Wilton."

"Yes."

The room went absolutely silent.

"William!" she corrected. "His name was William."

Cairn smiled and slipped his palm behind her neck. Her hair felt warm and soft against his knuckles, suggesting other places that would surely be warmer and softer still. "It's cold in the dungeon, Megs. Dank and dark. And lonely. If you're lucky enough to have a cell to yourself."

She raised her chin a fraction of an inch. It was small and peaked beneath a delicately squared jaw. "I just arrived on your isle. Check the captain's log if you do not believe me."

Her hair was heavy and dark. Shiny as the North Star, it swept over her shoulders and around her well curved hips. *Bonny hair*, murmured Hoary.

"There will be a record of my passage."

"What's that?" Cairn asked, speaking over his nether parts.

"The ship," she said. "It was called the *Melody*. Its captain was named Mr. Beuren. He will remember me."

"I am certain he would," he said and skimmed his thumb along her throat. Damn, it was soft. "And I suspect you called yourself Mrs. Mulgrave, aye?"

"I called myself that because that is my name."

"And you came all the way from London alone?"

"No. I had . . . a companion."

He raised his brows. *Companion?* Hoary said. "Companion?" Cairn repeated.

"I asked Ralph to accompany me. I had never been to Teleere before."

"Ralph?" he asked. He had no particular reason for his interest, of course, but he was curious as to the relationship she had with this companion.

She blinked. Her eyes were enormously wide. She must not have seen more than eight and ten years. Barely old enough to dress herself. *I'll help her*, Hoary volunteered

"I commissioned him to accompany me here," she said.

Running his hand down her back, Cairn felt her shiver at the descent. "You hired a man to accompany you?"

Her gaze shifted slightly. Perhaps it was the first true sign of weakness he had seen in her story. True, she had misstepped when he'd said Wilton instead of William, but that could have been an honest mistake. Now though, he saw the first signs of uncertainty.

"Yes," she said, and gathered her composure like a miller might gather bits of chaff. "I had heard the wharves of Teleere could be dangerous, so I opted for a . . . bodyguard of sorts."

"I can't imagine you had to pay him much," he said, and drew his hand away. Hoary complained vociferously.

"I am not a thief," she said. "Regardless what you think of me, I am an honest citizen with a goodly income. I paid him quite handsomely. In fact I could—"

"I meant I doubt you'd have to pay any man a great deal to guard your body so long as his treasures are safely hidden elsewhere."

She opened her mouth to speak, then closed it suddenly. "I will pay you." Her tone was crisp and ultimately self-assured.

He raised a brow. Some had called him a pirate, some a privateer. He tried not to take offense to either. Piracy, after all, was as honest as most enterprises. "Pay me?"

"For my release," she explained.

He canted his head. "Perhaps we can come to an agreement. What can you offer?"

He noticed that she had stopped breathing. Perhaps he was watching her bosom a bit more closely than caution necessitated, but it seemed that she was hanging on his every word.

"What do you want?" she asked.

"Wheaton's whereabouts."

"Damn you!" she swore, and swung her hand up to slap him.

He caught it easily, inches from his cheek. Passion. It shone in her eyes. Did Wheaton always evoke such passion in women? Even women like this small, cool thief? Had Elizabeth been passionate in his arms?

"I know no one named Wheaton," she hissed.

He held his temper, but not so easily as he held her wrist. She was not a strong woman, not even in proportion to her size.

"Then how will he pay your ransom?" he asked.

"Ransom?" Her face went absolutely white, and her knees buckled.

He scooped an arm about her back, pressing her up against his chest and scowling into her eyes.

"Ransom?" Her voice was weak.

"For your safe return to London," he said.

"Oh, yes." She nodded and straightened with an obvious effort, but he didn't let her go, for she felt wonderfully soft against the bare skin of his chest, beautifully right against his belly. "I . . ." She cleared her throat and tried to move away. He tightened his embrace a mite. "My . . . family . . . Will you please . . ." Her face was no longer pale, but flushed a bonny pink, and her breathing came hard and fast. "Let me go."

"But you will not give me what I want." He realized that what he wanted had just changed. Hoary's back-alley morals seemed to have taken over. "Therefore, I think I should take what I need." Leaning forward, he kissed the corner of her mouth and drew slowly back.

She stared at him for a full second, then, "Do not do that," she whispered.

"This?" he asked, and, pressing his mouth to hers, swiped his tongue gently along the crease.

She pushed against his chest. "Don't!" she insisted, but he barely noticed, for she'd lost her scarf, and they stood chest to chest. Skin against wounded skin.

"You don't like it?" he asked. He might not have Wheaton's heritage. After all, Lord Wheaton was the old laird's legitimate nephew, and even though his father and all his immediate family had been exiled for treason, the blood was still true. Still, Cairn was the laird of the isle, and even without that distinction his face had opened a few doors for him, though most of them were back doors to places not meant for nobility.

"I . . ." She was breathing hard. " 'Tis not right."

"But better than the dungeon."

"Are you threatening me?"

"A man might take offense to having his proposition called a threat, Megs."

"Proposition?"

He could feel her ribs against his fingertips, curved and firm and perfect.

"I admit Teleere's prisoners might miss your company should you choose to stay here with me."

He watched the blood drain from her face, and perhaps a niggle of guilt seeped into his consciousness. Aye, he was threatening her, compromising her. But he was not doing it for his own passion's sake. Hardly that. He was no ugly ogre she must choose, and if she spent a night or so in his arms, she would surely leave her loyalty to Wheaton behind, bettering her life. Perhaps saving her life.

"I . . ." She shook her head. "I cannot," she said, but she was weakening.

"Cannot what?" he asked, and bent to kiss her throat. It

was long and smooth and lovely, framed by her mink-soft hair.

She caught her breath on a strangely high note.

He pressed his kisses lower, traveling down the smooth slide of her glossy body. He could feel her heart beat in her chest. Could feel her breasts rise and fall.

Succulent breasts!

"Quit!" she ordered, and thumped her palms against his chest.

Pain shivered through him, and he released her with a grimace. She stumbled out of his embrace, breathing hard.

Cairn watched her, felt the pain subside and the desire roar back to life.

"I would not hurt you," he said. His voice was damnably low, pushed down by the hard edge of his desire.

"I cannot," she said.

"Why?"

"Why? Surely 'tis obvious, even to you."

"Even to me?"

"It would be wrong."

He ground his teeth. "How did Wheaton win such loyalty?"

"Wheaton again! Are you mad?"

"Aye. Perhaps. Which do you choose, Megs?" Anger felt hot in his gut. Hotter even than Hoary's burning interest. He took a step toward her.

"Leave me be." She backed away. "I've done nothing wrong."

He laughed as he followed her. "I seem to have a hole in my chest, bonny Megs. That alone surely warrants hanging."

"Hanging!"

"I gave you a choice."

"Choice." She choked a laugh. "A choice between the impossible and—"

"So 'tis impossible for you to share my bed."

"'Tis impossible for me to tell you that which I do not know."

He had cornered her again. Perhaps she had yet another impromptu weapon behind her back, but he found it difficult to care, for rage had spilled over his good sense. Damn her for choosing Wheaton!

"So you would rather die than cuckold him?"

"Who?"

He managed a smile. "Your lover."

"I have no lover."

"So you are untried?"

"Y—No. Of course not. I was . . ." Her breath was coming hard. She was pressed back against the desk, her spine bent as she tried to avoid him. "I was married."

"Of course." His gut twisted. "And yet you choose the dungeon to a night with me. Not very flattering, love," he said, and slipped his palm across her cheek.

"Let me go." The words were stuttered. "Please."

Let her go. Now there was an unexpected eventuality. Who would have expected Hoary to be a softy? Generally, he was pretty hard-edged.

"Tell me where he is, Megs. Tell me and no harm will come to you. I promise you."

"I cannot," she insisted.

He remained as he was for a moment then straightened with an effort and nodded once. "Good luck to you then.

"Peters," he called.

The door opened in an instant. Aye, Cairn had ordered him to take his meal, but perhaps the good lieutenant had no need for sustenance so long as he could serve the lord of Teleere. "You have need of me, my lord?"

Cairn's stomach knotted. "Aye," he said. "Take the maid to the dungeon until she sees fit to talk."

Chapter 4

∽⟍⟍⟋⟋∼

The night groaned on forever. It was cold and dank in the silent darkness. Worry gnawed, and time creaked along with miserable slowness.

Damn her! Cairn paced his chilly bedchamber yet again. Not a candle had been lit. Why wouldn't she talk? What magic did Wheaton employ to engender such wretched loyalty? Did she know his true nature? Did she know and cherish him regardless?

But he needn't worry. He would know the answers soon enough. One night in Westheath's dungeon would surely quell the girl's spirit. But the damned night dragged on interminably, cramping old injuries and making his head ache until he could no longer bear the wait.

The sun had not yet risen when he gave up his vigil and clattered down the stone stairs. Beneath the castle, deep in the roots of the ancient fortress, there was a hole in the earth. Rarely had it been used since Cairn's arrival in Teleere, for there had rarely been a need. It was the place this Megs belonged, however. It was the place she would learn that he meant what he said. She would talk, or she would suffer.

Down another flight of stairs, around a corner. He scowled into the blackness, and found—nothing. The cell was empty, the door open.

He cursed aloud, then spun away, taking the steps three together.

Peters appeared in an instant, his eyes wide. Despite the hour and the fact that he should have been in the barracks long ago, every hair was in place, every garment wrinkle-free. More often than not, he slept in the hallway just down from his laird's chambers. More often still, he didn't sleep, but stood, fully dressed, standing guard for endless hours. "Something's amiss, my lord?"

Cairn grabbed the man's pristine tunic in one fist, drawing him up close. "She's gone!"

Peters went pale if paler he could be. Confusion clouded his normally cool features. How had she managed to dupe him? Was it seduction? Trickery? Perhaps she truly was magical. "Who—who is gone, my lord?"

"Who!" The girl had turned the man's mind to mash. "Megs. The thief. She's gone."

"Nay! She cannot be. I delivered her to Pikeshead myself."

"Pikeshead." Cairn loosened his grip on the guard's shirt-front, careful of his temper. "You took her to Pikeshead?"

He made certain his tone was neutral, but perhaps there was something frightening in his expression because Peters took a cautious step to the rear. "Aye, my lord." He swallowed once, his Adam's apple bobbing. " 'Twas where you said to take her."

"I said the dungeon." He articulated precisely and clenched his fist once, lest he reach out and snatch the man up close again.

"Aye the . . ." Peters began, but in a moment his gray eyes widened. "You meant here at the castle."

"Where is she?"

Peters looked as pale as a shade when he shook his head. "I but delivered her to the gate master there. I do not know where they placed her."

Cairn gritted his teeth, but refrained from reaching out. Bert had assured him that violence was not the answer. But perhaps Bert didn't know the question. "Fetch me a steed," he ordered.

"A—" Shock was stamped on Peters's freckled features. "A carriage, sir?"

"A saddle horse, you twit. Get one before I roast you alive!"

Tatiana Octavia sat huddled against the stone wall. The cell was dark, dank, and smelled of things she dare not consider. Her stomach had been unsettled for days, and she had no wish to test its endurance. Instead, she steadied her breathing and glanced stiffly about. She could not tell the dimensions of her cell for she had been delivered after dark. But perhaps darkness forever dwelled in this nightmarish place.

She shivered once and wrapped her arms more tightly around her knees. A highborn lady was above fear, she told herself. Nay, 'twas the cold that made her quake. The cold and fatigue. She was exhausted, but she dared not close her eyes, for she was not alone. Rats quarreled somewhere in the distant dimness, but it was not those vermin that she feared.

Her terror was closer to hand and human. At least they were said to be human.

"Are you asleep yet, lassie?" someone asked. The voice was something between a hiss and a croon. She swallowed the bile in her throat.

"Nay." She found her voice with some difficulty, but she

dared not remain silent, for only fear kept these particular vermin at bay. "I am awake and vigilant."

"Vigilant?" A chuckle issued from the odious darkness. "Don't she talk pretty, Lute?"

"Aye. And she wields a rock even better, aye, Reek?"

Reek cursed vehemently. They had come at her shortly after her arrival, had knocked her down, had planned some evil she refused to contemplate, but she had found a stone in the waiting darkness and fought with a strength born of desperation. The bolder of the two would bear a bruise on his temple for some days. But maybe there were more than two. She had no way of telling for certain.

"She'll sleep soon enough," hissed Reek, and sidled closer. She couldn't see him in the darkness, but she could hear his shuffling approach and felt her throat close up with fear. "Then we'll see how feisty she be."

"I'm thinkin' you'll be needing more than your one arm to tame this 'un," said the other. " 'Praps I'd best take 'er first and—"

"She's mine!" Reek hissed. Something struck the wall. "And don't you be forgettin' it, you sawed-off little bastard."

"Bastard am I?" croaked Lute. There was a scuffling in the straw, accented by heavy breathing and raspy curses.

"Sod off the two of you afore I call the warden!"

Tatiana jerked at the sound of another voice. It came from her left, not far away and clear as the day. Perhaps it was a young girl, but her tone suggested experiences Tatiana had not shared.

"Sod off yourself, you lil' tart," Reek said, but the scuffling had ceased.

"Tart am I, Stinky?"

"A whore more like."

"Leastways I confine me interests to me own species," she said.

"When the girl 'ere sleeps I'll show you where me interests lie," Reek said, but he came no closer.

Lute muttered something, and the girl snorted, but finally all was quiet. Silence stole in, nearly as suffocating as the darkness. Tattiana shivered. Odd, fermenting odors made it difficult to breathe. It wasn't fear that made her throat close up, for she was above such mundane emotions. She did not lower herself to extremes, but kept herself always on an even keel. A true lady did not shout, did not cry. Still, when she escaped this hellish nightmare MacTavish would pay. That much was certain.

From the far end of her cell, someone began to snore. So one of them was asleep, but what of the other? She waited. Minutes ticked away, aching in the blackness. The night wore on. Images flitted through her mind. Her mother's face. The duchess of Fellway had been cool and unapproachable the entirety of her daughter's life, but there was a security to that, a constancy. All was well for Mother would make it so. But she was gone now, dead these past five months. Her father had died long before. No help there. But Nicol. She steadied her nerves and let her mind dwell on the viscount of Newburn. Nicol's crooked smile shimmered in the hopelessness before her.

"I but said you should not marry the first sniveling cur that sniffs out your crown," he said. *"Not that you should sneak off and marry the bastard lord of Teleere."*

"But you said he was strong, Nicol."

"Yes." His voice was uncertain, his dark eyes intense. "He is that."

"And fair-minded."

"He seems to be, from what I could see, Anna, but—"

"Then I shall go there and see for myself."

"And what of your throne? What of Paqual? You cannot trust him in your absence."

"No," she agreed. "But I can trust you, can I not?"

He watched her for a long moment, his face atypically somber before he shook his head. "No. Trust no one," he said.

And in that moment she awoke. Something was wrong.

Nightmarish reality screamed back in. Someone was close, within reach. She jerked to her feet, jumping backward.

From the darkness close at hand, Reek cursed and straightened.

"Quick little bugger ain't you, lassie."

She could see him now for the first time. His face was twisted into a parody of a smile.

"Come now, old Reek ain't goin' to 'urt you."

"No." She straightened her back and clenched her hands to fists to still their shaking. From the corner of her eye she could see Lute. He was small and scrawny, his eyes eerily bright in the predawn grayness. "You are not."

Reek chuckled. "There's a good girl. Come on over 'ere now, and we'll 'ave us a bit of fun."

"Fun!" The word escaped on hysterical laughter.

Reek stiffened, then took a step toward her. "You thinkin' you're too good for the likes of old Reek?"

Terror coursed through her. She couldn't move, couldn't speak. But her mind was still working, spinning away like a whirling dirvish. She snapped her gaze to Lute and back.

"Yes," she said, and suddenly her course was set. There was no turning back. Her legs felt stiff. She braced her back against the cold stone of the wall behind her and prayed. "I am far too good for you. As is every living soul. In fact, I pity poor Lute."

"Lute!"

"At least he has decency to leave me unmolested."

"Decency!" Reek laughed and turned his gaze toward his cellmate, who stepped forward a jittery pace. "Aye, 'e 'as the decency to wait till I'm through with you afore 'e takes what's left over."

She felt the wall behind her, searching for some unseen weapon, but there was nothing. "You should not judge others by your own depraved standards," she said.

"Depraved!" He took another step closer. It was impossible to breathe. He was too close, only a couple yards away, but she dare not dart away. There was nowhere to go anyway.

"Yes," she said. "You are depraved. While Lute—"

"I'll learn you to—" Reek began and stepped closer, but Lute came with him.

"Leave 'er be," he ordered.

Reek stopped with a jolt. His eyes bulged as he turned his glare on his companion. "What's this then?" he rasped.

"You 'eard 'er. She don't want nothin' to do with you."

Reek coughed a laugh. "And I guess 'er ladyship wants a tiny wick like you."

Lute clenched his fists. Shifting his eyes to her and away, he licked his lips and took a step toward his adversary. "Aye. She's mine."

Reek snorted, then shrugged and turned, but in the same instant, he launched himself at his rival.

Lute grunted as Reek's shoulder caught him in the gut.

They went down in a jumble of flailing limbs. Reek swore. From behind her, someone yelled. A woman cackled, and Tatiana screamed for the guards, grabbing the lattice-work metal bars in both hands and shrieking for help.

It all happened in an instant. Light burst in her eyes. The door sprang open, and she was flung aside. Her head struck the wall. Men rushed in, but reality was already blurring. Someone yelled. From a great, foggy distance she thought she heard the name Megs, but perhaps it was just a fragmented portion of her dreams.

Light glowed blearily. Someone bent over her like a

looming shadow. There was a whimper of fear. Was it hers? The thought floated groggily through her mind, but it didn't matter. She let her eyes fall closed and heard someone growl an oath.

For a moment she tried to sit up, but her body felt strangely heavy, then she was rising, floating mistily from the filthy straw and lifting languidly upward.

Death. She sighed. It didn't feel half-bad.

Chapter 5

"**F**orgive me, my lord." The voice was quiet but fraught with tension. Was she in hell? No one answered. Apparently Satan was the laconic sort. "I thought you meant to punish her."

Punishment. So it was hell. Nicol had been right. She should not have been so haughty, so aloof. She should have tried to understand the plight of her subjects. Should have listened when she could, done more to set things right when possible. Still, even in hell it felt good simply to lie in silence and let time slip quietly past her.

"I had no way of knowing she meant something—"

"Peters!" Satan growled. "Shut the hell up."

Someone chuckled.

"Yes, my lord. Am I dismissed, my lord?"

There was another growl, which she failed to comprehend. A door opened and closed. Too loud. It echoed in her head. She moaned and lifted a hand tentatively to her brow. Lights sparkled in her cranium, rocking her world.

"Here, put your hand down."

She opened her eyes, but only to slits, for the light seemed ungodly bright, blurring her vision.

"Who—"

"Quiet now," he said.

"MacTavish!" So he was the devil. Of course. She attempted to sit up. He wrapped a hand around her upper arm and pulled her upright.

"So you've finally learned my name." His voice was rough, his touch the same. It took little enough effort to hold her. Hell was intimidating, even for a princess.

"Here. Drink this," he ordered, and pressed something to her lips.

She would have enjoyed refusing, but she was horribly thirsty. Sitting was difficult. He steadied her with a hand to her arm and tipped a mug forward. Too fast. She sputtered and gagged as the herb-laced wine burned her lips and throat.

She coughed, winced, coughed again, then opened her eyes to glare at him. "I'd think Satan would have better seduction skills."

The boyish expression of yesterday was gone, replaced by a brooding glare. "You're raving," he said, and felt her forehead with the back of his hand.

She jerked her head to the side and was rewarded with a quick jab of pain through her eyeballs. She gritted her teeth and spoke nevertheless. "Threats and imprisonment and drowning in cheap wine. Is that the only way you can convince women to sleep with you, MacTavish?"

Someone chuckled again. She turned her head painfully, sweeping her gaze past a tumble of hazy artifacts to land on a man near the door. It was a giant dressed in fur and plaid. He raised a loaf of bread to her in a sort of salute and chuckled again.

She scowled groggily and turned back to her captor.

"What's next? The cat-o'-nine-tails if I don't capitulate?"

He was silent for a moment. "The dungeon is generally incentive enough for most maids."

"I am not most maids," she said.

"The indomitable Magical Megs," he said, and leaned back slightly, his hand leaving her brow.

She laughed. The sound was gritty and coarse, befitting her location perhaps. "Even in prison you called me Megs. I would think you would know my true identity," she said. "Given your . . . station."

"My station?" He was ungodly handsome, but of course Satan would be. Some thought the god of the underworld old and ugly, but she had always known better. Beauty disguised a host of sins and drew admirers all at once.

"God of hell," she explained, though reality was seeping painfully into her head.

Anger sparked in his eyes. "So you prefer last night's accommodations?"

She refused to shudder, refused to dwell on the stench of the dungeon he had saved her from, for he had also been the one to put her there. She tightened her fingers in the blankets that covered her. Memories from the day before sluiced in, and she glanced down quickly, but she was still clothed, though her sleeve was torn.

So she was well, basically uninjured and virtually untouched. Circumstances could be worse. She raised her gaze back to his and pursed her lips.

"Let me go, MacTavish, and I'll not seek vengeance."

"Vengeance!" He didn't laugh, but it sounded like a close thing. Instead, he jerked to his feet and paced back and forth before the enormous bed she found herself in for the second time. "And tell me, Megs, how would one in your position go about seeking vengeance?"

She longed to tell him the truth, to inform him that she had an army at her disposal, but she had said too much already, for she had no way of guessing what his reaction to her news might be. Instead, she remained perfectly still and watched him in silence.

"If you think Wheaton will avenge you, you're a greater fool than I believed."

"Tell me, MacTavish, how long have you been obsessed with this Wheaton fellow?"

Anger flashed in his eyes, and for a moment she thought he might strike her, but he settled back onto the mattress and watched her instead. "I might ask the same of you."

"And I might tell you . . . again . . . that I know no one by that name."

He smiled. It held no charm, no lightness, no joy, and yet, as pure physical beauty went, it was stunning. If she cared a whit about physical appearances, she might have been moved, but she had learned long ago that it mattered not at all. Her mother had been a rare beauty, yet she had no warmth for her only daughter.

Reaching out, he touched her cheek. She refused to draw away, but met his gaze with her own hard stare. Nicol had once said she could freeze the Cocklewall Falls if she turned her glare on it.

Unfortunately, MacTavish did not freeze. "Maybe you don't realize what I can do to you, Megs," he said instead.

"I think you already did it," she replied.

The giant chuckled.

MacTavish turned to glower, but Tatiana didn't shift her gaze. Her statement was not entirely true, of course, for he had saved her. Why? If he meant to have her tortured, Pikeshead Prison seemed a good place to start. Even in Sedonia they heard rumors of it. So why was she back here in his private chambers?

"Don't you have something else to do?" MacTavish asked, and she realized he was talking to the giant.

"Nay, lad, not at the moment. Since it seems I'll have to wait to torture the girl."

She snapped her gaze from MacTavish to the man by the door. The difference between them was shocking, for surely there were never two men whose looks were more at odds. The giant was as homely as his lord was beautiful. She liked him immediately.

"What is your name?" she asked.

Both men turned toward her in unison, and she realized her mistake. Most women, even wealthy widowed women, would not assume to question a man in such a situation. Still, she had already spoken, and it was too late to draw the words back. She kept her gaze fast on the giant.

"Me Christian name be Olaf." He said the words slowly, as if wondering why she'd asked. "Me friends . . . and the bastard here . . ." He motioned toward MacTavish. "They call me Burr."

"You are of Swedish descent?"

"Norwegian," he said. "Late of Kristiansund."

She nodded, remembering traveling to that beautiful peninsula as a child, but MacTavish was scowling. Who was this giant of a man who could call the sovereign lord of Teleere a bastard and live to tell of it? Someone very foolish or very brave. Perhaps a meld of the two. It intrigued her.

"Tell me, Burr," she said. "Are you in need of employment?"

His heavy brows rose. "What's that?"

"I seem to have lost my guard. I but wondered if you might wish to take up that position."

The huge man shrugged. A shadow of a grin played around the peripheral edges of his mouth. "What do you pay?"

MacTavish swore under his breath.

She didn't glance toward him. "I will give you twice what he does."

Burr laughed. "That won't be difficult, lass, for he pays me nothing."

"Ahh. Just in my price range then."

He laughed. She smiled.

"Get the hell out of here," MacTavish ordered.

Burr glanced at his master in some surprise. "The lady made me an offer, lad."

"She's not a lady."

Burr smiled. "Better yet."

"Go check on Peters."

The Norseman turned his gaze on MacTavish finally, his eyes still laughing. "You worried he's going to kill himself for disappointing you?"

"I'm afraid he's not."

Burr snorted, then turned back toward Tatiana. "Me apologies," he said, and bowed at the waist. The movement was strangely graceful. "It seems I am being sent to rout wild geese."

"Consider my offer."

"Aye," he agreed, and nodded. "That I will. And if the lad here gives you too much trouble . . ." He bowed again. "You've but to call."

"And if I call, what will you do?"

He shrugged. His shoulders were the approximate size of a river barge. "I'd have to charge extra to kill him."

"I shall bear that in mind."

Burr chuckled as he turned to leave. The door shut solidly behind him.

She shifted her attention slowly back to MacTavish. "Loyalty is a difficult commodity to come by."

"I don't believe in loyalty," he said.

"Why is that?"

"Because there are women like you."

"You think me disloyal?"

He was still scowling. "Here," he said, and lifted the cup to her lips again. "Drink this."

She turned away, making a face of disgust. "It tastes like sheep dung."

"Which begs the obvious question," he said, but didn't explain. "Drink it before I pour it down your throat."

She considered arguing, but his expression changed her mind. "What is it?"

"Heather wine laced with arsenic."

"Then I am certain you will understand why I must respectfully refuse."

"You're in no position to refuse anything."

"What about Burr?"

He laughed. "You expect him to save you?"

She lifted her lips into a parody of a smile.

"From me?"

She said nothing.

"For a woman of the world you're a poor judge of people, Megs."

"Am I?"

"If you think Burr will set himself against me to save you."

"So loyal is he?"

He saw the trap just a moment before it snapped shut. Indeed, he almost smiled at his misstep. "I prefer to call it force of habit."

"He has been with you a long while?"

For a moment some unknown emotion crossed his eyes, but it was gone in an instant.

"Drink the wine," he ordered.

"I've a strange aversion to poison."

He looked tired, she realized. And older than she had first thought. "'Tis naught but herbed wine."

"And I should trust you?"

"I don't care if you trust me or not, but I'll not have you swooning again."

"Swooning!" Indignant anger bubbled up inside her. "Is that what you call it when one is struck on the head while defending herself from execrable brigands?"

"Execrable brigands!" He scoffed, perhaps at her choice of words. Nicol had once suggested that she spoke like a constipated scholar. "They were nothing but a one-armed petty thief and his dwarfed companion. If you totaled their ages, they were older than the stones of this castle."

She drew herself up. "I am sorry if my tormentors weren't to your liking."

He shook his head. "'Tis a sorry day when Teleere's premier thief can't best a pair of doddering miscreants."

"Again, my apologies."

The room went silent. He had the deep penetrating gaze of a peregrine falcon, though his eyes challenged the blue of the morning sky. "So you admit your true identity?"

"I admit that you are a spineless cur."

"You almost make me wonder why I rescued you."

"Rescued me!" She growled the words at him, though, if she remembered correctly, ladies were not supposed to growl. Drawing a deep breath, she steadied herself. "'Twas you who tossed me into their midst. 'Twas I who distracted them with their own witless brawling."

"You set them to quarreling?"

"I thought it preferable to rape."

For a moment she thought he would respond, but he remained as he was. "Drink the wine," he said instead.

"No."

"Drink it," he ordered, "or I swear, Pikeshead will look as rosy as an afternoon jaunt in the park."

She wanted nothing more than to resist him, but his eyes were deadly earnest, and she was no fool.

The wine tasted like yesterday's death. She drank it in one long draught, shuddering at the end, but forcing herself to glare up at him.

"Where else do you hurt?"

"What?"

"Besides your head." He said the words as if she were daft. "Where else are you injured?"

"Why? Do you keep a list? So many a day to reach your quota?"

"Dammit, woman! I'm surprised he didn't kill you, too."

Her stomach twisted. "You said he was only a petty thief."

MacTavish scowled. "Is that what he told you?"

"We didn't have a great deal of time to converse. What with his companion wanting to rape me and the woman in the next cell—"

"Christ! I'm talking about Wheaton."

She blinked, trying to assimilate this new information. "Whom did he kill?"

A muscle jumped in his jaw, and he drew a deep breath through his nose as if trying to steady his nerves.

"Where else are you hurt?"

"If you're so concerned for my well-being, you could have me see a physician."

"Hoping to escape, Megs?"

"Hoping to stay alive regardless of your cruelty."

"Perhaps you want me to check your well-being for myself?" he asked.

She glared at him. "Touch me again, and I shall not need Burr's help to dismember you."

"You threaten me again?"

"Nay." She raised her chin. He touched a finger to its center. She jerked away. "I tell the truth."

His eyes laughed at her. His mouth remained absolutely immobile. "So you would kill me." He dropped his hand to hers. Lifting it, he turned it over. "With this hand?"

She nodded. Regal pride was all she had just now, but it had stood her in good stead in the past.

Bending slightly, he kissed the center of her palm. Hot feelings shot through her like a flaming arrow, beginning at the point of the caress and streaking madly up her arm and off in a thousand sizzling directions.

"'Tis a soft little hand, for one who uses a threat so boldly," he said, and pushed her sleeve up her arm. The simple cotton fabric had a rent near the elbow. He ignored it. "And a frail arm," he added and kissed the veins that throbbed rhythmically in her wrist.

Her body jerked at the unaccustomed contact. "Cease," she commanded.

He raised his gaze to hers as if worried. "I didn't hurt you, did I?"

She sharpened her scowl. Her heart was beating overtime, and her breath was coming fast. Faster even than when he had threatened her. "Unhand me or you shall surely rue the day."

"Rue the day." He smiled at that. "You speak very well, for a murderous thief," he said, and kissed the bend of her elbow.

"Desist, MacTavish, or you shall regret your actions."

"I have many regrets," he said, and when he raised his gaze to hers, it seemed almost that she could see them there, shadowed by a veil of bravado, but still visible. "I doubt if touching you will be amongst the worst of them."

She stared into his eyes, trying to read his thoughts, trying to discern the regrets, but in that moment he grinned, laughing at her attempts. She yanked at her hand, but it was an exercise in futility, for he held it fast.

"Release me," she breathed.

He smiled. "I only wish to make certain you are unhurt."

"Then mayhap you should not have thrown me into prison with a pair of degenerate rapists."

Something snapped in his eyes again. "Surely you've been in worse places."

His hand was easing up her arm toward her shoulder.

"Let go of me."

"Does that hurt?" He squeezed her upper arm gently. She scowled.

"You are making a horrible mistake."

He skimmed his hand over her shoulder. "All is well here?"

"You do not know who you are dealing with, MacTavish."

Turning his hand slightly, he brushed his knuckles along her collarbone. "I believe you said your name was Linnet Mulrooney."

"Mulgrave," she corrected, but his knuckles were inching downward, sapping her strength. They skimmed as slow as sunrise over her bodice, not detouring an inch as they slipped over her nipple.

"Nothing amiss there?"

She stilled a shiver. "Let me go now, and I'll not seek retribution."

He smiled. Something knotted in her gut. "Tell me, lass, who would do the retributing?" he asked and laying his hand flat, pressed it gently down her ribs.

"*Retributing* is not a proper word."

His smile remained. No, she did not care about a man's

looks, but his smile did unfathomable things to her insides.

"How would you seek revenge, wee Megs?"

"I have friends."

"Any not wanted for murder and rape?"

"You are not the one to speak of rape," she said.

His eyes darkened, but finally he nodded. "You're right. I am surely not above a little rape. Still, I should have known better than to send such a fragile thing into a den of . . ." He paused. A muscle jumped in his jaw. ". . . miscreants."

"*Miscreants.* 'Tis a pitiably weak word for the beasts I endured." His hand skimmed over her hip and onto her thigh.

"He who wastes not, wants not. I'm saving my best words."

He was tugging at her skirts, lifting them up her leg, baring her shins, her knees. She stared at the progress, then raised an imperious brow. She could do so, she knew, without a single wrinkle showing in her forehead. Nicol had dubbed it the ice princess glare. "If you hope to frighten me, MacTavish, you will be sorely disappointed, for I fear I've endured far worse than you."

"I'm flattered," he said, and, wrapping his hands around her ankle, eased them up her leg. "But nay, sweet Megs, I don't mean to frighten you."

She held her breath as his fingers squeezed up her knee.

"Any pain there?"

"What is your intent?"

He smiled. "You may be a murderous thief, Megs, but you are a bonny murderous thief, and I am currently without a mistress."

She felt her body go momentarily numb, and though she ordered herself to remain still, to withstand his ministrations, she could not. Instead, she jerked her knees up to her chest, slapping her skirts down below her feet as she did so.

"I will never lie with you!" she hissed.

He watched her in silence, like a spider might watch its slowly suffocating prey. "To me or with me?" he asked.

She glared, and he laughed.

"It will not be so hideous," he assured her. "You may even enjoy it." He reached for her again, but she scrunched against the rowan wood head of the garish bed, trying to control her breathing, to keep her expression impassive.

"This I can promise you." She raised her chin. "I shall never enjoy it. Not with you, MacTavish."

"Not like you did with Wheaton."

She stared, her mind churning madly in her head.

A muscle ticked near his mouth. "Tell me what magic Wheaton possesses then, lass. Perhaps I can learn from his expertise and pleasure you against all odds."

She sat frozen in place. His eyes smoldered with anger, but when he lowered his gaze to her breasts, there was a new light in their depths.

"Tell me, Megs, do you cherish him so very much? Or do you give him all because of fear?"

"Let me go." Her voice sounded deceptively calm, though her heart was thundering like wild horses in her chest, and her breath came hard.

"So that you can return to him?" He shook his head. "I think I'll keep you here, and maybe, if he cares half so much for you as you for him . . ." Leaning forward, he pressed a kiss to her throat. Feelings sparked like summer lightning, branching away on frayed electrical currents. "Maybe he will come for you."

"MacTavish." Her voice wavered now. "Do not be a fool." He kissed her again, in the hollow of her throat. She swallowed hard. Did a man's touch always elicit such feelings? "Save yourself."

"From Wheaton?"

"From me."

He straightened slightly. They were inches apart, his gaze absolutely steady on hers. Her limbs felt weak, but she was in a tight spot. It couldn't be the effects of his nearness.

"There are many things I should save myself from, wee lass," he breathed, and skimmed a finger along the edge of her collarbone. "But I don't think I care to save myself from you," he said, and bent to kiss her neck.

She jerked away and skittered off the bed. "Then you are a fool."

He descended the mattress and stalked after her, his strides smooth. He resembled nothing more than a tawny cat, sleek, confident, undeterred.

"Tell me, Megs, are you worried what Wheaton will do if he learns you've been in my bed?"

She was nearing the door. Perhaps if she could make it through, Burr would be there and maybe . . .

But in that moment MacTavish leapt. She shrieked and darted, but he caught her by the arm and spun her about. They were chest to chest, thigh to thigh. She could feel the tight expanse of his body against hers, and there, in the middle of his being, the hard evidence of his desire was impossible to mistake. Even the highest-born lady knew something of men.

Fear choked her. She pushed on his chest. "Nay." The word was weak, pathetic, her strength the same.

"You must pay your debts," he said. "Here or in the dungeon. Surely one night in my bed would be preferable to a lifetime in Pikeshead."

"You're making a mistake."

"Hoary disagrees," he said, and, bending his head, kissed the high flesh of her breast.

She gasped. He smiled. The door flew open.

"My lord!"

Her gaze darted across the room. A stranger stood there. He was immaculately dressed in dark waistcoat and tight pantaloons. He was as thin as a spindle and as small as an elf.

MacTavish didn't turn, didn't loosen his grip, but he spoke, nevertheless. "Sir Albert," he said. His tone was weary.

"My lord," he said again, his tone tight with disapproval, "tell me 'tis not so."

She felt his grip loosen the slightest degree. He turned with a scowl. "I thought you were in Paris."

"I have returned, and just in the nick of time, it seems." He lisped slightly, and his lined face was pinched.

"That'd be yer opinion."

"That *would* be *your* opinion," Albert corrected, tight-lipped. "If it cannot be said correctly, it should not be said at all."

"What do you want, Bert?"

The little man drew himself even straighter. His height barely exceeded her own. "You cannot keep this"—his gaze skimmed her—"woman . . ." She had felt a host of emotions emanating toward her throughout the years—jealousy, avarice, hope. But never had she felt such utter disdain. ". . . in your chambers."

"Aye," MacTavish disagreed, but he had released her entirely now. "I can."

She wouldn't have thought the little man's back could possibly get straighter. "Then pray, what is my purpose here?"

"I've wondered that meself." MacTavish's language was deteriorating by the minute. A strange thing.

"How will it look if word of this becomes loosed?"

She could almost feel MacTavish sigh. "How will what look?"

"The mighty lord of Teleere with . . ." He indicated her

with a sweep of a soft, long-fingered hand. "Her!" He couldn't have sounded more disapproving if his master had been found abed with two sheep and a handful of snails. "Really, my lord!"

MacTavish rubbed his eyes, but perhaps there was the hint of humor quirking his lips now. "So you've heard of her, Bert?"

"Yes." He didn't sniff, but he might have just as well. "Lieutenant Peters informed me of her presence."

"Did he say he put her in Pikeshead?" There was something in his tone she could not quite decipher.

"My lord . . ." The little man's voice had lowered to little more than a whisper, as though he barely dared to say the words. "You should not have gone there yourself."

"To Pikeshead."

"You must think about your reputation. Your safety."

He smiled. "Aye, I'll have to do that."

"You think I jest."

"No. I'm sure you don't."

"Your father—"

"Was a true gentleman," MacTavish finished.

The little man nodded. "And not one to take in . . ." He paused as if he had no wish to offend her, but his expression did that for him. "If one has . . ." He paused again as if searching for the perfect words. "If one has *needs* one should keep himself to himself."

MacTavish's smile widened. "I'm sure you're not saying what I think you're saying."

The little man actually blushed.

"This is not a matter lightly taken."

"I've rarely taken sex lightly."

Sir Albert drew himself even straighter. He had a beard, neatly trimmed. Even that seemed affronted. "If you hope to shock me, you will be sorely disappointed, my lord."

MacTavish laughed out loud. "And if you hope to discourage me from bedding who I will, you're barking up the wrong tree."

"She's not the proper sort."

"I've always liked the improper sort, Bert."

He pursed his lips. "So you've no wish for an heir, my lord?"

MacTavish scowled. "I doubt that bedding the girl will make a difference on that front."

"You think a proper heiress will want you after you've soiled yourself on her."

"Aye. I think a proper heiress will want my money regardless."

"So jaded, my lord." He sniffed sadly. "It pains me to hear it."

"Damn." He sounded immensely tired suddenly. "Have you come here for a reason, Bert?"

"What of disease?"

"What?"

"Look at her. The wastrel of the streets. Might you believe that she's kept herself pure?"

MacTavish glanced at her. She stared back. "I hope not."

"'Tis not a laughing matter, my lord. Aye, she may be comely enough to look at if you've a weakness for that sort . . ." Again she imagined a sniff. "But is she worth the loss of an heir?"

MacTavish opened his mouth, but Albert hurried on.

"'Tis said it falls off."

"What?"

Sir Albert's face was beyond red now, beaming like the inner core of a blacksmith's fire. "Your . . ." He cleared his throat. "Your most private parts."

"They can fall off?"

He pulled back his shoulders. "I have heard it said. Surely, you do not wish for that."

"No." MacTavish shook his head slowly. "No I don't."

"Then think long and hard, my lord. Think what you've accomplished since coming to this isle. How much more might you achieve if you keep your head."

Perhaps there was something of a pun there, for MacTavish smiled ruefully.

"Aye, I'd like to keep my head."

"Then send her back to the dungeon. 'Tis surely where she belongs. Forget this foolishness with Lord Wheaton. It can only cause you grief."

Burr stepped into the doorway. "Bert," he said, toasting the other with a spiced custard he held in his gigantic hand. Part of it toppled down his vest and rolled to the floor. "You're back from old Parree, aye?"

Sir Albert turned slowly. Rarely had she seen more disdain on a man's face, not even when he'd looked at her. "Aye." He bowed his head slightly. "I have returned from Paris."

"The lads there are a lively lot, I hear."

The tiny man's thin lips pursed. "Was it your idea to bring the chit here?" he asked.

"The chit?" asked Burr, then nodded. "You mean Magical Megs, here? Nay. It wasn't me own idea. She swooned all pretty at Cairn's feet. The lad thought of it himself. You can hardly blame him for taking her to his bed." He paused, looking Sir Albert up and down. "Or maybe you can."

The room fell silent.

"She should be returned to Pikeshead."

"Pikeshead? The lass be too clever to stay there for long." Something flashed in Burr's eyes. "Besides, the place is crawling with murderers and sodomizers. Surely you wouldn't wish that on your worst enemy." His gaze sharpened. "Maybe your best friend, but—"

"You go too far!" Albert's voice shook.

"Leave the lass alone. She's done you no harm."

"If she harms my lord MacTavish, she harms—"

"What do you think she's likely to do, the wee slip of a thing? Wrestle him to the ground and have her way with him?"

"I know her type."

"I rather doubt it."

"She deserves to be hanged."

"Have you nothing better to worry on, Bert? Napoleon invades Russia. England's regent is a fool, and trouble brews in Sedonia, threatening to bubble over on Teleere itself. But you are worried that the lad here might find himself a bonny lass, dashing your hopes for—"

"You are a cretin and a degener—"

"Get out, the two of you." MacTavish sounded tired.

"My lord—"

"Shut up," he ordered.

"Tav—"

"You too," he said, and strode toward the door. They turned to follow him. "Peters." His voice was just short of a yell. His lieutenant appeared in less than an instant, his face strained, his eyes wide.

"Yes, my lord."

"I'll be gone for some hours. I'm leaving the girl here. Can I trust you to keep her safe?"

"Yes, my lord. Without a doubt, my lord. I'll not fail you again, my lord."

MacTavish nodded curtly and continued through the door. She heard his voice from the far side. "Get her a meal and a change of garments."

"Yes, my lord."

"And a bath."

"Yes, my lord."

"And do not let her escape."

"No, my lord. Of course not, my lord. I'll watch her every moment."

"Every moment?" MacTavish's tone was strange and suddenly clearer, as if he'd turned back.

"Well not . . . not when she's bathing, my lord."

"Very well." She heard footsteps again, then, "And Peters, relax. She's only a lass. I'm certain you can handle the job."

Chapter 6

He took a carriage to Pikeshead, gritting his teeth against the jostle and jolts of the horrid contraption. Carriage rides had never improved his disposition. As a lad he had learned that horses tended to be fractious and unpredictable, opinionated and sour-minded. Not like the sea, where he could see a swell coming for miles and guess every dip of his vessel. Some might think the sway of a carriage was reminiscent of the pitch of a ship, but some were idiots. A frigate's roll was rhythmic and soothing. A carriage trip was tantamount to suicide. But he was in a hurry.

The streets of Portshaven deteriorated as they wound their way southward. Cobblestone gave way to clay, clay to mud, and mud to ruts as deep as his funk. The buildings became shabbier, the children dirtier. He scowled out the window and disembarked after a final jolting halt in front of Pikeshead Prison. It loomed over him like a gray, foul cloud. Somewhere to the east a crow broke the silence with its harsh call. It sounded like nothing less than the raucous laughter of a ghost.

Cairn stepped out of the carriage. It rocked beneath his feet, and he held tightly to the doorframe lest he be pitched into the street. He had insisted that he come alone, but he knew better than to believe that his wishes had been met. Olaf Burroun, master intimidator and frequent pain in the ass, was nearby.

Pikeshead's gate master was a tall man with hair gone gray and a somewhat ghoulish expression. He bowed at Cairn's approach.

"My lord," he said, and straightened. "I swear I did not know there had been a mistake. I was told to imprison the girl, and I did so. Had I—"

"Tell me," Cairn interrupted. "Do you keep such watchful care over all your prisoners?"

The warden licked his lips and shifted his eyes side to side as if debating if this was sarcasm or a question truly asked. "I am not certain of your meaning, my lord."

"I mean, do you simply throw every prisoner to the wolves, regardless of his crime or station?"

"They are . . ." He paused for a moment as if baffled. ". . . criminals, my lord. Incarcerated as a punishment for their crimes."

Cairn scowled and straightened slightly. The man was right, of course. They were criminals, here to be punished. Cairn had never been squeamish about punishment. For God's sake, he'd spent most of his life on a frigate, and there were few milieus in the world that boasted harsher conditions. He had a score of scars to show for those years, and yet, the idea of punishment irked him now, eating at his consciousness, gnawing at his gut.

"It matters naught if they are female or male, hardened criminals or tender maids?" he asked, though he supposed it would have been a fine time to keep his mouth firmly shut.

"Tender maids." The warden looked affronted at best.

"My lord, 'tis true, they sometimes look mild, but this I know from experience—they would as soon rip your heart from your chest as do an honest day's labor."

He considered arguing, but his chest ached from the puncture of a certain compass, so he only scowled instead.

"But . . ." The warden continued to look anguished. "Had I known you favored her, my lord—"

"I do not favor her." He made certain his tone was chill. "But I am laird of this isle and 'tis my duty to look after even the lowliest of my subjects."

The warden looked confused. Cairn gritted his teeth and exhaled between them. This was getting him nowhere.

"Did you recognize her?" he asked.

"Your pardon, my lord?"

"The girl," he said. His impatience was mounting, for though he had been fortunate enough to leave Burr out of sight during the journey, the irksome giant had left his steed behind and now stood a few yards away. He had leaned a huge shoulder up against a wall and appeared to be busy with his own rudimentary thought processes, but Cairn knew better. The Norseman heard every word, dissected every nuance. Damn him and his barbaric facade. Why the hell couldn't he be a cretin who thought like a cretin? "Did you know the girl who was brought here last night?"

"I believe the lieutenant said her name was Megs."

"But you hadn't seen her before."

"No, my lord, but as I have said, there are brigands and vermin aplenty in Portshaven. I cannot know them all."

Cairn drew a deep breath and refrained from knocking the warden upside the head just for sport. "I need to speak to the girl's cell companions," he said instead.

The jailer blanched. "Surely not, my lord. They are—"

"Brigands and vermin," Cairn finished.

"Exactly, my lord, and not fit for your esteemed company."

And yet he had spent most of his life in just that sort of company. With any luck, he could make some new friends here. Burr's companionship was becoming wearing.

"I'll be speaking to them," Cairn insisted grimly, and the other capitulated with a bow. There were certain advantages to being lord of all. One could coerce without even issuing a decent threat. But sometimes he missed the opportunity.

On the other hand, even his title did nothing to induce Megs's two cellmates to talk. When they were led into the light, they were blubbering and incoherent. He asked them much the same questions he'd asked the warden, but they knew nothing, or at least, in his glowering presence, they professed to know nothing of the girl called Megs. They had thought her just another cell rat. They'd had no intention of harming her. Just fooling they were.

Memories knotted in Cairn's mind. The stench, the screams, the sight of tiny Megs unconscious. He was tempted to wring their scrawny necks, but they were so piti-ful, so low and wretched already that he could do nothing but send them back to their hole.

Cairn gritted his teeth as they were led away. He turned back to the guard. "Were there any others there last night?"

"No, my lord. Just the two."

He scowled, remembering. "*Even in prison you called me Megs.*" But he hadn't called her. God only knew if he had spoken at all. Rage was a primeval thing.

"Was there another she might have spoken to?" he asked.

The warden looked nervous, shuffled his feet and blinked. "There may be others she spoke to in the adjoining cell. There is no way to keep them from conversing though we—"

"I want to see them."

"My lord?"

"Anyone who may have spoken to the girl. But don't tell them my title."

His wish was granted, but not happily. Five people were ushered into a barren, rough-stoned room. They came one at a time—a tattered old man, so debilitated he could barely speak, a woman who cackled when she spoke, but was not above trying a bit of seduction should it better her lot, two boys barely into puberty, and a young woman. A girl really.

Cairn stood in the nearly empty room. A wooden chair adorned the chamber, but there was little else. The walls were stone. The floor the same. The girl eyed him carefully as she entered, but if she were afraid, she was careful not to show it. Behind him, Burr said nothing.

"What's your name?" Cairn asked her. The corner of a grin lifted her lips. Her hair might have been red. It was matted and her face dirty, but under other circumstances, she might have been pretty. Under any circumstances she would have been scrappy. That much was clear in every move she made.

"That depends," she said. "On why you be askin'."

He remembered saying something similar on his first day at sea. Ten stripes should have taught him better, but punishment didn't always have the desired effect, for he would guess this girl had known her share of stripes, yet she spoke as if she hadn't a care in the world.

"I am asking because I wish to know." He employed his best upper-crust speech. It came in handy now and again, and he was not above using it, unless Albert was within hearing, of course.

"Oh?" She sounded bored, irritated even. "And who are you that I should be sharin' my name?" she asked.

He paused a moment, taking in her appearance. Her gown might have been blue at one time. Now it was an undistinguished grayish hue, faded almost white at the ends of her ragged sleeves.

"MacTavish," he said, and let the word sink in for a moment. "My mother called me Cairn."

She paled, but she didn't cower. "Bloody 'ell," she murmured, and he laughed despite himself.

"What's your name, girl?" he asked again.

She straightened her spine. "I don't need ta—"

Burr shifted his feet, settling his weight more comfortably against the wall. The girl looked nervously past him to the giant. At first glance one might think he'd died in an upright position. At second one might guess the other was merely bored. It took some brigands a good deal of time to realize he was watching every move. By that time they were usually already dead. But the girl seemed to have gotten the gist of his personality already, for she swallowed once and turned her gaze rapidly back to Cairn. "They calls me Gem," she said.

He repeated the name with a nod. "Do you know a lass named Megs?"

"Megs, you say?' She glanced at Burr again. He was like an unsightly wart. Hard to ignore and harder to be rid of. "No, me lord, I don't believe I do."

He watched her carefully. It was the first time she'd given him any sort of proper address. Why this sudden civility? "Why are you at Pikeshead, Gem?"

"Me?" A corner of her mouth lifted again as she glanced about. "I enjoy it 'ere, guvner. Don't you?"

The smart mouth was back. He liked to think he himself had shown some bravado under duress, but she was a common thief, and he was the king of her world. It was entirely possible even he would manage to show a little more caution in the same situation.

"We usually hang murderers," he said. It wasn't that he didn't admire her spunk, but he had things to learn, and a subtle threat seemed the most expedient means to that end.

"Murder!" She stumbled back a step when she said it, then snapped her gaze to Burr, as if expecting him to produce a noose from beneath his tunic. Her eyes were wide. Perhaps he should have felt guilty for the threat. But guilt was wearing and of little real value if you came right down to it. She narrowed her eyes now, thinking. "I didn't do nothing but steal some bloke's snuffbox."

"Really?"

"Aye. Bloody lot of good it did me, too, cause it weren't even silver."

"Are you saying that's the only thing you stole, Gem?"

"On my honor, guvner, I never took nothin' else."

He smiled. "I hope you're a better thief than you are a liar, Gem."

"You callin' me a liar?" Her hands were formed to fists, her bright mouth pursed.

"Aye," he said, and nodded once. "I am that."

She watched him for a moment, lifted her gaze to Burr, watched him again, then shrugged. "Suit yourself."

Cairn smiled. He had forgotten how much he enjoyed common thieves. "About Megs—" he said.

"I didn't kill 'er."

He paused in his thoughts. "Is she dead then?"

"I . . . I . . ." She shifted her attention back to the giant and shrugged, striving for a casual demeanor once again. "How would I know, guvner? I was thinkin' you 'ad found 'er dead, what with the way you was talkin'."

"So you didn't kill her, but you know her."

She looked momentarily disoriented. "Who was you asking about?"

"A girl called Megsan or perhaps Margaret?"

She shook her head.

"Megs?"

She scowled as if thinking, then shrugged again. The

movement was casual. Too much so, but perhaps a certain amount of taut bravado was to be expected under the circumstances. Burr shifted against the wall again. She scowled, not glancing toward him, but obviously aware. "There was a chit named Megs brought in last night. Or so's I was told."

His breath caught, but he forced himself to remain relaxed. "From whom?"

"I 'eard the warden say it."

"So you've not heard of a lass called Magical Megs?"

For a moment her face showed absolutely no expression, but then her eyes widened dramatically. "Was that Megs 'erself?"

"You've heard of her then?"

"Magical Megs? Course I 'ave."

"Could you identify her?"

She shook her head slowly, her eyes wide again. "Like I told you. I only stole that one time."

"The snuffbox."

Her expression became enormously sad. She blinked as if fighting tears. "Seems a harsh sentence for one foolish mistake don't it?"

"Your lying skills seem to be improving already."

Anger flashed across her mobile features, but one quick glance at Burr, and she shrugged again. "I does what I can."

"Aye." He stood, turned away, then slowly swiveled back. "How long will you be visiting Pikeshead?"

The sad expression was back immediately. "Six months. If'n I lives that long."

He let her words sink into the silence. "What if I set you free?"

"What?" She started suddenly, but her eyes narrowed a moment later, like a small red fox, sniffing a trap.

"If you came to Westheath and identified the thief called Megs, I'd see that you went free."

"Magical Megs's at the castle?"

He gave her a noncommittal stare.

"Is she alive?"

"Would you care?"

A rainbow of emotions arced across her face, but finally she shrugged. "Like I said, guvner, I don't know 'er personal."

He nodded once, then turned away. A moment later he could hear her heckling the guards as they escorted her back to her cell.

Burr was silent as he fell in beside Cairn. Their footsteps echoed in dull tandem down the stone hallway, but above that noise it seemed Cairn could hear the giant's mental wheels churning.

"What is it?" he said finally.

"What is what?" rumbled Burr.

Cairn snorted, immediately irritated by the other's silent reflection. Reflections rarely showed him in a favorable light it seemed. "Next time you find me lying helpless in a pile of rocks, leave me there."

Burr nodded agreeably. "I won't even offer me assistance."

There was silence again except for their footfalls. "You going to ask why I spoke to the girl?"

"I assume you're improving your circle of friends?"

"She's lying," he said.

The other shrugged. The movement might have been reminiscent of the young girl's, but Burr's shoulders were huge and round and closely resembled the lumbering motion of a circus bear.

"Why?" Cairn mused.

"Maybe she's afeared of you. After all, you're the laird of the isle."

"For today."

Burr grinned.

"Why do you think she lied? Even if she didn't know Megs, she'd surely say she did, just to get a chance to be free of this hell."

"She's naught but a thief."

"A onetime thief."

Burr snorted. "You come around asking 'bout a lass named Megs. Showing a good deal of interest. She hears you got the lass up to the castle."

They exited the stifling confines of the prison. Cairn scowled across the cobbled street toward the waiting carriage. The team was a quartet of dark bays. Stallions no less, bred for speed and fretfully groomed. Their coats gleamed with mahogany good health as they fidgeted with distraught energy. His gut clenched. He should have known better than to allow Burr to choose the team. In fact, he was going to go out tomorrow and purchase a pair of plow horses—maybe something in their second century of life.

"Anyone in their right mind would be scared," Burr said.

Cairn flashed his gaze from the restive stallions to the giant.

A smile lurked just beneath Burr's stoic features. "I'm talking 'bout the girl," he said.

"Of course."

Burr grinned.

Cairn swore in silence. "She didn't seem scared."

"Maybe she's a better actress than your Megs even."

"Tell me . . . Olaf . . ." He felt the Norseman's dour glare, but continued on. "Is there any conversation I've had in the span of my life that you haven't listened in on?"

Burr thought for a moment. "Once when you were a lad you spoke to a man named Grady."

"I'll give it some thought," Cairn promised, "and try to let you know what was said."

"I'd appreciate it."

A liveried footman lowered the carriage steps with a bow and a flourish, as if he were swinging wide the pearly gates of heaven.

Cairn grabbed the window with a deadly grip and levered himself into the rocking casket. Burr swung his tremendous weight casually up behind him and wedged himself into the opposite seat.

"What are you doing here?" Cairn asked. There were few things worse than letting another witness his weakness. And if he had to choose the person to do so, Burr would be the last on his list. As far as Cairn knew Burr was unimpressed by death itself. "What about your horse?"

Burr shifted in his seat, widening his personal space. "I missed you, my laird."

Cairn scowled. "Curious about my visit here?"

"Not atall."

"Really?"

Burr gave him a baleful glare and pulled a curved pipe from somewhere inside his furry vest. "'Tis pitifully obvious, lad."

"Oh?"

"The lass has bored beneath your skin."

Cairn carefully controlled both his surprise and his irritation. It was best to show Burr no emotion whatsoever, but Cairn was not the stoic sort. Emotion and actions rode hand in hand in his world.

"The lass." Burr sighed as he leaned his back against the plush upholstery of the red velvet cushion and put a light to his pipe. "She's made you sit up and notice."

"Interesting theory for a barbarian. You know she stole my mother's brooch."

The other shrugged.

"And she's Wheaton's accomplice."

"Ahh. So we finally get to the crux of the matter," Burr said, and puffing once, thrust his arm out the window to rap twice on the carriage's sleek mahogany siding.

There was a word from the driver, and the vehicle lurched forward. Cairn gritted his teeth. Burroun's eyes seemed strangely bright as if he were enormously happy.

"You're making less sense than usual, Burr. I didn't know it was possible."

The big man smiled. "You want me to speak plain, lad?"

"It'd be a change."

"Very well then." He leaned forward and looked Cairn in the eye. "The young laird of Teleere is enamored."

"Enamored." Cairn said the word dryly as if tasting the flavor of such an impossible term, but the other raised a mocking brow and continued on.

"Aye, he's met a wee maid. Bonny she is and fair, with a quick wit and a bold manner. A maid who stirs his interest and his blood like none of the highborn lassies what have come before her."

"Remind me to check for a vacancy in Portshaven's asylums."

If Burr heard him he gave no indication. "But the pirate laird dare not let down his guard, so he proclaims her to be a thief and a—"

"She is a thief," Cairn reminded him. "She stole my brooch."

Burr held up one stubby finger. "And not just a thief, but Wheaton's accomplice. In case one death sentence isn't satisfactory for the isle's grand sovereign."

"Perhaps it's you who is enamored," Cairn suggested.

Burr raised his brows as if considering. His forehead wrinkled like an aging hound's. "She *is* a bonny piece. If you've got no use for her, I'll—"

"Stay away from her," Cairn ordered.

Burr grinned. "My hairy ass, but you're almost too easy."

Cairn ground his teeth and managed a rough smile at the same time. "She's my link to Wheaton."

"Ahh, so that's it. You're not aching to have her for yourself then?"

"I've little use for conniving women."

"Had your fill with Elizabeth, did you?"

Cairn's stomach churned. "Leave her out of this, Burr."

"Dammit, lad!" The grin was gone. "It's been all of two years. When might you be planning to cease your brooding?"

Cairn clenched his teeth. If his stomach weren't churning like a Mediterranean whirlpool, he might just have taken a punch at his lifelong companion, even though he rather suspected that his title would do him little good in the way of protection.

"You know what you need?" Burr's tone was deep. He puffed again, watching carefully.

"I can only hope you'll enlighten me."

Burr nodded his agreement. "You need to be bedded."

"I'm flattered," Cairn said, careful to keep his tone dry. "But you're not my type."

Burr snapped his pipe from his teeth and leaned forward in his seat. "And what is your type, boy? Some milk-fed princess who speaks of everlasting love, then spreads her legs for every handsome liar that smiles her way?"

Cairn's teeth hurt from clenching them. "She was my wife, Burr."

"Aye." He nodded curtly. "That she was, lad, but she's dead now. Dead and gone."

"You think I hadn't noticed?"

"Aye, you noticed that, lad. But little else. Since her death you've been like a walking corpse, but it's time to wake up now. You're not some wayward bastard, leaping with the waves anymore. You've a country to rule now. Open your eyes."

"I'm awake."

"And the guilt is eating you every minute."

"Guilt." He stared at Burr in honest surprise. "Why would I be guilty?"

"Because you wanted her dead."

Besides the whirring of the carriage wheels, the world seemed to have gone absolutely silent.

"If you've an accusation to make, Burr, you should take it to a magistrate."

"Damn Bert and the fancy words he put in your head!"

Cairn watched the Norseman in surprise. He rarely swore.

"There was a time I could get a straight answer out of you, lad."

"I didn't kill her if that's what you're asking."

Burr's face turned red. His hands clenched to mallet-sized fists, clasping the pipe hard in short, broad fingers. For a moment Cairn thought the other might reach out and strangle him. Well let him come; he was spoiling for a fight.

"You must think me the daftest fool in Portshaven. Of course you didn't kill her, but you might as well have for the flogging you give yourself."

"You're a far cry off course, Burr. I have no guilt."

"So it wasn't your fault that she went to Wheaton's bed."

Cairn tightened his grip on the window and said nothing.

"She would have lain with the devil himself if she thought it would hurt you." Burr's voice was suddenly quiet.

Cairn turned to look out the window, but he saw nothing except Elizabeth's face, twisted in anger, in hatred. It was entirely possible there had never been another human being who had despised him with such hot intensity. Funny, as a young, ragged lad, he had believed a lady's every thought would be filled with peace and light. Her smile would be radiant, her love would be pure. Elizabeth had taught him much.

"I didn't resent her early affairs," Cairn said to the blur of the passing trees.

"She was a whore, lad. Everyone knew it."

Cairn turned slowly toward his oldest friend. "She was my wife."

The Norseman nodded once. "But it's not your fault that she chose her bedmates poorly."

The window called again. "I should have stopped her."

"How?"

"I am the laird of Teleere."

Burr snorted. "Since when does a laird overrule a woman, lad? You couldn't have stopped her, not without killing her yourself."

"Maybe I should have."

"Aye." Burr sighed as he leaned back again. "Mayhap. But Wheaton beat you to it, and so you make others suffer."

"The girl knows where to find him."

"Does she?"

"Aye. And she'll say eventually."

"Planning some torture are you?"

"I thought I'd leave that up to you, Burr."

"You've always been generous. Even as a lad." He sighed and settled back into his seat.

The wheels lurched, launching them into the air. Cairn gritted his teeth and swore between them.

Burr shook his head and grinned. "I love them bays."

Cairn turned his gaze to his companion and allowed a thin smile.

"What is it?" Burr asked, his brow furrowing.

"I have a plan."

"Does it involve me risking me life?"

"Aye," Cairn said. "That's my favorite part."

Chapter 7

Tatiana paced. Outside her door there was at least one guard. She gave a passing thought to the man she had hired. Where Ralph had gone was impossible to guess. Although he had already been paid a goodly portion of the sum agreed upon, he seemed the sort to continue searching for her. MacTavish's plans, however, were more obscure. She knew she had to escape, and the hour was getting late. Though she'd never been unusually strong, she was hardly fragile. Nay, she was stout enough, but it was a bit too optimistic to think she could overwhelm an armed guard with physical strength. Therefore, she'd best think.

The Viking called Burroun had gone with MacTavish. That left Peters at the door. She focused her thoughts on the lieutenant for a moment, reading his personality. Who was he really? Aye, he was determined to do his lord's will, perhaps obsessively so. But what was his lord's will? What were MacTavish's plans for her?

He despised her. That much was clear, for he'd had her imprisoned. But he'd also seen her released. It seemed obvious, then, that he did not want her dead, but was keeping her close at hand in an attempt to capture Wheaton. Therefore, it stood to reason that he would be careful to keep her alive. And Peters would be more careful still.

She turned like a cornered badger to face the door. Yes, he would be careful, and she must be the same.

She longed to pace again, but she forced herself to wait, to sit on the bed, to plan. Perhaps it did not take long before the knock sounded at her door, but it seemed like forever.

"Who is it?" She made her tone soft, and if there was the slightest quaver to it, it was not altogether planned.

" 'Tis Lieutenant Peters." His voice was the antithesis of hers—commanding, brash, a young soldier with much to prove.

"Come in, Lieutenant."

The door snapped open, and he stepped inside. Behind him came two others, one bearing a tray, the other bringing a bottle and a mug.

Peters stood very straight, though he didn't look directly at her when he spoke. Perhaps he felt some shame for the debacle of the night before. After all, he had delivered her to Pikeshead, and his master had fetched her back. And although she'd heard little of the following conversation between the two of them, she could assume that MacTavish was somewhat irritated. Why then, she wondered, did he continue to put her care in his hands?

"My lord commanded me to bring you sustenance," he said.

She blinked and kept her hands tightly clasped. "My thanks," she murmured. "But I fear I am not hungry."

He shifted his gaze quickly to her and away. A scowl marred his freckled features. His back was perfectly straight, his brightly polished boots aligned just so. "Lord MacTavish ordered me to make certain you eat."

She wrung her hands. "I . . ." she began, then let her gaze fall to her fingers. "I've no wish to cause you any trouble, Lieutenant."

She could feel his attention shift to her again, though she did not raise her eyes to make certain. "But I . . ." Parting her hands, she touched her fingers to her forehead. "I fear I am not well."

"Not well?"

"Dizzy," she said. "Sick to my stomach."

His scowl deepened, and she forced a weak smile. "You needn't worry. I'm not about to perish and disparage you in front of your lord."

"Perish!" He looked paler than ever.

She brightened her tremulous smile a bit. "I will be fine. I only need to rest."

"Food will help settle your stomach," he said, and motioned one of his men to set the tray beside her on the bed. "Eat."

"Perhaps you are right."

He stared at the wall again. "I am."

Tatiana retrieved the loaf of bread from the tray. It was made of well-milled flour, soft-grained and white. She broke off a piece and ate it, then finished off the wine.

Peters watched her in some amazement. His shoulders were only slightly behind vertical.

"Shall I bring up a tub, Lieutenant?" asked the second-closest man. He was short and stout and dark of hair. But his eyes were very blue.

"There is no need, Cormick," said Peters. "There is a bathing area in the adjoining chamber."

"Right there?" The young man sounded awed. Peters kept his expression stoic.

"Shall we fetch water for it then?"

"It is piped up."

"Piped up, sir?"

Peters scowled. "You are not an oarsman on some wave-tossed frigate any longer, Cormick. Try to remember that."

"Yes, sir."

"Go now and fill the vessel."

"Aye, Lieutenant," Cormick said, and hurried across the room to the far door. He opened it, stepped through, and whistled low.

An expression of perturbation crossed Peters's face but he said nothing. Indeed, she couldn't help but notice that he didn't turn toward the other chamber, though the sound of splashing and chuckles echoed in the place.

Tatiana nibbled on her bread and tasted her pie. It was pigeon, mixed in a savory broth and baked to bubbled perfection. Regardless of MacTavish's host of faults, he kept a good kitchen, but perhaps a night in prison would heighten anyone's appreciation for cuisine.

She said nothing as the tub was filled, but concentrated on her meal.

"How do you feel now, madam?" Peters asked. His tone was stiff.

She smiled, employing her most girlish expression, but if truth be told, she was not one for maidenly glances and girlish giggles. Being in line for the helm of the country, even when the possibilities were remote, tended to eliminate flippancy. Being her mother's daughter negated flirtations. Nevertheless, her life depended on her ability to do just those things, so she glanced up through her lashes and fiddled with her mug.

"I am much improved, Lieutenant. Thank you."

"The water . . ." said Cormick, entering the room and grinning like a prankster. "It's warm." Tatiana noticed that his sleeves were wet well past the elbows and his trousers damp about the knees.

Peters gave him a disdainful glance and turned his attention back to Tatiana. "I will leave you to your bath then." She would not have been the least surprised if had clicked his heels together.

"My thanks," she said, and stood, but as she did so, she wobbled slightly and lifted her hand to her brow as if she were about to swoon.

Peters grabbed her elbow in a steely grasp. "Are you unwell?"

She took a moment to answer, then, "Nay," she said, and straightened with a brave effort. "Nay, I am well. Do not concern yourself."

His scowl deepened. She almost smiled.

"You needn't worry," she said as she made her way into the adjoining chamber. It was small and close, almost filled by the round copper tub that stood near the wall. Steam curled like silvery fronds into the air. But it was the window that captured her attention. It was long and narrow, but surely broad enough for her to squeeze through. Her heart leapt to her throat, but she planned carefully. Long ago she had learned her capabilities . . . and her weaknesses. She skimmed the room again. It was not so cluttered as the bedchamber, but it was far from empty. A tall, brightly woven basket with an hourglass shape stood beneath the window, its cover slightly askew. Wooden shoes with curled toes were nestled against an earthenware pot, where a miniature pine tree grew at odd angles. "I am not about to drown," she said, and glanced over her shoulder at Peters. "Or escape through yonder window."

The lieutenant paled visibly. "Perhaps you should wait before entering your bath."

She smiled. "Your lord may return at any moment, and despite what you think of me, I have no wish to disrobe in front of him."

Peters's paleness was gone, immediately replaced by a rush of color. "I did not mean to imply—"

"I will be fine," she assured him, and closed the door behind her.

There was a rap on the other side in less than a heartbeat.

"What is it?" she asked.

"I've no wish to disturb you, my lady . . ."

My lady. She almost smiled.

"But I cannot allow you to remain in there alone."

Slipping out of her shoes, she padded silently to the window, but one glance told her that her initial assessment had been correct. She was too high up. She would not escape by that route. Turning back toward the tub, she loosened the ties at the back of her simple gown.

"Surely you are not suggesting that you watch me bathe," she said.

"Nay." He sounded appalled, then cleared his throat. She could almost see him straighten. "But I must insist that you leave the door ajar."

"But . . ." She let her voice waver again. "Lieutenant, 'twould not be seemly."

"I assure you I've no interest—That is to say, I will not watch you. I only wish to ascertain your safety."

She opened the door and granted him the smallest of smiles. "In other words, you want to make certain I do not escape."

He cleared his throat again, but didn't look her in the eye. "I can see the window from this chamber," he said.

It was her turn to scowl. "And you will not . . . dishonor me?"

If his back were any straighter, he would surely keel over backward like an axed pine. "You have my word, my lady."

She bit her lip. "Very well then. But you will stay well back by yonder wall?"

He glanced over his shoulder, past the menagerie of unidentified objects toward the bedroom's only door. "I will guard the portal," he said. There was a host of places to sit, including a small satiny couch of sorts that curled dramatically at one end. There was also the bed, which seemed the most welcoming, but he would use neither of those. No, she was certain he would stand hour upon end like a stone sentry and be perfectly happy doing so.

She nodded, then left the door ajar and pattered out of sight. His footfalls were distinct as they paced from the plush weave of the carpet, onto hardwood, and back onto softness.

She skimmed the room quickly now—the tub, the plant, an ungainly statuette. It seemed to be a figure of a man. It was not large, perhaps twelve inches in height, but what it lacked in stature, it made up for in earthy suggestiveness. The figure's penis was nearly half the length of its body and as erect as an oak tree. Her hands shook as she lifted it. It was heavy, solid, substantial. A fine weapon. A noise brushed from the other room, and she stiffened. But in an instant it was silent again. She exhaled heavily and set the figurine quickly aside.

This was no time to hesitate. Straightening, she set her hands to her laces. She was not accustomed to dressing herself, but her costumes were usually more elaborate. This gown was simple enough to remove. She did so, controlling her breathing and glancing furtively toward the door. Not that she didn't trust Peters. If she were reading him right, he would take a sword through the heart before he would dare displease his lord, and if there was one thing the princess of Sedonia was adept at, it was reading people. She had learned long ago to know whom to trust and whom to fear. All fawned, few cared. She had been a duke's daughter since the day of her birth, a commodity, an heiress, and now a sovereign. Like so much gilded treasure, to be carefully hoarded and well spent.

In a moment her shift had joined her gown. Her stockings came next, and she drew a deep breath as she shed her long cotton stays.

The clothes reeked. That much was true. She needed a bath, but that was hardly her reason for agreeing to this foolishness. She stepped into the tub. The temperature was perfect. She wouldn't have suspected Cormick for a lady's maid.

The water slipped steadily up her body. It was almost tempting to relax, to let the warmth soothe her frazzled nerves, but of course she had no time for that. She had been less cautious than her situation warranted, true. She had made a misstep, had lost her guard, but she was no fool, and she would prove that.

Reaching up, she splashed the water a bit and glanced toward the door. Not a sound came from the adjoining room. Her heart was beating heavily against her ribs, but she forced herself to pick up a canister of dried herbs that sat beside the tub and spread them across the water. Lavender perfumed the air. She relaxed a smidgen. There would be little enough time for such a luxury. So she lifted the bar of soap and tried to hum a tune. But for the life of her, she could think of nothing. She splashed again, thinking, then finally remembered Beethoven's *Eroica*.

She hummed it softly. Her voice wavered a little. She steadied it and continued on, splashing and washing.

Not a sound issued from the bedchamber, but from the bailey below, she heard a horse nicker. She stiffened. Had she waited too long? Had MacTavish already returned? She remained frozen in place, listening with her entire being, but all was silent again. No one entered, no one exited, no one spoke. There was nothing she could do but continue with her plan.

She hummed again. The dramatic symphony sounded frenetic, but her heart seemed to be pounding in her very ears, and her hands shook on the scented soap.

She could wait no longer. Holding her breath, she said a silent prayer, then lifted the well-aroused figurine from the floor. Letting her arm droop over the side of the tub, she gave a small whimper of sound and sank quietly below the surface.

Thoughts swarmed like wild bees in her head. She'd been too quiet. Peters hadn't heard. But suddenly the hard tattoo of boots echoed against hardwood. Even beneath the water, she heard Peters rasp an expletive. She waited, breath held, but still he didn't reach for her. Instead, he turned and ran for the door. Panic seized her. She should have guessed he would be leery of touching any woman found naked in his lord's bedchamber. She should have known . . . but at that moment she heard Peters turn back, heard him falter, and then he reached for her, hauling her out of the water, cradling her against his chest. In that instant, she struck.

She crashed the figurine against his skull with all her strength. His eyes opened wide, and then, like a loosened marionette, he crumpled to the floor, bearing her with him.

She scrambled to her feet, wanting to cry, to check his pulse, to call for help, but she did none of those things. Instead, she dropped the figurine and grabbed the pistol from Peters's belt. It felt heavy in her hand, but she didn't delay. Yanking the door open, she brandished the weapon. Not a soul was in sight. She jumped into the hallway and leapt toward the corner. She would duck into a room, find a disguise, and then she'd be—

It was at that very second that MacTavish rounded the corner. She hit him dead on, striking his chest with the impetus of her weight and bouncing off like a ricocheting cricket ball. Her bare buttocks slapped against the floor. The pistol flew out of her hand, struck the wall with a wooden thud, and exploded nearly in her ear.

By the time she sat up, dazed and disoriented, Peters had stumbled around the corner, Cormick was grinning like a demented monkey, and MacTavish was staring down at her in utter glaring silence.

It was Burr who finally spoke. "I like her," he said. "She's got spunk."

Comrick's grin widened.

"And she's not shy 'bout being naked," added the Norseman. " 'Tis a rare quality in a maid these days."

"Peters." MacTavish never shifted his attention from her.

She scooted backward, found her feet, and rose with shaky determination. Every instinct in her insisted that she cover herself, but it would do no good, so she balled her fists at her sides and raised her chin in tremulous defiance.

"Do you think you can manage one simple task?" MacTavish's tone was dry and dark.

The lieutenant nodded, looking as pale as an Easter lily beneath his freckles.

"Fetch a blanket."

The soldier turned rapidly away, but MacTavish spoke again.

"And Peters."

The man pivoted, wobbling slightly. If Tatiana weren't terrified for her own safety, she might have felt guilty. As it was, she truly did feel sick to her stomach, and a bit lightheaded. But swooning seemed out of the question. Chances were good that if she passed out again, they would simply toss her out the nearest window.

"Yes, my liege." The lieutenant's voice was as pale as his complexion.

"One more damned blunder and you'll be having your meals at Pikeshead. And it won't be as a guard."

There was absolute silence as MacTavish's meaning came home to Peters, but he finally swallowed. His Adam's apple bobbed, and he nodded once before hurrying away.

Chapter 8

The bedchamber was absolutely silent.

The girl stood in the center of the room with nothing but a tattered plaid blanket wrapped tightly about her shoulders. Her hair was a dark mess of silken chaos running down her back. And yet she stood as straight as a mizzenmast, unbowed and unembarrassed. But what did she have to be embarrassed about? Cairn had seen her body. Hell, they'd all seen her body.

He ground his teeth and circled her. She didn't turn, but watched him from the corner of her eye until he was well out of sight.

The candles lit to ward off the impending darkness gleamed on her kitten-soft hair. "Why naked, Megs?"

She didn't respond for a moment. Indeed, for several seconds, he thought she would not.

"I tire of this game, MacTavish," she said finally, and she did sound tired, but in a bored sort of way, as if they sat in some well-appointed parlor playing faro in the wee hours of the morning.

He felt his brows rise, but not so much as other body parts. "And what game is that?"

"This game of make-believe," she said.

"Is that what we're playing?"

She nodded. Her chin was tilted up slightly, perhaps to enable her to look into his eyes, but perhaps it was simply her attitude. Take no prisoners, bow to no man. "But I seem to be the only one with a fictional name."

"It does seem to be the case," he agreed.

She gave him a nod for the twist of her words and continued. "Mayhap I shall conceive one for you. I believe I like the name . . ." She paused as if thinking. "Norman."

He waited a moment, then, "You know I could have you executed, don't you?"

If he had planned to frighten her, his goal was sorely missed, for her chin notched up another fractional inch. "Truly?" she said, fluttering one hand to her chest. She was the very mistress of sarcasm. "And all the while I was only dashing about in the altogether for the sheer joy of the romp."

Something tightened in his gut at the memory of seeing her naked. Hoary had tightened, too. Joy would not quite describe his own feelings, but if truth be told he was entirely at a loss to guess at hers.

"I can understand why you might want to bash Peters on the head," he admitted. "I'm tempted to do the same meself at times. Taking his pistol . . ." He shrugged, feeling a spark of admiration. The top of her shiny little head barely reached his shoulder. " 'Twas a good try. I'd have done the same meself if I—"

"I am so flattered," she interrupted.

He paused. She made him grit his teeth. All the time. As if he were braced against some deviant pain. "Flattered?"

"That the great MacTavish might actually choose the same course I myself undertook." She pressed a splay-fingers hand to her breast, which was something of a silly gesture, since her other hand still held like a recalcitrant hound to that damned, ragged blanket.

He nodded once as if accepting her compliment at face value. "Aye," he said. "I would have taken the pistol." He paced again. "The only difference is . . ." He shrugged. "I would have taken a garment or two with me. And I would have succeeded, of course."

If she was angry, the emotion didn't show on her face. In fact, few situations ever seemed to change her expression. As if she were untouchable, far above his reach, except those few times he had reached through her defenses. And that stoicism made him feel all the more edgy. Pirates were not known for their sterling control over their emotions. But he managed a smile and let his gaze skim down her form. It was a wasted effort, for she was bundled like a newborn babe and seemed oblivious to his disdain. Damn her.

"I'm ever so sorry to offend your sensibilities with my nakedness," she said, and curtsied. "But if you would hand me my clothes, I might shield my shame from your sight."

"Shame." He felt a muscle dance in his jaw, calmed it with an effort, and circled her again. "I begin to think you have no shame, Megs."

"You bas—" She never completed the thought, but caught herself immediately as if she were about to say something rather uncomplimentary. He smiled and realized she seemed as surprised as he by the truncated outburst. Perhaps she was not so unaffected after all.

He raised a brow.

She drew a deep breath through her nose. Her nostrils flared slightly. Above the blanket, her phenomenal breasts rose. Her dark hair was slicked back from her heart-shaped face, and her body was wrapped in green plaid, narrowing at her thighs, then sweeping toward the floor. And despite all the good sense he believed he might possess, he couldn't help but think she looked like a mermaid come to land. But not just any mermaid, a sea princess, gracing the lesser folk with her presence.

"You are the one who should be ashamed," she said. "Holding me here against my will. Threatening me at every turn. Taking my clothes."

He hadn't taken her clothes this time, but he didn't mention that fact. "And of course you have done no wrong?"

"No, I have not."

"You did not steal my brooch, allow a criminal to escape?"

She was shaking her head.

"Stab me with a compass? Knock my lieutenant unconscious?"

Her head shaking ceased, and for the briefest instant, her eyes flickered away. "Aye, I did that one . . . those last two things."

And suddenly he wanted to laugh, but it would surely not seem very "lordly." He should probably be calling for the executioner even now and bellowing, "Off with her head. Off with her head," with a good deal of fanfare and pomp.

But she had such a proud, witty head. And it was attached to such a fine, luscious body. Surely she would miss it if she were parted from it.

"If you're going to kill me, why wait?" she asked.

He wondered vaguely if she could read his mind. But nay. It was far more likely that she was only watching his expressions. Anger was an emotion he bent to his will. 'Twas what came of having the face of a prepubescent lad while trying to keep a score of seasoned sailors from wreaking havoc.

"You think I'm going to kill you, Megs?" he asked.

She shrugged. The motion reminded him suddenly of Gem. They were not unlike, those two. Which made him wonder about the scheme he had set Burr to. Would it work?

"Is that your plan, my liege?" she asked.

My liege. The words were naught but a mockery from her lips. He should have been insulted, he supposed. But her lips were exceptionally full and lusciously bright. "No," he said, and pulled his attention from her mouth. "Not yet at least."

"Why?"

"Maybe it's because I can learn something from you."

"From me? A common thief? Again, I am flattered."

She had a gift for conveying the opposite impression of her spoken words.

"As well you should be."

"What is it you wish to know?"

A half dozen questions jockeyed for position in his mind, but he squelched the most vociferous one. After all, it hardly mattered if she felt any desire for him. Did not matter if she felt as breathless as he when they touched.

"Do you always escape while naked?" he asked, and realized that sometimes Hoary had more influence over his verbalization than he liked to admit. After all, he should be asking about her connection to Wheaton. But he'd tried that already, hadn't he?

"You ordered me to bathe," she said. "I could hardly disobey my sovereign lord, for surely he knows what is best for a lowly—"

"Save the sheep dung for the gardener, Megs," he said. "And answer me straight."

"It was the time Peters would least expect my escape!" she spat.

It made some sense. For while Peters might be obsessive about protecting his laird, he was less than comfortable around the fairer sex and might never have considered she would compromise herself to outwit him. Naïveté was a cruel master.

"So you planned to seduce him?"

Maybe there was something odd in his tone, because she narrowed her eyes at him, like a cat watching its prey. Wasn't she supposed to be the prey?

"So you would add whore to my list of sins?" she asked.

It was a harsh word, but she was in a harsh situation, and surely if he were in her shoes, or barefoot as she happened to be, he would not be above a bit of seduction, but perhaps that truth didn't need to be voiced.

"How far did you go, Megs?"

"In my plans for seduction?" It was her turn to pace. Her full lips were pursed, her eyes disdainful. "The truth is, MacTavish, I tire of your questions." She said the words as if he were excused. He raised his brows.

"I want to know exactly what happened."

"Then ask your lieutenant."

In fact, he already had, but the story was so pathetic, so simple, that it was near impossible to believe. She had taken a bath while Peters watched the door. Suddenly her humming had ceased and he heard a gasp and small splash. Thinking she was drowning, he'd rushed in to save her. At which time she trounced him on the head and disappeared with his pistol. The entire laughable tale put the freckle-faced lieutenant in a very poor light, so there seemed little reason for the man to lie.

The girl was watching him closely. Then the corners of her mouth raised slightly. It was an intriguing sight. Like the dawning of a smile on a fairy face. "You already asked him, didn't you?"

Obviously, but Cairn would almost rather believe she had seduced the poor lad than that she had tricked him with such pitiable ease. Hell, the stiff-backed fool was lucky she hadn't decided to drown him while she was at it.

"He was merely following your orders, MacTavish," she

said. "You told him to make certain I bathed and to keep me safe."

Was she defending him? "I don't remember telling him to be bashed over the head and let you escape with his pistol."

"Perhaps he was improvising," she said. "I certainly was."

Naked improvisation. Maybe it would catch on. "With Dimitri?" he asked.

She frowned a question, so he strode into the bathing chamber and retrieved the impromptu weapon.

"Dimitri," he said, lifting the defamed figurine high. Its penis had been broken clean off. "He was a fertility god."

"He was ugly."

"Aye, well now he's castrated."

She shrugged with absolute unconcern. The blanket had slipped. An inch or so of golden shoulder peeked into view. Hoary raised his horny head. Desire tightened Cairn's body like fear, and suddenly he found that he didn't care if she were good or evil, if she were the widow she claimed to be or the thief he believed her to be. He wanted her regardless.

He glanced at the statue. Is that how he would end up? Was that his fate? Castrated by a woman with no soul? Was she another Elizabeth? But no, Elizabeth had been groomed to deceive. Brought up by conniving nobility and taught to believe that everything belonged to her. Everything she desired. Everything she touched. Everything she saw.

This Megs, despite her attitude, could not believe the same. And even if she did, he could take advantage of her charms and let her be. Send her on her merry way. There was no reason to believe she wouldn't enjoy it as much as he. Women didn't tend to shudder with distaste when he passed them on the thoroughfare. He was not presently without a mistress because of lack of interest on their part. Rather, he needed time to himself. Or at least he had. But circumstances had just changed. This was the lass he would take to his bed, and when they parted ways, there would be no royal parents to contend with. No threats of war, no political entanglements.

Besides, she was Wheaton's companion. How much more enjoyable she would be, knowing he would ruin her for him. Aye, it was clever to use her as bait. But why not enjoy her charms while he did so?

He leaned a hip against his desk and watched her. "So your faith in Wheaton is already waning?" he asked.

She said nothing.

"Else there would be little reason for your attempt to escape."

"Tell me." She watched him with no expression on her perfect features. "What makes you so deluded?"

Deluded? Maybe he was, but he didn't care at that precise moment. Maybe it was because he enjoyed the game, maybe it was her near nudity, or maybe it was the knowledge that, despite everything, she would be his. The decision had been made. "You still insist you don't know him?" he asked.

"Because I do not."

"Then why the bravado, Megs? If not because of assurance that he will save you? Are you not afraid? Are you not worried?"

"Is that what you want?"

He thought for a moment. "It might make me feel better."

"Then I am sorry to disappoint you."

"You don't disappoint me," he countered, and found that it was immensely true. Every move she made fascinated him. "I but wonder how you can be so certain of your escape from my dastardly clutches."

She shrugged. The blanket slipped another half an inch. "You seem loath to do bodily damage."

"There are fivescore of seamen who would argue with that."

"Your obsession with Wheaton is too consuming. You believe, against all sanity, I might add, that he will come for me. And until then you will keep me alive."

"Alive, yes," he agreed. "But there is no guaranteeing your condition."

"So you would torture me?"

He shrugged. Perhaps she had paled a mite, but her chin hadn't dropped a whit. "Why wouldn't I?"

"Because of Sir Albert."

He was surprised. Surprised at her answer, surprised at her attitude, surprised she even remembered his effeminate tutor's name. "Albert."

"Yes," she said, and, taking a few steps to the right, seated herself on a lavishly upholstered chair. She looked incredibly at home there, as if she weren't a prisoner, as if she weren't threatened, as if she were a sea princess, sitting comfortably on a coral reef as her clansmen gathered round to honor her. "You are a barbarian."

"I'm not sure how that attribute will make me want to keep you safe and well, Megs."

"You are a barbarian," she repeated. "But you are also the lord of Teleere."

He stared. She shrugged. "Thus your need to prove yourself."

"You think I won't harm you because of my need to act . . . elite?"

"Torturing a young foreign woman for unproven crimes might seem less than noble."

"But couldn't I have you tortured in private?"

Perhaps this was an idea she hadn't considered, because she paused, then rose and finally spoke.

"Someone would know."

"Someone?"

"Burr. Peters. Sir Albert."

"Ahh."

"Thus I suggest a compromise," she said and paced the room with mincing steps.

"I'm listening," he assured her, but mostly he was watching. Watching as the blanket slipped another inch. Watched her lips move and her tongue moisten her lips. He watched and waited and felt his senses vibrate at her nearness. The very air felt different when she was in the room.

"You release me this very day," she said, "and I will make sure there are no repercussions for your egregious actions."

"Egregious," he said, and stepped toward her. She stepped back, toward the bed.

"Yes." She nodded, but she swallowed and tilted her chin up at the same time. "Let me go, and all will be well."

He took another few steps. She did the same, but in a moment she was up against the mattress, and he could not help but reach for her. She plopped down onto the bed, ready to scurry backward, but he was quicker and pinned her there, one arm on each side of her body with her legs bent beneath him. Their faces were inches apart. Their breath melded, and in that moment he could think of nothing but feeling her beneath him, of sweeping his hand up the curves of her body. Of possessing her.

Her breath was coming hard. But so was his. He leaned in and kissed her lips.

Lightning struck him, shaking him to the core, but in a moment he realized her hand was on his chest, splayed against the rapid beat of his heart.

He drew away with a hard effort. Her eyes were wide and stunned, her plump lips parted and moist. He leaned in again, but she pressed him back.

"Let me go, MacTavish," she breathed.

It took a moment before he could manage to shake his head, longer still before he could speak.

"I can't let you go, Megs," he said. "But I can make love to you."

Chapter 9

"**M**ake—" She couldn't seem to quite force the words past her erotic lips.

The blanket had slipped sideways, exposing half her left arm and the high portions of her chest. Cairn smiled. "I won't hurt you, lass. In fact, if you quit your foolishness and—"

"Foolishness! You call protecting my virtue . . . protecting my very life—"

"Quit braining my lieutenant," he explained, and because he could not help himself, he gently kissed the point of her shoulder.

She jumped like a startled quail beneath the caress. Interesting.

"Quit trying to escape," he added, and kissed her collarbone. "Sleep with me." The words came unbidden.

"No," she said. The single word was breathy, but whether it was from fear or desire, he could only guess.

He glanced up. Her eyes were as wide and bottomless as tidal waves, her pupils all but swallowing the vibrant green of her irises. "No you won't quit braining Peters or—"

"I won't sleep with you!" She was breathing hard. "Ever."

He eased his weight off her the slightest degree. She drew her feet onto the mattress, ready to escape, but it only served to displace the blanket, for he still held her captive. She was all but naked now, and that fact left him breathless, for she was stunning.

Judging by the size of her breasts, one would assume she was stout, but she had virtually no belly. He swept his hand over the concave expanse and down. Her hips were as narrow as a sapling, her thighs lean and long.

"But you would have slept with Peters," he said, running his hand down her leg. She quivered in his wake. "And he has freckles."

"I did not say I would sleep with him."

"You implied it."

He scooped his hand behind her thigh, then around and down, so that he cradled her bottom in his hand. *Nice. Nice nice bottom*, Hoary said.

"MacTavish!" Her voice sounded panicked, her eyes looked the same. "I lied to you."

He stopped his hand, held his breath. "You did?"

She nodded and licked her lips. His hand remained immobile on the luscious curve of her buttocks. "I did not come here with only one companion."

What new lie was this? He commenced breathing and skimmed his fingertips along her bottom.

She swallowed, breathing hard. "There were others. I was to . . . meet them."

He left the lovely curve of her buttocks with some regret, easing his palm over her thigh to her knee.

"They . . ." She was breathing hard. "They had my possessions."

"Possessions?" He paused and found her gaze, but her

body called again, and he turned his attention back to the compelling sweep of her satiny skin.

"I am a wealthy woman, MacTavish. Let me go and when I find my—" His fingers bumped over her knee. It was sharp and cute and strangely enough, begged to be kissed. He moved down in that direction. "Friends." Her voice was raspy. "When I find my friends I will reward you. Handsomely."

"I'd much rather have this," he said, and kissed her thigh. Her stomach contracted. Her lips parted.

"Quit!" She was breathing hard through her mouth. It did strange things to his gut. "Don't do that."

"Why?"

"It is not right."

"It feels right." Tugging the blanket gently, he fully bared her left breast. "It looks . . . phenomenal," he said, and, easing up her body, kissed the outside curve of that one succulent breast.

She bucked against him. "MacTavish! I—Cease! Let me go."

"You needn't fear, lass."

"Let me go!" She sounded panicked. Where threats of decapitation and hangings had barely made her blink, the idea of sex seemed to send her teetering toward the edge of hysteria. Why? He narrowed his eyes in thought.

"Did he hurt you, Megs? Is that why you're afraid?"

"No."

"Did he warn you not to lie with another man?" he asked, and brushed her nipple with his finger. She jumped again.

"What are you talking about?"

"Wheaton." He was patient now, ultimately so, for his mind was elsewhere. Or perhaps nowhere at all. His body had taken over. "Did he threaten you?"

"No. As I've told you before—"

But he kissed her breast again, and her words stumbled to a halt, left hanging on a breathy note.

"No threats," he murmured, and skimmed the flat of his hand down her midline. Her eyes fell closed, and her body arched slightly. It was in that moment that the truth struck him like a mallet to the head. She might be afraid. She might be terrified. But she was also aroused. Wee Megs liked sex. Craved sex. So why was she fighting it. But when his hand reached her pubic hair she bucked like a storm-tossed schooner, nearly escaping. He drew her back by the barest of margins. But the blanket had abandoned her completely, doing nothing now but cradling her lovely rear. Her back was against the headboard, and her knees were bent, but it was her breasts that held his attention. They were capped by nipples that were dark and full and peaked like small, precious jewels. And they moved, up and down almost violently with the force of her breath.

"Don't do this, MacTavish!" Perhaps it was a plea, but it sounded more like a warning.

"Why?" he asked and stroked her calf.

Her eyes dropped closed again and her head fell back slightly, but she rallied in a moment, though she didn't manage to speak.

"You're not afraid of Wheaton." He caressed her toes. She pulled them back against her buttocks with a shudder. He moved to the other ankle. "You're unattached." He trickled his fingers up the back of her leg. She swallowed hard. "And though I don't pretend to know women well . . ." He smoothed his knuckles down the length of her thigh toward the destination he so desired. "Methinks you do not detest the idea of copulation." He moved in for a kiss. "So—"

"I'm a virgin!"

He reared back, cocked his head, and stared at her. Seconds ticked away. He cleared his throat, then shook his head once and held it canted to the side. "I was in a battle some years back," he said.

She didn't interrupt him, didn't speak, just stared into his eyes like a cornered kitten. Hissing and ready to claw.

"A powder keg exploded nearby and I think . . ." He scowled, trying to do just that. "I think I lost some hearing in my right ear because I thought I heard you say you were a—"

"Virgin."

Her legs were tucked tight against her fancy bottom, and her arms were wrapped around them, but her gorgeous breasts swelled beside her knees, and it seemed that if he made the right move, she would unfurl like a summer rose beneath his hands

"I am sorry, lass, but . . ." He drew a deep breath, trying to slow down, to consider. "I'm having a bit of trouble believing that Teleere's most infamous thief is—"

"I'm not Megs."

He nodded again. "Then you are—"

"Linnet."

"The widow."

"Aye." She licked her lips, shifted her gaze sideways, and turned solemnly back to him. Her eyes were tremendously large and ridiculously bright. "About that . . ." She cleared her throat.

He waited, fascinated.

"My husband—"

"Wilbur."

"William. William and I never . . ." She stopped and shook her head.

He raised his brows and waited some more.

"We never . . ."

He leaned closer as if that would help him hear the unspoken words.

Turning her eyes sideways, she snagged the blanket and tried to pull it over her nakedness, but he was sitting on it, and all she managed to cover was her feet. It was unfortunate but he could live with it.

"I never . . . knew him."

"You didn't know your own husband."

"I *knew* him. Of course I *knew* him. I just didn't . . ." She winced. "*Know* him." She closed her eyes as if shutting out this entire scene. He remained silent. She opened her eyes with a snap, and lo and behold there was anger there.

"You know exactly what I mean," she said.

He would have laughed, but all his energy had headed south, and he found he lacked the ability for such a Herculean effort. So he drew a deep breath and rallied. "You never swived your own husband?"

"That's . . ." She pursed her lips and straightened her back against the headboard. If she'd had clothes, she would have looked quite proper. As it was, she simply looked delectable. "That's a very crass word, sir."

He did laugh now, but the sound was unnatural. "Are you correcting my grammar, Megs?"

"I am *not*—"

"That's right. You're Linnet. The widow, who never . . . *knew* her own husband."

"I am telling you the truth."

"Really? Then explain. I'm fascinated. Why would a woman like you . . . a woman who obviously . . ." He skimmed her body, but he did not touch. "Who obviously does not . . . detest the idea of *knowing*—"

"He was unable," she interrupted.

"What?"

She cleared her throat and nodded violently. A slick sable curl bobbed across her nipple. He watched its progress breathlessly. "He had been . . . injured."

"How did—"

"By a bull."

"I thought he was a tailor." He couldn't resist her any longer, but reached out to brush that teasing hair from her breast.

She drew a hissing breath but spoke fairly steadily. "His father was a landowner. As was mine. Rupert. His father's name was Rupert. His mother was called Martha. But he called her Fah. I don't know why. It was silly really. They farmed a piece of land near Midhurst. He planned to be a farmer as well. In fact, he said to me once . . . 'a man isn't really a man without' . . ." He skimmed his fingers across her breast to her arm. She closed her eyes. "Land." She finished the sentence on a shiver.

"I've seen some bonny sights," he said, and stroked her arm. Her lids lifted with slow deliberation. "The sun climbing, red as cranberries, out of the Caspian Sea. The flight of a sailfish as it soars for the heavens. But you, lass . . ." He shook his head, knowing he should detest her, should despise her, should at least be wary of her. But her skin was so soft. "You are the most beautiful thing yet."

She stared at him in disbelief for a moment, then, "He intended to follow in his father's footsteps," she whispered.

He slipped his fingers into her hair, stroking it over her velvety shoulder.

"But then the bull—"

He traced a waving strand down her arm. Her lips parted slightly. No words came.

"Gored him?" he suggested.

"Yes." She nodded, but the expression seemed almost sleepy. "Yes. She gored him."

He smiled. She was always lovely, even when she was trying to kill him. But now, with her eyes wide with desire and her breasts bare to the world . . . Triton's balls She was a sight to behold.

"I don't pretend to be well versed in animal husbandry, lass," he said, and trailed a finger beneath her left breast. "But I believe bulls are male."

"Oh." The sound was little more than a sigh. "Yes. Of course. *He* gored him."

"Before or after you married him?"

"Before," she said. "Otherwise, we would surely have . . ."

"*Known* each other."

"Of . . . of course."

"Which explains your frustration."

"My . . ." She sighed as he stroked her forearm.

"Frustration," he repeated and shrugged. "Because you've not been *known*."

"I am not frustrated."

He trailed his fingers up her arm. She shivered.

He watched her eyes.

"It is not frustration. It is—"

"You will enjoy it."

"What?"

"Let me make love to you."

"Nay. I—"

He kissed her knee. She started.

"It's been a long time for me, too. Who knows? It might do us both some good."

"I—I cannot."

"I'm sure you're wrong."

"I mean I will not."

"Even if I let you go?"

"What?"

He regretted the words as soon as he said them, but they were out and he was horny. "If you don't enjoy it. If you can look me in the eye and say it didn't please you"—he shrugged, probably because he was a raving lunatic—"I'll let you go."

"Free?"

"Aye."

"You lie."

He shrugged again. "I can't say I haven't lied in the past."

"So you *are* lying."

"Take a risk, Megs. Why not? Even if I am lying, you'd be no worse off than now."

"Not true. I'd be compromised, and—"

He kissed her thigh. She exhaled softly between parted lips.

"With child."

"Surely you don't think women get pregnant every time they . . . *know* a man."

She stared.

"Do you?"

"Of course not." She sounded breathless and innocent.

"You won't get pregnant."

"How do you know?" Her voice was a whisper.

"I give you my word."

Uncertainly shone like sunrise on her perfect features. "And if I don't like it . . ." Her words trailed off.

"I'll let you go."

"But what if I fabricate the truth?"

"Is that the same as lying?"

She nodded.

"When I'm dishonest it's called lying, and when you're dishonest it's called fabricating the truth?"

She scowled, not easily distracted. "What if I lie?"

"I'll know."

"Ahh." She pursed her lips. Everything below his waist ached with anticipation. "So that's it. Even if I say I abhorred it, you will call me a liar and keep me bound here. You have no intention of—"

"If you look me in the eye and tell me you . . . abhorred it, I will let you go."

"How do I know you are telling the truth?"

"You don't."

She shook her head. "Then—"

"I could call Peters in. I could sign my name in front of witnesses."

Her jaw dropped. Perhaps she was beginning to understand the depth of his own frustration.

"Do you want me to?"

"Nay!" she gasped.

He couldn't help but smile. Neither could he seem to keep his hands to himself. "Then—"

"Very well." She said the words quickly, as if she were afraid that if she didn't say them hastily, they wouldn't be said.

"You agree?"

"Aye, if you vow, as a gentleman—"

"I'm not a gentleman, Megs. And I don't pretend to be."

She scowled. "As a lord—"

"I promise," he said. "As a man."

She bit her lip, glanced toward the door, and scowled. "Very well," she said slowly. But that was it. She didn't move. Didn't touch him. Didn't smile. In fact, she looked as stiff as a longboat's oar and just about as eager.

He couldn't help but chuckle. "I'm not planning to tie you to the mizzenmast and flay you," he said. "You can relax."

She swallowed. "What is a mizzenmast?"

He kissed the corner of her mouth, gently, then drew back with a hard effort.

"It's the mast aft of the main mast," he explained, and kissed her jaw.

"Oh," she said, and tilted her head slightly. "What's a mast."

He kissed her throat. "How can you live on an island and know nothing of ships?" Letting his fingers skim her jaw line, he kissed her collarbone.

She sighed, but quietly, as if she didn't want him to know. "I don't live on an island. I live—"

He froze. Her eyes popped open.

"In London," she said.

"With Winston."

"William," she corrected. "And he is deceased."

"And you never *knew* him."

"No. I did not."

"Did you see him naked?"

"What?"

He smiled at the shock in her voice. He was certain she wasn't a virgin, but he would never again doubt her acting ability. "Surely he must have removed his clothes from time to time."

"Yes. Of course. He . . ." She swallowed. "Disrobed."

"Then you won't be shocked by the sight of me."

By the look in her eyes, he would guess that might be a false assumption.

"Will you?" he asked, and brushed aside her hair to kiss her neck.

"He was not—" She was breathing hard again. It was, perhaps, the most beautiful sound he had ever heard, like the soft lap of waves against a swift vessel's prow. "He wasn't like you."

He drew back and raised his brows. "The bull must have done a hell of a job."

"I did not mean—" She inhaled slightly and pursed her lips. "You are making light of this."

"Am I?"

"His injuries were quite serious."

"Were they?" he asked and stroked her neck.

"Yes. He almost died."

"Did you nurse him back to health?"

"I did in . . ." She paused as he kissed her hairline.

"Was he naked?"

"You keep coming back to that."

He smiled. "I don't want you breaking down the door in your rush for freedom if I unbutton my shirt."

She swallowed. "Are you going to?"

"I was hoping you would do it for me."

"Me?"

"Aye," he said, and, sliding his hand down her arm, lifted her fingers in his own. Bearing them to his lips, he kissed them gently. "After all, you nursed your husband back to health. Surely it will not be a shock—"

"I told you. He was not like you."

"He did have a chest, didn't he?" Cairn asked, and set her hand against the front of his shirt.

She licked her lips. "Of course he had a chest."

He shrugged. Her fingers shifted slightly over the play of his muscles. Her eyes widened.

"Then how were we different?"

Her hand remained exactly as it was, pressed lightly over top of his right nipple.

"You could take a look if it would better help you remember."

For a moment he wondered if she really would flee for the door, but instead she drew a deep breath and lifted her other hand.

His shirt sighed open with breathtaking slowness.

"Well?" he asked.

She cleared her throat and raised her gaze to his. "He was not so . . ." She paused as if revising her original thought. "Sun-browned as you."

"He probably didn't spend a lot of time topside."

"Topside? No." She glanced at his chest again and licked her lips. "He was a—" Cairn moved a fraction of an inch closer. "Tailor."

"You told me that."

"And very good at his appointed task."

"Appointed task." He liked the way she used her words. Execrable. It was now one of his favorite words. And it had been given to him by Magical Megs. But just now she didn't seem like Teleere's most infamous thief, but rather like some fine lady just dropped into his lap, like a delectable bit of ripe fruit.

"Yes." Perhaps she was insulted, because she stiffened slightly and drew her hand away. He was immediately sorry he had spoken because he missed the feel of her hands against his chest.

"So Wallace was a good tailor."

She pursed her lips. "William. And yes, he was."

He wondered vaguely if it seemed strange to her that she was sitting buck naked telling stories about her fictional dead husband.

"So he could have made . . ." He paused and slipped out of his tunic. "This shirt?"

Her mouth dropped open. Her gaze was glued to his chest. "Megs?"

She jerked her eyes upward. "Yes. Yes. He could make it. Could have made it. Could—"

"And the trousers?"

For a moment he thought she might leap right off the bed. But she calmed herself with an effort and raised her chin even more.

"Yes, he could have made those, too, and you needn't remove them for me to be certain," she added quickly.

"But it would make getting to *know* you simpler."

"I . . . I think you know me well enough."

He laughed. "You play the innocent maid very well, Megs," he said, and reached for his belt.

She licked her lips and glanced toward the door.

"What of our deal?" he asked.

She shifted her eyes back to his. There was panic there, but it was not real, he reminded himself. Still, she was an incredible actress. The stage was sorely lacking.

"I do not trust you," she said.

"You don't think you'll enjoy it?"

"I do not think you will let me go when I do not."

He smiled again. "Then call it quits, Megs. You're welcome to stay here indefinitely."

"Or until you execute me."

"Or that of course."

She stiffened. "I guess I have little choice."

"You're hard on a man's ego," he said, and setting his hands to his trousers, removed them with ease, barely noticing the wound that haunted him. Hoary sprang to attention.

Candlelight flickered in her eyes, which she refused to lower. But he could no longer read her emotions. If indeed, she had any.

He took a step toward the bed. She scrunched back even farther as he eased onto the mattress.

"Really, Megs, some women find me somewhat preferable to death."

He watched her swallow. Again, he couldn't read her mood. He only hoped it wasn't disdain. He'd had enough of that to last a lifetime.

"In fact," he added, "there are a few who might envy your position."

"Truly?" There might be tension in her body, but her voice was a cool as river water. "Any you could contact immediately?"

He laughed again. She was good at insults. If you were careful, you might miss that completely. You had to like that in a murderous thief.

"Lie back, lass," he ordered. "Relax."

She remained exactly as she was. Scrunched into a ball the size of a pillow. "Which do you want?" she asked.

He raised a brow.

"I can lie back or I can relax. Both would be quite impossible."

"I am starting to believe there is nothing impossible for the Magical Megs. Lie back."

He thought she would refuse, but she finally did as told, scooting stiffly downward, so that she lay stretched out before him. Still, her arms managed to cover a surprising portion of her more interesting parts. But then they were pretty much all interesting.

Her legs were ridiculously long for such a small frame. Her hips were narrow, her belly nonexistent, and her breasts . . .

They were stunning, full and heavy with pale mocha skin topped with checkerberry nipples.

Impatience stroked him like a playful whip. Hoary whimpered. But he'd made a deal, and he would stick with it.

True, he was certain she would not do the same. He was certain she would swear she felt nothing and leave him forever. But he would know the truth, and that would be enough.

So he stroked her gently. She shivered beneath his fingertips. His own body reciprocated, seeming to absorb the rush. But still he wouldn't hurry. It had been a long while for him. But when she returned to Wheaton, she would return knowing he could move her. And eventually Wheaton would know the same. So he caressed her until her tension eased. He kissed her arms, her waist, the delicate indentation of her navel. And finally, when he thought he could bear no more, her tension returned, but it was a different sort of tension now. Impatient, writhing.

"Megs."

She moaned, and he slid his hand between her thighs. They parted like magic, baring the sweet fruit of his labor. She was sleek and wet. Did she get so wet for Wheaton? The question tormented him, but he shoved it back. Concentrating on her alone, he eased down beside her, stretching full length along the hot iron of her body.

"Are you ready, lass?" he asked.

She was breathing hard, and for a moment she lay absolutely still, but finally she nodded, and there was something about that movement, something about the width of her eyes, the tempting stillness of her body, something that made him pause. Could it be that she was telling the truth? Could it be that in all her years on the street she had protected her innocence? He scowled at the thought.

"Maybe," he said, holding her gaze. "It could be that there will be a little pain—" He was a fool to believe her an innocent. An absolute fool. "At first. But it'll pass in a moment. Don't be afraid."

She said nothing, but shivered once before closing her eyes and kissing him.

Heat scorched him, but he drew back, trying to think. Could she have told the truth? He skimmed his palm down her belly. She drew air softly between her lips. Her eyes remained closed, her lashes dark shadows against her satiny cheeks as she turned her head and arched against his hand.

And that was all it took. He could wait no longer. Damn Wheaton to hell, he thought and, easing between her legs, reared up.

He was there, a moment from utopia. Her body was warm and slick. Hoary salivated. Cairn pulled back, ready for the first thrust.

And lightning exploded in his skull. He didn't have a chance to turn or flee or defend himself.

In fact, the last thought he had before blackness took him was that he should have hurried.

Chapter 10

～～⁓◯◯⁓～～

Tatiana moaned and writhed. She was burning, boiling, cooking slowly from within. Damn Sedonia and virginity and her mother's cool admonishments. She would do this. She would take him inside of her, would quench the fire, would seize this moment of passion and remember it forever.

MacTavish reared over her. She held her breath, but suddenly there was a thud and a gasp. Jerking her eyes open, she watched him topple limply onto the mattress.

She stared in bewilderment, but a shuffle of noise caught her attention. She glanced upward. It was then that she tried to scream. In fact, she opened her mouth to do just that, but nothing issued from her but a breathy rasp of shock.

"Megs!" whispered a girl. Her voice was frantic, her hair was snarled, and in her hand she held Dimitri. "You all right?"

Tatiana scooted back against the wooden headboard, all but kicking MacTavish aside as she did so, her mind spinning wildly. "Who—Why are you here?"

The girl scowled. Candlelight flickered across her mobile

features. Her gaze skittered sideways and back. "I comes ta bust you out."

"Bust . . ." Tatiana began, but the rest of the words got caught in her throat. She was naked, bewildered, and shocky.

The girl leaned closer, motioning wildly. There was dirt beneath every nail. Even in the wavering candlelight, Tatiana could see it. She leaned away.

"Come on," she rasped. "We ain't got all night."

Facts were clicking along slowly in Tatiana's mind. She was a prisoner. This girl thought she was Megs, and she was offering her a means of escape. Of course she might very well be killed if she accepted it.

Her heart clanged like a smithy's hammer against her ribs. She stalled for time, trying to think.

"How did you get in here?"

"Through the window of course. Weren't no great feat. They ain't watchin' now. Not with 'is 'ighness in 'ere with you," she hissed, and scowled. "Funny, a great laird don't fall any 'arder than no other man."

Tatiana glanced breathlessly at MacTavish. "Is he . . . dead?"

"Dead?" She shrugged, but her face looked pale beneath the coat of grime. She glanced rapidly toward the window, as if longing to be off. "Don't think so. But 'e's gonna 'ave one 'ell of a 'eadache when 'e wakes up. And that ain't goin' to improve 'is mood. We'd best be off."

Tatiana stared at MacTavish. His buttocks glowed in the candlelight. His right wrist lay across the toes of her left foot and his fingers were twitching.

"Mary and Joseph!" the girl gasped, and grabbed Tatiana by the upper arm. "Come on, we's out of time."

She was dragged from the bed.

"Clothes! I need—" she began, but the girl was already throwing an unidentified garment at her. She slipped it over her head, but even that simple task was difficult, for her hands were shaking like maple leaves in a hurricane.

"All right then. Out you go," hissed the girl.

"Out—"

"Careful of the first step. She's a right bitch, but there's a small ledge off to your left," she whispered, and veered toward the bed again.

Tatiana could only stare. "Who are you?"

The girl turned abruptly toward her. The candlelight cast her sharp features in stark relief, the bright eyes, the peaked chin, the frown wrinkling her brow.

"What'd 'e do, Megs, knock you senseless? I'm Gem, you knows that."

Tatiana stared and the girl glanced at MacTavish before snuffing the flames off the candelabra with her grimy fingers. The room burst into blackness. "Blast them pretty lads. You can't trust 'em be they king or clown? But you'll be right as rain soon nuf, Megs. We just got to get you 'ome."

"'Ome?"

The girl grasped Tatiana's arm, propelling her toward the window. "Aunt Ned's"

"Aunt—"

"Shh." Gem's fingers tightened like talons on Tatiana's upper arm. Outside the door, footsteps rapped up, then passed by. The girl's relief was palpable. "Go," she hissed.

And Tatiana went, because she could think of nothing else to do, because she had been threatened and bullied. Because the lord of Teleere was lying unconscious and possibly dead on the mattress they had shared only minutes before.

She glanced over the windowsill. Thirty feet below her, candlelight flickered from the bailey. Her heart got stuck in her throat, making it difficult to breathe, impossible to move.

"'Urry up."

She tried to say she couldn't. That she was frozen, but

Gem gave her back a shove. She stumbled forward and wobbled one foot onto the windowsill. Somebody moaned. Possibly it was herself, but maybe the noise came from the bed.

"Bloody 'ell," Gem rasped. "Go!"

Another moan echoed in the chamber, but it was most certainly MacTavish this time. She dangled her leg over the sill, dragged the other beside it, and gazed into eternity.

"Turn around! Climb down! Shit, Megs, 'e's wakin' up."

She would have sworn she didn't have the nerve to move, but suddenly she *was* moving, shimmying downward with her knees quaking and her arms stiff with fear. She couldn't breathe, couldn't see. In the darkness, her toes searched for a hold. Her fingers clawed at the stone.

"'Urry up. 'Urry up!"

And she did. She swore she did, but suddenly Gem was all but atop her, clambering down behind like a monkey on a rope, stepping on her fingers, kicking her in the head. If it hurt, she didn't realize it, for she was certain she was about to die, about to crash to the earth a mile below and break up like a clay doll on a rocky shore.

"Let's go!"

Tatiana glanced sideways, and suddenly Gem was there, grasping her arm, dragging her along. And she realized in some dim part of her consciousness that she had reached the ground, that she had not died. Gem yanked her down behind some unseen obstacle. The smell of hay filled her nostrils. She fell to her knees.

Off to their left, a man laughed.

"So Lord MacTavish is busy this night."

"Aye." A pair of footsteps rapped past. Lanternlight swung in their wake. "Aye, he is that. Busy with the thieving little trollop what stole his mother's brooch. Like they say, you don't take from the pirate lord without paying pretty."

"And she is."

"Pretty or paying?"

"Both," said the first man.

They laughed in concert. Tatiana felt sick to her stomach, but there was no time to retch, for Gem was already pulling her into the darkness.

And then things got worse. They slunk through holes no bigger than a rat's chamber and splashed like hunted deer into a millpond, hiding in the fermenting shadows until a guard passed by.

They crawled out like drowned ferrets and scrambled away, down back alleys that smelled of vermin and a dozen things she dared not think about, over fences, past growling dogs, and through a back door that listed badly and squeaked like coffin hinges as it was carefully pushed closed.

" 'Ere we are then," said Gem, and sighed deeply as if she had settled onto a velvet chaise after a long day of lawn bowling. The air smelled of rancid urine and spoiled wine.

Tatiana turned carefully. Utter darkness was combated by a single flame above a smoky, tallow candle. But even that feeble bit of light showed too much. Perhaps the building had once been a decent house, but now it was rubble. The smell of decay filled the stagnant air, and somewhere in a far corner, she heard the scurrying sound of rats.

"Where are we?" she breathed, and Gem chuckled.

"We're 'ere, 'ome sweet 'ome."

Tatiana's stomach churned, and in that instant someone grabbed her hair, yanking her head back. She squeaked in fear and tried to jerk away, but knuckles were up tight against the back of her skull, and against her throat she felt the hard edge of a blade.

" 'Oo's this then?" a man rasped. His breath was fetid against her ear.

"Cott." Gem's voice was low, and despite everything, Tatiana could hear the fear in it. Her own stomach twisted. "What are you doing 'ere?"

"I come to collect what's due me."

"I . . . Listen. About the coin. I don't 'ave it just now," Gem said.

"Don't you?" The knife eased along Tatiana's throat, drawing forth a whimper. "That's unfortunate, Gemmy. How 'bout your friend 'ere? She got anything?"

"Let her go, Cott." Gem's voice actually wavered. "She ain't got nothin' to do with this."

"Don't she?" he asked. "Then I might as well slit 'er throat and be done with."

He moved his hand.

"No!"

Cott froze.

"She's Megs."

"What's that, Gemmy?"

"She's Magical Megs."

"You're lyin'," he said, but his hand had moved back a bit. Tatiana squeezed her eyes closed and tried to breathe, to remain alive, one second at a time.

"Ain't you never seen 'er afore?" Gem's tone was only slightly derisive.

"Maybe I 'as and maybe I 'asn't. But I knows this much, if she's Megs, she'll 'ave something on her to brighten old Cott's day huh?" he said, and suddenly the knife was removed and she was propelled across the floor, flung forward to crash into the far wall and nearly drop to her knees. She turned there, terror closing her throat as effectively as the knife had.

"What do you say, girlie?" he asked, and approached, stalking her like a fetid cat, the knife still in his hand. "You Megs?"

Past his shoulder, Tatiana could see Gem nodding. Fear. Her eyes were bright with it. What would make a girl like Gem afraid? A girl who could storm Westheath Castle and defy all?

Tatiana straightened slightly, finding a sliver of resolve amidst the terror and fatigue. "Yes," she said, and felt her heart tattoo in her throat, "I'm Megs."

The man stopped in his tracks, and then the corner of his parched lips lifted. He was missing a tooth, his arms were bare beneath a tattered tunic and high on his stringy right biceps, a tattoo shown blue in the candlelight. His hair was as white as combed wool. "Then there ain't no reason you can't pay yer friend's debt, is there?"

Tatiana felt the wall behind her, hoping for some sort of weapon, but there was nothing. Nothing to protect her. No guards. No title. Not even a fertility god.

She swallowed hard and stiffened her knees. "That depends." Instinct made her stall, though she had no idea how it might help her.

"Depends does it?"

"Yes." Her legs were bare from midthigh down, and her knees were quaking. So she maintained eye contact and prayed that he would not realize her fear. For she knew without a doubt that he fed on terror. "It depends on how much she owes you."

The villain chuckled. The sound permeated the room like a noxious gas. "She owes me 'er soul, little Megs. You think you can pay for that?"

She shrugged, but even with that simple motion she felt her hands shake, so she crossed her arms against her chest and stared him down. "I can't say for certain," she said. "What are souls worth these days?"

Cott threw back his head and howled at the roof, and it was in that moment that she saw the edge of a wound rising just past the top of his tunic. When he lowered his head to grin at her, it disappeared from sight.

Outside, someone yelled. Footfalls clattered along a hard-packed surface. Cott shifted his bloodshot gaze toward the door and back.

"Listen, it's been fun chattin' with you girls, but I've got to be off. What you got to give me?"

"You?" Tatiana asked. Could it have been a night watch that she'd heard outside? "I've got nothing for you."

He turned back toward her and drew his lips back like a rabid dog when he smiled. "I don't think I much care for your friend, Gemmy."

"She's 'ad a 'ard time of it lately, Cott. That's all."

His eyes never left Tatiana's. "Yeah?"

"She's been in Pikeshead."

He chuckled. "I go to Pikeshead when I need to relax," he said, and approached her slowly, eyeing her blatantly as he did. "Or when I need a bit of new meat."

It seemed as if her heart dropped out of her chest, as if the floor had fallen from under her feet, but she kept her chin up, kept from whimpering, kept from passing out. Instead, she dropped her hands to her sides and sidled to the left. There was a rotting mattress on the floor, and near its end, a stick leaned against the wall. Perhaps it had once served as a staff, but whatever its original purpose, she saw his wound in her mind's eye now. She couldn't best him in strength. She couldn't outrun him. And if he got close enough to use the knife, she was dead. She knew it beyond a whisper of a doubt. But a plan had begun to form.

"Is that what you do, Cott?" she asked. "Prey on children half your size?"

He shook his head as he veered to follow her. "No. I prey on women, and I don't care what size they be. Tall, fat." He shrugged. She dropped her gaze to his chest. But she couldn't see the wound. Still, it was there. "Saucy like you."

"Really?" The word sounded breathless. Her head felt light. But the stick was behind her now. Within reach. She was sure of it. Almost. "Then it's true—what I always heard about you."

"Yeah?" he said. "What'd you hear? That I 'as a dick like a cart 'orse?" he asked, and laughed.

"No." She smiled herself and prayed she wouldn't faint. "That you're a coward."

The room went absolutely still.

"Gemmy." His voice was soft, breathy. "I'm afeared I'm gonna 'ave to kill yer friend," he said, and in that instant he charged.

Chapter 11

〜◦◯◦〜

atiana grabbed the stick and screamed in terror or rage or some emotion so feral she couldn't guess at. But he kept coming, careening into the staff. It struck him full in the chest, and for a moment she thought it would remain there, but it did not. It clattered to the floor. Still, he staggered back, clutching his wound. His knife wobbled and fell to the floor, but he straightened with a growl, pulled a pistol from his trousers, and fired.

Agony struck her chest. She staggered away. But he was after her.

She screamed as she felt the sweep of his hand past her shoulder.

"Cotton!"

He pivoted wildly toward the sound of his name. She turned in unison, panting hard.

A woman stood there. She was tall and slim and as regal as any queen.

"You will leave my house now," she said.

He snarled a chuckle. "I don't think so, old witch."

She smiled, and in the flickering glow of the candlelight, her face looked perfectly serene. "Then be prepared to suffer the consequences." He cursed, but his eyes darted right and left as if searching for hidden demons.

Still, he drew himself up and shook his head. "I ain't afraid of you, you crazy old crone."

"Perhaps that is because you are brave. But I rather suspect it is because you're a fool. For as you said, I am a witch," she said, and dramatically raised one hand.

Cotton crouched. His face contorted, then he snarled something and pivoted away. Still holding his wound, he stumbled past her and out of the house.

Tatiana stood like one possessed, waiting to wake from the nightmare, for surely it was a dream. Surely. But the throbbing pain seemed hopelessly real, though her head was spinning wildly, twirling the floor away from her feet.

"Gem." The old woman's voice seemed to come from far away, down a long tunnel perhaps. "Put her on the bed, lass."

"Ned."

"Hurry now."

They were the last words she heard for some time.

Tatiana's head still felt light when she awoke, but the pain in her shoulder had been reduced to a dull pulsation. She lay in silence, letting memories swirl around her.

"So you are the infamous Megs."

She opened her eyes. The old woman sat on a three-legged stool beside the bed. Pulled back in a tight knot at the back of her head, her hair was as silver as moonlight. Her eyes were nearly the same hue, and her face pale.

"What time is it?"

"I find it strange," said the other slowly, "that when people awake their first concern is the time of day."

Tatiana studied the woman's face. It was virtually unlined, and yet it showed age as surely as hers showed youth.

"As if they may have missed something so ultimately important that they dare not remain asleep another instant." She smiled. Ned, Gem had called her. Memories were flittering erratically back into Tatiana's hazy brain. Aunt Ned, an old woman in an ancient house. "What is it you had to wake up for, lass?" She spoke softly, and yet there was strength in her tone.

Cotton—

The memory of her attacker screamed into Tatiana's consciousness, and she flinched.

"All is well." The old woman touched her hand. "He is gone. You will heal."

Tatiana glanced at her shoulder. It was bandaged in a grayish cloth.

"He shot me." She was still surprised. Surely this could not have happened to her. She was Princess Tatiana Octavia Linnet Rocheneau. Untouchable.

"Yes." The old woman nodded soberly. "But I was able to remove the bullet without undue trauma," she said. Her hand was gentle upon Tatiana's knuckles. "And you are young." Her expression was wistful and wan. "You will heal well."

"You tended me yourself?"

Ned smiled. Fatigue stretched the expression tight. "I have learned to do much for myself in the past few years," she said, and in a moment she drew away and rose to her feet. She faltered a little, then steadied herself on the wall before moving on.

Tatiana winced as she tried to sit up. Pain burned like hell through her shoulder. She ignored it as best she could. "You are Gem's aunt?"

"I am everyone's aunt." The old woman didn't turn from where she squatted by the crumbling hearth, but poured a measure of broth into a metal bowl and straightened slowly. "Here then, lass, drink this."

It smelled strongly of onions and some spice she couldn't quite name. "What is it?" she asked.

The old woman's eyes shone, as if smiling was too tiring, but she couldn't hold back the expression entirely. "I do not work at cross-purposes, girl."

Tatiana took the bowl, scowling her question.

"There would be little reason to remove the bullet if I meant to poison you the very next day, lass."

"Poison me!"

"Is there some reason one might wish to poison you?" The old woman watched her closely for a moment, then nodded. "You can trust me, my lady. Drink—"

"My lady!" Tatiana remained frozen on the bed, her heart thumping in her chest. "I am not nobly bred."

Ned watched her solemnly, then smiled a little. "Very well then, lass, what would you have me call you?"

"My name is . . ." she began, but the old woman's eyes bored into her, making her pause. "Gem calls me Megs."

"Very well. Megs it is, but I warn you, lass, once you begin down this path 'tis difficult to make your way back."

Tatiana opened her mouth to argue, but Ned interrupted.

"Drink your broth now. You will need your strength."

She did as commanded, using her left hand to hold it and barely managing to prop it up with her right. The soup was all but tasteless. She lowered the bowl, but the old woman was watching.

"All of it," she ordered.

Tatiana did as told. "Who are you?" she asked.

"You must rest now."

"Why did you take me in?"

She looked mildly surprised and a little amused. "I didn't take you in, lass. You came in on your own."

"You could have thrown me out."

"I must look terribly strong."

"I mean—"

"I know what you mean. Sleep now," said the old woman, and, turning her back, left Tatiana alone with her questions.

"Eat it." Gem's voice woke Tatiana, though it was quiet enough.

The old woman's voice was no louder. "Your friend will need sustenance in order to regain her strength." The room was dark, with only a shadow of light seeping through the one unbroken window.

"Megs?" The girl laughed, and even in the dimming light, Tatiana could see her offer the loaf once more. "You needn't worry about 'er."

"You did."

"Me?" Gem shoved the bread into the old woman's hands and rose jerkily to her feet. "Not 'ardly."

"Then why did you bring her here?"

"She's Megs," Gem said, turning back abruptly. "Magical Megs. Think o' what she can teach me."

The room was silent for a moment, then, "To steal."

"Aye, just that."

"As you stole this bread."

"Listen, old gammer," Gem said, her voice hard, "I don't 'ave t' come round 'ere, y' know."

"No you don't."

"So you want me to leave you t' starve t' death?"

"I won't starve to death. I have work yet to do."

"Slavin' for the rich folk?"

"That," Ned said, "and making sure you are safe. Making sure you are happy."

"'Appy! You think I'd be 'appy bound to that balding crock o' shit what wants to bed me?"

"I'll have no cursing in this house, Gem, and marriage is

not bondage. At least it is not if you are with the right man."

"Well 'e ain't the right man, and I'll do as I please," insisted the girl, and pivoted away, but she stopped at the door. Her knuckles looked pale and sharp against the wood. "I didn't steal the bread," she said, and hurried outside.

The old woman held her back straight for a moment longer, then dropped carefully into a tattered chair. Old age descended with her, graying her features and dulling her eyes. But perhaps it was not just years that dimmed her.

Tatiana stirred. "Are you ill?"

"Ahh." The old woman smiled, but the expression was weak. "So you're awake. Good. 'Tis time to eat," she said, and rose unsteadily to her feet.

Taking an oaken board from beside the hearth, she set the loaf atop it. It was small and dark and sprinkled with rolled oats.

Swinging a metal arm from the smoldering embers of the fire, she wrapped her hand in a rag and retrieved a hanging kettle. In a moment she had poured tea into an earthenware mug and was bearing the board to her patient's bedside.

"You're feeling better?" It was more a statement than a question.

Tatiana nodded, and Ned settled herself carefully upon the mattress before placing the tray beside her.

"I'll have a look at that wound," she said.

Tatiana considered arguing, but the old woman was already slipping the gown from her shoulder and loosening the bandage. Her expression was somber as she eased the cloth away, but finally she tied it back up with a nod.

"You're stronger than you look, lass."

"Why did you take me in?"

"As I said before—"

"Do you plan to betray me to MacTavish?"

The old woman showed some surprise for the first time. "He is the lord of this isle."

She dropped her gaze. "He accused me of crimes I did not commit."

"So you are not a thief, Megs?"

Tatiana raised her eyes to find the other's sharp upon her face. She pursed her lips. "I did not do what he said I did."

Aunt Ned made no comment, but seemed to delve into Tatiana's mind. "No, you did not," she said. "But you may yet if you do not go back to him."

"Go back— He would have me executed."

"There are worse things than death, lass."

"If there are, I've no wish to do those things either."

The old woman smiled wanly. "Perhaps you have underestimated him. Perhaps your original assessment of him was correct."

Tatiana's mind was reeling. "Who are you?"

For a moment she thought she would receive an answer, but finally Ned sighed and rounded her frail shoulders.

"I am who I always was, though people see me differently now."

And what did that mean? "I owe you much, madam," Tatiana said finally. "I but wonder why you have taken it upon yourself to help me."

"Because you need help."

"And do you help all who need it?"

"When I can."

"But not Cotton?"

"He has not asked."

"Or you would?"

She didn't answer directly, but gave her a shallow shrug. "Perhaps that is why he thinks me crazy."

Tatiana studied her for a moment. "Evil cannot comprehend goodness."

The old woman watched her with silver-bright eyes. "You are wise for one so young," she said, and nodded slowly. "You will be good for him."

"For whom?" Tatiana asked, but the old woman had turned away.

"Eat now."

"Will you turn me in?" Tatiana asked.

Ned glanced at her from the fireplace. "How badly does he want you back, lass? Will he offer a reward?"

"What?" The idea took her by surprise.

The old woman shrugged. "Portshaven is not London, lass, but it is goodly sized. He's not likely to find you here even if he dares come to the south side. But if he offers a reward . . ." Her gaze was sharp. "You would be surprised what people will do when they are hungry."

Tatiana raised her chin. "I have been hungry."

"Have you?"

"Of course."

"Then perhaps you are not such an accomplished thief as Gemma believes."

There seemed no way to avoid this woman's eyes, no way to avoid the truth. Reaching out, Tatiana tugged the blanket aside.

"You're not mended enough to leave."

"As you said, I am stronger than I look."

"But not strong enough to overcome Cotton."

Tatiana stopped where she was. Fear congealed like pig jelly in her stomach.

"Or a thousand others of his ilk," Aunt Ned added. "Eat."

She eyed the loaf. It was as dark as the bread they fed the carriage horses in Sedonia. But it smelled heavenly, making her mouth ache at the sight of it. She lifted it in her hand, then glanced at her hostess. The old woman's cheeks were hollow, her complexion gray. Guilt tightened Tatiana's stomach.

But she did as she was told.

* * *

"Megs." The voice was neither hushed nor loud. " 'Tis time to be off."

Tatiana awoke with a start, then shielded her eyes with the back of her hand. A single taper glowed not ten inches from her bedside. Gem's face looked taut and intense in the light of it.

"Be off?" She scowled. Suspicion soured her gut. "Where?"

"There be a cockfight over t' the slaughter'ouse."

"Cockfight?" The world had gone mad. She sat up with an effort.

"I knows it ain't your usual fare and all, but my belly ain't gettin' no fuller. Thought you might be able to teach me a bit of sleight o' hand."

Tatiana's heart sped up a notch. It didn't seem wise to present her true identity, for this Gem might be just the person to turn her over to MacTavish if a reward was offered. "Where's Aunt Ned?" she asked, hedging carefully.

Gem's expression softened the slightest amount, but in a moment it was hard again. "She ain't got 'ome from work yet."

"Work?"

"Mendin'. Stitchery. That sort o' thing."

"She's a seamstress?"

"Some say she's a duchess."

"What?"

Gem shrugged. "It don't matter. She's a stubborn old bat won't take what I brings 'er." The momentary expression of tenderness brightened her face again, then blankness. "But that ain't for the likes of us, aye? Not when there be pockets what need pickin'."

Tatiana scowled, trying to look dismayed. It wasn't difficult. "I'm afraid I'm not going to be up to my customary standards."

"Up to your customary standards." Gem chuckled. "You could always talk pretty when you wanted to, aye? But no, you'll 'ave t' take some time to loosen up. Tonight you can give me pointers and act as decoy."

Decoy! Her throat felt dry. She tried to think of an excuse, a lie, a protest, but in that moment her stomach rumbled.

Gem chuckled. "Come on," she said, and, retrieving a much-mended gown from a nearby peg, tossed it onto the bed. "Get dressed. We don't want to miss the wagerin'."

Chapter 12

⌒◯◯⌒

The smell of blood permeated the air, blown in on a chill, wet wind. They'd walked forever to reach the slaughterhouse. It loomed in the night like an evil dream. The darkness, dank and smothering, was held back by nothing more than a few faltering torches and a wood fire that barely illuminated the gray stonework of the building. The flames smoked into the night air as if hell itself were steaming, and milling about the fire was a raucous crowd. All men, mostly drunk.

Tatiana's legs felt stiff. Her breath came hard. Sweat moistened the back of her neck, yet she felt cold despite the servicable woolen gown she wore to replace the one Auntie Ned was mending.

"What do you make of the crowd?" Gem asked. "Is it best t' be a 'ore or a beggar?"

Tatiana turned with a start, trying to think. "What?"

"The old fella near the cage . . ." Gem nodded almost imperceptibly toward the right. Near the flickering fire, an enclosure made of willow branches gleamed in the uncertain

144

light. But the bird inside was clear enough as he was lifted from his prison. His comb was as red as autumn apples and upon his legs, metal spurs had been affixed. "'E looks t' be the grandfatherly sort."

Tatiana dragged her attention from the cock.

"Don't y' think?"

"What?" She was trying to cope, to survive, to function. But her mind was roiling as wildly as her stomach, and her shoulder ached.

"The fella with the cane. You could tell 'im bout your ailin' granny. Tell 'im you needs a bit o' coin to buy 'er elixir."

She found the old man Gem was referring to. He was tall and somewhat stooped, but his expression was hard and his eyes narrow.

She choked a laugh. Panic was threatening to swallow her whole. "He's not going to give me money."

Gem shrugged. "Maybe not, but 'e'll look y' over long enough for me to nip 'is pockets, aye?"

"No." The word escaped on its own.

Gem scowled.

Tatiana shook her head and straightened her back with an ungodly effort. She would do what she must. "He may be a short step from the grave, but he'll take the cane with him and maybe one of us if he cracks us on the head."

"Ahh." Gem nodded. "Aye. Right y' are then. There be plenty o' other blokes 'ere what don't 'ave no weapon close t' hand." She glanced about, then straightened her skirts as she looked pointedly away. "The fella in the top 'at. 'E's a ripe plum for sure. 'E's got a bulge in 'is trousers pocket." She grinned. "And 'e ain't even seen us yet."

Tatiana found him immediately and shook her head shortly after. "Look at his shoes."

Gem did and even by the glow of the firelight, she was sure to see they were scuffed and worn. Mother had said more than once that if a gentleman didn't care for his footwear, he wasn't a gentleman at all, but just a man in scuffed shoes.

"But what of the bulge?" Gem asked.

Tatiana glanced at his face. There was anger there and bitterness. "A gun," she guessed.

Gem narrowed her eyes, assessing Tatiana in the darkness. "Could be yer as good as they say, Megs. Could be."

They strolled around the perimeter of the crowd then, talking softly and seeming to have business of their own. Gem suggested several others, but Tatiana read them easily, seeing through their facade to the men beneath. Thievery, it seemed, was not so different than politics. Lies were written upon many faces. It was her job to find them.

But finally their travels brought them round to the far side of the wagering. Within the circle of ruddy-faced men, two roosters faced off, Maddened by teasing and their own foolishness, they flung themselves toward each other, soaring for a moment above the heads of the spectators and gleaming like winged seraphim in the firelight before falling back into the roar of the mob. Tatiana could feel her heart thrumming in her throat, echoed by every step of her shoes against the uneven turf.

"That one," Gem said with final decisiveness.

Tatiana glanced in the direction indicated. The noise of the first fight was already dwindling. The winners were collecting their bets while the losers cursed and lamented.

Gem's mark was young, brash, loud, and inebriated. He had also just won a fat roll of cash. The perfect victim. But just then another fellow slapped him on the back, granting Tatiana an easy excuse.

"Too many friends," she said, but fate was against her, for in that moment he waved to his comrades and wandered sloppily into the crowd.

"A fool and 'is money," crooned Gem. "'E's all but beggin' t' be robbed. 'Twould be rude t' disappoint 'im. Go on, Megs, work yer magic."

"I—" Tatiana grappled for a viable excuse, but the girl was already slipping into the dark folds of the crowd. Tatiana's stomach squeezed tight in her belly, and she followed, breathing hard and trying to think.

But in moments she had lost her mark. She turned about, grateful and scared. Her stomach rumbled.

"Looking for someone?" She jumped, and a man nearby laughed. "Goodness, you're skittish. Though I can't say I blame you. This is hardly the place for such a young beauty."

Her heart rang like a smithy's hammer in her chest, and she failed to speak. Like a country bumpkin who had just stumbled off the dogcart and into the city.

"What's your name, sweeting?" He was dressed well but conservatively in a dark waistcoat and tails. In his right hand, he carried a wooden walking stick with a round brass knob at the top.

"I am . . ." She held her breath, her mind reeling. "Lady Linnet."

"Ahh," He took her hand and kissed her knuckles. "With a name as lovely as her face. And tell me, my lady, what brings you to this den of iniquity?" He held her gaze with his own. "Please tell me it's not your husband."

"No." She found her voice with an effort and straightened slightly. Her hands were shaking as was her voice. What a wondrous actress. "I'm not married."

He had a winning smile. "Your father then?"

"No," she said, and glanced through the crowd again. She longed to flee, to scramble away as fast as she could, but where would she scramble to? She had no friends here. No family. And no way to return to where she would.

"Not a beau I hope," he said.

She focused on him. There was no one else to save her. No one else to feed her. Not a servant or a guard, and she was starving. "My brother." The words slipped out on a breath, although she couldn't guess where they came from.

"Of course." He laughed. "Only a brother would leave a pretty lass like you stranded." He slurred his words slightly. He was intoxicated but not incapacitated. "Want some help finding him?"

She almost said no, but she desperately needed help, and she was in no position to judge harshly.

"Yes. I . . ." The words came hard. "I need help."

He smiled and placed a proprietary arm around her shoulder, leaning close. His breath smelled of sweet wine. "You're shaking," he said. "You poor thing. Come on, lass, I've a redingote in my carriage. We'll get you warmed up, then we'll find your brother. You needn't worry. I promise."

They weaved through the crowd. She shivered again, and he pulled out a flask from some hidden pocket and handed it to her.

"Here you go, sweeting, drink up."

She did, fortifying her spirits and glancing about once. She dared not turn back now. Up ahead a dark bank of carriages stood in a row. The mob thinned, leaving only a few scragglers to stumble off in the direction of the fights.

She handed back his flask. "Thank you, sir," she said, and he flashed her another smile.

"You're not from Portshaven."

She drew a careful breath. "No. I am not. In fact . . ." She glanced nervously behind her. "My name is not Linnet."

The smile again, as bright as summer lightning. "You lied?" he said in mock astonishment.

She swallowed and raised her chin. "And I have no brother."

"Oh?"

" 'Tis a complex story and I fear . . . not easily believed."

"I might believe anything from lips as lovely as yours. But here . . ." He motioned to a nearby phaeton, then set his walking stick against the polished vehicle and opened the narrow door. "You're still shivering. Get in out of the wind and tell me your tale."

She stepped up with some misgivings, but it felt lovely to sit on the upholstered seat, to leave the rush of the wind behind. He followed her inside and pulled the door shut after them. Retrieving the promised redingote from the seat beside her, he wrapped the fitted coat about her shoulders, pulled it close around her neck, then settled back on the seat, watching her in the darkness.

She couldn't think of where to begin, how much to say, what words to use.

"Let me guess," he said, "you've lost your money and you need a bit of coin to feed your ailing granny."

"No!"

He drew back slightly at the force of her answer, and she managed to relax a mite.

"No." She searched for words. "It is imperative that I return to my homeland."

He smiled and, leaning closer, took her hand in his. "Imperative?"

"Yes." She nodded numbly. "If you can assist me, there will be a great reward for you."

He laughed and stroked the back of her hand with his thumb. "What kind of reward?"

"Money." She scowled at him as he moved closer. "My people will pay you whatever you like."

"Don't tell me you're wealthy *and* beautiful."

She lowered her eyes to her lap. Never had she had to beg. It was difficult, burning her soul. "But I fear I cannot pay you in advance."

He brushed her hair away from her face. "And what kind of assistance do you require, my bonny lass?"

She drew a careful breath and listened, though she wasn't sure what she listened for. But all she heard was the sound of the wind and the distant roar of the crowd. "I need to return to Sedonia."

"Sedonia?" His surprise was evident.

"Yes. And it must be soon."

"Ahh." He nodded as if he suddenly understood. "In a bit of trouble here in Portshaven are you?"

She crunched her hands to fists in her lap and forced herself to think clearly. "Will you help me?"

"Well . . ." He scowled as he exhaled through his mouth. "Sedonia is quite a voyage. It would be expensive."

"As I said—"

"The reward. I know. But I would have to pay the fee with no guarantee—"

"You would have my word."

"Aye," he said, and smiled as he stroked her cheek. "And spoken from such luscious lips. But I am not a wealthy man, and—"

"You will be," she vowed. She was close now. So close to returning home that she could feel the excitement like wine in her veins. "If you but get me to Sedonia, I will see that you are rewarded well beyond your dreams."

He scowled as if considering, then shook his head. "Maybe if I had some kind of payment in advance."

Fear swamped her. She was too close to fail now. But she raised her chin. "If you do my bidding, you will not regret it," she said. "But I have nothing to give you immediately."

"That's where you're wrong, love," he said, and, wrapping an arm around her back, pressed her down against the cushioned seat and kissed her.

She knew then. Knew she had been duped. Knew she had been a fool.

"Relax," he crooned. "If you're good, I will make certain the authorities don't find you."

She wanted to scream, to buck madly against him, but she did not. Instead, she remained very still, quieting her terror, closing her eyes.

He stroked her cheek and she shivered.

"Eager little sprite aren't you," he breathed.

"Yes." She opened her eyes with an effort. "But I must not do this. Not here."

He skimmed his knuckles down her throat. She gritted her teeth, but kept her lips closed lest he guess her true feelings.

"And why not here?" he asked.

"You were right." She skimmed her gaze to the right, as if she could see through the narrow door to the night beyond. "I must not be caught here."

"What was it, lass? Thievery or something worse?"

She pried her teeth open and licked her lips. He watched the movement of her tongue.

"There is an inn not far from here," she said.

"But I'm happy here."

She forced a smile. Perhaps it was suggestive. Perhaps it was ghoulish. "You will be happier there, my lord, I promise you."

It was his turn to smile. "What can we do there that we can't do here?"

She glanced through her lashes at him. "If you don't know, my lord, someone has been negligent in your education."

He stared at her for a moment, his mouth open, and then he laughed. But he eased off her in the same instant. "Very well," he said. "I shall fetch my driver."

She could barely breathe for the hope that swamped her.

But she dare not falter now. "Hurry," she whispered and licked her lips again, but slowly this time.

"Jesus!" he rasped, and, stumbling from the carriage, rushed away.

Chapter 13

Tatiana waited to the count of five, then slid across the seat. Her hands shook like windswept leaves, but she steadied them on the doorframe and forced herself to get out of the carriage.

Someone stood there, inches away, looming in the darkness.

Tatiana gasped, but before the sound was loosed a palm was slapped across her mouth, stifling the sound.

"Hush!" Eyes gleamed white and round in the darkness. Gem's eyes. "You want 'im ta 'ear you?"

Tatiana's heart slammed hard against her ribs. She let her eyes fall closed, remembering to breathe, and shook her head. Gem eased her hand away.

"Did you get the goods already?"

"What?" Tatiana's voice sounded shaky, pressed out on a gasp of quick breath.

"I was just about to pinch the other fella, then 'e turns around sudden-like and looks me straight in the eye. 'Bout

153

peed in my knickers. And all the while you was targeting another bloke."

Tatiana steadied her knees.

"What's 'e got then? Any ready coin?"

Tatiana shook her head, but reality remained vague, blurry, as if she were living in a strange half dream. She glanced to the right. "He's coming back. He'll be right back."

Gem scowled as if confused by her demeanor, then brightened. "Ahh, of course. A bloke like that . . . 'e ain't gonna 'ave 'is cash on 'is person. Too easy to pinch it. It's 'idden in 'is carriage."

Tatiana tried to respond, but the girl was already scrambling inside. Scratching noises issued from the interior, but in a few moments, she poked her head from the carriage. "I can't find nothin' . . . 'ceptin' this," she said, and bringing her hand forward, displayed a shiny, silver-plated pistol. "We'll be eatin' good this time tomorrow."

"Tomorrow!"

Gem shrugged. "Less'n you know a better fence than Hobbs."

Tatiana's stomach twisted up hard. The man had meant to rape her, had pretended to befriend her, had betrayed her trust. He owed her a meal—at least. "There's no money?" She felt desperate. Hungry and defiled and beaten.

Gem shook her head. "'E probably spent it all on the fights," she said, but in that instant, Tatiana noticed his walking stick. It leaned against the rain-slick carriage, gleaming dully in a tattered shaft of moonlight.

Lifting it in one hand, Tatiana examined it for an instant, then set her fingers to the brass knob. It unscrewed creakily beneath her fingers

"Balls!" Gem hissed as Tatiana drew out a chunky roll of bills.

It was like holding lightning in your hand. Like possessing magic. Like grasping life itself.

Tatiana raised her gaze to Gem's. They smiled in unison.

"Blimey," said the girl, handing over the gun and taking the paper notes reverently between her grimy fingers. "I guess we'll be eatin' well for breakfast."

They ate like queens. Fresh barley bread still hot from the baker's stone oven, newly churned butter, and clover honey fresh from the comb.

When they returned to Ned's, they found her gone. They slept most of that day, then visited the market again.

Gem turned out to be an excellent cook, and by the time Aunt Ned returned, stew bubbled alongside an onion pie.

The old woman paused in the doorway, seeming to sway slightly. Gem rose to her feet.

"It's a gift," she said. "From Megs."

The old woman's eyes were filled with longing, but she straightened her back and spoke slowly. "Was it honestly gained?"

"Like I says afore," Gem said, glancing quickly at Tatiana and away, "Megs's rich as God."

Ned's faded gaze turned toward Tatiana.

"I am indeed wealthy," Tatiana said. "And I wanted a chance to repay you for your kindness to me."

Whether Ned believed her or simply wanted to believe her, was impossible to determine. But something like relief flooded the old woman's face, and in a moment they were seated around the table.

The fare was simple, the crockery chipped, and their chairs nothing more than old crates and battered wine casks. But never in all her pampered life had Tatiana enjoyed a feast more.

"Mr. Banks, said I . . ." Ned's voice was regal and smooth as she told her tale. Her cheeks were flushed, and her eyes seemed brighter. Tatiana had caused it. Through her own hard efforts, she had bettered another's life. "Marry me and you marry my poor friends as well."

"And what'd the old gaffer say?" Gem asked.

"He said yes of course," Ned said with a sweep of her hand to indicate their abode. "Thus my luxurious lifestyle of today."

For reasons unknown, it struck them as funny. Soon they were bent over their abused plates, laughing like witches gone mad.

"Aye," Gem said between gasps, "I am the queen of England, you know."

"And—" Ned began, but she paused and her eyes grew wide. "Dear God. Remain calm. Please—" she began, but in that instant the door burst open. It crashed against the wall and shivered on one hinge.

Burr stepped inside, and behind him came his laird.

Tatiana snatched the pistol from beneath her skirts and pointed at MacTavish with trembling hands. But his men were already fanning out, weapons drawn. One glance toward her companions told Tatiana that Gem had grabbed a knife from the table and stood with her back to Ned, her eyes wild and her arms flung sideways as if she were prepared to take on the laird and his entire army.

MacTavish pulled his gaze from the two other women to pin it on Tatiana. Silence settled like toxic fumes into the house.

Tatiana's hands shook on the pistol.

"Put that down before you hurt someone," MacTavish ordered.

She shook her head frantically. "I fully intend to hurt someone unless you get out and leave us in peace."

"Peace." He said the word softly, but his eyes belied his tone. "'Tis a fine word for you to be spouting, lassie, when I haven't had a moment of it since the day I laid eyes on you."

"Get out." Her voice trembled. She swallowed hard and waved the gun. It was small and solid, but if truth be told, she wasn't entirely sure how to fire the thing. She could feel sweat moisten her upper lip. "I haven't done anything against you, MacTavish."

Reaching up slowly, MacTavish rubbed a spot on the back of his head. He winced as he did so. "Nothing, Megs?"

She steadied her arms. It didn't seem like the tiny weapon should be heavy. Who could have known that holding off the laird of the isle and his guards would be such tiring work? "Even you cannot blame a maid for defending her honor."

Perhaps his men's eyes widened a little at her words, but if they were shocked, they said nothing.

MacTavish smiled, and in that moment hot memories stormed into Tatiana's mind. The thought of his hands on her skin, his voice in her ear. "Even if a maid like you had honor," he began softly, and took a step toward her, "she would surely find a better way to convince me of her innocence than to brain me while in the throes of—"

"Stop!" she commanded, louder than she'd meant to. "Stay where you are." The gun wobbled wildly. "Or so help me God, I will shoot you where you stand."

"You owe me, Megs," he said.

"I owe you nothing." Her voice was hissed and low.

His smile lifted a mite. Satan had a gift. "Think again, lass."

"I did not take your brooch."

He shrugged and took another step toward her. "Maybe not. But at the least you owe me a prisoner."

She opened her mouth to object, but he raised a hand to shush her. "Fair is fair, Megs. You appeared. Wheaton disappeared. But . . ." He glanced toward the women by the table. Gem's eyes were as wide as Swedish oysters. Ned looked as if she were supporting herself by sheer strength of will. "If I take these two miscreants, perhaps we could call it even."

Tatiana's stomach twisted. "They've got nothing to do with this."

"Nothing? So it was you who struck me on the back of the head while we were about to—"

"Silence!" Tatiana ordered, and MacTavish smiled again.

"I think the girl already knows what we were up to, lass." She glanced toward Gem.

"Burr worked like hell to figure out a way to make her escape from Pikeshead seem like an accident," MacTavish said. "I knew she'd try to free you. Though I admit my timing was a bit off."

Hot memories flooded in again, but she shoved them rudely out of her mind.

"Go away, MacTavish. Get out before it's too late."

"You're going to shoot me?"

"Yes." The word only bobbled a little. The movement of the gun was a bit more aggressive.

"You just might," he admitted. "But not before my men fire their weapons."

"You'd still be dead."

"Do you know how to work that thing?" he asked, and stepped toward her.

She cocked back the hammer. "I am learning fast," she assured him.

He smiled. "I bet you are. But you can't take us all down. You're outmanned."

"I only have to shoot you."

"And they only have to shoot you," he countered.

She narrowed her eyes and aimed directly at his heart. Damn him to hell then.

Some emotion crossed his face. It almost looked like the shadow of admiration, but it was gone in an instant. "Or they could shoot them," he said, nodding toward the women.

She felt the blood drain from her face. "You can't harm them." Her voice was no more than a whisper.

"I'm Laird MacTavish," he argued. "The pirate bastard."

"Ned is nobility," Tatiana said. She herself didn't believe it was true, but everything was unbelievable just now.

MacTavish nodded once. "Lady Nedra, Baroness of Lark, accused of witchcraft some years ago I believe."

It was true?

"There is a harsh punishment for witchcraft," he said, "not to mention the girl's fate."

Tatiana darted her gaze across the table. Gem had risked her life to save Tatiana. True, she had mistaken her for another, but the debt was still owed.

"She's a known thief, Megs, and the citizens of Teleere are tired of thievery."

Tatiana winced, remembering the stench of the gallows. The dead man's purple tongue.

"I wouldn't need a reason to execute her, but I'd have one."

"You're a bastard," she said.

"It's common knowledge," he agreed, and shrugged. "The choice is yours, Megs. You or them."

"If I . . ." It was impossible to breathe, to force out the words. "If I come with you . . ." Her head felt light and her arms strangely heavy. "Will you let them go?"

His eyes were sharp and fragmented, like shards of broken glass. The devil through a stained-glass window. "I'll consider it."

She raised the gun. "And I'll consider blowing your nose off your face."

The corner of his lips lifted a quarter of an inch. "I've seen you fight in the past, Megs." He shook his head once and took another step toward her. "It was not a fearsome thing."

She gritted her teeth and tightened her hands. They hurt like hell from her death grip on the weapon. "I didn't have a pistol then."

"Are you sure it's loaded?"

She refused to blanch, to look at the gun, to let him shake her, but her soul quivered. She didn't even know what it should be loaded with.

"Do you care to find out?" she asked.

His smile was full-blown this time, and from that single expression, she was pretty sure he would. "I guess I'll know soon enough."

"Don't come any closer."

"You're outmanned, Megs."

"And you're outwomaned."

"True enough," he said, and lunged.

The gun exploded like a cannon in her ear. Her back crashed against the floor. Air ripped from her lungs. Gem screamed. Ned gasped, men yelled, and footsteps thundered.

When the haze cleared and the roar in her ears subsided, Tatiana realized that MacTavish was lying half under her. The pistol was gone. With one hand he'd immobilized her wrist. His other arm was bent, tight as an iron band around her back.

"I'll say one thing, lass." His voice was low. "You know how to keep life interesting."

Chapter 14

Men rushed up, Peters at the forefront. "My liege, are you well?" His freckled face was so pale even his lips seemed to disappear.

Cairn rolled onto his back and forced himself not to wince at the stab of old pain in his thigh. Shit, she'd seen enough weakness in him already. If he were a proper lord, he would have killed her twice by now.

"My liege, are you—"

"I'm fine," he said, and pushed himself to his feet. His men were already dragging Tatiana onto hers.

"My apologies, my lord. Forgive me. I should have tackled her myself. I should have—"

"Take her to my carriage."

"Your—*Your* carriage, my lord?"

Cairn stared. Peters swallowed.

"Yes, my liege," he said, and, pulling his pistol from its holster, directed it at the girl. "Outside," he ordered.

Cairn swore. "She's not a damned cannibal."

"But—"

"Put the gun away."

"But—"

Cairn swore again, more vehemently this time, and Peters holstered his weapon with haste.

They left the ramshackle hut together, with the lieutenant holding the girl's upper arm like she was a damned murderer. Which she . . . *may* not be. Though he had to admit she had shown considerable improvement in her fighting skills. Still, she looked so small, a strange meld of fairy goddess and waif. Soft and . . .

He felt Burr's gaze on him and turned with a frown. The giant was standing not two feet away, staring at him with raised brows.

"What are you looking at?" Cairn asked.

Burr smiled. "So you don't worry about folks believing you're getting soft, aye?"

His temper flared. "Want to try me, old man?"

Burr laughed out loud, then tilted his head toward the two women by the table. They seemed to be frozen in place. "What do we do with them?"

Cairn glared at the two. Who were they? How were they important to Megs? Damn! She'd been ready to give herself up for them. The idea made him fidgety and mad as hell. Loyalty was not a trait he wanted to find in her. It was bad enough that he'd found it in Peters. It made life damned inconvenient.

"Bring them along," he said.

Burr's grin widened. "In your carriage?" he asked, but there was no reason to answer. Burr knew better than to push his luck too far.

Outside, the bays worried at their bits. The carriage rocked in their fractious wake. Cairn gritted his teeth and approached the door.

Peters bowed from the behind the front wheel. "She is inside, my lord."

"I can see that."

"Yes, of course, my lord."

Damn, he thought, and, gripping the handle, pulled himself inside.

She sat in the very center of the tufted red seat. Her face was inscrutable and her hands clasped in her lap, like a praying nun or a scolding schoolmistress. Nothing at all like a thief, but like someone in power who was currently displeased.

"What do you plan to do with them?" she asked.

He watched her. She had an exotic look to her, not like most Teleerian maids, who tended to be fair and seem plump whether they were or not.

"I'll have an answer," she insisted, drawing his attention back to her question.

"If you've got a yearning to worry about someone's continued survival, you might put some thought into your own, lass," he warned.

She pursed her lips. "I've done nothing wrong."

His chest hurt where she'd stabbed him just a few days ago. He refused to rub it. "Some think it wrong to threaten their laird—bad deportment, as Bert would say."

"Some think it bad form for the laird to execute his subjects for no reason."

"Execute . . ." he began, and gritted his teeth against the bays' boisterous jolt into their collars. "Is that what I should do to you, Megs?"

She winced. Beneath the soft mocha hue of her skin, she seemed to pale slightly.

"My name is not Megs."

"Still?"

She ignored him, glancing out the window instead.

He should let her stare, of course. Should cease such worthless dialogue, but her distance irritated him. "Gem seems to think you're Megs," he said.

She was quiet, as if considering that. "What do you plan to do with them?" she asked again.

"Are you suggesting that I should not execute you and your friends, Megs?"

"They're not my friends, and I'm not Megs."

"But you'd give yourself up for them."

"That would be foolish," she said, and faced him, her expression unreadable, "since I had only just met them."

But he knew the truth, had seen it in her eyes when she'd held him off with a pistol. She would have given her life to keep the others safe.

God damn it!

"So the girl, Gem. Does she often risk her life for someone she's never met?"

"I believe she, too, may have mistaken me for the one you call Megs."

"May have."

"Yes."

It occurred to him that their conversation was foolishly polite, as if they were traveling in luxury to some grand ball instead of jolting through knee-high ruts behind four murderous stallions. Did she make every situation seem like this? "But you're not Megs," he said.

"No."

"And you didn't steal my brooch."

"No."

"And you don't know Wheaton."

"No."

"So you can't help me find him."

"I'm afraid not."

"Then you're little good to me, are you?"

She raised her chin a notch.

"But maybe your friends will be of more assistance. The girl, at least, seems like someone who might be persuaded to help."

"They know nothing about me, MacTavish." Her expression was strained. "Leave them be."

"Because they're good, lawful citizens."

She glanced out the window again, watching the country gallop along beside them.

"Like you," he added.

Her brows lowered slightly as if she were deep in thought. Her hands were still clasped in her lap.

"They are like me in many ways," she said. "Far more so than I knew."

"You're all thieves?" he guessed.

"I am not—" she began, then paused and glanced at her hands again. "I did not steal your brooch."

Damn. If she weren't such a liar, she might be convincing. "But you've stolen other things," he said.

She raised her chin and met his gaze again. "Tell me, MacTavish," she said, "why do you think people become thieves?"

Wasn't this supposed to be his interrogation. Shouldn't he have pulled out the cat-o'-nine-tails or at least the thumbscrews by now? "You tell me," he said. "Why did you become a thief?"

Her gaze was enormously steady, her eyes strangely old. "Because I had no choice."

"So you admit your guilt?"

"I suppose I do."

He wanted to strangle her. "But you're not sure."

"I am sure of this much," she said, and in her face he saw deep sorrow. Good God, what an actress. "One would not choose such a life if one had other options."

He wanted to laugh at her, but in that instant he saw that a pinkish stain had seeped through the shoulder of her shabby gown. Blood! Something cramped in his stomach.

"What happened?" He nodded toward her shoulder, trying to keep his tone casual.

She glanced at it, then away in a dismissive manner, but her face was pale. "Perhaps a thief is no better a friend than a nobleman."

"Destroyed your belief in honor among thieves, did they?" he asked, and, reaching out, tugged her sleeve downward. It only slipped a bit, but even so he could see that the skin was red and irritated above a swath of bandage.

His teeth hurt immediately. "What happened?"

"I am told it will heal well."

"By whom?"

"Aunt Ned has some skill as a physician."

"Aunt Ned."

"Lady Nedra I believe you called her."

"Why?"

"Most probably because that is her name."

He ground his teeth. "Why did she tend your wound if she doesn't know you, Megs?"

"I asked the same question myself."

He waited, then counted to ten in Latin. Actually he counted to nine, for although he was an excellent mathematician, language was not his forte. Bert was eternally distressed. Apparently great lords were supposed to be able to cipher *and* speak.

"What did she say?" he asked.

"It is what she does," Tatiana said. "She helps people."

Silence echoed inside the coach, accentuated by the crunch of the wheels and the too fast step of the horses' hooves.

"Do you think . . ." She paused, but it seemed as though she were talking to herself. Outside the window, beside the muddy road, a ragged boy tended his sheep. His face was dirty and solemn as he watched them pass. "Do you think if you are of noble blood, you are inherently a superior being?"

Inherently. He liked that word. Unfortunately, he didn't have a clue what it meant, but he was careful not to scowl. He had a dictionary at Westheath. And Bert, ever thrilled to instruct.

"Or wealth," she said. "Do riches make one noble?"

"Perhaps I would say yes if I had not been born a penniless bastard."

She eyed him carefully, and though it would have taken a pretty fine rack master to make him confess the truth, he felt a little nervous under her scrutiny.

"Is that why you steal, lass, because the rich are *inherently* better?"

"It seems to be a myth perpetrated by the rich."

Perpetrated. "Is that yes or no?"

She shook her head. "Perhaps there was a time when I believed such a thing."

"And now?"

"Now I believe it is difficult to be noble when one is hungry."

"Some think if we do not keep them hungry, they will rise up and overtake their . . ." He paused, remembering his own ragged childhood. "Betters."

"Betters." She watched him carefully. "Better than who? A lad who protects his sheep with his life? An old woman who risks all to tend another?"

"So wealth doesn't mean superiority."

"No more than poverty means depravity."

Depravity. Balls! "And what has made you come to such a deep conviction, lass? Tell me, have you seen the light?"

If she realized his sarcasm, she didn't acknowledge it. Instead, she glanced out the window again. "I once had a friend."

God damn, her stories were slow. He'd hate to rely on her in a battle. But there was an unlikely scenario. She was damn poor in a fight, being the approximate size of a cricket, as she was. Still, she was a cricket with steam in her craw, as Burr would say.

"He was born of a noble family," she said, and found his eyes with hers. It was strange how she always managed to make him feel at a slight disadvantage, just a bit off-balance. Damn! And how the hell did he have time to formulate complete sentences in the time it took her to draw a breath. "He was handsome, dark, and witty."

An itch started to form at the back of Cairn's neck.

"He was neither demeaning nor obsequious. Or perhaps he was demeaning to everyone equally. Whatever the case, he believed that every person was of equal value. We would oft debate just that point."

"When you weren't fucking him."

The coach went silent. Why the hell had he said that?

She scowled at him as if coming back to the present and disliking the reality she found there.

His chest ached dully, but not so much as his thigh. "I've heard others extol Wheaton's virtues," he explained idiotically.

"Wheaton! I—"

He gritted his teeth. "Don't!" He held up one hand. "Don't lie again, lass."

"I have never—"

"Don't lie again, or I'll flog you meself," he gritted. Damn the pirate talk.

She pursed her lips, sad and small and still defiant. "I have never met a man named Wheaton."

He cursed with feeling, but just then the carriage jolted to a halt.

Peters's face appeared in the window, as pale as ever and as nervous as hell.

"My apologies, my lord, but we have arrived."

"Arrived?" MacTavish growled, staring at the man.

Peters paled even more, but he managed to speak. "At Pikeshead, my lord. I assumed . . ."

Damn it all! Cairn tightened his fist against the foolishly tufted seats. He should leave her there, of course. Should shove her from the carriage and whistle a tune all the way back to Westheath. "Drive on," he ordered.

"Your pardon, my lord?"

"I said, drive on," he gritted.

"But surely you wish to deposit—"

"Damn it, Peters, if you don't want to spend the rest of your life chained to a slave ship in Madagascar, you'll tell Galen to put the whip to the horses."

"But what of the two women, my lord?"

Cairn glanced at the girl across from him. Her expression was stoic, her eyes unreadable, but her lips . . . Damn her fat, trembling lips.

"Take them with us."

"To Westheath, my liege?"

"Now!"

"Yes, my lord," snapped Peters, and rode ahead, probably to inform the driver of their lord's lunacy.

A chuckle sounded from outside the window. Cairn turned back only to find Burr there, leaning a gargantuan forearm upon the pommel of his huge, dappled steed.

"To Westheath, aye," he said, and winked at Megs. "Good thinking, lad. 'Twill be a better place to do the flogging."

Cairn considered reaching through the window and dragging the giant from his horse. But they were already on the move, and Burr was as tough as old boot leather. And perhaps he had proven himself a big enough fool without letting some overgrown Norseman beat him senseless.

Chapter 15

"I'm not going to hurt you," Cairn said. The girl called Gem stood in the middle of the solar at Westheath Castle. She looked filthy and out of place against the bright tapestry that adorned the wall. "Not if you answer my questions."

The girl nodded, shifted her gaze to Burr, and nodded again.

"What's your name?" Cairn asked.

The girl smiled. "Me name be Gem as I've told you afore."

He smiled back. They were oh so civilized. "I meant your given name," he said, and motioned to an old man who carried in a silver tray. Even from his vantage point Cairn could smell the fresh lemon patties.

"'Tis the name what was given me," Gem said. "Might you think I took it?" She laughed. Her eyeteeth were crooked, slanting in toward each other, but she had a dimple in her left cheek, and her eyes were damnably bright, as if she were always one step ahead of your average bastard laird.

"The name your mother gave you," Cairn explained.

"Didn't have no mother," Gem said, eyeing the tray that old Roland lowered before her.

Cairn smiled again, lest his carefully won patience slip into the abyss of his slowly simmering anger. "I would have thought that impossible."

She tilted her head at him. "Is them treats for me?"

"How'd you get in?" Burr rumbled.

Cairn turned toward the Norseman. He stood beside the door, one gargantuan shoulder resting against the wall.

"What's that?" Gem tensed as she narrowed her eyes and turned toward the giant, all congeniality gone.

"How'd you get in?" he repeated. "To the castle."

"You brought me. Don't you remember?"

Burr gave her a level stare. She swallowed as if she were facing a hooded henchman. Triton's balls! Cairn was the damned laird of the isle. Menace oozed from him. He was sure of it. But she could lie to him outright and not blink an eye. What was it about Burr that made her swallow her tongue. Of course it might be that he was the approximate size of Mount Hess.

"Oh. you mean when I came t' get Megs." She shrugged. Her gown was nothing but rags, her hair was still tangled, and he was pretty sure there was a distinctive odor wafting from her person. Something between rotting mackerel and sheep dung.

"I walked," she said.

"You walked," Burr repeated.

"Aye." She fidgeted a little. "About them treats . . ." she said, but she directed her question to Cairn when she spoke.

"Help yourself," Cairn said, then, "Why?"

She snatched up the closest dessert and shoved it into her mouth. "She's Megs," she said, speaking around the delicacy.

He merely stared.

"Magical Megs."

Cairn was careful not to blink.

"Go on," she scoffed. "Sure, you've 'eard of 'er. She can steal yer eyeballs clean outta yer head and never even disturb yer sleep."

He nodded, making a face of admiration.

"How'd you get past the guards?" Burr asked.

"They was lookin' elsewhere."

"So this Megs . . . she's clever," Cairn said.

She nodded. "And tough. Tough as an old 'ore."

Burr shifted his weight. She glanced toward him and back. The whites of her eyes showed clearly.

"So she's good in a fray," Cairn said.

"She could kill you just as easy as look at you," she said, taking another patty, though her mouth was still full with the last one.

"But she didn't," Cairn said. "Why?"

The girl shrugged. "'Tis 'ard to say with Megs. 'Oo knows what's in 'er mind?"

"How well do you know her?"

She was still eating, munching away like a cow in a wheatfield. But she shook her head. "Ain't nobody knows 'er real good. She keeps to 'erself, she does."

"So you know her as good . . . as well as anyone?"

She shrugged and licked her fingers "Don't know."

"How about Lady Nedra? How well does she know your Megs?"

Her chewing ceased, though her mouth was still full. "Ned don't know her atall," she said.

"She took the girl into her house."

"I took her," she said and swallowed. "I took her into the 'ouse."

"The duchess let her stay."

"That's just 'ow she is. She'll tek anyone in. She's daft.

Everybody knows it. That's why folks protect her. That's why some is scared of 'er. She's daft in the 'ead. And she can read your mind."

"She tended Megs's wound."

Gem shrugged, but she didn't continue eating. "It weren't no terrible injury."

"Not for Magical Megs."

"Nah." She reached for another patty. "It weren't nothin' much. 'E only 'ad a little pistol."

"He?"

"A fellow called Cotton."

"He shot her?"

She slowed her chewing for a moment. "Yeah. But just in the shoulder. Not in no vitals nor nothin'."

Cairn turned abruptly.

Burr raised his brows. The corner of an evil grin lifted his lips. "Where you goin', lad?"

"See to the girl," he ordered instead of answering, and headed toward the door.

Burr followed.

Cairn turned to glare. "What the hell are you doing?"

"You said to take care of the girl."

"I meant this girl."

"Oh." When the Norseman tried to look surprised, he only managed stupidity. "But what of the other lass? Gem here says she's been shot."

Cairn looked into his eyes for a instant. The huge man's face was almost completely impassive, as if he didn't know what was going through Cairn's mind. As if he didn't realize that his gut was churning. As if he didn't know Cairn was going to her this very instant.

"Someone should see to her wound," Burr said, still straight-faced.

"Shut the hell up," Cairn said, and Burr laughed as the door closed and the laird of the isle disappeared from sight.

"Well, lass," Burr said, turning back to the girl. "It looks like you've been left in me own hands then."

Her manner changed abruptly. She was not a tiny lass compared to Megs, but she was young, and she was thin. Defiance only made her seem more so. "I'll tell you somethin', Viking. If you lay so much as a finger on me, you'll be feelin' the pain till the day you die, and you won't 'ave long to wait."

He raised his brows. "Are you threatening me, lass?"

She smiled. Her crooked eyeteeth winked in the candlelight. "So yer not so dense as yer size suggests. 'Tis good to know."

"And yer a mite small to be so mouthy."

"What you gonna do, Viking? Hit me?" She raised her chin, but her face seemed unusually pale. "It's been tried afore."

He paused a moment, watching her. "I bet it has," he said. "Come along."

Her eyes changed, though he couldn't have said how exactly. "Where to?"

"You stink like a privy."

"Then don't stand so damned close."

"You need a bath."

She snorted a laugh. "Not in this lifetime."

"You got something against good clean water, lass?"

"Nay." Her tone was dismissive, though her eyes looked wild. "But I 'as something agin' oversize brutes loomin' like trolls whilst I get meself naked."

He stared at her for an instant, then threw back his head and laughed.

She was scowling at him. "If you'd tell me the jest, I might laugh, too, oaf."

He glanced at her and chuckled. "You stink, you've a

mouth like a sailor, and you're a child to boot. You can believe me in this, lass." He leaned closer, so that their faces
were only inches apart. "I've no interest in you whatsoever."

"Really?" She drew back slightly, scowling at him.

"Aye," he assured her.

She shrugged and stepped toward the door. "Then I might
just as well be on me way."

He grabbed her arm as she passed, and she jumped,
pulling away.

He let her go, but watched her carefully. "As I've said,
lass, I've no interest in you meself, but if the lad says to see to
you, I'll see to you. You can bet on that, wee one."

Cairn opened the door to his bedchamber and stepped inside. Relief flooded him when he saw her in a chair by the
desk, but he shushed it, for of course she was still there.
Where else would she be?

She was sitting very straight, her lips slighly pursed, her
hair gleaming dark and rich in the candlelight that spilled
from the candelabra behind her. A book was in her hands. *Animal Husbandry* was printed in faded gold along the spine.

He said the title aloud, ridiculously glad that Burr had
taught him to read years ago. "Planning on doing some farm-
ing, Megs?" he asked.

"I beg your pardon?"

"The book," he said, motioning toward it. "It's about raising livestock."

"Yes." She scowled slightly, as if he were daft. "I realize
that."

"So you can read."

Again, the daftness. "Yes," she said.

He took a few steps toward her, drawn against his will.
"Read me a few lines."

"To prove myself?"

"Humor me."

She turned back to the printed word, regal as a princess, and began to read. There was no purpose in letting her go on for long. Animal husbandry wasn't his first interest, though he had made an attempt to learn a bit. Sheep thrived on the Teleerian hills, and wool was a profitable export.

"Where'd you learn to read?"

"My mother taught me."

"So you had a mother?" Perhaps she would quit looking at him like that if he would quit spouting lunacy, but his conversation with Gem had done little to clear his mind.

"Does not everyone at some point?" she asked.

"I would have thought so." He seated himself on the desk beside her and crossed his arms against his chest. "You didn't tell me you'd been shot."

She was staring at him, her siren's lips pursed. "You did not ask," she said.

He forced himself to relax a little. She was crowding his patience, which had never been outstanding. "Who shot you?"

She drew a deep breath through her nostrils and closed the book, carefully, as if she had no wish to lose her place on such a scintillating subject as swine management. "I did not ask his name," she said.

"And you didn't know him?"

"I do not generally associate with such people."

"Because you're a seamstress."

"Yes."

"From London."

"Yes."

"But you don't have a London accent."

She shrugged. "We lived in Sedonia for some years."

"You and Wildon."

"My husband's name was William," she said. "And no. I lived there with my parents."

"Who taught you how to read."

"Yes."

"Isn't that unusual?"

"In truth, it's never been my goal to be usual, MacTavish."

"Then I guess you've achieved your goal admirably. A thief who reads like a scholar, speaks like a princess, and lies like a soothsayer. Your parents would be proud."

She raised her chin slightly. "What do you plan to do with me?"

Damned if he knew. "I plan to take a look at your wound."

She pursed her lips again. Damned if she didn't have the most ridiculously seductive mouth he had ever seen.

"Ned tended it," she said. " 'Tis healing well."

"Take off your gown."

Her expression didn't change a whit. Nor did she move to accommodate him.

He sighed. "I know something of injuries," he said.

She remained silent for a moment, then, "Does it still hurt?" she asked.

He scowled. "What?"

"Your leg."

He watched her carefully. "What of it?"

"Your physician has not been able to ease the pain?"

"I hate to disappoint you, lass, but I am not in pain."

She watched him soberly, then spoke. "You are more the lord than I realized."

He canted his head.

"Unwilling to admit a weakness," she explained.

He laughed. "I'm flattered you think me so royal, Megs, but I'm afraid piracy discourages weaknesses, too. If I had one, which I don't, I would have likely had my throat cut long ago."

"Do you wish you were one still?" Her expression was tense now, as if she were more than casually interested.

He watched her eyes. "A pirate?"

She nodded.

"Pirates are often hungry and tend to die young and bloody." He shrugged. "Being the sovereign ruler isn't so bad. People have to do as I say. Such as removing clothing."

She didn't blink.

"If I insist that a woman remove her garments, she must do so without question," he added pointedly.

She didn't move a muscle, and he sighed.

"You may be the most stubborn maid I have ever met."

"Because I refuse to disrobe in front of you?"

"There are other reasons."

"Tell me," she said. "Do most women simply drop their gowns at a glance from you?"

"That's my preference."

Her lips parted the slightest amount, as if she were about to smile. He watched them, then pulled his gaze away with a dogged effort.

"I'll be seeing the wound, lass," he warned.

"If you are so worried about my well-being, perhaps you should release me."

"It irritates me when my prisoners die prematurely."

"Are you a physician then?"

"No. But I was an excellent pirate."

"What good would there be in revealing my wounds to a pirate?"

"I'm the lord of the isle, and therefore have indisputable rights."

"And I am a human being, and I have moral rights."

"So you would rather die of gangrene than show me the injury?"

"I would rather maintain my morals than bend to your commands. Indeed—"

"Dammit woman, I'm not going to eat you. Just lower your gown."

"And what if I refuse? Will you stretch me on the rack?"

He refrained from rubbing his eyes in weary frustration. "My favorite rack is out of commission just now."

"What a pity."

"Isn't it? On the other hand, I could just tear the damned gown off you myself."

"Fitting for a barbarian, but not quite right for a lord."

He watched her for an instant. "Luckily, I am more one than the other."

"But which do you want to be?" Her eyes were somber and wide as though she were delving into his very soul. For a thief she had a wide range.

"Well, barbarians tend to lose limbs and attract fleas," he said. "On the other hand, lords seem to lack power over their subjects."

"Sometimes I almost believe . . ." She paused, her expression deadly serious. "If there weren't this misunderstanding between us. If circumstances were different, you might prove to be a decent human being."

He laughed. "Triton's balls. I don't know if I should thank you or behead you."

"You should thank me," she said with utmost sobriety. "It is not something I would say to many even though they are highly bred and gently born."

Truly? He almost said the word out loud, but he managed to refrain. Magical Megs, after all, was the very mistress of manipulation. But how was it that she knew of his self-doubts? And what of his leg injury? Only his closest advisors were privy to the extent of the damage. Only Burr knew of the intermittent pain.

But of course. Elizabeth had told Wheaton, and Wheaton had in turn told Megs. The humiliation of that knowledge ground into him like salt into an open wound. Who was she to him? he wondered, but he did not ask again, for she would only deny knowing him, and he was so damned tempted to believe her, for she was beautiful and soft and everything a man would want in a woman. But he had learned a hard lesson with Elizabeth, and he was not fool enough to forget it easily.

"Take off your gown, Megs," he ordered, and perhaps there was something in his tone this time, for he saw her tense.

"I will not," she said, but there was fear in her eyes.

And that was good. She should fear him. She was his enemy, but her eyes were so large and her lips so seductive.

He kept his tone steady. Damn her eyes and her stupid, pouty lips. "Show me your wound."

She didn't move.

"Do as I say," he ordered. "I don't wish to hurt you."

"Then let me go," she whispered.

He shook his head and reached for her.

She leaned away. "You first!" she rasped.

He drew back. "What?"

"I will . . . bare my injury if you will do the same."

"I told you, I don't have—"

"Then neither do I." She raised her chin, and in her eyes was such damnable pride that he wanted to weep. Why the hell was he drawn to these haughty women? These women who could tear him to shreds without batting an eye.

"You don't have an injury?" He kept his tone carefully level. Surely he could manage to play her game.

"No more grievous than yours. But you are too cowardly to admit to the truth."

He stared at her for a long moment, then, rising to his feet, he rucked up his plaid.

"What are you doing?"

He raised his brows at the panic in her voice. "I am baring all."

"I just . . . I only asked to see the wound."

"It's on my thigh."

"No. 'Twas your knee that was injured when thieves broke into the castle."

Thieves! His knee! It was the story they had loosed to the public. So she had heard that version of the tale and not the truth?

Nay, they had not spilled the truth to Teleere's populace for none needed to know how close he had come to impotency. Neither did they need to learn of Elizabeth's betrayal. He had protected her reputation rabidly at the time of her death. No one needed to know she had taken her husband's nemesis as a lover. No one needed to know that enemy had killed her. Cairn had failed to protect her in life, but he would do so in death. Or so he told himself. Yet in the back of his mind, doubt ate at him. Perhaps he only protected himself.

He pulled up his plaid along with the tunic beneath and Megs's gaze followed its accent. Her gasp was soft when he bared the wound. It ached even now, more than ever, burning with hot humility. Aye, he had been stabbed, and yes, the cut hurt, but he had also been cheated, surprised, cuckolded.

And Magical Megs, queen of the damned, dared sound surprised at the sight of his humiliation when Wheaton had surely told her the truth of the tale.

He dropped his plaid back into place and stared at her.

"Now yours," he said.

For a moment he thought she would refuse. For a moment he almost wished she would, for anger had replaced every other emotion, and it felt good, safe. She was Wheaton's. He knew it, and yet she lied. For him. Just as Elizabeth had.

He waited, then her hands moved, slowly reaching for the ties on her gown.

Her gaze never wavered from his. Her expression was unreadable as she watched him, and he saw, as the gown slipped lower, that her shoulders were perfect, and her breasts . . . They were phenomenal. Large and round and as bold as her temperament, they bulged outward as if begging for attention, and they were his, legally and otherwise. There was no reason he shouldn't take her. Revenge, after all, was sweet. It was a documented fact.

But then she slipped the bodice lower and every thought came to a screaming halt. For while the wound was small and healing and did little to distract from her beauty, her hands, where they supported her gown, shook. They trembled. Like a child's. Like an innocent's.

A myriad of emotions quivered through him. Rage and lust and a dozen other feelings he dare not admit.

"Put it back on," he ordered.

"What?" Her voice was breathy.

"Put your clothes on," he said, and pivoted woodenly toward the door. It was strangely difficult to open his fist enough to turn the latch. He managed it with some effort, then turned back toward her.

She hadn't moved. Her breasts were still partially bare, but in that instant she broke free from her trance and pulled the gown up.

"I am sending in a physician," he said. "You will let him see to it?"

She nodded. He scowled. So it was just her laird who was not allowed to touch her. The thought scored his mind.

"But I shall accompany him."

She said nothing, made no objection. He deepened his scowl.

"And be prepared, because afterward there will be a lesson."

She tipped her chin up a notch, but the haughty attitude lacked something now, for he had seen her trembling hands. "A lesson?"

"Aye." He clenched his jaw and turned the latch. "You will learn to defend yourself."

Chapter 16

"The physician," Burr said. His tone held no inflection. His face remained unmoved. He stood with his gargantuan legs spread and his back to Gem's bedchamber door. A scrape issued from inside the room, followed by a soft, muffled dispute.

Cairn scowled but continued on. "Yes," he said.

From the far side of the door, voices could just be heard, rising in disharmony.

"You want the physician to see to the thief's wounds," repeated the Norseman.

Cairn ground his teeth and refused to reiterate his request. "Where is he now?"

Something solid struck the wall inside the bedchamber.

"He's with the elderly lady, as ordered."

"What has he learned?"

A feminine voice squealed from the far side of the door.

Burr shrugged as if he heard nothing. His shoulders were slightly hunched as if in battle, despite his careful nonchalance. " 'Tis hard to say," he admitted, his brows lowering the slightest amount, perhaps in concession to the rising noise that issued from the adjacent room. "Since I have been playing nursemaid this whole morning."

"Nursemaid?" Cairn said, then brightened at the thought. "For Gem?" he asked, and nodded toward the door.

Burr's scowl only deepened.

Cairn grinned, just a little, letting his tension ease slightly. "Averse to bathing, is she?"

"I believe—" Burr began, but at that precise moment a shriek sounded clear as a bell through the nine-foot wall.

Cairn raised his brows. His day was improving. "Sounds like they could use your help, Burroun."

"They'll work it—" Burr began, but his platitude was interrupted by another shriek, a curse, and a bevy of screams.

Burr glanced behind him, hesitated an instant, then whipped the door open and strode into the storm. Cairn followed.

Inside the chamber, women were everywhere, gasping and swooning and shrieking, and in the center of the melee, was Gem. She was spread-eagle atop another maid, who was screaming like a banshee and thrashing like a trout.

Burr waded resolutely into the maelstrom. He grasped Gem by the back of her gown with a deep-throated growl and fished her out of the pile like a hooked mackerel. She came up swinging, limbs pistoning wildly. But he held her at arm's length until she swung about and landed him a blow on the chest. His expression didn't change a whit. Not a muscle twitched.

The second blow caught him in the groin.

He grunted softly and doubled slightly, and in that second Gem glanced up.

Her face went white, her arms quit swinging, and the room fell absolutely silent.

"Mr. Burr!" she rasped.

His glare was enough to sour cream. His lips twitched as he forced himself to straighten.

"What the devil's going on here?"

She was still hanging from his fist by the scruff of her gown, but she lifted her chin and glared at Carolyn, who was scrambling ponderously to her feet.

"That old cow tried to steal me hair."

Cairn glanced at Burr and back at Gem.

The room went silent again, then, "What the bloody devil are you talking about?" asked the Norseman.

"'Er!" Gem shrieked, and spat in the direction of the rapidly retreating maid. Carolyn did rather resemble a cow. Still, she had been Elizabeth's favorite. But Elizabeth tended to surround herself with plump plain-faced maids. "She 'ad a scissors in 'er 'and, she did." And indeed a scissors lay on the floor, alongside a hairbrush, three petticoats, and a bar of scented soap that had been cracked down the middle.

Burr glanced at the girl's hair. It stood out from her head a good nine inches, like a wasp's nest gone mad. "My laird gave orders to see you cleaned," he rumbled.

"Aye, well . . ." She'd lost a bit of steam, but her hands were still formed to fists and her brows were down. "'E won't be cuttin' me hair."

Cairn glanced happily at Burr and back.

"The lad orders," said Burr. "I enforce."

The girl swallowed visibly. Half the women were now hiding behind Burroun. The others were backed prudently against the walls.

Carolyn pointed a shaky finger at Gem. "She's possessed with the devil. I'll have nothing to do with her."

"I ain't possessed, you old witch!" shrieked Gem, and the room exploded back into chaos.

Burr stood in a sea of women, like a rat drowning in perfume, looking more tense by the second.

Cairn actually chuckled.

Burr glanced in his direction, saw his liege's happy expression, and straightened his back with a scowl.

"Quiet!" he roared.

The chamber went absolutely silent to the count of five, then burst back into confusion.

"Get out!" His voice was quiet this time, but somehow the word carried above the din.

The women stopped in midsentence, their mouths still open.

"Get out," he repeated. "All of you."

Gem swiveled toward the door, but Burr kept his fist tight in the back of her gown, and Cairn took that opportunity to go about his business. In moments, the room was all but empty.

Only Burr and Gem remained. Burroun loosed his hold on the girl's garments and settled her heels onto the floor with a scowl.

He glared at her. "You are a thief," he said. "And a liar. Laird MacTavish could see you executed before nightfall if he so wished." Staring into her eyes, he saw that he'd gained her attention. "But he has vowed to see you fed and clothed and hear you out before he decides your fate."

The girl swallowed and blinked owlishly. "She ain't 'avin' me hair," she whispered.

Burr ground his teeth. Right this minute he could be back on the high seas, storm tossed and starving. Ahh, the good old days.

"She doesn't want your hair," he assured her, skimming the mess atop her head. "But you'll not be seeing the laird whilst looking like that."

"I ain't never asked to talk to his mightyship."

"No. You simply broke into the castle and took the girl who's caught his interest."

Her eyes brightened slightly, but her face was still pale. "Megs?"

He shrugged. "Can you get that rat's nest out of your hair yourself?"

"My 'air ain't no rat's nest."

He glared. She swallowed.

"Aye. I can take care of it."

"And get cleaned."

She nodded, all starch gone from her demeanor.

He lowered his brows. "Try to escape, and I'll feed you to the pigeons. Do you understand me?"

She dropped her eyes. "You was right, guvner," she said softly. "Lord MacTavish 'as been decent to me, and I've repaid him poorly. I'll do as 'e asks from here on in."

He stared at her. She bobbed her gaze up and back down.

"You won't try to escape?"

She shook her head. "No, guvner. You 'ave me word of honor."

He stared at her for another moment, then said, "Good, because I'll be watching you the whole time."

Her eyes came up with a snap. "What's that?"

"While you brush your hair, while you bathe, while you dress," he growled. "I'll be right here."

"I gave you me word to stay put."

"Aye, and I'll help you keep it."

She swore at him then. As cursing goes, it was fairly impressive, he thought, and he'd spent most of his life with sailors. He waited for her to finish.

She pursed her lips and glared into his downturned face. "I'll not 'ave you gawkin' at me in the altogether, you great leering oaf."

Bending down, he retrieved a hairbrush from the floor and offered it to her.

"I won't do it," she repeated.

He took a step toward her. She backed away. "I know yer sort."

"I doubt it."

"Takin' advantage of a young girl like me. Gettin' 'er with child then—"

"Hah!"

She stopped in midsentence and narrowed her eyes. "You find somethin' amusin'?"

"You are a child," he said. "A scrawny, lying street urchin with diseases that haven't been named yet."

"I am not diseased."

He didn't reply.

"*You're* diseased, you whoremonger."

He stretched a smile across his teeth and considered drawing her across his knee. "Why don't you quit your cursing so I won't feel a need to paddle your behind?"

"Damn you, you—"

"These are the rules," he growled. "You don't try to escape. You don't steal anything, you don't strike anyone, and you don't curse."

She opened her mouth. He lifted a brow. She shut her mouth.

"Abide by those rules," he added, "and you'll be treated well and kept safe so long as you're in my care."

"Care! Hah! It's rape you have on your mind, you lecherous old—"

"But break my rules—" he interrupted, "and you'll miss a meal for every violation."

"So it's starvation you plan for me."

"Your life's your own to decide, lass."

"And me life was perfectly fine until you came along."

"Aye." He looked her up and down. "I can see all was going well for you."

"F—"

He pointed a warning finger at her.

She raised her chin, but backed off another step. "I'm not afraid of you."

"You can't be as daft as all that."

She glared.

"Now, lassie, are you going to get in that tub, or am I going to have to throw you in?"

"Try it, you—"

He cocked his head.

She pursed her lips and narrowed her eyes. "I'll do it meself, but you'll 'ave ta turn yer back."

He sighed. "I wish I could."

Propping her hands on her hips, she sharpened her glare. "And what are you meanin' by that remark?"

He didn't reply. He'd have to be a fool to let a scrap of decay like her get his dander up. But there were more than a few who had called him a fool.

"Are you sayin' you don't like the look of me?"

He didn't respond.

"Are you sayin' I don't raise yer flag, old man?"

"Watch yer tongue, girl."

She cocked her head, studying him as if he were a rare reptile. "Are you that ancient then?"

He wasn't sensitive about his age, of course, but paddling her sounded better by the minute.

"If I'm wanting fleas, I can always bed down with the hounds," he said.

"I don't 'ave no fleas."

"Maybe it's the stench that keeps them at bay."

For a moment he thought she would curse him again, but she closed her mouth, straightened her back, and reached for the ties on her gown. The garment slipped rapidly away from her shoulders. Even they were dirty. He shook his head and strode across the room to lean against a nearby wall. When he turned back to her she was scowling. She was also naked to the waist. Her breasts were small and firm and high. Her ribs were prominent, and her gown hung askew about her narrow hips.

He yawned and rubbed his tired eyes. When next he glanced her way, she was stepping into the tub.

Her buttocks were tight and white and as round as twin buckwheat loaves.

And his erection ached.

Damn him. If only he were as old as she thought.

Chapter 17

$$\sim\infty\sim$$

Tatiana sighed in her sleep. She was warm and comfortable and someone was stroking her hair, easing it along the length of her arm. It felt quite lovely, though even in the depths of her dreams, she realized that none was allowed to touch her. The duchess's daughter was far above such mundane activity as physical contact.

"You're different. I'll give you that."

She opened her eyes with a gasp and a start.

MacTavish was sitting on the slipper-shaped couch beside her. Candlelight gleamed in his honey wheat hair. His chest was bare, his stomach flat, his hip only inches from her thigh. She stiffened but refused to scoot away.

"What are you doing here?" she asked.

He smiled at her. She'd raised her head to stare at him, but her hair remained draped across the ivory-toned satin of the couch. He curled a stray lock around his wrist, watching the shine shift as he bent it to the light of the candelabra. "It's my chamber, Megs, remember?"

She sat up. Pain niggled at her shoulder, but the physician

had seen to the wound and assured her that all would be well. If only she were a believer.

"You didn't don the bed gown I sent."

She pursed her lips and refused to glance away, though if the truth were known she had found a slim, primitive dart amongst his treasures and had pinned it into her underskirt. At some point she would have another chance to escape, and she would need every possible advantage.

"The color would look right on you."

She said nothing.

"Innocent. Untouched." He shook his head as if baffled. "If I didn't know better, I could almost believe that you don't belong in prison," he said, and took her hand, turning it over in his. Her hair loosened on his wrist, but remained twined softly against the golden skin of his arm, stroking the taut tendons. "Your hands are soft." His fingers were gentle against her palm, his eyes thoughtful.

She licked her lips. "The life of a seamstress oft consists of long hours, but rarely entails heavy labor."

"Entails," he repeated, and raised his brows slightly. "You've an extensive vocabulary for a thief."

"I am not—"

"Or a seamstress," he interrupted, and stroked her palm again, skimming his thumb along the smooth line beneath her fingers. "I suppose Walden did all the manly labor?"

She blinked in dismay at her hand. It was not a particularly sensitive area, after all, and yet, sensations kept sprinting wildly up her arm every time he touched her. He caught her gaze, and she swallowed. "William," she corrected numbly. "And yes, he did."

He nodded, absorbed by her hand again as he rubbed a slow circle into the center of her palm. "So if I brought in a length of cloth, you could stitch me a doublet?"

Panic struck her like a rock, but she remained as she was,

though every instinct told her to wrest her hand from his grasp and run like hell. Aye. Perhaps she should have considered this eventuality, but if she were to worry now about all the things she should have done, she would be paralyzed until her death, which might be in the very near future if she didn't think hard and fast. So she canted her head slightly and forced a prim smile. "Are your tailors all ill?" she asked.

He held her gaze for another few seconds, then called out, "Come in."

An elderly servant entered, carrying a bolt of gray fabric. Behind him, another brought a basket filled with scissors and thread and a dozen items she couldn't name but assumed any seamstress with half a mind would be able to identify.

Tatiana's heart was thumping in her chest. She glanced at MacTavish, making certain her expression was partly mocking, partly bored. It was the same look that had made the king of Denmark back down in chagrin. "So this is what you meant when you told me to be prepared to defend myself?"

He shrugged.

"And all the while I was desperately trying to choose between the crossbow and the lance."

"And it looked like you were merely sleeping."

"'Tis strange how appearances can deceive," she said pointedly.

He smiled again, but her heart could hardly beat faster than it already was. "A needle's the only weapon you'll need, lass," he said, and, taking the bolt of fabric, sent the men from the room. "I'm told this is linen."

She glanced at the material, then nodded smoothly. "'Tis good to know your subjects wouldn't lie to you. About cloth at least."

The chamber went absolutely silent, then, "Stitch me a doublet fit for a king, lass," he said. "And I will set you free."

For a moment her heart ached with hope. Freedom—

within reach. Nearly hers. But the truth came hard on the
heels of hope. She could no more stitch a doublet than walk
on water.

Her mind was spinning and her hands were shaking more
dramatically, so she swung her feet to the floor, perhaps to
distract him, perhaps to keep herself occupied, lest her brain
burst from her skull. But she did so slowly, as taught from
birth, "*like a princess, not a ragged street urchin*," as Mother
had often said.

Her arm brushed his as she slipped from the bed, and her
hair trailed along his fingertips like a dancer's veil. Standing
up, she paced to the fabric and spread it upon the coverlet.

She eyed it leisurely as if she were in some fine market
with wares spread about for her royal inspection, as if her
very next words would not condemn her to death. He
watched her from uncomfortable closeness.

"I'm afraid there's not enough fabric," she said.

He remained exactly as he was, and yet there was a
change, a stiffness, almost as if he waited with bated breath
for her next words. Almost as if he were disappointed. "Cy
assured me there was," he said.

"Cy?" She raised one brow, trying to read the nuances.
After all, she was a queen. All revered her, few liked her. It
was a matter of life and death that she know the difference,
that she be able to differentiate between those who were
looking for independent gain and those few who had her best
interests in mind. She had learned well, for she knew that she
could count on one hand those who truly cared.

"Cy was my father's favored tailor," he informed her.

"Ahh." She gave him a small shrug. "Well, I do hate to
make Cy feel unneeded. Perhaps he should craft the garment
himself."

"I want you to do it."

"And if I do . . ." She flitted her gaze to the fabric and up, feeling an odd catch in her stomach as though it had twisted in on itself. "You'll set me free?" It was difficult to force the words from her constricted throat, but to her own ears the words sounded almost normal. 'Twas another trick she had learned at a selfish court.

He was watching her like a hunting falcon: his gaze absolutely steady, his mouth immobile. She refused to lower her eyes. After all, raptors followed movement. They liked their prey fresh and frightened. "Why not admit that you aren't a seamstress, Megs?" he asked. "Things can hardly get worse for you."

"Not true," she said, and ran her fingers leisurely along a fold in the fabric. "I am still alive after all."

"Ahh." He leaned back to watch her. "So you're a maid who expects little from life."

She gave him a single, noncommittal nod. "A humble lass," she agreed.

He laughed a little. "One would expect humility in a thief," he admitted, "but one would be disappointed. The dichotomy piques me interest."

"Dichotomy," she repeated and tilted her head at him, much as he had done to her. "I'm impressed."

He shrugged. The movement was strangely boyish. "The good people of Teleere seem to think their laird should be able to say more than, 'yo me hearties.'"

She laughed, then, wondering at his expression of surprise, she sobered immediately, feeling nervous under his stare, her gaze flitting foolishly to the side.

"So Magical Megs has a sense of humor," he said.

"I am not M—"

"Then stitch me a garment."

She almost winced, but managed to keep her face impassive and her hands steady. "I cannot."

Seconds ticked by in silence.

"No?" he asked.

"The truth is . . ." She paused, waiting for inspiration, for breath, for her mind to kick back into gear. "You see . . ." She shrugged, hoping she looked charmingly defenseless. "William did all the actual labor."

"William?"

"Yes."

"Your virginal husband."

She fiddled with a frayed edge of fabric. "I never said he was virginal."

"Only that you are."

She cleared her throat and dropped her gaze to her hands. They were clasped together in front of her body now, and she wondered with a kind of vague distraction when she had linked her fingers. One could hardly tell they were shaking at all.

"I believe my . . . marital status is none of your affair," she said.

MacTavish rose to his feet with slow, leonine grace, watching her every second. "My laird," he said.

"What?"

" 'Tis what you might say in this situation," he said, pacing slowly toward her. "I believe my . . . marital status is none of your affair, my laird."

"Of course," she said, and raised her chin, though her soul trembled at his nearness.

"Who are you?" he asked.

"I believe—"

"But I don't," he said, and, lifting his hand, brushed his fingers along her cheek. He was larger than he seemed. Perhaps it was his beauty that created the illusion. Perhaps it was his physical perfection that made him seem less intimidating, but now she was aware of every inch of him. "In truth, I don't believe much of what you tell me." He traced his fingers along the curve of her ear. She tried to control the shiver, but experience was everything, and she was not accustomed to being touched, to him. Even her mother had avoided such a personal contact. "You say your name is Linnet, but Gem denies that. You say you are a seamstress, but there you call yourself a liar. You say you don't know Wheaton, but circumstances prove otherwise. You say you are a virgin . . ." He paused. "It seems to be the only thing you've left to convince me of."

She didn't speak. Indeed, she was quite sure she was incapable of doing so. Instead, she raised her chin and drew a careful breath.

"Where do we start?" he asked.

Her heart fluttered like a songbird in her chest, but she was certain her face would show nothing.

"I'm told there are several ways to prove your statement," he said.

So he had been discussing her with others. Perhaps his physician, and somehow that knowledge made the humiliation that much worse, but she showed nothing in her gaze.

"Oh?" she said, as if she were only mildly interested.

He watched her with hot intensity, and for the first time in a long while she wondered if her mask had slipped, if he could see past her well-polished defenses into her quivering soul. "I could call the good doctor back in to examine you," he said. "Or—"

"If you mean to humiliate me, you needn't try so hard, MacTavish."

His eyes were hard now and his expression unfathomable. "But I've hardly tried at all yet. You should experience being stripped to the waist and tied to the masthead."

"But I feel belittled already and not a masthead in sight.

Belittlement must be a gift of yours." She tried to step back, but he slid his hand onto her shoulder, keeping her close with a light pressure. " 'Tis not very noble of you," she added.

"Amusing, isn't it?" he said. "I am a laird who acts like a pirate, while you are a thief who acts like a princess."

She tried to scoff or laugh or deny. She managed none of those things, but stood like a trapped mouse beneath his hand.

"How do you explain it?" he asked, and, leaning forward, kissed the corner of her mouth.

She licked her lips as he drew away. "Perhaps it is because you *are* a pirate."

He skimmed his hand down her arm and stepped closer. She could feel the heat from his half-naked body. She was eighteen years of age, had visited more countries than she could remember and spoke a half dozen languages, but never had she seen a man unclothed. Her mother had been careful about that, all but obsessed with the idea of keeping her pure. A pure lady was a valuable lady.

But his chest was mesmerizing, hard and rounded, with small, peaked nipples. Below that, muscles marched in double rows down to a fine strip of golden hair. For a moment she was almost tempted to reach out and touch it.

"And you?" he said.

"What?" Had she been staring at his chest? Had she lost so much control?

He smiled slightly, but there was something other than humor lighting his eyes. "I *am* a pirate," he said. "While you . . ."

"I am naught but a humble seam—"

He tsked a warning and slipped his arm about her waist.

"The . . ." She was breathing hard. "The widow of a humble tailor," she corrected.

"The virginal widow," he added, and kissed her lightly on the lips.

Terror melded wildly with unknown emotions and shivered up her spine. "Please—" It was the only word she could seem to force out.

"Please what, princess?" he murmured, and leaned close again.

"Let me go." She breathed the words against his mouth.

He drew back slightly, but the smile was gone, replaced by an expression of tension. He closed his eyes and exhaled softly, his breath warm against her cheek.

"You steal me property, cause Wheaton's escape, and lie at every turn, lass. How can I let you go?" They were pressed together now. His eyes held her gaze as firmly as his hand cradled her bottom. It did strange things to her equilibrium, shattering her concentration, unbalancing her thoughts, and yet she had no desire to shift it. In fact, something in her ached to move closer still, to feel his hand slip more intimately against her body, to let her own fingers taste the flavor of his skin.

She fought the insanity. "I tell you again, I am not what you believe me to be." She whispered the words, as if they were an awful secret.

"Then what are you?" Was there desperation in his voice?

"I am innocent," she whispered.

"Innocent," he repeated, and stroked her hair away from her face.

She closed her eyes and nodded. Her lips felt swollen, and between her thighs, she felt strangely warm and heavy.

He slipped his hand beneath her hair, cradling her neck and tilting her head back slightly. Then he kissed her again, slowly now and so thoroughly that her knees threatened to buckle.

Desire steamed through her. Unexpected and unwanted, it melted her resolve and dimmed her reason. She kissed him back, pressing against his heat, tasting the hard strength of him.

He drew back a fraction of an inch, breathing hard, and in his expression she thought she saw some of the same raging insanity she felt.

"Dammit, lass!" His tone was ragged. "Where did you learn to kiss?"

She couldn't think, couldn't see straight. All she could do was feel. The heat of his skin. The strength of his hands. She shivered and, slipping her fingers into his hair, pulled his head down for another kiss.

For one frantic second, she thought he might resist, and then he was growling against her mouth, kissing her with wild passion. She answered with every aching fiber in her body.

He pulled away, and she mewled desperately, trying to draw him back. But his hands never left her. In an instant, her gown was gone. And she was all but naked.

"Lass." His voice was a low rumble of desire. He stared down at her, his eyes hot as he skimmed his hand over her breast.

She closed her eyes, shivered, and pressed her hips to his.

"Damn Wheaton!" He breathed the words like a prayer and lifted her into his arms.

The world ground to a halt.

"What?" she rasped. "What did you say?"

She could feel his heart beating against her breast, could feel the heat of his gaze against her skin.

"You've a body like a sea siren and passion like a blaze." He kissed her again, but her eyes remained riveted to his. "Damn him!" he said, and carried her to the bed.

Chapter 18

❧

"**W**heaton!" Tatiana hissed and scrambled wildly from his arms. He tried to hold her, but she had the force of surprise and managed to stumble to her feet. "Wheaton!" It was hard to breathe, impossible to think. "You would bed me to hurt another."

"Lass—"

"You still believe I lied."

His eyes narrowed. "Are you saying you've been honest?"

Her chest hurt with the force of her emotion. "At least I've been honest with my feelings."

"Feelings?"

"Yes. I—" She stopped the words short, realizing what she'd said. Panic consumed her. She stepped back a pace.

"Feelings?" he repeated and followed her.

"Do not touch me," she warned. "Never again, or I swear on my father's grave you will rue the day."

"Is that what you said to Wheaton?" He was stalking her, following her in a slow circuit about the congested room.

"Damn you, MacTavish," she said.

"And what of that?" he asked, and, quick as a serpent, he reached out and grabbed her arm. "Did you tell him that, too, or did you only moan his name as you spread your legs?"

She slapped him as hard as she could. He turned his head, but his grip didn't loosen, and in an instant he turned back to stare into her eyes.

"Is that what you did to discourage him, lass? A little tap on the cheek? Is that how you piqued his interest? By acting the innocent, then moaning like a whore?"

She slapped him again. This time he didn't even turn away. Instead, he smiled.

Anger boiled like tar inside her, burning her soul.

"Has there ever been a single man you've managed to discourage like that?"

"Touch me again, and I'll kill you, MacTavish."

"Kill me!" He threw back his head and laughed. She raised her hand to strike again, but he caught her arm with no effort at all. "Megs," he said, feeling her puny biceps, "you couldn't kill a flea with a hammer. But you know that, don't you?"

She glared at him and he stared back, watching her with narrowed eyes.

"You had no intention of stopping me, did you?"

She quivered with unaccustomed rage. She would make him pay. Somehow. Someday.

"You only planned to egg me on, to arouse my interest, to act like an innocent that could no longer resist me." He nodded. "How many men have you enticed this way?"

"Let me go." Her voice quivered—with rage or humiliation or a strange blend of the two.

"Why?" he asked. "So you can kiss me or strike me?"

She straightened her spine and found her pride. "So I can kill you," she said.

He smiled. "You don't want to kill me. I've too much to offer you."

She said nothing.

"You may have the finances of a thief, but you've got the morals of a duchess."

"You—What?"

"You don't want to damage me, princess."

She canted her head at him. Rage still simmered inside, but she could now control her hand. Never had she struck another living creature—until she met *him*. "Yet again I'm surprised at how often you can be wrong," she said.

"Truly?"

"Yes."

He glanced around the room, then dropped her arm and stepped away. Retrieving a magnifying glass from his desk, he hefted it in his hand for an instant, then smashed it against the wall. Brass bent and glass shattered. He twisted the remaining metal away from the handle. Pacing across the floor to her, he lifted her hand, placed the broken handle against her palm, and curled her fingers tight around it.

It felt heavy and hard. She scowled at it, then at him.

"Strike me," he said.

She raised her brows. "What?"

"Hit me," he said.

She shook her head in bewilderment.

"So I was right. You never intended to discourage me advances."

"Believe what you will." She felt tired suddenly, tired and spent. "Do what you will."

"Come now, lass. Surely Wheaton's whore has more spirit—"

She never meant to swing, and apparently he didn't expect her to, because she caught him solidly on the chin. He rocked back on his heels like a hobbyhorse, teetered there for an instant, then settled back onto his feet and stared at her.

Raising his hand, he tested his jaw. His gaze never dropped from hers, and she held it like a bulldog.

He nodded judiciously. "That was better," he admitted.

Better! Hell, it was wonderful. She stepped toward him. He raised his brows.

"Want to try again?"

Perhaps she nodded. Perhaps she just dived in, but suddenly she was wrapped in his arms, her fist stretched out in front of her, her shoulder against his chest.

"You've got to stay balanced. Don't overreach," he said, and slapped her bottom as he released her.

She swung even as she turned. Her knuckles skimmed his shoulder, but he danced back.

"Good. Never let your enemy settle in. Never let him know what you're thinking. But you're good at that, aren't you? The mistress of manipulation. That's how you snared Wheaton."

She swung again. He sidestepped easily, shaking his head as he did so.

"I expected that one. You're too frail to use strength alone, even with a weapon. You've—"

"Damn you!" she growled, and swung again.

He danced to the side, grinning now.

"Surely you know you're frail, Megs. Even you can't be that deluded."

She jabbed wildly. He laughed as he backed against the wall.

"Triton's balls, you're hardly big enough to make a decent meal."

She strode in. He feinted left. She followed.

He dodged right, smiling as she stumbled past.

"Still," he said, his eyes gleaming as he stared at her breasts as they bobbled above the laces of her shift, "you're more than a mouthful."

She barely stopped herself from falling, but came around hard, swinging her fist wildly upward as she did so. It was a poor effort, but he was distracted and she had rage on her side. Her fist caught him right between the legs.

He grunted loud and doubled over, his mouth twitching as he did so.

She backed cautiously away, amazed, silent, watchful.

He remained as he was, his knees slightly bent, his eyes closed, his arm laid protectively across the abused area.

"That . . ." He nodded slightly and exhaled carefully, but he didn't straighten. "That was a good, solid strike."

An apology was on the tip of her tongue, but his gibes were still clear in her mind. She straightened her back.

"Shall I call the physician?"

He squinted up at her from his bent position. "And tell him what? That I've been hit in the balls by a woods fairy with a brass handle?"

"Are you hurt?"

"No. No." He shook his head and straightened a couple inches. A muscle spasm in his cheek. "You're too frail to hurt me, remember?" His tone was rueful.

"I didn't mean to strike you . . . there."

He straightened some more, closed his eyes and gritted his teeth. "Why not?"

She winced as he levered upward. "It's not . . . very . . ." She was watching him carefully, wondering if he was about to keel over like a rotten parsnip. "Sporting?"

"Sporting." He gained his full height with some difficulty and frowned at her. "What kind of thief are you?"

"I told you—"

"Then what kind of woman are you?" He sounded more peeved than when she'd first hit him. "I'm a man, fully grown and bent on ravaging you. Hell, I was taunting you. If anyone deserves to be hit in the balls, I do. And you want to be . . . sporting?"

"I'm not . . ." They were talking conversationally, as if she weren't naked, as if he didn't plan to execute her, as if she hadn't just hit him in the balls with the handle of a magnifying glass. "I never claimed to be a fighter."

He eyed her carefully. "How do you survive, lass?"

There was something in his eyes. It was disconcerting and arousing and frightening. She turned away. "I am highly intelligent."

"Then why haven't you learned to defend yourself?"

She raised her chin. "Not everyone has your opportunities, MacTavish."

He nodded once, skimmed his gaze down her body, tightened his fist, and nodded again.

"Get some sleep," he said, and, shuffling toward the door, made an inelegant exit.

"I'll not do it!" Carolyn's back was arched with prim dismay, her thin lips pursed and her pinched face disapproving. "She's a thief and a heretic and other things my good graces keep me from mentioning."

"I gave you an order." Burr's voice was deep.

"I'll not—"

"I wish to speak to Burr alone," Cairn said, giving Carolyn a nod of dismissal as he approached.

Her eyes widened slightly. "Yes, my lord," she said, and curtsied hurriedly before making her way down the hall.

Cairn waited until she was out of hearing. "Troubles, Burr?"

"Nothing I can't handle," said the Norseman, but he turned a miserable eye toward the door as he did so.

The irritation on the giant's face made Cairn feel somewhat better. His own night had been endless, for while he had found a comfortable bed not far from his own chamber, his damn cock ached in concert with his head, and his balls didn't feel so good either.

"You look like hell," Burr said, seeming to read his thoughts.

"*Me laird*," Cairn corrected mechanically, and Burr grinned and nodded.

"Aye, you look like hell, *me laird*."

"Do you remember Lord Remmy?"

Burr narrowed his eyes, which were generally narrow to begin with. "The fencing instructor?" he asked.

"Yes. Didn't he teach other forms of . . . defense?"

"Aye, I believe he did."

"Contact him. Have him come to Westheath."

Burr remained unmoved for a moment, then grinned and nodded as his lightning quick mind caught Cairn's intent. "Aye, 'tis a good idea, lad. Teach Teleere's master thief to defend herself. 'Tis a grand idea."

His head hurt. "I didn't say the lessons were for her."

Burr laughed happily. "Then the lass must be scrappy indeed if the pirate laird feels the need to hire a bodyguard."

Cairn gritted his teeth. "I didn't sleep well," he said. "So you may want to keep your clever comments to yourself."

Burr shrugged. "What are you going to do? Have the lass avenge your wounded pride?"

Cairn tightened his fists, then swore softly and rubbed his brow. "Just get word to Remmy," he said, and turned away.

"As you wish," Burr agreed. "Lord Remmy. He's the right man for the job. Always had an eye for the maids, he did."

Cairn turned back. "What the devil do you mean—" he began, but the door behind Burr snapped open, and Gem stepped out.

"I thought—" The girl's words stopped short. "Oh," she said and bobbed a curtsy. Her face was clean, but she'd donned her old, much-abused gown and her hair was frayed and snarled. She blinked once at him. "'Scuse me fer sayin' so, but you look like 'ell, me lord. Are you feelin' good?"

Cairn pivoted away, and Burr grinned before transforming his expression and turning toward Gem with a scowl.

"You'll not speak to Laird MacTavish that way."

She scowled aggressively in return, but she backed up a pace. "What be you doing 'ere, Viking? I thought them ladies were to primp me 'air."

"Aye, well perhaps the ladies weren't in the mood to be mauled by an undersized urchin with more brass than brains," he said.

She grinned. It was like watching an imp peek through a window glass. Her slanted eyeteeth made her look somehow foxy.

"What are you smiling about?"

"Do you mean she refused ta challenge me again?"

He saw no reason to answer, but her grin lifted just the same.

"Fer such a mean old toad she couldn't tek much abuse, could she?"

The maid's disposition could stand some improving, and no, when it came right down to it, she hadn't stood up well to the narrow girl named Gem, but Burr refused to let himself smile.

"Don't think yourself so smart, girl. You're in deep trouble here."

"I ain't done nothin' wrong," she said.

"Of course not. You're the pillar of society."

"Just cuz I weren't born haughty-tauty like you don't make me no thief."

"Haughty-tauty." Him. He almost laughed out loud. "So you're not a thief."

"'Course not," she said, and tried to look affronted. She only managed hair-frizzled surprise.

"Then you shouldn't look like one," he said, and skimmed her with a cool gaze.

She settled her tattered gown into place around her narrow hips. "I bathed right and proper. As I'm sure you recall, you old lech."

He shrugged "I do seem to remember a skinny little scamp stepping into the tub," he said. "But I wasn't sure whether it was a lass or a walking stick."

"Hah!" she croaked, and he shook his head as if offended by the very sound.

"Things might go better for you if you'd cease sounding like a heavey horse and rid yourself of that rat's nest atop your head."

"Really?" she said, sounding suddenly coy. "So you think if I fix meself up, Lord MacTavish might be interested in me."

"Laird MacTavish?" He grinned a little, not because he was amused, but because nothing would give him more pleasure than irking her just as she irked him. "I'm afraid the lad's interests lean toward women who can speak without spitting," he said. "But I'm thinkin' the hounds might find you tolerable if you got yourself cleaned up."

She glared at him. "Don't pretend you ain't interested in me," she said. "I saw you watchin' me whilst I was bathin' last night."

"Aye," he agreed. "I feared you were so skinny you might slip down the drain with the muddy water you left behind."

"Miss me, would you, Viking?"

" 'Tis hard to fool the likes of you, I can see that, lass," he said. "Now get inside and do something with your hair."

"Me hair's fine. I washed it meself."

He snorted.

She bristled. "And I suppose you can do better, you great galloot?"

"As could me steed."

"Sure then, come on in," she said, and swung the door wide.

He snorted. "You may not have noticed, lass, but I'm a long shot from a lady's maid."

"Oh I know what you are," she said. "Yer the master's puppet. Bound to do what 'e tells you to. You've got no choice, do you now?"

He said nothing, and she scowled as she bent toward him slightly. Her eyes shone suddenly with crystal-bright tears.

"I've done nothin' against you or yer lord," she said. "Yet you hold me 'ere. And why? Just becuz 'e tells you to."

He kept his expression absolutely stoic, pretending her eyes weren't filled with tears. Pretending it wouldn't matter if they were. "What would you suggest, lass?"

Her face became intensely earnest, her small mouth pursed. "Let me go, old man, and I'll make it worth yer effort."

"Will you now?"

"Aye," she said, her voice low and intense as she laid her hand on his chest. The fingernails were still rimed with dirt. "You've got yer eye on me. I know you 'ave."

He didn't respond.

"But you'll not 'ave me without a fight. No one 'as yet. Though there've been more than a few what 'ave tried."

He watched her intently. She was an odd mix of elements—pride, fear, and cleverness to name a few. "How old are you, lass?"

She shrugged her narrow shoulders. "Old enough to tame

your fires, old man," she said, and slid her fingers down his chest.

He watched the movement for a moment, then took her hand in his own and placed it by her side. "Why don't you start by taming your hair, lass."

Her fists tightened like small mallets. "Is that what cranks yer crossbow?" she said. "A great mound of silly 'air piled atop me 'ead? If that's what it takes to gain me freedom, then send in the fat old cow."

He refrained from smiling. "She refuses to have anything to do with you."

"She refuses!" She drew herself up as if mightily offended. "She was the one what tried to steal me 'air."

He eyed it, noting the amazing tangled heights. "Any idea why she might want it?"

"Them fancy ladies in London and whatnot would pay a fortune to get their 'ands on 'air like mine."

He didn't respond.

She bristled. "Send the old bat in."

He shook his head. "That ship has sailed, lass."

She scowled at him for a moment, then shrugged. "I guess you'll 'ave te let me go, then, since yer lord don't want no audience with no scraggly-'aired peasant?"

"He wanted you cleaned."

"I am cleaned."

"And coifed."

"Well that's damned tough then ain't it," she said. "Cuz we can't always get what we want."

"MacTavish can."

"You got another royal simp out there who's game to tame me 'air?"

"Aye," he said, and took a step toward her.

She raised her chin another couple inches and backed away. "What the devil are you doin'?"

"Hand me that brush and sit down."

"I will not."

"Sit your skinny arse down," he warned, "before I think of more fitting things to do with a hairbrush."

Chapter 19

"*S'il vous plaît*," said Sir Albert.

"Go away," ordered Cairn.

"*S'il vous plaît*," repeated the tutor.

"Get the hell out of here," gritted Cairn, and Albert, finally taking the not so subtle hint, arched his spine in deep afront and headed for the door.

Cairn sighed and paced to the window. Far below in the courtyard, a team of grays jangled their bits and rolled their white-rimed eyes.

"*Lord Remmy always had an eye for the maids.*" What the hell did that mean? Not that he cared. If Magical Megs wanted to seduce the man, she was free to do so. Hell, she could seduce the devil himself if she wished, just so long as she told him what he wanted to know. But until then she had to stay alive. Thus the lessons. He couldn't afford to have anything happen to her. A titter of guilt crossed his mind. He didn't mind lying, but it had always seemed foolish to lie to himself. And the truth was, it was unlikely that the girl would fall into trouble here at Portshaven. Then again, she had been

215

here when she was taken last time. When she was taken and shot. He closed his eyes. Damn! She could have been killed. And what would happen next time? Not that there would be a next time. After all, he had her carefully guarded.

But the truth bedeviled him. Eventually she would leave—would escape by her own confounded means or be turned loose, for despite everything, he would not harm her. No, she would leave Westheath. She would leave him, and she would fend for herself.

He winced and ground his teeth as he paced, for she was barely the size of his pillow, and like his pillow, she was soft and . . .

Triton's balls! He growled a curse and paced again. She was not defenseless! She was Magical Megs. She had lied, had stolen. That was why he held her here because . . .

His thoughts shambled to a halt as his memory burned back to the sight of her asleep on his couch, the feel of her in his arms, her lips soft against his, her body . . .

Damn! He paced again. Did he detain her because she was guilty, or did he hold her because he was too weak to let her go? Perhaps he had no right to keep her. Perhaps she had loved ones who awaited her return. Perhaps there was a man. And perhaps that man was Wheaton. The thought scoured his mind. He ground his hands to fists. Aye, maybe she would return to Wheaton, but if she did, she would not go defenseless. Thus the lessons. It all made sense. He winced at his own logic.

But Burr's words rang in his head. "*An eye for the maids!*"

"To hell with that," Cairn growled, and marched down the hall once again.

The door to Gem's bedchamber was closed, the hallway empty. Cairn scowled as he glanced about. It wasn't like Burr to leave his post. The man might be a looming barbarian, but you couldn't say that he was the kind to abandon his duties.

He would tear his head off and throw it at a prisoner before he'd let her escape.

It was then that he heard a moan. It was low and pained and came from inside the nearest chamber. Drawing his dagger, Cairn burst into the room.

Burr and Gem were near the window. The Norseman stood behind, her before. Her hands were splayed against the stone wall. In profile, with her expression blissful and her eyes closed, she was truly pretty. But Cairn's intrusion jerked them apart. Gem gasped. Burr growled. They turned in unison. The girl's expression was somewhat dazed, but Burr stood at the ready, his legs spread, his feet planted, and his huge arms flung wide. In his gargantuan right hand, he held a hairbrush.

Cairn let his dagger droop down by his side.

The room went absolutely silent, and Cairn let the silence fall, waiting.

Burr cleared his throat and lowered the hairbrush, which he'd held like a damned scimitar. "I was just . . ." He paused, scowled, then pointed the brush toward the girl. "The ladies refused to see to her hair."

Cairn said nothing.

Burroun cleared his throat again. "You said to see her cleaned up proper."

"You were . . ." Cairn tried to wrap his mind around the situation, but it didn't seem possible that Burr, the pirate, Burr the brigand, Burr the deadliest bodyguard in all of Teleere, had been caught playing nursemaid to some ragamuffin street urchin. "You were brushing her hair?" he asked.

Gem's expression, usually as sharp as a highwayman's blade, was still vague, as if she'd reached utopia and dreaded the return. But even as he watched, her eyes began to focus. "'E's right 'andy with a 'airbrush," she said. The words came out on a sigh.

Cairn couldn't have stopped the grin if he had tried. He didn't try. "You were brushing her hair?" he asked again.

"'Twas in the line of duty," Burr said. "The ladies were loath to tackle the job so—"

"So you braved the task."

Burr's expression darkened considerably. "Is there something you needed . . . *me laird*?"

Cairn's light mood vanished. "Aye," he said, remembering his mission. "I've changed me mind about Lord Remmy."

Quiet settled in again. Burr watched him for a moment, then, "Decided your skills be good enough to match the lassie's, have you, lad?"

Tension cranked into Cairn's muscles, but he loosened them with an effort and gave a languid shrug. "I don't want to keep you from your brave deeds, Burr," he said, and turned toward the door. "Carry on, man, I think there may yet be a tangle left to conquer."

Cairn would have liked to enjoy having the final word, but his mind was atumble, and Megs, the magical thief, was only a short distance down the hall.

He nodded to Peters as he passed him, then opened his bedchamber door with no prelude.

Megs sat very upright on an ivory-hued upholstered chair. She was completely clothed, every button holed and every hair in place. Her shoes, though scuffed, were laced tightly and perfectly aligned, the heels together just so. As the door opened, she turned her head slowly, like a princess about to be coronated, not like a prisoner awaiting her sentence, and for a moment he was stunned by her regal beauty.

He closed the door slowly behind him.

She set her book aside, and they stared at each other, neither speaking for a moment.

"Stand up," he said finally.

"What?"

"Stand up," he repeated.

"Time for my execution?"

"Don't tempt me."

She did as told, but slowly, as if she had all the time in the world, as if her subjects watched every graceful movement.

He scowled. "Come here."

Again, she did as commanded. She was dressed in the gown he'd first seen her in. It was a decent garment made of sturdy brown linen with dark piping at the ends of the sleeves and around the modest bodice. But somehow it didn't suit her. And he had no idea why that foolish notion should bother him.

"Turn around," he said when she was less than a full yard away.

"Why?"

"Because I'm the laird," he said, "and I've ordered you to do so."

She did as told. Her deep sable hair shone in the candle-light, and as he reached out, his fingers brushed it, scattering the gleam, but he ignored the seductive softness as he wrapped his arm around her neck. He took a deep breath and settled his mind. "What would you do if I meant you harm?"

"You do mean me harm."

He gritted his teeth. "If I were a brigand."

"You are a brigand."

"Listen." He turned her about rapidly, nearly spinning her off her feet so that she faced him. "I'll not have you so ill protected."

She was staring at him as if he'd lost a good portion of his mind, but he refused to drop his gaze, though it was a close thing. "Peters is at my door," she reminded him.

"Peters can't chew his own food."

"Then why do you keep him about?"

"Because loyalty deserves—" He stopped himself. She

hardly needed to know how he valued loyalty, especially since he'd told her he didn't believe in it. Drawing a deep breath, he slowed his speech. "If word got out that Teleere's premiere thief is feeblish, we'd be the laughingstock of all Europe."

"Because I can't protect myself," she said, as if trying desperately to understand his lunacy.

He didn't shuffle his feet. "That's right."

"And you still think me a thief."

"Aye."

"But you want me to be able to defend myself."

Yes, he was as daft as a turnip. "Norway has Rupert," he said as proof.

"I beg your pardon?"

He sounded like a blathering idiot in the presence of a princess. "Rupert," he repeated. "He stole the crown from right off King Charles's head, then held off fifteen guards with nothing but a staff until he made his escape."

She stared at him for a full ten seconds, then turned pointedly and headed toward the door.

He scowled. "Where are you going?"

She didn't respond, but lifted the latch and stepped into the hallway.

"Lieutenant." Her voice was absolutely earnest. "I fear your lord is not feeling well."

There was a moment of quiet, then Peters burst into the room, his face pale as winter and his eyes bulging. "My liege!" he said, his gaze rushing to Cairn. "You are ill?"

Cairn eyed him levelly. "Get back to your post, man."

The lieutenant looked confused at best. "But—"

"Our prisoner is amusing herself, Peters."

Confusion turned to bafflement.

"She jests," Cairn explained.

Peters scowled. "About your health, my lord?" His tone

was beyond shocked. His thoughts were clear; surely no one would joke about Lord MacTavish's well-being. The idea was bewildering. There had once been a time aboard the *Skian Dubh*, when, while fishing, Cairn had mistakenly landed a shark. It wasn't a huge creature, but it was large enough to take a chunk out of its captor's leg. The entire crew had laughed for a week, and not a single soul had offered to bandage his wounds.

"Return to your post," he repeated.

"Yes, my lord." One quick glance at Megs, and Peters left with floor-rapping precision, closing the door firmly behind him.

Cairn exhaled and scowled. "You are my link to Wheaton."

She continued to stare. No expression shown on her face. As if she were above simple emotion.

"You were right when you said not everyone has my opportunities to learn to fight," he said, and shrugged. If he couldn't do stoic, he'd settle for nonchalant. "Burr thrashed me regularly until I learned to defend meself."

Her face was solemn. "Thrashed you."

"Well,"—another oh-so-casual shrug; damn, she was beautiful—"he challenged me. It turned out to be pretty much a thrashing. I'm guessing you didn't have that advantage."

"No," she admitted. "Nary a Norseman to pit myself against."

"Did you have a father?"

"Most do."

"Didn't he worry? You being so . . ." He avoided the word frail. She didn't seem to like it. In fact, his balls ached at the thought. "Delicate," he said instead. "Didn't he teach you any sort of self-defense?"

"I fear not," she said, and offered no more.

It frustrated the hell out of him that he had no idea what

kind of past she had experienced. He kept the thought to himself. "If you're killed, Wheaton will have no reason to return here," he explained.

"And you're afraid I might be accosted surrounded by a dozen guards . . . and the walls of Westheath Castle."

"If I remember correctly, you already left our kindly protection once."

She nodded in mild concession. "That is because you threatened to hang me." She said it matter-of-factly, as if there were no hard feelings, as if, in fact, there was nothing he could do to pierce her cool calm. And perhaps there was not. Not again, though he remembered her losing her refined demeanor on a few occasions. Aye, he remembered her heated words, her hot caresses, and he would not soon forget, for he enjoyed a little honest fire. Since Elizabeth he saw a good deal of value in fishmongers' aromatic wives and giggling goosegirls. And yes, in thieves. But not in thieves who acted like duchesses. Hell, if they were going to act like duchesses, they might just as well have the funds to match. As it was, he would not marry again, not to deepen Teleere's coffers, not to form an alliance, not if the entire continent threatened to explode like black powder around his ears.

"Do I have your word that you will not try to escape again?" he asked.

She paused, blinked, remained perfectly still, and said, "No."

"Then I have little choice but to help you defend yourself."

"Lest I escape."

"Aye. So that you are safe until I find you again."

"Tell me," she said, "was your mother closely related to your father? A sister perhaps."

He gave her a sardonic grin. "My mother was the daugh-

ter of a Scottish wagonwright and a Welsh milkmaid," he
said. "My father was Anthony Penworth, laird of this isle."

"Still—"

"I'm not daft," he said, though he wished he could believe
his own words. "I'm merely cautious."

"This is ridiculous," she said. "I—"

"Did you know he murdered my wife?"

The blood drained from her face. "What?"

"Wheaton," he explained, and found that his tone was admirably steady. "He killed my wife."

"No." The word was little more than a whisper.

"Aye," he said, and the story spilled out. "They were
lovers. He was exciting, I suppose. The son of a banished, aging earl. Still, some thought he should be next in line for the
throne. Elizabeth thrived on excitement, and on my humiliation." He shrugged. "But she'd cheated so often in those first
two years. By the time I learned of Wheaton, her infidelity no
longer mattered."

"I am sorry."

He watched her carefully for a moment, then continued
on. "When I failed to care . . ." He paused for a moment.
"She meant to put a stop to their trysts, I think. Or perhaps
that's just what I wish to believe. But Wheaton is not one to
be set aside. He killed her, in her own bed, in my bed, here at
Westheath.

"Making it look as though you did it."

He said nothing.

"And you think that could happen to me. Hence the lessons."

His gut hurt, and his throat felt damnably tight, but he
shrugged with casual disregard.

She walked toward him, never losing eye contact. "Mac-
Tavish, I am so—"

But he could not bear her sympathy, so he stopped her. "I will tutor you," he said, "and you will remain safe."

She said nothing, but in a moment she nodded and turned about.

He shoved aside a dozen distractions and wrapped his arm about her neck, but her scent penetrated his barriers, and that was strange, for he had given her no perfume. Nothing to make her smell so tantalizing, and yet she did.

"Are you ready?" she said.

He brought himself back to the business at hand and tightened his arm. "What would you do if I came at you from behind like this?" he asked.

"I am unsure," she said. "What should I do?"

He focused hard, shoving old memories behind him. "Anything you can."

"What?"

"What do your instincts tell you to do?"

"I would surely feel the urge to grab your arm and try to wrestle myself free." She raised her hands to his forearm, holding it with both hands.

"Good. Then what?"

"I would pull."

"Don't pull. I'm stronger."

"Then what should I do?"

"Faint," he said.

"What?"

He shrugged. "Granted, you're no bigger than a mite, but if I have to support your weight . . ." he paused. "Lift up your feet."

"What?"

"Make me bear your weight," he said. "It'll surely pull me off-balance. Then you'll have the advantage."

She lifted one foot tentatively.

"No. Fast. Jerk them up. Catch me unawares."

"I'm afraid that is impossible since you are the one giving me the instructions."

"Pretend."

She rose to her tiptoes, then settled back onto her feet. "I am not a very accomplished pretender, my lord."

Frustration born of a thousand troubles swamped him. "What the hell kind of thief are you?"

"Apparently I am not your renowned Rupert!" Her temper was rising, and somehow that knowledge comforted him.

He drew a deep breath. Glancing over her shoulder, he skimmed her body. From this vantage point, he could see a good deal of her cleavage, the soft mounds of her breasts rising invitingly above her gown. "Tell me, Megs, how did you survive so long? Distraction?"

"What do you mean?"

He glanced down again. "I think you know."

"No. I do not." She turned slightly, brushing her bottom against his growing erection.

"You'd make a whoremaster wet himself."

She straightened her spine with a jolt. "I beg your pardon!"

He laughed. Damn, it felt good to get a reaction out of her again. "You know exactly what I mean."

"I fear I do not."

"You've got great tits," he said.

There was a second's delay, then she slammed her heel down on his instep.

He stumbled back, pain burning his foot as she twisted about.

She stood perfectly still, staring at him with flames snapping from her eyes.

He winced once and glared at her as he settled his abused foot to the floor. "Well, what the hell are you waiting for?"

She simply glared.

"Come on!" he commanded. "You've injured me. 'Tis not the time for shyness."

She scowled.

"Hit me!" he ordered. "Or stab me or something. Don't just stand there and look daft."

He waited in silence with his arms slightly spread. Nothing happened. He shook his head, relaxed, and scowled.

"You've got to take advantage of my weakness, lass, or you'll find yourself hanging upside down on the mizzenmast before you know what hit you."

She raised one brow. "It seems unlikely."

He motioned her over. She stepped closer, looking uncertain. But she finally turned around, and he captured her with his arm again.

"Are you ready now?"

"For what?"

"To defend yourself."

"This is foolishness."

He stiffed a groan, then, "You've got great tits," he repeated, and tensed.

From his vantage point, he could see her scowl, but she refused to turn toward him. In fact, she tilted her head away slightly, so that all he could see was the firm angle of her jaw.

The room went silent, then, "What is it about them you find . . . exemplary?"

He raised his brows, scowled, and relaxed his stance. "What's that?"

She cleared her throat. "Were you . . ." The pause was painfully tense. "Were you jesting?"

Here was an interesting development. He turned her around so he could examine her face. "You've got a stunning body, Megs. I'm sure you know that."

She snapped her gaze to his and away just as quickly. "I've always been healthy."

"Healthy." He laughed and skimmed her stiff form. "Hell, lass, you'd put Cari to shame."

She lifted her chin and found his gaze again. "Cari?"

"The mermaid on the *Skian Dubh*'s prow."

"Your ship."

"Aye."

She nodded and said nothing.

"You don't have to pretend modesty, Megs. A maid like you would have to be a fool to be unaware of your . . ." He considered his choice of words, remembered his throbbing instep, and said, "Your charms."

She still didn't speak. Why? Curiosity had always been his weakness. Hence the time he'd inadvertently spent on the mizzenmast.

"Men must have been crowding you for a long time," he added.

Her lips moved slightly, then she stilled and finally spoke. "In my . . . formative years . . ." She paused again. "There were other things to consider. More important things than . . ." She glanced toward the door. "I had much to occupy my mind."

"I suppose your childhood wasn't easy."

She said nothing for a moment, then, "No, not easy, I suppose."

"So you learned to make your own way in the world."

"I had assistance."

He nodded. If not for Burr, he himself would not have survived childhood much less have grown to manhood aboard the *Skian Dubh*.

"Someone must have taken you in," he said. "Taught you the fancies."

"Fancies?"

He shrugged, feeling suddenly foolish, like a ragged lad in the presence of royalty. "The way you talk. The way you stand. Your hair." What the hell was wrong with him, he wondered, and reached out to brush a few wayward strands back amongst their mates. His fingers brushed her ear. She shivered, and her eyes fell closed, but she opened them in an instant and took a cautious step back, putting distance between them. He watched her—her feline eyes, her flawless skin. "You know," he said.

There was tension around her tempting lips, but she canted her head slightly. "Know?"

"That you're beautiful beyond words."

For an instant, for just a fraction of a fragmented second, he thought he saw honest surprise on her face, but before he could analyze it, her expression had returned to its usual coolness. Still, she couldn't seem to hold his gaze. Very strange.   •

"Men must have been telling you so for years."

She turned back toward him briefly. "No," she said. "You are the first."

He knew he couldn't hide his surprise as well as she. "You lie," he said.

"Generally, I do not."

"Wheaton never told you how beautiful you are?"

She cleared her throat and lowered her gaze to her hands. They were clasped neatly together. "As I have told you, I do not know—"

Cairn stepped forward and brushed his knuckles across her cheek. The bones there were high and regal. "He never told you he couldn't keep himself from touching you."

"No."

"And the others?"

"What others?"

A stab of inexplicable anger flitted through him. "The other men in your life, Megs."

"Oh. No." She didn't turn her gaze away this time, but kept it pinned to his. "'Tis not something one says to a . . ." She paused. "A person like myself."

What did that mean? Men didn't find her worthy of praise? Had they thought her so lowly that they would take her against her will without a word of kindness or comfort? He ran his fingers down her throat. She didn't close her eyes this time, but swallowed, as if there were some great battle going on within her. Perhaps she was not used to tenderness. Perhaps she had only known brutal copulation. Only . . . But no. What the hell was wrong with him? She was lying again.

"There's no need for you to pretend, Megs. I set little stock in innocence."

She said nothing.

"And there is no need to fish for compliments."

He skimmed her collarbone with his knuckles. She inhaled a long, careful breath.

"I'll give them freely." He brushed over the rounded tops of her phenomenal breasts and felt her shiver mirror his own. "You are amazing to look at. Better still to touch."

Her lips trembled, and though he gave it his best effort, there was nothing he could do but kiss her.

"So who won the first bout?"

Megs jerked around at the words. Cairn turned more slowly.

Burr stood at the door, his barbaric face impassive, his expression innocent.

"Remind me to have Bert teach you to knock," Cairn said.

Burr laughed. "I'll do that, lad. And what of you, lass?" he asked. "You look a mite flushed. I hope my lord hasn't been working you too hard."

"No." She studied her clasped hands for an instant. "He

was simply . . ." She cleared her throat. ". . . teaching me to defend myself."

The Norseman nodded. "And not a moment too soon."

"Did you want something, Burroun?" Cairn asked.

"Did he teach you how to knee a man yet?" Burr asked. " 'Tis well worth learning. Of course, half of Teleere is fretting over the lack of an heir. So if you decide to kick him, don't make it too hard."

She glanced at Cairn. Was there panic in her eyes? It was impossible to tell, and yet something welled up inside him, some sort of misplaced protectiveness mixed with overt frustration.

"Get out, Burr."

The big man's brows lifted, then he grinned broadly and bowed. "As you wish, *my laird.*"

The door closed firmly behind him.

Cairn wasn't sure, but it looked as if Megs was holding her breath.

"Well, you've probably had your fill for today."

She cleared her throat and raised her chin to regal heights, but her eyes still seemed strangely dilated. "Thank you for the . . ." He could see a tiny vein throbbing in her throat. ". . . the tutelage."

Cairn dropped his gaze to her bosom. Why not take her? He was the laird. She was a thief. But one glance at her eyes, and he turned on his heel, leaving the room without another word.

Chapter 20

"It's what the girl said." Burr's voice seemed to echo against the solar's stone walls. The room was all but barren since Elizabeth's death, and it made Cairn uncomfortable. He liked to be surrounded by tangible things, things he'd collected, things he'd purchased. Perhaps being a penniless bastard did that to a man. Or perhaps he was just an oddment.

"And you believe her?" he asked now.

Burr shrugged. "Could be Gem's telling the truth. Maybe she *was* mistaken when she claimed the lass was Magical Megs."

"And the old woman—what does she say?"

"She says we should think hard before we judge the lady too harshly."

"Lady?" Cairn rose abruptly to his feet and paced once across the floor. "What the devil does that mean?"

"I can't say for certain. Lady Nedra's an uncanny one. From what I hear there are more than a few who think she can read minds. That's why she gave up her duchy. She thought the poor were better folk than the rich. They deserved her funds more than the people she usually dealt with."

Cairn snorted. "Well, she pegged Megs all wrong. I've seen her myself, you know."

"Stole your brooch, I think you've said."

"Aye."

"So where is it?"

Cairn scowled. He didn't like the direction this conversation was taking. "What do you think, man, that she'd keep the damned thing on her?"

The giant shrugged as he puffed on his pipe. Silvery smoke curled from his lips and up over his head, looking like an unlikely halo in the soft candlelight.

"Nay," Cairn answered himself. "She'd be rid of it. If she's half as smart as she seems, me brooch would be gone at the first opportunity. Hell. She stole it from the laird of the isle. She'd have to be an imbecile to keep it about."

"She stole it from the laird," Burr repeated. "Maybe that's the reason she would keep it. Maybe she's an admirer."

Cairn snorted then scowled. "Even if she did keep it, she wouldn't have it on her person. She'd have it hidden away somewhere."

"Where?"

"How would I know?" Frustration was mounting.

"I thought you might ask."

"You think I haven't asked?" He felt like strangling someone. But strangulation was frowned upon, even for the laird of the isle.

"Could be if you could find the brooch, you could find Wheaton. Or the other way about."

Cairn gave him a wry look. "The thought crossed my mind."

Burr shrugged. "Maybe a well-placed threat might—"

"I've threatened everything but her damned dog."

Burr's eyes seemed unreasonably bright, as if he were struggling not to laugh, and Cairn sighed.

"Threats don't seem to move her a great deal."

"Maybe she doesn't believe you."

"That could be," he said, sarcasm ripe in his tone. "She treats me like a damned indentured servant."

Burr chuckled, then sobered at Cairn's stern glance. "That's unfortunate," he said. "I could talk to Graves."

Cairn turned back. "What?"

Burr shrugged heavily. "Aye, he's a bit rough, but he's got a gift for getting information when—"

"If you let that bastard within ten feet of her, I'll—" Cairn caught himself, recognizing the bait a moment too late.

Burr's eyes were dancing now, and his mouth quirked. "You're not becoming attached to her are you, lad?"

"Damn you," he said. His tone sounded tired. Exhausted really.

"She's a wee bonny thing."

"She's a liar and a thief."

"As was Elizabeth. And a whore to boot. But you married her."

For a moment Cairn considered striking out, but he checked himself. Life had changed since the *Skian Dubh*, where a rousing fight was always welcome. "You think I forgot?" he asked.

"No, lad." Burr's voice was suddenly serious. "I think you remember everything."

Cairn paced to the window. In the courtyard below, a host of lanterns were lit and swayed gently in the evening breeze. A woman's laughter floated to him in the darkness.

"She's not Elizabeth," Burr said.

"No. She's Magical Megs, Teleere's master—"

"Is she?"

.

"Don't tell me you have doubts just because Gem said she might be wrong."

"I've heard you threaten her," Burr said. "Doesn't it seem strange that she wouldn't buckle under, give up Wheaton's location?"

"She's loyal." And didn't that beat the hell out of everything. He was the laird of the entire damned island, and he'd found no way to gain his wife's allegiance. And yet Wheaton, the son of an ousted traitor, still held Megs's loyalty in a tight grip.

"Perhaps you should try a bribe," Burr said.

"Hell!" Cairn turned away again, tormented. "I've offered her a dozen chances to be free, and she's taken each one and thrown it back in me face. She's made a fool of me a hundred times."

Burroun sighed. "All men are fools where women are concerned."

"Aye," he agreed. "But I am the laird of fools."

"And she's the princess."

Cairn scowled. "What the devil do you mean by that?"

"Think on it, lad, the way she talks, the way she carries herself. She's a damned sight more elegant than you will ever be. Sir Albert or no Sir Albert."

"It's an act. She says she's a seamstress. But she doesn't talk like a seamstress."

"And so she's a thief?"

"Do you have a better explanation?"

"Gem says the girl's different than she remembers."

"Gem says!" Cairn glared. "You're believing a thief about a thief."

Burr reddened slightly. "The girl's seen some rough times."

"You're hard for her!" Cairn accused in amazement.

Burr snorted. "And some say you've got no sense of humor."

Cairn grinned, sure of the truth suddenly. "You hope to bed her," he said.

"She's not half my age."

Cairn laughed. "No one's half your age, Burr. In fact—"

The giant rose suddenly to his feet, looming like an enraged bull in too narrow a space. "Haven't I taught you to keep your mouth shut regarding things you know nothing about?"

Cairn bristled, spoiling for a fight. "You've tried."

"You saying I failed, lad? Cuz I'm willing to make it right now."

"My lord." A servant stood in the doorway, looking tense. Cairn couldn't remember his name. There were too damned many of them. "A package has been sent for you."

Cairn scowled. "Have it delivered to M—to my prisoner."

"Gem?"

He gritted his teeth. "Megs."

"Very well, my liege."

The room fell silent.

Burr stared. "What was that?"

"None of your business."

"I made it me own business when I fished you out of that rock pile a score or so years back."

Cairn sighed. Tension washed out of him. "Haven't I ever taught you to keep your nose out of other people's affairs?"

Burr snorted. "You giving her gifts now?"

"Don't be a lackwit. If you can help it."

Burr shook his head. "Don't know how she's going to resist your interrogation with you turning the screws like you are. She'll sure break before dawn. Why—"

Burr's voice droned on as a half dozen scenarios flitted

through Cairn's mind. His favorite involved himself hitting the other square on the nose. But the man was as big as a damned whaler, and although the idea of pummeling and getting pummeled was strangely appealing, he had other things to do.

Tatiana lay awake, curled against the satiny slope of the couch. She had scoured the room a dozen times, had found a score of items that might assist in her next attempt to escape, but just now she merely lay there—trying to rest. But sleep refused to come. Normally, she found solace in slumber. Not now. But who could blame her? She slept in MacTavish's bedchamber with no guarantee that she would be left unmolested. Hardly that. In fact, he might burst into the chamber at any moment.

Her heart picked up a beat at the thought. Fear was unbecoming in a highborn lady, she remembered, but in the back of her mind lay a festering question. Was it fear or was it something else? Something more dangerous. He'd touched her. Caressed her, and she'd felt . . . something. Something she'd not felt before. But then she'd not been a prisoner before. Of course she would be confused.

A noise sounded at the door. Her heart jumped, but it was a woman who stepped inside.

"So you're the thief," said the stranger.

Tatiana sat up and raised one brow in question. "And who are you?"

The servant was plump and pretty. "Ain't you the uppity one."

"Did you have a reason for breaching my quarters?"

The woman looked as if she planned to retort, but finally she scowled in confusion. "I been told to deliver these to you." She laid a bundle of clothing on a cluttered chair.

"They're gent's clothing." She paused. Tatiana stared. "You're to put them on."

She would not show her surprise. "Very well."

"They're gent's clothes," she repeated, as though Tatiana hadn't heard. As though she weren't shocked. But "*a lady keeps her thoughts to herself,*" or so Mother had said.

"I believe you said that," Tatiana said dismissively, and the servant turned away.

The door shut heavily. Tatiana crossed the floor and lifted the garments from the chair. It was a simple cotton tunic and a pair of buff trousers.

Why? she wondered, but at that moment she heard a noise on the far side of the door. Bringing the tunic to her chest, she held her breath and waited, but the noise died down, and she was left alone.

There seemed nothing to do but don the garments and see what happened. She had barely slipped into the trousers when MacTavish stepped into the room. He stopped when he saw her, then closed the door behind his back and crossed the floor.

"Elton and you must be the same size." His eyes skimmed her. "In some places."

"May I ask why?"

His nostrils seemed to flare slightly before he found her eyes with his again. "Of course."

She swore in silence. "*A lady does not curse.*" "Why?' she asked.

"It will be easier for you to learn the art of defense."

"Ahh. So you are still insane."

"Of course," he said, and pulled a knife from a sheath at his side. Despite his position, it was not an ornamental blade, but a dark, deadly, serviceable weapon. "This is a dagger."

She said nothing.

"I'll teach you to use it."

"You jest."

He smiled. God almighty, when he smiled one could almost believe that he was sane. Or that his mental stability didn't matter either way.

"You should keep one on your person at all times."

"Very well. Hand it over."

"I mean you are to keep one on you when you are no longer here at Westheath."

"No more plans for the rack?"

He shrugged. " 'Tis late," he said, hefting the blade. "My master torturer is already abed."

"And it would be rude to wake him."

He gave her a look. At least she could pretend to fear him. But then he was offering to teach her to defend herself. Maybe it weakened his position. "This blade is not for peeling quince," he said, shushing his logic.

"That is not what I had in mind."

"What were you planning?"

She smiled.

He smiled. "Hoping to have your way with me, Megs?"

"Hoping to get away *from* you, MacTavish," she corrected.

"When the hospitality here is so fine."

"Are you planning to relinquish that knife?"

He stared at her for a moment, as if considering a dozen possibilities, then, flipping the knife into the air, he caught it by the blade and handed it to her. "Relinquished," he said. "Now what?"

She glanced at him, at the blade, at him. "I stab you?"

"A fine idea."

She actually considered it. After all, he seemed to want her to, and he was lord and master here. But even though her mother's cool tutelage hadn't covered this ordeal, she was pretty sure ladies didn't stab sovereigns, no matter how daft they might be.

"Come ahead," he said. "Begin."

She remained immobile.

"Do I have to talk about your body again?"

She raised her chin, possibly in warning. He sighed.

"First off, you can't hold it like it's a damned daffodil." Reaching out, he wrapped his hand around hers, tightening her grip. Heat radiated from his palm. "And remember what I told you about fighting hand-to-hand. It's not a costume ball, so don't be polite. Concentrate on the weak spots."

"Weak spots," she repeated, but she was having a difficult time concentrating at all. His own attire was similar to hers tonight. Simple, comfortable, open at the throat. And, strangely enough, it was his throat that fascinated her. It was so broad and sun-darkened and strong.

"The eyes, the vitals, the groin."

"Of course." She had no idea what he said.

"Very well." He stepped back a pace and motioned to her. "Come ahead."

"I beg your pardon?"

"Stab me."

She still stared.

"Balls, woman, stab me!"

She lowered the knife. "Would it not be more efficient to simply allow Peters to execute me?"

"What are you talking about?"

"What do you think will happen if I injure you?"

He stared at her for a moment, then threw his head back and laughed. She watched, annoyed.

"You are amused."

"Aye," he said, wiping his eyes.

"Because you think I cannot win."

"Aye."

"So I should add 'faulty memory' to your lists of flaws," she said.

He raised his brows, then nodded in understanding. "Because you hit me before."

"Just so."

He was still smiling. "I'm not going to let you stab me, Megs."

"Then perhaps you should cease insisting that I do so."

The smile faded softly. His eyes became somber. "Where would a seamstress learn to speak like you do?"

She didn't drop her gaze. "My mother hoped to see me married well. She insisted that I become a lady in every possible manner."

For a moment, she almost thought he believed her, but then he spoke.

"Draw my blood, Megs, and I'll let you go."

"What?"

"You heard me, lass. One scratch, and you're free."

"Or dead."

He watched her for a moment. "Remind me to tell Burr he was wrong."

She watched him.

"He thought you had some backbone," Cairn explained.

She pursed her lips.

"Turns out your spirit is as weak as your body."

"I am not weak."

He chuckled. "I've seen bigger midges," he said, "and stronger."

"I hope your physician is skilled," she said, and struck.

One hour later she was flat on her back.

"That was better," MacTavish said.

She was sweaty and tired, and her breath came hard. Of course, he was lying on top of her, constricting her lungs.

"Let me up." Her voice sounded strange, like a feral growl. Not resembling a queen regnant in the least.

"I think you've had enough."

"And I think I'd like to kill you."

He grinned. "Maybe Burr was right after all."

"Get off me."

"'Tis a strange thing. Most times nothing can touch you. Cool as a highland stream, you are. But at other times . . ." He pushed a stray strand of hair away from her face. "Might you have a temper, princess?"

"No. I do not."

He laughed and she scowled. "You provoked me."

He lay half on his side, watching her face. "Have you never been provoked before?"

She blinked.

"Megs?"

"Of course I have been provoked."

He smiled. Something twisted in her gut, low down, near her thighs.

"Sometimes you seem so worldly-wise, so hardened by life," he said, "and sometimes you seem like you have just awakened. Like a butterfly breaking free of its cocoon. Cool on the surface but fire underneath. Is that an act, Megs?"

His voice was soft and when he touched her cheek, she closed her eyes. Emotions rushed in, unwanted, unacceptable. Feelings crowded thought, pushing hard.

"If we are finished with the instruction, I would like to rise."

"Who are you?"

"Let me go, MacTavish."

"I can't," he said, and kissed her.

Her body responded like a parched flower, like a love-starved hound, like a traitor.

She kissed him back, slipping her hand behind his neck and slanting her lips across his. His erection was hard against her thigh, and between her own legs she felt an unaccustomed need.

He kissed her throat, then slid his hand up her body to cradle her breast and kiss the high portion. She moaned in frustrated ecstasy, writhing beneath him, and it was in that moment that he kissed her nipple. A swath of cotton lay between his lips and her breast, but her breath stopped just the same, frozen in her throat just as surely as her body froze.

He suckled it lightly, wetting the fabric. She arched against the feelings. Breath exploded. She wrapped her fingers in his hair, pulling him closer, and he gladly came. His cock throbbed against her belly. She found his lips with her own. His hands felt hot against her skin as he tore at her clothes, and she shed them gladly, for she was ablaze, burning like red embers beneath his hands. Her tunic was gone in an instant. Her breasts were free, bare, glorying in his touch. She arched her head back and moaned as he suckled her, but he was sliding lower, kissing her ribs, her belly, pushing her trousers down until his lips touched her hair.

She froze. Reality rushed into her brain like ice water. She kicked madly, scrambling to her feet. He half followed, crouched like a snarling animal.

"Megs!"

"No!" She could see the outline of his erection through his pantaloons. "I can't."

"Can't?" He rose slowly to his feet.

"Stay back." Her voice wobbled. She was losing control, losing herself.

He took a step toward her. Bending, she snatched the dagger from the floor. It quivered like a loosed fledgling in her hand, but she remained slightly bent, watching.

"Do not come closer, MacTavish."

He scowled, baffled, and who could blame him. Her own emotions felt raw. "What's this then?" he asked.

"This . . ." She raised the blade slightly. "I am told . . ." He took a step forward. She took a step back. "Is a dagger."

"Why—"

"You are not my husband." The words spurted out of their own accord.

He shook his head once. "Nay."

"Nor my betrothed."

"A moment ago that didn't matter."

"Of course it matters." He advanced. She retreated. "Don't push me, MacTavish."

"But it didn't matter with Wheaton."

"Stay back."

"Or is he—" He stopped suddenly and his eyes widened. "Are you wed . . ."

She stared.

"To Wheaton?" he asked.

"As I've said before, I do not know any man named Wheaton."

"Aye. And you have said you've known no man. But you lie."

She didn't bother to disagree, for it took all her concentration to think, to remain steady, to stay out of his reach.

He shook his head. "No untried maid kisses like you do."

"And how have you determined that, MacTavish? Have you kissed them all?"

"You're Wheaton's wife," he said.

She laughed. "And you are insane."

"Then tell me the truth, lass. Tell me who you are."

"My name—"

"Not Linnet Mulgrave, the widowed seamstress," he said, and shook his head. "Spare me that tale."

She swallowed hard. " 'Tis not a tale."

"Nay, 'tis a lie, lass, and I tire of it."

She said nothing. Indeed, she was certain she could not, for his chest was bare and so hopelessly alluring that she felt lost in feral feelings.

"Wheaton's wife," he repeated. His face was expressionless, but his eyes sparked with hot emotion. "Here beneath me own roof." He nodded and drew a deep breath. "I've been thoughtless, Megs."

She remained tense, waiting for him to strike, but he did not.

"It would have been wrong to lie with you," he said.

She tried to nod, but wasn't sure if she did, for her body was still thrumming.

"Nay." He shook his head and suddenly he was there, inches in front of her with an arm about her back and a fist wrapped around her knife hand. In a moment she was disarmed. Her head fell back unnoticed. Her breath came hard. "Wheaton's bride deserves a special seduction," he said and, kissing her once, took the knife from her hand and left the room.

She stood like a sun-dazed kitten. Good Lord, what was wrong with her?

She had kissed him, and grabbed him, had all but begged for his touch. And even now . . .

She stopped the thought.

One thing, and one thing only was clear.

She had to escape, and it had to be soon.

Chapter 21

Tatiana paced the bedchamber and glanced out the window now and again. The day was dark and overcast, in sync with her mood. She'd slept poorly on the previous night. She'd tossed and turned. Dreams plagued her. Dreams she shouldn't be dreaming. She couldn't tolerate much more. She must leave. Must escape, and she had a plan, but it was a desperate plan, and it must be utilized soon, before it was too late, before she gave in to his pressure. Not that he tempted her. Hardly that, but it was impossible to think, impossible to concentrate when she was kept hostage as she was, when she had no way of knowing when he would appear. When he would speak to her. When he would begin her foolish defense lessons again. When he would touch her.

Her heart clanked in her chest at the memory. She must not let him kiss her again. She must think, keep her wits, hold firm. Surely that was not so difficult, but just at that moment the door opened.

An errant ray of sunlight shone through the gray clouds behind her and fell with unerring precision on Cairn MacTavish.

He wore a plaid again today, and though he was always ridiculously beautiful, he seemed right in a tartan, at home, himself.

"Good morning," he said. His eyes were bright, his smile just below the surface.

She wrung her hands. Dear God, when had she begun wringing her hands? And was it still morning?

"Did you sleep well?"

She watched his mouth move. It seemed that his lips were perpetually quirked, as if he were just about to smile or had just finished smiling.

"Why are you here, MacTavish?" Her tone was cool.

"I thought we should start your lesson early today, lass."

"My lesson." She raised one brow the merest amount. Her mother would be impressed. Cold as a north wind.

"Aye," he said. "Villains don't always attack from behind, you know."

He wore a fresh tunic. It was an ivory hue, open at the throat and closed down the front with broad wooden buttons. Three of the oaken spheres remained undone.

She swallowed.

". . . from the front?" he asked.

She raised her gaze to his face and grappled wildly for lucidity. "What?"

He scowled a little. The expression made him no less beautiful. "Brigands," he said. "They could just as easily come at you from the front." He stepped toward her, hands open, arms bent at shoulder width. "What then?"

On later inspection, she could only believe that madness took her, because in that instant, in that one wild moment of insanity, she reached out, grabbed him by the front of the tunic—and kissed him.

For one second he was frozen in shock, but he rose almost

instantly to the occasion. Wrapping his arms about her back, he drew her into his embrace. His lips were hot, his arms like iron.

Need met need and roared like a hurricane in her ears. He kissed her lips, her throat, her chest, all the while pressing her toward the bed. She stumbled backward. The back of her knees struck the mattress with a jolt and at that simple movement, reality rushed in. Her terrible plan came with it.

"I know where he is!" she rasped.

"What?" His eyes were glazed, his breathing harsh.

She shivered violently. "Wheaton!" she gasped.

The very air seemed sucked from the room.

"What about Wheaton?" he asked, and drew away an inch.

Her skin felt hot and cold all at once, burning on contact. "I know . . ." She scooted sideways, praying hard and putting space between them. "Where 'e might be." The guttersnipe accent came almost of its own accord, not so strong as Gem's but a far cry from that of Tatiana Rocheneau.

She watched his expression, but it showed little. The pirate's face had been replaced with a politician's. Devoid of emotion, except perhaps a tenseness. "Where?"

"I . . . I cannot tell you."

"Ahh," he breathed, and reached for her again.

She scrambled away. "But I know . . . I can show you how to get there."

He followed her like a cat. Dangerous, sleek, unpredictable. "Then tell me."

"No, I . . . 'e's very secretive. Even with me."

"Then how do you know where to find him?"

"I've been there, but—"

The world went silent.

"So you are his mistress?"

She raised her chin. Her soul trembled like mad. "I don't think—"

"Do you sleep with him, Megs?"

"No."

"I'd like to believe you, lass, but it seems you've lied from the very beginning. Only now you lie with an accent."

"I told you I was smart." The slurred speech came so easily. Dear God in heaven, what had she gotten herself into now? But panic had set in, driving out any logical thought.

He watched her.

"And a smart lass don't give nothing away for free."

"So you are innocent because of financial reasons instead of—"

"Innocent." She laughed. It sounded hysterical to her own ears. "Don't be a fool, MacTavish. I'm about as innocent as you. And you ain't—"

"Why now?"

She shut her mouth and watched him for a moment. Her mind was spinning wildly. "What?"

"Why are you telling me this now?"

Her heart was beating fast, but her training as a duchess held her in good stead. She could keep her face absolutely expressionless. Any duchess worth her jewels could. But she let the shadow of a frown show. "Even thieves have their illusions." She almost winced at her choice of words. Gem would have chosen something more simplistic.

"Illusions?"

She shrugged, letting a shade of shame gleam into her expression. "Could be I thought 'e loved me."

He took a moment, then, "Wheaton."

She nodded.

"You thought he would come for you?"

She hunched her shoulders and shrugged.

"But he won't?"

She shook her head, then caught his gaze and raised her chin defensively. "You should be flattered."

He raised a brow.

"Looks like Drake's fear of you overshadows even the promise of taking me maidenhead. He'll not be back for me."

"Drake?"

"That's what I call him."

"An endearment?"

She shrugged, and he nodded. She had no way of knowing if he believed a single word.

"What of honor among thieves?"

She laughed. "Was a time I thought you had some wits about you, MacTavish."

"I'm thrilled to hear it."

"Thieves don't have no honor. No more honor than the nobility does." She canted her head slightly. "Question is, is there honor amongst pirates?"

She could have sworn she could hear her heart beating in the impending silence.

He crossed her arms against the hard strength of his chest and gave her a sideways glance. "I don't like to be . . . obsessive about honesty."

Her heart stopped. "Are you going back on your vow?"

He smiled. "I can't decide who I trust less," he said. "The honest thief or the dishonest lady."

She corrected her speech hastily. "You said you'd set me free."

"And you said you'd never met Wheaton."

"That's cuz 'e'd kill me if 'e knew."

"If he knew what?"

"That I betrayed 'im."

His expression hardened for a moment, then lay flat, without emotion. "Deliver him to me, and I'll release you."

She licked her lips, delayed an instant, and spoke. "And what else?"

A muscle jumped in his jaw. "Your freedom's not enough?"

She shook her head.

"The rack has been repaired."

She didn't blanch. "You can't do no worse than Wheaton would."

The silence seemed to last for an eternity. "He won't hurt you." His voice was low and deadly earnest. "I'll make sure of that."

Anger exuded him like a foul odor, but she forced herself to laugh. "You'll 'ave te do better than that, MacTavish."

"Money?"

"And fare out of Teleere."

"You can trust me not to pursue you, Megs, no matter what you think."

She subdued a shiver. Perhaps it was faked, perhaps it was real. She could no longer tell. "It's not you I'm worryin' on, MacTavish."

"You think I can't best him?"

She shrugged. "You're the laird of the isle. With an army an all, I'm thinkin'. But 'e's. Well . . ." She shrugged again. "'E's Drake."

He stared at her for what seemed an eternity, then he nodded slowly, his face absolutely sober. "Where will you go when you are free, Megs?"

She gathered her senses and kept carefully back from him, lest she reach out, lest she weaken. "I can't tell you that."

"Then I'll give you a horse."

She shook her head, though she was tempted to snatch at the opportunity. A steed at her disposal would certainly better her chances, and she'd noticed Westheath's stock. It was nearly as fine as her own. "Nay."

"Why not?"

She glanced toward the door almost imperceptibly. "Horses is too slow."

"Westheath's stables are renowned, or so I'm told."

"You're told?" He didn't know. Didn't care. Her initial assessment was correct. He had a strange aversion to horses. And suddenly she longed to teach him the glory of riding, to help him appreciate the soaring utopia of a fine steed beneath his legs. But that was not to be. Ever! And his aversion was good, for she would use it. Would pretend she shared his feelings and gain that much more chance to escape.

"I've been busy since becoming laird," he explained. He might not be a conventional lord, but he was a man, with a man's distaste for admitting weaknesses.

She shrugged. "It don't matter 'ow fast the 'orses be. They won't get me cross the sea, will they? Naw. You'll 'ave yer Norseman take me to the docks and order 'im ta leave me there with enough coin ta go where I will."

He watched her forever, his eyes intense, his face unmoved. "Very well."

She exhaled softly, pretending to hide it. "Good then. We 'ave us a deal."

"Then we can continue where we left off," he said, and stepped forward.

She tripped backward like a startled dairy goat. "Nay!"

He followed her. "I thought you said you were smart."

"What has that got to do with anything?"

"You must see the possibilities."

She continued to back away. He continued to follow.

"I'm a very wealthy man. Not to mention me being laird," he added.

She came to an abrupt halt, her heart beating hard. "You'd make me a whore?"

His brows rose and she knew her mistake immediately. "Is that beneath you, Megs?"

She forced a shrug. "'Ores got their place same as anyone. But I won't do no 'orin' lessen I 'ave to."

"And you don't have to now?"

"I'm already givin' you what you want most."

The world seemed very quiet suddenly.

"You're wrong," he said, and reached for her.

She jerked away, but her back struck the wall, and she stopped short, breathing hard. "You sure? If'n you 'ad to choose. Which you do . . ." She raised her chin as if she had some power. "Who would you take? Wheaton or me?"

"You're a far sight bonnier," he said, and, reaching out, stroked her cheek.

Her mouth went dry. Her eyes fluttered closed, and her hands trembled. But she licked her lips, yanked her eyes open, and clasped her fingers together in fervent supplication. "You ain't seen Drake by candlelight," she said.

He drew his hand slowly away. The fire in his eyes died slowly.

"Be ready at dusk," he said, and left.

"So if'n you weren't 'ighborn, how'd you 'appen to end up with the laird of the isle?" Gem's voice was quiet. She sat very upright on the only chair in the room. Her knees were together and her baby's mouth pursed. Burr sat on the bed and could see her lips from above, ridiculously pink against her winter white skin. It was disturbing. What the hell kind of thief had an infantile mouth like that?

He pulled his attention from her lips and spoke without thinking. "I found him," he said. "In a pile of rocks."

"Found 'im?" She peeked sideways, but not enough to disturb his brushing.

"Aye. He was sitting on a boulder with his mother beside him. But she'd been wounded by brigands on her way back to Portshaven." He remembered in silence for a moment. "She was almost dead already, with barely a word left to say."

"So you tended 'im."

He shrugged, drawing himself from his reverie. "There was little else to be done. He was a scrawny, bawling brat, with no way to take care of himself."

"And you didn't know 'e was to become the old man's heir."

"He didn't look like much, though in years to come he had a way with a sword." He smiled at the memory of the fencing lessons. The lad was an exceptional duelist, though Burr would never admit it to his face. "We spent most of his early years at sea."

"So 'ow did you learn 'e was the old lord's get?"

"He had a brooch," Burr said, "that his father gave his mother. I didn't think it was more than a bauble, but . . ." He sighed. "The old laird was aging. Mayhap he saw his strength slipping away. And mayhap he saw that same strength in the lad when he first met him. Whatever the reason, he was certain Tav was the one to take his place."

"Like a fairy tale, it is," Gem murmured.

"Aye, though raising the lad was no treat." In fact, the boy had been bold and rude and opinionated, not unlike himself, or the girl who sat beneath his hands. "Still, I got Falcon out of the bargain," he said, and stroked the brush downward.

"Falcon?" she asked on a sigh.

"Me stallion. The old laird gave him to me for me troubles. As fine a steed as ever there was in all of Teleere. In all the world, mayhap."

"I've never been a horseback."

Never. He scowled at the thought, for logic told him she never would, even if she lived to reach maturity.

"When you was young, did you take your sisters ridin'?" she asked, changing the topic suddenly, as she often did.

But Burr was no longer in the mood for reminiscing and knew he had told her too much already in the hours spent brushing her hair. "Quiet now," he said, and stroked the brush down her scalp for the hundredth time.

She sighed, fell silent for a second, and spoke up again. "What was their names?"

"Were," he corrected gruffly. "What *were* their names?"

"Yeah."

"'Tis none of your affair, lass."

Silence fell again. Her brows lowered slightly and her mouth quirked. "They didn't . . ." She paused. "There weren't nothing bad 'appened to them, were there?"

"What?"

"You said '*were*.' They're all right, ain't they? Yer sisters?"

He should correct her, but there was something in her tone. Something intense and deep and strangely wistful.

"Viking?" she said, and tilted her head up to look at him. Her throat seemed as fair as a snowy dell and ran down gently to where her breasts, small and firm, lay barely hidden by her tattered gown. He refused to look past her eyes.

"They're fine now."

She scowled. "Now?"

He cleared his throat and called himself a fool. "Rosie's first husband . . ." He stopped, remembering. Some men deserved to die. And some did, earlier than they planned. He shrugged, pushing away the memories. "He shouldn't have struck her. It wasn't wise."

She absorbed this news in silence, and he knew that she understood his meaning.

"But they're safe now?"

"Aye, the three of them," he said. "All wed and fat and happy with roofs over their heads and babies at their breasts."

He winced. Damn him. He shouldn't have said the word "breasts," but she didn't seem to notice. Instead, she pursed her mouth again and faced forward, but the hint of a smile lifted her raspberry-sweet lips. The room fell into silence.

"You found their 'usbands for 'em?"

"*Husbands*," he corrected. "Nay. You put a bonny lass out in the world, and the laddies'll find them."

"But you 'ad to give yer consent since yer father was gone."

He shrugged. "I was their closest male kin."

She nodded again and sighed softly as he stroked her hair. It gleamed beneath the boar bristle brush like sunset waves and curled like magic down to her too small waist.

"How many babes do they got?"

She was a baby herself, and yet it was disturbing, being this close to her. "Didn't I tell you to pipe down?"

"Do they got any girls?"

She'd been afraid of him only days before. He missed that now, for then she was sometimes quiet for whole minutes at a time.

"I'd like to 'ave me a girl someday, but . . ." She shrugged and let the statement fall into meditative silence. He felt like hitting something.

Damn it to hell! With the course she was on, she'd be lucky to live out the year, much less hold a babe of her own.

"Viking?"

He realized abruptly that she was looking up at him, glancing through her sunlight lashes into his face. For a moment he wondered what she saw there, but he knew the truth. MacTavish had once compared him to a troll. And Mac-Tavish was his best friend, except for his steed, of course. He scowled, which almost certainly didn't improve his features.

"What do you want?" he growled.

She smiled despite his tone, and in that second she looked younger than ever. "Don't you want to have yourself no wee ones?"

He held her gaze for an instant longer, than jerked to his feet. "You babble—" he began, but she had already grabbed his arm, and it was strange, for while her skin looked pale as winter and baby-soft, her fingers felt rough against his wrist.

"No. Don't quit," she said. "I'll shut me trap if'n you—"

The door opened. Cairn stepped inside, and Burr immediately realized how it must look. They were standing mere inches apart. She was holding his arm and gazing into his eyes, while he stood like a great gaping love struck ape.

But Cairn didn't chuckle.

"I need your help," he said simply, and that was that.

Chapter 22

❧

"**B**lindfold me," Tatiana said.

They sat in an elegant landau. The exterior was polished to a high sheen. The horses were blooded bays, sleek, fast, and breathtaking. Inside the carriage, the seats were upholstered in plush scarlet velvet, but MacTavish's knuckles looked white in the deepening darkness. She had been correct. Horses made him nervous, and somehow that knowledge made her want to cry.

"What?" he asked.

"Drake . . ." she began, though it was hard to speak around the lump in her throat. She swallowed it and concentrated on the mission at hand. She had no choice. She would be free. "'E 'ad me blindfolded."

"I thought it was dark."

"I told you 'e was cautious."

MacTavish leaned forward to request a blindfold, but at the same moment the door opened, and Burr handed in a sash.

MacTavish took it without question and tied it around her eyes. She settled back against the cushions.

"Are you ready?" he asked.

She counted in silence, listening for the sounds of hoof-beats outside the carriage. There was Burr on his giant polished gray, certainly. Peters, Cormick, and three other men she didn't know. There was also the driver. That made seven without counting MacTavish himself. Her stomach crunched cruelly. She swallowed her bile and let her hands shake. There was little reason to hide her fear.

"Megs—" he began.

"Aye." She took a deep breath. "I'm ready."

The team jolted into action, jerking her back against the cushions. She held her breath for a moment and squeezed her hands together. Her stomach quieted a bit. She could do this, for it needed doing. Nicol had told her of a place. An old ram-shackle inn where he had first met the girl called Birgit. Despite the poor garments of a common laborer, she had looked so much like Tatiana that for a moment he had thought they were one and the same. It was that girl whom he had trained, that girl who now sat on the throne.

"Head west you said." MacTavish's voice was low.

"Yeah. Even through the blindfold I could tell the sun was sinkin' low ahead of us."

The iron-rimmed wheels of the landau rattled across cob-blestones, then quieted as they finally rolled out of the village. She let the silence surround her, pretending she was listening for every sound. But she did not have to. More than once Nicol had described Portshaven to her. And more times still, he had told her of his meeting with Birgit. It had all been very clear. Clear enough so that Tatiana could have given directions, but of course she would not, for it would do her little good to send MacTavish off by himself. No, she must lead him there, must get free of Westheath and maybe, somehow, if fate was kind, she would escape.

"Water." She said the word well enough, as if drawn from her reverie. "I remember hearing that before."

"It's the mill," he said. "So you think we're headed in the right direction?"

"Aye." She scowled, but the expression might have been wasted beneath the dark fold. "But just after there was . . ." A sheep bleated, low-voiced and homey. "There it is. I remember sheep."

He said nothing. They traveled in silence. Once she made them stop and turn back. The night fell dark and heavy around them.

"How much longer?" he asked finally.

Her hands shook again. "Not far."

"An inn you say?"

"Aye." The road dipped down rapidly, leaving her stomach behind, and she knew. "It's just ahead." She didn't have to fake the tremor in her voice.

MacTavish rapped on the side of the carriage. It jolted to a halt.

Burr came back through the darkness. "This it?"

For a moment MacTavish remained silent, then, "We'll know soon. Stay with the girl."

Burr snorted in answer.

Cairn swore at the man's insubordination, then called for Peters.

Hoofbeats thudded in the darkness. "Yes, my lord."

"Tie your mount to the carriage and stay with the girl," MacTavish ordered. "We go in on foot."

"Yes, my lord."

Leather creaked as the lieutenant dismounted.

"She's your responsibility," MacTavish said, but he was already speaking from a lower point. So he had left the carriage. It was almost time.

Men murmured in the darkness, then footsteps crunched softly into the distance. The landau creaked as Peters entered it. She waited to the count of fifty before speaking.

"Might I remove me blindfold?" she asked softly, and felt Peters's attention turn toward her. He delayed for a moment.

"My lord didn't say."

"It was my idea to have the blindfold at the start."

She could almost hear him scowl, then, "I suspect it could do no harm."

She untied the sash herself. Grayness moved in, replacing the blackness.

She realized immediately that Peters's mind was wholly occupied elsewhere, for he was gazing out the window in the direction his lord had gone.

As for her, her heart was pounding out of control.

She steadied her nerves and remembered to breathe. "Lord MacTavish is brave," she said.

"I should be at his side." His tone was rife with excess loyalty.

Her mind was spinning. *Now what?* she wondered frantically. But in that instant, gunshots burst into the night. She gasped. Peters jerked toward the door

From the distant darkness, a man shouted.

"My lord!" Peters rasped and launched himself from the carriage.

For a moment Tatiana was paralyzed, then she moved, throwing herself after him. She hit the ground with a jolt, rolled, scrambled to her feet, and leapt toward his horse.

Gunshots pounded into the darkness. From behind, she heard a gasp, but she already had the reins untied. Her foot was in the stirrup. One glance told her Peters had turned, but she threw herself into the saddle. The gelding was game. He leapt forward like a hare, but a man can beat a horse for a good thirty feet. She knew it, heard Peters's roar, and then he was upon her, throwing himself at her back. His fingers snagged her hair, and she was ripped from the horse, falling in a heap on the earth.

"You'll not betray my liege again. You die now!" he rasped, and suddenly she felt the cold barrel of his pistol against her temple.

Pandemonium seized her brain. Trauma shook her reserves. She'd been close. So very close. Her limbs quaked. She felt the hard bump of Peters's gun as he cocked it, and she began to babble.

"What the hell happened?" Cairn demanded, rushing up.

"My lord!" Peter's face looked as white as death in the darkness. "You are well!"

"Aye."

"But the shooting!" said Peters.

"Damn it, man, I told you to watch her."

"Yes, my lord. But she fled. Stole my horse. She's a traitor, delivering you into Wheaton's hands."

Burr appeared in the darkness. He'd been running, but his breathing hadn't escalated a whit. "Wheaton wasn't there," he said.

Cairn swore, then glanced down at Megs, who was still babbling incoherently in a seemingly foreign language. "Who was there?" he asked Burr.

He shrugged. "Highwaymen. Brigands. Our sort of folk."

Cairn cursed again, but silently this time. "You're certain?"

"Aye. Once they realized who you were they were eager to spill the truth, but they knew of no Wheaton."

Cairn glanced down at the girl. "Megs."

She continued to mumble. Her hands were clasped in front of her chest, but even in the darkness, he could see that they were shaking.

"What the hell did you do to her?" he asked, lifting his gaze to Peters.

"Nothing, my lord. She tried to escape. I merely—"

"Let go of her hair."

"She's a traitor, my lord. Execution would be too good for her."

Cairn glanced at Burr. The Norseman shook his head. He, too, failed to understand zealots.

"Let go of her hair," Cairn repeated.

"Yes, my lord." Peters did so slowly, but the girl remained exactly as she was, sitting on the earth with her legs spread-eagle in front of her, her hands clasped tightly and her lips moving almost inaudibly.

He scowled. "Stand up, lass."

She didn't respond. Cairn shifted his gaze toward Peters. The lieutenant shuffled his feet uncomfortably.

"Did you strike her?"

"No, my lord. Shall I?"

Cairn swore again, more vehemently this time. "Megs, no one's going hurt you. Stand up."

Nothing changed.

"What's she saying?" Cairn asked.

Burr shrugged. Peters shook his head. "I do not speak Sedonian."

"Sedonian?" Cairn turned to him with a jolt. "She's Sedonian?"

Peters jerked back a step. "I—I do not know, my lord. I just—I—"

Cairn didn't wait for an explanation, but bent down. Grasping the girl around her torso, he draped her over his shoulder and rose to his feet. Getting her inside the carriage was not an easy task. But once there, she gave him no trouble. He was barely terrified by the carriage ride on the way back to the castle, for his mind was spinning. The girl seemed all but comatose, though she made it out of the horrific vehicle and into Westheath under her own power. He followed her up the stairs and into his bedchamber, closing the door behind them.

She walked across the room like one in a trance, but she held her head high and her gait was steady. She went to the window and gazed out on the street below. He waited. But to no avail. Time marched on.

Someone knocked on the door, and in a moment a servant handed in a bottle and two goblets.

Cairn filled them both and handed one to the girl. She took it without a glance and emptied it immediately. He managed to repress his admiration and refilled it.

She took it and drank it without any seeming effects, though he watched her closely.

"Did you intend to have me killed, Megs?" he asked finally.

She said nothing.

"This may surprise you, but it's frowned on to ambush your sovereign lord, even if he is a barbarian bastard."

She turned slowly. "Tell me." Her diction was perfect again, though her words were faint. He would give his Keralan coconut cracker to speak as well as she did. How much easier would it be to influence the noble families? How much easier to make them understand the needs of the poor. "If you were . . . captured, accused of heinous crimes and imprisoned, would you not try to escape?"

He shrugged. "Yes, but I'm a barbarian bastard."

"And what would you call me?"

He waited, watching her. Beautiful was the first word that came to mind. He made certain it didn't reach his lips. "Sedonian?"

She sighed and let her eyes fall closed. "Yes, I lived in Sedonia for a time."

"Who did? Megs or Widow Linnet or the real you?"

For a moment she paused and for a moment he thought

she might actually spill the truth. But he was to be disappointed again.

"There is only one me," she said.

"I don't doubt that." He almost smiled, for despite the terror she had obviously felt at Peters's hand, she had recouped. Indeed, he'd seen seasoned sailors who would not rally so quickly. "But who are you?" he asked.

"I only told you I was Megs to gain an opportunity to escape."

"So you are really . . ." He paused, waiting for her to complete the thought.

"Lady Linnet. What I told you is true. I was the wife of a tailor, but my mother was a baroness. My family . . ." She paused. Her expression was tense. "We fell out of favor with the king and lost our property, so it was necessary that I marry wisely."

He sighed. "I should thank you, I suppose," he said, and turned toward the window though he could see little in the darkness below. "I was cheated out of the stories a mother might share with her son. But since meeting you . . ." He shrugged. "You have already given me enough tales to last a lifetime."

"You are not required to believe me."

"Thank you. So Wart was a successful tailor?"

She raised her regal little chin, looking disapproving at best. Disdainful at worst. Perhaps he should have been insulted that she showed him such disdain, but he had just seen her subdued and disoriented, and though he knew he was a fool, he found he much preferred her thus.

"William," she corrected, then, "Yes. It was a bargain of sorts. He got a lady bride, and I got to continue to eat."

"And where is William now?"

"As I told you before, he died shortly after our marriage."

"How shortly?"

"What does it matter?"

"I'm wondering if you're sticking with your tale of virginity."

She pursed her lips. "I am not the person you think I am, MacTavish. I am not a thief. I am not a traitor. I am a simple lass who wishes for nothing more than to find her way back home."

"In Sedonia?"

Was there the slightest bit of tension in her stance suddenly?

"As I said, I lived in Sedonia for only a short while."

"Long enough to learn the language."

"Yes."

"Do you speak other languages?"

She hesitated a moment. "Yes, I do." A pause. "A half dozen or so."

"A half dozen." He was lucky to have mastered his mother tongue.

"Aye."

"*Parlez-vous français?*"

"*Oui.*"

He shrugged and glanced at his goblet. It was not yet empty. "That's all I know," he admitted.

"I speak French, English, Sedonian, and the Gaelic quite fluently. I am not so accomplished at Italian and Spanish."

He stared at her.

"I can converse well enough in Norway."

Triton's balls.

"And Swedish is similar, of course."

"Of course."

"We traveled a good deal when I was a child."

He had, too, but he doubted they'd shared the same vessel. Possibly not even the same wind.

"Where did you learn to drink?"

Perhaps she looked a bit sheepish when she glanced at the floor. "My father had a small vineyard. He let me sample his wares."

"Was there any left when you were through?"

She scowled, and he almost smiled despite everything.

"Where do you live now, lass?"

"London."

The same story with a slightly different twist. "So why are you here?"

She glanced away. "The truth is an embarrassment to me."

"Or not the truth at all."

"I suppose I cannot blame you for your skepticism."

He gave her a wry glance. "Why are you here?"

"I came to find a husband."

He shook his head once. "I think you're losing your touch, lass."

She stared at him.

"Your earlier lies were better."

"It is not a lie, MacTavish." Her eyes were absolutely earnest. You had to admire a woman who could lie like that. "I swear on my father's grave, I came to find a husband."

"Strange," he said. "Last time I was in London, the eyesight of the average fellow seemed good enough."

"I—" She stopped, scowled, dropped her gaze and lifted it nervously back to his. "Are you saying I am pretty?"

"And lucky for you, or Peters might well have executed you before I came along."

She glanced away again. "How did you return so quickly?"

"Since I've known you, you haven't actually told a single truth, lass. I thought it unlikely that you'd started now."

"You were skulking in the trees? Watching the landau the whole while?"

She looked honestly offended. He couldn't help but smile. "I don't think lairds are allowed to skulk."

"You waited to see what I would do. You expected me to try to escape."

"And I left Peters's horse to make it more tempting. You acted as if you're afraid of horses." He shook his head. "But I doubt you fear anything."

She watched him, her slanted eyes wide.

"Perhaps I should apologize," he said, "but I'm laird of the isle, and . . ." He shrugged. "I have no idea who you are. Or why you are here. Or what you—"

"I am desperate."

"I would have believed that earlier," he said. "Now you just look irritated. So what's the word of the day, lass? Do you know Wheaton?"

"I fear you may be disinclined to believe me even if I tell you the truth."

"Disinclined." He nodded. "Could be."

"Then why waste the words?"

"Judging from past experience, I would say 'because I'm laird' will do me little good."

"I do not know Wheaton," she said.

"Do you swear it . . . on your father's grave?"

"I do."

"Then how did you know of the inn we just visited?"

"That you will not believe."

"Why not take a chance?"

"A friend told me of its existence."

"Maybe you should expand your circle of friends, lass."

"I knew you would not believe me."

"So you had no reason to think Wheaton would be there."

"No."

"And you have no . . ." He paused, searching his memory for a word he had particularly admired. "No animosity against me?"

She opened her mouth, then closed it more slowly. "You have abducted me and held me against my will, MacTavish. I've been shot, beaten, and nearly raped. It tends to strain a relationship."

He tried not to wince. "You have no animosity against my country?"

"No."

"And you want to be set free."

She raised a single brow at him. It was amazing. She could do so without causing a single wrinkle to furrow her forehead.

"Yes or no?" he asked.

"Yes."

He stared at her, trying to read her, but there was no hope.

"Tell me, Megs, would it be worth endangering your life to be set free?"

"I believe I have already answered that once this day."

The memory of Peters's gun against her temple stormed through his mind, leaving a chill aftermath. "Why?" he asked. "Why now? I've not hurt you. In fact, I thought we had come to something of an understanding."

"Understanding?" She watched him narrowly.

"You're a bonny lass, Megs. And though I admit it may be somewhat suicidal, I have admitted my attraction for you."

"Hence you thought . . ." She paused. "You believed I would sleep with you to atone for my sins against you."

He shrugged. "That's as good a reason as any."

"It is not."

"What reason would be?"

"A marriage."

He felt his eyebrows rise. "Generally my marriage proposals are channeled through my advisors, lass, but—"

"I am not proposing, MacTavish."

"Ahh."

"I'll not sleep with you."

"Not even for your freedom."

"No.

Hoary remained resolutely hard, despite his disappointment. He was like that. Cairn merely nodded. "Then I've another proposition."

Chapter 23

"Proposition?" Tatiana asked. Her world spun around her. There was too much, too fast. Too many emotions, fears, desires.

"Don't look so skittish," MacTavish said. "It couldn't be so horrible as sharing my bed."

Tatiana didn't respond. Couldn't, in fact.

"Two men will be meeting at the Seaport."

"The Seaport."

"It's an alehouse," he said. "You haven't heard of it?"

"No."

"Bert tells me it's not a place I should frequent. Mostly sailors gather there for drinks and a bit of sport."

She stiffened. "No."

"What?"

"I'll not prostitute myself for my freedom."

"You think I would ask you to bed another?"

"What else?"

He looked somewhat baffled, but continued on. "I want you to listen in on a conversation."

She scowled. "I have heard that men are not good listeners, but surely one could manage—"

"Barton thinks they won't be speaking the Gaelic."

"Barton?"

"He gathers information for me."

"A spy?"

"Of sorts. He tells me we'll need an interpretor."

"So I, too, would be a spy?"

"I have other people who might do the job, but they are occupied elsewhere."

"Where?"

"Trouble brews on many shores. So what say you, Megs? Will you act the spy, or is that beneath you, too?"

She walked to the window, her mind churning. "Who are these men?"

"No one you would know."

"And what of Lady Linnet? Would she know them?"

"Nay."

She remained silent for a moment.

"Neither would the little people."

She didn't bother to acknowledge his goading. Perhaps he had reason for his skepticism. "And if I do as requested, what will become of me?"

"I would tend to believe you are not a traitor."

"How will you know I am telling the truth if you do not speak the language?"

"Maybe you should simply tell the truth this once, Megs, and leave the rest to me."

She pursed her lips. "Very well then."

He looked surprised. There were times when every emotion showed like lightning on his face. "You'll do it?"

"Yes."

Perhaps she expected him to be happy, but he scowled instead. "It's not the kind of place a baroness would frequent."

"Lucky I am only a baroness's daughter then."

His scowl deepened. "You'll need a disguise."

"I could be a thief," she suggested, and glanced askance at him.

"Did you just make a joke?"

"I never have before."

"Can you pretend to be a barmaid?"

"If you tell me what it is, I am certain I can be one."

"You don't know—"

"That *was* a jest, MacTavish."

He looked uncommonly owlish. Strange. He'd seemed ambivalent when she'd tried to escape, impressed when she'd kneed him, and all but giddy when she'd stabbed him. "The innkeeper is a friend. He'll accept you without question."

"Very well."

He seemed angrier still. "It'll never work if you continue to talk like that."

She canted her head. "Would this be more to your likin' then, luv?"

His scowl deepened. "And what of your costume? You'll need to be rid of that prudish gown."

"This is not prudish."

"Not for a sister of the Holy Order of Mary."

"What would you have me wear?"

He paused as if unspoken ideas were skittering through his mind, then, "Something that doesn't spook the patrons."

"They must be a skittish lot."

He snorted, then glanced sideways, scowling out the window into the darkness. "Can you handle a pistol?"

"What?"

"A gun," he said, turning back toward her. "Do you know how to use one?"

"This may surprise you, but neither tailor's wives nor baroness's daughters generally find the need to shoot—"

"And what of thieves?"

She shrugged. "I know little of thieves, since I am not one."

He watched her for a moment, and now, for the first time in some hours, she could not guess his mood. But there was no need to try, for he turned and walked away without another word.

Burr knocked twice on Gem's door. There was no answer. He rapped again, then waited. Perhaps she was asleep. He shifted his weight from foot to foot. There was no window in her room. He'd seen her just minutes before when servants had delivered her bathwater. Of course she was still in there. Where else could she be? he asked himself, then barreled through the door when the answer came home to him.

Gem jerked upright. Water streamed down her red-gold hair. It looked to be as soft as a vixen's hide. Her eyes were wide, her baby's mouth circled in surprise.

He skidded to a halt, tightened his fists, and cleared his throat.

"Gem."

"What—What is it?" Her voice was breathy, devoid of that brash harshness with which life had imbued it, and without her usual rags, her body looked as genteel and lovely as a princess's.

"Me apologies," he said, and backed toward the door. "I knocked." He nodded toward the portal as if she might not realize where he had been when he'd knocked. "When you didn't answer I thought—"

She'd found a towel and held it in front of her breasts, but it did little good, for truth to tell, every inch of her fascinated him. The hard exterior, the soft interior. Despite the harshness of her formative years, she looked as soft and delicate as an orchid petal.

"You thought I had escaped," she said, and grinned. Her crooked teeth winked at him.

Even that sight entranced him. He scowled. "You may continue your bath," he said, and turned for the door, which had slammed against the wall and bounced nearly closed after his arrival.

"Viking."

He drew a careful breath, tightened his fists for a moment, and pivoted slowly toward her. His heart was beating far faster than a heart his age should beat, and his cock was equally as foolish. "What is it?"

And that's when she did it. She stood up.

He felt his knees weaken. Like a smooth-faced boy. Like a lovesick calf.

"I need to talk to you," she said.

He kept his gaze steady on her face and felt that his brows were pulled low over his eyes.

"Is there a problem, sir?" asked Peters, and pushed at the door. "I thought I heard—"

Burr turned with a start. "If you don't get your nose out of the door, there sure as hell will be, lad."

Peters stepped back, and Burr closed the door. Then he turned, placed his back against the heavy timber, and remembered to breathe. "I've things to do," he said gruffly. "Is there something you need?"

She stepped from the tub. The towel was wide and plush, but only managed to hide the mid portion of her body. The outside of her thighs, the gentle curve of her hips, and the graceful length of her arms were exposed. He was in trouble.

"Something wrong?" His tone was as coarse as sea coral. Still, he was surprised he could force out the words at all. It was sad really. He'd eaten cheese older than her, and here he was, all but trembling at her advance.

"I . . ." She stepped toward him. "I been wonderin'—"

"I have been wondering," he corrected. Poseidon's frigid ass! He was turning into Bert. A hand-wringing old woman with a lisp.

"I have been wondering." She could mimic like a parrot. It made him wonder if she had ever heard correct speech. If she'd ever had a chance. True, his own childhood had been something short of idyllic, but at least he'd had enough to eat. "If maybe I could see Auntie Ned."

"Why?"

She shrugged. Her shoulders were absolutely white, like the pearlescent swirl of a conch. "No particular reason. Just thought I might talk to 'er. Ain't much for me to do 'ere."

He stared at her.

Her lips were sunrise red and slightly puckered, tempting beyond all reason and in that moment he almost weakened beyond forgiveness, but her mouth quirked the slightest amount. "Isn't much," she corrected, "for me to do here."

He scowled. "I told you that as long as you are under my protection you needn't worry. Not about yourself and not about her."

Gem's gaze spurted to his, her defenses dropping into place like a well-oiled portcullis.

"I ain't worried."

He said nothing, only watched her. She held his gaze for a good several seconds, then cleared her throat.

"She ain't been feelin' well lately."

He said nothing.

"Not that I care particular, but she—" Gem shrugged and paused.

"She needs to eat more."

"What?"

"Dr. Leonard." He paused. "The lad's physician. He says she'll be fine so long so she eats proper."

"He—" She stopped, her eyes round as marbles, her voice breathy. "The doctor saw 'er."

"Aye."

The room went absolutely silent.

She swallowed, licked her lips, darted her gaze to the side, then spoke. "Thank you." Her voice was very soft, her eyes hopelessly large, like a lost fawn's. His hand was sweating on the door latch behind him.

He shook his head. "I ain't no nursemaid, girl. It wasn't—"

"I *am not*," she said.

He scowled.

"I am *not* a nursemaid," she said, and smiled.

Maybe it was those two damned slanted teeth that captivated him, or maybe she truly had the most entrancing smile in all Christendom. He gripped the door handle harder, holding himself there by sheer force.

"Can I see 'er?" she asked.

He shook his head, but truth to tell, he wasn't sure why. Was he denying her request or insisting that she stay back?

She stared hopefully up at him. Only a few scant inches separated them. His kneecaps were sweating.

"It's the laird's orders," he said. "He wants the three of you kept separate."

She nodded. Her face had filled out a little in the past few days. "I just thought . . ." She shrugged again. His heart leapt a little with the movement. "Maybe I could peek in."

He shook his head. "Like I said, girl, I ain't no nursemaid."

"Ain't you?"

He deepened his scowl.

"I been thinkin' 'bout your sister. Milly."

He said nothing.

"How you nursed 'er when she was sick."

He should have never told her about his sisters, but when

he brushed her hair in the evenings, it seemed wise to fill the silence with some kind of blather. Now he realized his mistake. The last thing he needed was for this scrap of a girl to think him soft.

"Anna took care of her," he corrected. "Not me."

Her smile brightened and her brows rose. "Are you afraid, Viking?"

He glowered at her, and she laughed.

"You can admit you cherished 'er," she said. "I won't think you're weak. Not with them muscles."

He glanced at his biceps, almost flexed and caught himself just in time. He stared back at her and realized with a start that she'd advanced. They were all but toe-to-toe now.

"You're the biggest fella I ever seen," she said. " 'Ceptin' for once when the carnival come ta Ports'aven. I was just a wee thing then."

"Not like now." His voice rumbled in the room like a death threat. Heaven help him.

"What?" she said, and placed a hand on his arm. Warmth spurted off like frightened doves.

He stiffened. "You aren't the size of an underfed gnat," he said, and made sure his tone sounded no more effusive. "Aren't they feeding you?"

She nodded, but her gaze remained on his arm for a moment before lifting to his face. "The food is so grand. Sometimes . . ." She paused, and in that instant he realized there were tears in her eyes. "It's nice is all. And there be times when I think I could almost be safe with . . ." She paused again and swallowed. A crystalline tear slipped down her cheek.

"Lass," he breathed.

Behind him, the door opened. He turned with a growl. "What the hell do you—" he began, but Cairn stepped through.

He glanced at the girl, then at Burr, at the hand on his arm.

Burroun cleared his throat. "Were you wanting something, lad?"

Cairn raised his brows only slightly. His mouth quirked the same amount, but he shifted his attention back to the girl.

"Can you shoot a gun?" he asked.

She wiped at her cheek with the back of her hand and nodded rapidly. "Aye," she said. "I can if I needs to. Everyone I knows can."

Chapter 24

Tatiana sidestepped quickly, avoiding the man at the corner table. There was a miniature gun shoved under her garter and a knife in her sleeve, but the lush still tried to grab her bottom. Maybe it was because her bodice drooped halfway down her bosom. Maybe it was because her skirt was hiked up between her knees. And maybe it was simply because he was a pig.

He straightened in his chair and leered at her. "Quick little snippet, ain't you?" He was drunk and leering and smelled something like a wine vat gone bad. She considered having him executed, but remembered with some disappointment that her army was no longer at her beck and call.

"Did you want a bit more beer, luv?" she asked instead.

"Nay." He was eyeing her breasts. Was there spittle in the corner of his mouth? "I want a bit o' that."

His companion chuckled blearily. "Looks like she got plenty te spare don't it, George?"

The first genius grinned. "What do you say, lass. I've some coin if'n you have some time."

Her feet ached, and her head pounded. She'd been here most of six hours. Fatigue wore at her like the plague.

"I'd like te and all." She tried a smile again, but it was entirely possible that she snarled instead. "But then I'd have ta kill—"

The door opened. She felt the draft and turned, and somehow she knew it was the man she'd been waiting for. He was casually dressed in gray trousers and fawn waistcoat, and yet there was something about his bearing that spoke of importance. He glanced about the room, caught her gaze for a moment, half smiled, and folded his tall frame into a chair near the door.

An arm curled around her shoulder, and she was jerked to the side.

"Old George was talkin' to you, girl."

The lush had risen, and, despite his inebriated state, he felt incredibly strong. She was crushed against his side like a rotten pear.

"And George don't like to be ignored. Not for a piece o' shit like that." He nodded toward the newcomer. "I got twice the tail that's got."

"Let me go." She tried to push away, but he was far stronger. Panic felt hot in her throat.

"Let you go where? To my room?" he asked, and chuckled as he pressed his groin up against her hip. Bile rose like high tide.

"Release me," she ordered, and realized too late that she'd dropped her Seaport dialect.

But George was far too intoxicated to give her accent any importance. "Release me," he mimicked and chuckled. "Did you hear that, Mug? We got us a princess in tart's clothing."

"I wouldn't mind being in her clothing."

They laughed together, then George dropped his arm from

her waist. She nearly darted away, but in the same instant, he caught her wrist and began dragging her toward the door.

She dug in her heels, resisting madly, but he glanced back as if barely noticing and yanked her against him. She bounced wildly against his sloppy body, and he chuckled again.

"If you knew what I 'ad in my pants, you'd be beggin' fer attention," he said. She shoved the panic back and found the knife in her sleeve. It came away in a shaky fist. She pressed it to his groin, low and steady.

"And if you knew what I had in my hand, you'd be begging for mercy," she growled.

The color drained from his cheeks like river water as he felt the knife's tip penetrate his trousers.

"Hey there, missy . . ." His face contorted. It may have been a smile, but it was difficult to tell for sure. "I didn't mean no harm."

"Let me go." She found that if she gripped the blade firmly enough, it barely shook at all.

"You're makin' a mistake, girl."

"Then you had best depart," she said, "before I mistakenly kill you."

His face reddened, but he dropped her arm and stepped back a pace. "Come on, Mug," he said, not looking at his companion. "The girl ain't in the mood right now, but I'm bettin' she will be soon." He grinned, but the expression was evil and threatening. "Real soon."

Mug stood up unsteadily, and the two of them left, wending their way between the tables and out.

Tatiana waited breathlessly. It seemed that the world might end, or she might faint, or at the very least, someone would rush to her side with words about her bravery, her boldness. But the world did not stop. No rescuer came.

From the rear of the tavern, a skinny man with a beard yelled for ale, and she stumbled toward the kitchen to fulfill his request.

Her hands shook as she filled two mugs, and when she reentered the common room, she saw that the tall stranger had been joined by another man.

Her stomach coiled hard in her gut and her throat felt dry. They were here then. This was it, a chance to prove herself. A chance to win her freedom, but she must not rush in. She must not appear too eager, so she tended a pair of old men and a sailor before making her way between the patrons to the appointed table.

She wiped her hands on her apron and tried a smile. Although her face felt stiff with panic, they didn't grimace and draw away, so perhaps the expression wasn't quite so ghoulish as it felt.

"You gents lost?" she asked, though in truth they did not stick out so drastically as they might. Obviously, they had dressed to fit the occasion, but perhaps they, too, had not realized such wretched places existed.

"No," said the newest arrival, but the first man smiled.

"Perhaps I am," he said. "Is this not Westheath Castle?"

She laughed. It sounded crazed, but she swept her straying hair back with a weary hand and tried to hide the tremble. "You're a bit off the mark," she said. "This 'ere is 'ell."

The first man laughed. His hair was fair, his features comely. The second finally smiled. "Ahh," he said. "I understand. She jests."

And in that instant she recognized his accent. He was Sedonian. She smiled, though her heart was beating hard and high, making her certain they would see it pounding in her well-exposed chest.

"What can I bring you?" she asked.

"A pint of beer," said the first man. She almost nodded,

then realized suddenly that he hadn't spoken in Gaelic, but in French with a soft Teleerian accent.

She scowled and shook her head. "Me apologies," she said. "'Fraid I don't speak no Italian."

He smiled and repeated his order in the common tongue. The dark Sedonian asked for Scotch.

She scurried off. Why French? Why would he speak French but to test her linguistic skills? She didn't rush back to them, but cleared a table and hoped her heart rate would fall back into normalcy. It did not, but she could wait no longer. Finally, she filled a pair of mugs and toted them back to the twosome, taking her time and approaching from the rear, but their conversation was banal, revolving around recent voyages and natural disasters.

She deposited their libations and turned away, but the men at the next table stopped her, wanting meals with their drinks. She shambled into the kitchen, carrying their orders in her head, then returned minutes later with bowls of stew and loaves of bread.

There were complaints all around. Too stale, too cold.

The night wound away interminably. She wandered near the appropriate table whenever possible. The Sedonian watched her, though he spoke to his companion. "You islanders raise your women well."

The Teleerian laughed as he sipped his beer. "She's half your age, Martinez."

"She is that, Douglas, but luckily, she's just my size."

They laughed, already well in their cups.

Patrons came and went. Tatiana delivered more drinks to the twosome in question and listened in when she could, but there was little to hear.

She dropped a pitcher of beer, splattering it in every direction. A sailor pinched her buttocks. Two fisherman threatened to brawl, and a trio of laborers called her over, but finally the patrons began to wander out. The place grew quieter, and in the midst of the softening conversations a single word caught her attention.

"The princess?" said the islander in French.

The word rang like a bell in her brain, stopping her cold. She stiffened.

"Girl," snapped a patron, and she refocused. It seemed to take forever to satisfy him, longer still before she could return to an empty table near the Sedonian. She wiped it down slowly, then bent to clean up an imaginary spill on the floor.

"I'm told your country is quite rich," said the Teleerian. He was leaning back in his chair, and his French was slurred. "Perhaps such a match would be advantageous for my country."

"Perhaps," said the Sedonian. "But it would not be advantegeous for my benefactor. Or for your pocketbook."

The fair man sat up suddenly. Tatiana flinched, but he took no notice of her. "You'd bribe me?" he asked.

The Sedonian stiffened. "I was told you were sympathetic to our cause."

"I am not," said the other brusquely, then laughed as he leaned back again. "I am sympathetic to my own. So tell me, who do you have your princess earmarked for, if not for our bastard lord?"

"'Tis not my place to know or care. But this I will tell you: Those I work for will not allow the princess to dally here."

"And if she does?"

"Princesses are a frail lot and can fall prey to a host of troubles." The Sedonian drank with casual disregard, then continued with a shrug. "But she was put on the throne at some risk, and my lord is loath to see her gone just yet. Thus—"

"You've waited for me."

Tatiana glanced rapidly up. George had returned and stood swaying near a table to her left, but he was not alone. Two thugs had come with him.

She stood up slowly, realizing belatedly that the room was nearly empty but for the two she'd been eavesdropping on. She glanced at the Sedonian, her countryman. He shifted his gaze toward the brutes and rose to his feet. "Perhaps we should continue our discussion elsewhere."

The islander caught her eye, then rose beside his companion. "Aye," he agreed and dropped a pair of coins on the table. "We'll leave you to your fun, lass."

They were gone in a moment. She turned with them.

George smiled. "You ready then, girl?" he asked, and lumbered heavily forward.

She stepped back. "If you leave now, no harm will come to you," she said.

"I like the way you talk," he said, and chuckled. "Don't you like the way she talks, lads?"

They followed their leader, closing in on her. Breath clogged in her throat. She grappled for the gun beneath her skirts. It came away in her hand, but it was gone before she could bring it to bear, snatched from her fingers.

"Girl!" shouted the cook from the kitchen.

She tried to call for help, but in that instant, George clasped his hand over her mouth and dragged her toward the door. She kicked madly, but it was hard to breathe, impossible to think.

They were outside in a moment, but there was no one in sight, no help to be found. She tried to shriek, but even as he shifted her under his arm, his hand remained over her mouth.

She bit him. He dropped her, and she scrambled wildly, trying to gain her feet, but he was on her in an instant, snatching her up by the hair and ripping her bodice away with one fist.

She cried out in terror, but he slapped his hand across her mouth, thumping her against the wall of the inn and grinding his groin into her.

"Here's a right fine place for a fuck then if'n yer in a hurry for—" Something swung out of the darkness. George crumpled sideways, spinning her about with his momentum, and when she found her feet, MacTavish was there.

He stepped toward her, as Burr grunted and let the other two fall.

Tatiana tried to be strong, tried to keep her back straight and her head high, but fatigue and the tattered remnants of terror corroded her will. She began to shake. A moment later she realized she was crying. Taking off his doublet, Cairn wrapped it about her shoulders and pulled her into his arms.

In the back of her mind, she told herself she should resist. After all, it was he who had endangered her at the start, but his body felt warm and strong. She was sheltered in the lee of his arm, bundled against the heat of his person.

The journey to Westheath seemed to be gone in an instant, but perhaps she had slept. The carriage jolted to a halt. She sat up blearily as Cairn stepped to the ground and lifted her back into his arms. Tatiana was certain she should make her own way up the stairs, but it was so much easier to remain as she was, listening to his heart beat against her ear, feeling his arms around her. His footfalls seemed far away and muffled. The world seemed strangely quiet. In a moment they were in his chambers. A single candle flickered on a thousand outlandish items, casting shadows and light across the unearthly room like a magical wand.

He closed the door with his shoulder and bore her to the bed, where he sat down. She kept her eyes closed and her face turned into his chest. The scent of pipe smoke lingered on his tunic and through the sheer fabric, she could feel the heat of his body. He held her close and swept his hand slowly

down the length of her unbound hair. It felt strangely soothing, but she dared not be soothed. She drew a shaky breath
and forced herself to straighten.

"I do not know if you could hear them." Her tone was
matter-of-fact, distinctly at odds with their positions. But it
was the only tone she had. "They spoke—"

"I'm sorry."

She glanced at him. They were close, their faces inches
apart, their bodies touching. She was painfully aware of each
point of contact. Her arm against his chest, her bottom
pressed against the hard strength of his thighs.

She took a deep breath, strengthening her resolve, though
not quite enough to force herself from his lap, and ignored
his words. "They spoke French."

A muscle jumped in his cheek. His brows lowered. "I
didn't realize they'd come back. When the two left we sent
men to follow them. I thought you would be safe. I thought—"
He stopped the words. The muscle jumped again. "Did they
hurt you?"

She watched him for a moment. "Do you have spies?"

"Besides you?" His tone was serious, his fingers light
when he brushed back her hair. She nodded.

"Aye, we have many. But you were as brave as any of
them. Barton himself would have been proud."

She refused to tremble, but could not maintain eye contact. "You lie," she said. "I fear I was not an exemplary spy. I
have—"

"The face of an angel."

"What?'

He watched her in silence for a moment. "The body of a
siren," he said, "and the spirit of a lion. Who are you, lass?"

She opened her mouth to speak, but found she'd lost her
train of thought. "I was . . . terrified and exhausted and . . ."
He was stroking her hair with a rhythmic cadence. "And I

couldn't help thinking that my people . . ." She caught herself. "That *other* people feel those same things with regularity. Every day. Every—" He was watching her intently. She closed her mouth and stared down at her hands, knowing she had said too much.

"And what of you, lass?" he asked. "Don't you usually get tired? Don't you get scared?"

"Perhaps I have been more sheltered than I knew."

He exhaled softly. She felt his breath against her. "There are times when I am sure you're a thief. There are times I believe you are a duchess. And there are times—"

"I am not a traitor, MacTavish. No matter what else you think of me, I did as you asked."

The muscle in his jaw tightened again. The movement fascinated her, but she forced herself to think of other things. Not his physical beauty, not on the feel of his hands.

"I believe you were correct," she said. "The smaller man, the darker man . . . he was Sedonian."

"Lass—"

She scowled at him. "I risked my life for this information, MacTavish. I . . ." She paused. "How do people live like that? And—" She shook her head. "Who were they?"

She thought he might try to shush her again, but he answered instead. "The taller of the two is an ambassador of mine."

"And the Sedonian?"

"He has ties to man named Lord Paqual."

Lord Paqual! She felt the shiver of betrayal shake her. Felt the heat of shame warm her. Lord Paqual had been her uncle's most trusted counselor and the man always eager to offer his advice. He was also instrumental in her coronation. Yet he had connived behind her back, had offered money to make certain she would not make the match she thought best for her country. Had threatened to see her gone if she did not conform to his wishes.

Aye, Lord Paqual had betrayed her. How many others had done the same?

Chapter 25

Tatiana's heart seemed to beat in slow motion. Loneliness hung like a heavy weight between her aching shoulders, but she dared not bend beneath the burden, for MacTavish watched her carefully as if judging her emotions, guessing her thoughts.

"You've heard of Paqual?" he asked.

"No," she said, but her own voice sounded far away, as if spoken by another. "How could I?"

"He's an important man in Sedonia. The old king's trusted advisor. Some say he is also the king's murderer." He shrugged. "'Tis sure the young princess values him, too, for he was instrumental in gaining her the crown. 'Tis said she is but his puppet. You've not heard of him before?"

"No."

"You're shaking," he said, and took her hand in his. She tried to pull from his grasp, but he held her fingers between his palms, and somehow the sight of his hands, large and strong, surrounding hers made her feel just a little less alone.

"You said you lived there once," he said, and turning her hand over, traced a line in her palm.

"Yes," she agreed. The simple movement of his fingers against her hand felt disturbing lovely. "But I was young then and . . . unaware of politics."

She tried to free her hand. The attempt was unsuccessful, so she tried not to be grateful, though the warmth of his fingers fortified her.

"What else was said?" he asked.

"Apparently the princess of Sedonia hopes to convince you that a marriage would be advantageous to your isle."

"Really?" His tone was sharp with interest, and with that interest a tangle of uncertain emotions brewed within Tatiana's breast. Uncertainty, frustration, and some feeling so dark and unfathomable, she could not even guess at its import. Certainly, she could not be jealous. Not of herself. "The princess of Sedonia?" he asked.

She lifted her chin slightly, battling the feelings like a bullfighter with a butterfly net. "Yes."

He smiled. "'Tis said she is quite . . ." His fingers were gentle against her wrist. "Bonny."

"Really?" she asked, then forced herself to lower her eyes and concentrate on the matter at hand. The matters of state— so much more important than the feelings his fingers evoked. "The Sedonian wished to make sure there was no match between you and the princess."

"Why?"

"They did not say."

"It doesn't matter." His eyes softened. "I am not looking for a bride." He slid his thumb up her wrist, seeming to drive the unsteadiness out of her hand.

She swallowed. "Sedonia is wealthy . . . or so I hear."

"And embroiled in intrigue. The old king died." Lifting

her hand, he kissed the veins that throbbed in sharp relief in her wrist. Blood scurried hotly through her, screaming the news of his touch to her heart. She licked her lips and remembered not to breathe through them. "The girl, his niece, was left to man the throne." His eyes were as warm as his fingers. "There will be a bevy of hot-blooded fools vying for her hand . . . just as many old bastards after her throat. Nay, Teleere doesn't need the troubles Sedonia would surely bring."

She tried not to wince. "Perhaps that is why the princess is considering taking a husband. To still the turmoil."

A slight frown marred his brow. But he shrugged, concentrating on her hand again and stroking it with careful attention. "Sedonia has nothing to offer us. Teleere has enough problems of her own without adding such instability to its troubles."

"Instability?" Perhaps she should be insulted, but the sensations caused by his fingers were all-consuming, though she did her best to concentrate on the conversation.

"Sedonia is rich, but her leader is young and untried, her counselors old and mercenary."

"So you will not consider her suit?"

He glanced up, drawing his attention from her hand. "Would you care?"

"No. I mean . . . of course not. I do not know the princess, after all. Her plight has little to do—"

"Would you care if I took another to bed?"

Her jaw dropped slightly. She drew a soft breath between her teeth. "It is hardly my place to decide whom you take to your bed."

"But it would get rather crowded if another were here," he said, and, slipping her off his lap, he kissed her.

Emotions buzzed like mad hornets, racing through her bloodstream, skittering through her nerves. Fear and relief and uncertainty, all screaming through her system. But it was desire that warmed her blood.

His tongue touched her lips, sweeping gently across them. His fingers tangled in her hair.

She pulled back in a panic, and he let her go. But still, he was horribly close. So close she could feel his heat, could feel the brush of his arm against hers. She shivered.

"You're still shaking," he said.

She tried to calm her breathing, her heart, her newly surfaced emotions. "I think I've earned the right. 'Tis not every day I'm accosted by living excrement," she said. Nor was it every day that she learned of a plot against her. It was difficult to say which was worse, but he smiled, and something inside her mewled like a baby at the sight.

"You've the heart of a bear, lass," he said, and stroked her cheek. "In truth, I wasn't sure whether to save you or them."

"I believe you made the right choice." Dear God, she should not let him touch her.

"Your voice was steady earlier." He watched her carefully. "Your hands the same. But now you tremble. Why?"

She wanted him. Desperately. Completely. God help her. "Delayed reaction I suspect."

"Or you are more afraid of what lies between us than of the bastards at the inn."

"You *have* offered to execute me."

"And you've never believed it for a moment."

"*Are* you planning to?"

"No, lass. But I didn't intend to make love to you either," he said, and, kissing her again, pressed her gently into the pillow. His hand was firm against the back of her neck, his chest was hard against hers. She kissed him back, though she knew with absolute certainty that she was a fool to do so.

His tongue touched her lips, and she opened for him, welcoming him in, slanting across his mouth and searching for more.

"Lass . . ." His breathing was just as hard as hers.

"We mustn't do this." She panted the words, but strangely, her fingers were already on his buttons, pulling them open, revealing the smooth, rigid slopes of his chest. Entranced, she brushed her palm across his nipple. He closed his eyes and shivered. The tremble traveled his arm, shaking the beautiful musculature to his fingertips. She watched, her lips slightly parted, fascinated beyond belief. "It would be foolish," she murmured, and, reaching up, gently suckled that same nipple she had just touched. "Wrong."

He jerked against her, arching back, and she drew away slowly, seeing that his teeth were gritted. His eyes opened, though not fully.

"Lass," he said, "I admit that I've no idea whether you lie or tell the truth, but if you are virginal—"

"I am," she said, and, brushing his shirt aside, kissed the other nipple.

It stood out like a small sentry on a glorious hillock.

"If you are," he repeated. He was breathing hard. His tunic was pushed off one shoulder, and every muscle stood rigid and ready beneath the golden sheet of his flesh. "It would be best to do this slowly."

"Slowly." She nodded, though she wasn't exactly sure what he had said. The muscle across his shoulder stood out in sharp relief, leaving intriguing hills and dells. She reached up to pet them, to feel them shift beneath her hand. He might have the title of lord, but he had the mind-numbing body of a god, or a pirate. She kissed his chest, just in the center, where the hard sinews and muscle drew together in a tight valley. "You do not look like most lords," she said.

"Oh." His tone was breathy. "And have you seen many?"

She realized her mistake, but somehow it was difficult to care, for he was nearly undressed, and she was wet. Wet and far past ready. "Just hearsay." Reaching up again, she brushed his shirt from his other shoulder, baring the entirety of his chest. "I have heard they are powerful," she whispered, "and skilled." She swept her palm down his abdomen. It rippled like high tide, but he stopped her with a hand on her wrist.

"Lass." His eyes were burning, his voice strangely raspy. "I am a man."

"Yes, you are."

Their lips were inches apart. She could feel his desire like the brush of a warm wind. And somehow that desire scorched her. He wanted her. Not for her riches, not for her influence or her title. But for herself. Her body, her spirit, her heart. She was not alone.

She curled her fingers inward, so that her knuckles brushed his skin. He closed his eyes, but opened them in a moment, finding hers.

"The fact that I am laird here . . ." He shook his head. She tried to move her hand, but he tightened his grip, stilling her movement. "It is little more than an accident."

She watched him. "And who should be lord, MacTavish? Who deserves the title?"

He shook his head.

"Burr? Peters? Me?" She laughed a little, because everything seemed ultimately clear, yet strangely vague. "The more I see, the more I think that everything is an accident. Luck." She swept her free hand down his arm. The stark white of his sleeve looked strangely incongruous against the golden strength of his fingers. "There are those who would have us believe that royalty is the divine will of God. But what now?" she asked. "The old lord is dead. You are left in his place. Does that mean that his death was also the Lord's divine will?" She shook her head in mild confusion. "Perhaps the experiences you have had, the hardships you have faced . . ." She paused, drawing her finger along a scar that crossed his shoulder. "Perhaps they make you a better ruler. A better man."

"But not a better lover."

"What?" She raised her gaze from the scar to his face.

"I am a man, like any other man."

She skimmed his body again. "I may be naive, Mac-Tavish, but—"

"If there is a secret, lordly way to satisfy women, the secret stayed with the old man."

"What?" she said again, but she realized with sudden, mind-blasting certainty that he was not, at this moment, worried about his ability to rule. He was worried about his ability to satisfy her. And she laughed. "You think that because you are the lord you should also be a phenomenal lover?"

He watched her askance. "You don't think so?"

"I think there may be some sort of mandate to the contrary."

"Elizabeth thought . . ." He stopped his words and bent down to kiss her lips. "You are as beautiful as you are brave," he said. "And maybe . . ." He scowled. "Maybe you are just as kind."

"What did Elizabeth think?"

His eyes were warm and deep. "You don't need to do this, lass, if you choose not to."

"What did she think?"

He drew a careful breath. "She hated me. For a time I thought it was because of who I am, a lowborn bastard set in the place of a lord. Then I thought she simply detested me." He shrugged. "Now I don't know."

"And it torments you?"

He shook his head, but she ignored his denial.

"It torments you because she was the Benelean king's youngest daughter. A lady of the purest blood. Surely she was all that is good in a woman."

"I've no desire for ladies," he said.

Again she ignored him. She could read him like a book. Cairn MacTavish, laird of the isle of Teleere, felt inadequate. And somehow that almost made her cry.

"Gem saved my life," she said.

He scowled at her.

"Gem." She nodded, and realized suddenly that her eyes had indeed filled with tears. "I'm nothing to her," she said. "But she kept me alive, saved me from . . ." She was unable to go on for a moment. "Saved me from a man some surely believe is a gentleman. She risked her life to escort me to safety." She smiled. "Or to relative safety." She shifted her gaze back to his. "I've seen you with your people," she said. "You are above them, and yet you are one of them. Lieutenant Peters. He could hardly make more mistakes if he put forth a concerted effort, and yet he remains."

" 'Tis only because—" he began, but she continued on.

"Most noblemen would not see fit to keep an uncouth Norseman in their households, yet Burr rarely leaves your side."

He shrugged. "I can't seem to be rid of him."

"Even Sir Albert, who surely disapproves of your unrefinement, cannot deny your abilities."

"Albert," he said, and winced. "I think he may be in love with me. I try not to be alone with him."

She smiled. "You've a gift, MacTavish. Do not belittle it."

Silence ticked by.

"Sometimes I can't decide." He was watching her carefully, his heavenly eyes narrowed, his mobile face expressionless. "Are you kind or are you clever?"

"Can I not be both?"

"Most aren't, lass."

"Then I shall choose to be honest. I've nothing to gain from you, MacTavish. You will set me free, or you will not. But while I am here . . ." She was calm now. Calm and languid, warmly wet, quietly eager. All seemed hopelessly right. She ran her hand slowly up the dramatic curve of his chest and curled it gently around the back of his neck. "I will learn from you," she said.

"The more I know of you, lass, the less I think there is anything I can teach you."

She smiled. "I am sure you are wrong," she said, and kissed him.

Chapter 26

~~⌒⌒~~

Desire burned through Cairn, hot as torched pitch. He kissed her in return, passionately, wildly. She tore at his shirt. It came away in her hands. He reached for her bodice, but her arms were in the way, working at his pantaloons.

Virginity was well overrated. Experience was easier. Passion was everything and so long missed.

She pushed his trousers over his hips.

He heard her intake of breath. Her movements slowed, but she didn't shift her gaze. It remained on his erection, which hugged his belly, tight and hard. He waited breathlessly, and then she touched it. He closed his eyes as she wrapped her hand around his length, stroking him. Desire bucked like a wind-tossed frigate in his veins, but he remained absolutely still, waiting.

"I did not expect . . ." She raised her gaze to his. Her cheeks were flushed, the black of her pupils all but swallowing her eyes. "It is large."

He was surprised by her words. Hoary was ecstatic and squeezed hard up against his abdomen.

She stroked it again. He gritted his teeth and shuddered. "Lass, if you hope to wait a bit, you shouldn't—"

"Will it . . ." She licked her lips. She'd lowered her gaze again and just the knowledge that she was staring at it made him all but burst with wanting. "Are you certain it will fit?"

"Damn!" he groaned. "Don't tease me, lass."

She lifted her gaze to his. Her eyes were huge, her lips slightly parted, and he could do nothing but kiss her. He crushed his mouth to hers, and she answered like a wild vixen, returning his caresses with mind-numbing desperation. He tried to slow the passion, but her hands were everywhere, stoking the fire until it was out of control.

He kissed her throat. She moaned and arched into the bed. Drawing her knees up, she cradled him between them and wrapped him in her arms. It was then that he realized she was trembling. Like a babe. Like a child, lost and alone. He calmed himself with a hard effort, drew himself back a few scant inches and kissed the corner of her mouth with gentle, tremulous care.

She laced her fingers through the hair at the back of his head, wrapped her legs around his waist, and devoured him. Perhaps he tried to fend her off, but Hoary insisted she was too strong for them. Too strong. They had to capitulate. Hoary had a great vocabulary.

Answering her wild kisses, he gave up his hopeless battle. He could no longer wait, could no longer think. Rearing back, he plunged into her—and felt her tear.

She gasped and stiffened. He squeezed his eyes shut and swore hotly as he tried to retract. But she was already re-couping. Wrapping her legs more tightly about him, she pushed tentatively against him.

He cursed again, just as heatedly, but if she noticed, she made no response. Instead, she pushed harder, and his body responded with aching need, pumping into her.

She answered savagely, squeezing him with unbelievable strength, sucking him in, driving him beyond control. He no longer tried to stop, for he couldn't. He was out of his mind, out of his depth, out of control. He pumped madly against her, and she bucked back, gasping for breath, taking him in, drawing him past release until he burst free and fell with a hard rush into satiation.

He collapsed atop her. Through the coarse fabric of her gown, he could feel her heart thumping wildly. Against his ear, her breath came hard and fast.

Guilt was the very next sensation he felt. And guilt made him mean. He was a pirate, for God's sake. Pirates had no room for guilt.

"Who the hell are you?" he growled.

She opened her eyes rather slowly. They were still dark, still wide, still so damned beautiful it made him want to cry like an abandoned babe. To pull her into his arms and beg forgiveness. He'd rather die.

"Is it . . ." Her lips, always full, looked swollen now and as red as a blossom. She licked them. He watched the movement and felt his mouth go dry, and his stomach pitch low in his gut. "Does it always feel like that?"

He swore again and pulled himself away from her. "You were a virgin."

She blinked. Her lips quirked. Perhaps it was a smile. Perhaps she was going to cry. He realized suddenly that he had no idea which it might be. How could he know so little of her mind when he knew her body like a glove.

"I told you I was," she said.

He shook his head and pulled his attention from her lips. "You knew I didn't believe—"

And then she kissed him, openmouthed, with passion as hot as a burning poker. He leaned into her, then found his mind and jerked to his feet. He was naked. But that seemed the least of his worries. He paced jerkily across the room and back.

"You knew I didn't believe you!" he repeated.

She sat up, but didn't bother to smooth her skirts. They rode high on her thighs, barely covering her hot core. Her shoes were still on, her stockings in place. But her hair had come loose and stroked her face like wild, darkling waves. Her eyes were wide and slanted, and her lips . . .

He tried not to moan, but perhaps he failed, because her lips quirked up again.

"You knew," he said.

Her gaze skimmed him, starting at his eyes and traveling down with languid speed. Her nostrils flared. "You did not answer my question, MacTavish."

He felt strangely breathless, as if he'd been battling.

She kept her gaze well below his waist. "Does it always feel like that?"

He felt himself swell, felt his balls draw tight against his body, but he shook his head, fending off the hard press of desire renewed. "I'll be the one asking the questions, lass."

She raised her gaze slowly back to his, but that did little good, for her eyes were deathly dark with desire. He crunched his hands to fists and held himself carefully from her. It was the hardest thing he'd ever done.

"What is it you want to know, MacTavish?" she asked. Her tone was perfectly level, as if they sat in a fine tearoom eating crumpets and discussing the latest antics of the *ton*.

Yet her voice was strangely husky. He swallowed. Even in a tearoom he would be hard-pressed to keep himself from her. "Who are you?"

"I told you—"

"Aye," he growled. "But you lied."

"Did I?" she asked, and rose slowly to her feet.

A nipple had escaped. He realized it with a shock for the

first time. The bodice, always low, had been misplaced during their lovemaking, and now the dusky peak of her left breast was peeking over the white gathered cotton. He shut his eyes and found he could see it just as vividly in his imagination.

"Aye," he said, and opened his eyes resolutely. "You did. Repeatedly. But I'll have the truth now."

"My name is Linnet," she said.

She was lying. Of course she was. But something deep inside of him whispered that he wanted to believe she was lying. Thieves were a problem. But ladies . . .

"Widow to the late Lord Waldon," he said.

She advanced. He managed to hold his ground, neither retreating, as his brain suggested, nor rushing in, as Hoary vociferously insisted upon. "Yes."

"*Virgin* to the late Lord Waldon," he corrected, and laughed.

She stopped and eyed him quizzically. "You find that amusing?"

"Amusing?" He sounded hysterical. Him. Cairn Mac-Tavish. Pirate. Bastard. Laird. Hysterical. It would have been funny if it weren't so damned scary. "Nay. It's not amusing. It's damned ridiculous."

She reached out. He watched her hand draw near and braced himself against the impact. But it was no good, for when her palm brushed his chest every living cell buzzed to attention, yammering insolent suggestions to his battered brain.

"Ridiculous?" she asked, and glanced up.

He was breathing too hard. As if he'd battled and lost. What the devil was wrong with him? Burr would laugh his damned ass off if he saw this.

"This late husband of yours," Cairn said, teeth gritted. "Was he breathing?"

She scowled slightly when she nodded.

"Was he male?"

"Yes," she said, and slipped her hand across his nipple.

His muscles jerked as if yanked by a cruel puppet master but he kept his teeth gritted against the razor-sharp sensations and remained as he was. After all, he could hardly go screaming from the room. It would be unseemly, as Bert would say. "*And just idiotic*," Hoary added. He shook his head. "There's where your story goes wrong, lassie."

Her eyes fluttered up slowly, as if it were difficult to shift them from his chest. Her lashes were thick and sable. Her cheeks were flushed. Hoary danced like a leashed hound.

"What do you mean?"

He laughed. It sounded wheezy. But his chest was on fire, so that could only be expected. He clenched his muscles and fought for some kind of normalcy. "No man could take you to wife and not have you."

Her honey-sweet lips parted slightly. Her eyes narrowed in thought, and her hand stilled just below his bottom rib. It made it damned hard to breathe. Harder still to keep from rising on his toes just to urge her hand a little lower. But he was thinking now. *Thinking*, he repeated. Hoary snorted.

She lifted her chin and moved her hand again. "Do you mean to say I am . . . attractive."

He barked a laugh. "Don't—" he began, but just then her hand slipped down, causing his breath to catch hard in his throat.

She moved closer. "Don't what?" she asked, and slipped her hand up his shaft.

He squeezed his eyes closed, and she brushed her lips against his chest. It would be girlish to tremble, he was certain, but he may have done just that.

He forced his eyes open, and she lifted her gaze to his. She rose up on her toes and kissed him, freezing the world.

"Is it a hoax?" he breathed.

"Hoax?" She scowled and moved her hand again. His cock pulsed, drawing her attention lower and causing her to tighten her grip.

He moaned.

"You think I faked my innocence?"

"Virgins don't usually—"

She licked his nipple, lapping it with the tip of her tongue. Every muscle in his body jerked up as tight as a bowline.

"Don't usually what?" she whispered.

Was he panting? "Damn, woman! You've the ways of a London whore!"

She blinked. "Truly?"

He would have laughed if he could breathe. As it was, every bit of energy went into keeping himself upright, keeping his hands to himself, trying to think.

She was scowling, but her hand was still wrapped around his erection, and her lush lips were still parted.

"How do virgins act?" Her hand moved.

"Virginal."

She stroked. He moaned.

"Can you expound?"

"I'm hardly an expert on the subject."

"Truly?" Her hand stopped. He missed the movement immediately.

"I'm a pirate. A bastard at—"

"A lord. With all the lordly rights."

"Aye, well, I've been busy." And injured. And Elizabeth had done little to enhance his desire for women. She, too, had seemed innocent at the outset, but proved to be well experienced. This girl had seemed experienced, but now, after lying with her . . . He deepened his scowl. It was all very confusing. But Hoary didn't care in the least. Hoary wasn't confused. Hoary could focus like a beacon. "But what of you?

Surely you haven't been too busy to . . ." She was stroking again, distracting him.

"No. Not too busy. Too . . . foolish. I did not realize how . . ." She paused and kissed his chest.

He swallowed. As it turned out, he truly had had no idea what a woman could do with her hands. Perhaps he was the innocent here. "How what?" he asked.

"It was not unpleasant, MacTavish." She said the words casually, but there was a taut earnestness to the words that made him pause. "I had no way of knowing your touch . . ." She stopped herself. "That *touching* would feel . . . It was not repulsive."

"You had no way of knowing?"

"As I told you . . ." It seemed almost that she tried to hold herself back. But she leaned forward finally and kissed his throat. He managed not to rip her gown off and reenact the entire deflowering process. He didn't quite manage to control his frustrated moan. "I was well protected," she said, and kissed his jaw.

He gritted his teeth in an attempt to think, to get his mind around this change in her. Hadn't she, just hours before, refused to lie with him? Hadn't she fought like a tiger to protect her virginity? "They must have pounced on you from every corner." It took him a moment to realize he'd spoken his thoughts aloud. "Men," he added. "How did you keep them at bay?"

"It was not so hard."

He could feel the sweet softness of her feral breast pressed with hot intimacy against his chest. "Not so hard, lass, they must have been tearing down your—"

She kissed his nipple.

"Balls, girl, who protected them from you?"

She drew back slightly, and he regretted his words immediately, for anything that stopped the touching could be immediately labeled "very bad."

"You think I've thrown myself at men?" she asked, and blinked, not as if she were insulted, but merely intrigued.

Her hand started up again, which surely would suggest that, yes, she had indeed thrown herself at men, but that could not be the case, not with what he now knew. She'd been a virgin just moments before, and if there had been the slightest chance for any breathing man to have her, that man would have taken it or died trying.

His brain felt hot. "Why me?" he asked.

"Are you not the lord of this isle?" she asked, and smiled a little. "My liege?"

He nodded, just now remembering. But the foolishness struck him immediately. Aye, he might not be as experienced as some, but he knew enough to realize that she was not giving herself to him out of some sense of— Hell, she was not *giving* herself to him at all. She was taking. Devouring. He stopped her hand before Hoary could guess his intent.

"Why me?" he asked again. "Why now?"

She tried to free her wrist. He tightened his grip. She scowled, looking young and vexed.

"Lass," he said, and lifted her chin with his free hand so that their gazes met. "Perhaps . . . Maybe you could trust me with just this tiny piece of the truth."

She stilled and her mouth softened. "I've told you the truth, MacTavish," she said. "I was protected, told to save myself. Indeed, I was ordered to save myself."

"But you were wed."

"Aye. To a man who could not . . ." She paused. He waited. "Could not do what you do." She said the words breathlessly from those damp plump lips. He hoped he wouldn't faint.

"And you didn't . . . miss it?" he asked.

She swallowed and glanced down. "We were not the demonstrative sort."

"We?"

"My family. My parents." She shrugged and looked up again, and in her face was an expression of awe, as if she'd discovered something so wondrous she could not yet fathom the truth. "We did not touch."

"What?"

"In any way. Not as punishment. Not as affection. Nor was I allowed to be touched by others. I was—"

He realized he was holding his breath.

"I was their little princess," she said. "Set above. Set aside."

"There must have been a slew of men trying to breech the fortress once they had seen you."

Her brows dipped momentarily. Then she raised her eyes and smiled slightly. It made his heart hurt, but he remembered the lies with a hard effort. "Do you find me alluring, MacTavish?"

He considered lying, or at least not telling the truth, which was entirely different in his own way of thinking. But there seemed little purpose. "A sand snail would find you alluring, princess, and you know 'tis true."

"No one said as much. Mother was . . ." She shook her head as if thinking back. "Some said she was the most beautiful woman in all of Europe. Perhaps in comparison I paled to—"

"It doesn't matter who you're compared to."

She stared at him for a moment, then leaned forward and kissed his lips.

Desire struck him again, but it was deeper now, slower, still burning, but it was not the hot flash of fire like before. Now it burned hot and red, like stoked embers.

"Are you saying you didn't know you were beautiful?"

"A person's physical appearance . . ." She shrugged. "Outer beauty oft hides a host of inner ugliness."

"Then why not choose an ugly man?"

"Are you assuming you are not ugly, MacTavish?" He didn't answer, and she laughed. "Truth to tell, I had no desire for a man at all, MacTavish."

"Forgive me for finding that hard to believe," he said. "Since I have scratches from me shoulders to me arse."

She cleared her throat and glanced away. It was the first time he'd ever seen her blush. And that couldn't be faked. Could it?

"I was ignorant."

He watched her. She glanced toward him and away again. She was strangely shy, for a nymphomaniac. Not that he had any sort of aversion to nymphomaniacs.

"I didn't know . . ." She paused, pursed her ungodly lips and tilted her head as if defying the world. "It was really quite pleasant."

He flexed his shoulders, feeling the scratches burn his skin. "Pleasant?"

"In truth . . ." She flitted her eyes down and up. "I would try it again if you are agreeable."

She stepped forward, and he retreated though he would not have thought he had the strength.

She gave him a questioning glance. He scowled in return and kept his hands carefully to himself.

"I don't make it a practice to deflower virgins."

"I am quite happy to hear it, MacTavish, but since the deflowering is already done . . ." She shrugged and stepped toward him.

He caught her wrist. "I will have the truth. Who are you? Some sorceress trained to seduce? A spy sent to defeat me?"

Her expression sobered. "If I am a spy, I am a spy for you," she said.

His emotions were roiling like storm clouds. "Tell me, lass," he growled. "Why are you here?"

For a moment, the sharp-edged lady of fortune stared up at him, but in an instant she softened and raised her hand to his cheek. Her palm felt soft against his face. "I am here for this," she whispered, and slipped her hand down his chest and onto his abdomen.

Sensations burned like magic. A thousand errant emotions screamed for attention, but he tightened his grip on her wrist.

"Nay," he said, and Hoary whined like a starved hound. "Not again. Not until I know the truth."

She opened her mouth to speak, but he knew it was a lie even before she spoke. So he backed away, snatched up his clothes, and fled.

Chapter 27

❦❦

"**Y**ou've returned." Burroun's voice rumbled as he entered the darkened throne room. The chamber contained very little; a few hanging tapestries depicting gloriously bloody battles, a carefully woven floor carpet, and a throne. Cairn hated this room.

He poured himself a mug of beer from a pitcher he kept on the oaken arm of the throne. The pitcher was made of silver. The mug was crafted of gold-encrusted ivory. He emptied it in one chug and filled it again.

Burr eyed him quizzically. "I see your mood has improved."

Cairn gave him a dark look. He had left the castle three days since to find answers and his wits. But he had waited too long to inquire about the ship called the *Melody*. In fact, the good captain had already sailed for France. Upon questioning the man's first mate, who had remained behind, he had learned that a young woman named Mrs. Mulgrave had indeed traveled on their ship. She had been accompanied by a largish man with limited intelligence, and she had come from Sedonia.

Cairn scowled. Aye, some of her story seemed to be true, but she had not said she was traveling from Sedonia. He raised his gaze to Burr's. "You've been giving her lessons in defense?" He had given up the task, for it was all too obvious that he could not touch her without bedding her.

The Norseman looked less than pleased. "Of course. My laird has deemed it necessary to train his prisoners in the art of self-defense. So I train them. Who am I to think it strange?"

Cairn filled his mug again. "Quit your whining, Burr. You make a poor fishwife."

"And you make a poor laird when you're mooning over the maid like a smitten harp seal."

A number of possible responses presented themselves to Cairn, but he had learned long ago that it was best not to get into a pissing contest with someone of Burr's phenomenal size. The man could flood the room before Cairn had opened his pantaloons, but it was late, he was tired, and not in the best of moods, as Burr had rather sarcastically suggested.

"Better a harp seal mooning over a maid than a whale moping over a child," he said, and quaffed the beer again.

Burr stiffened. "What are you trying to say, laddie?"

He shrugged, loosening his muscles. "Gem," he said and rolled one shoulder back, easing the tension there. "Couldn't you find a doxy old enough for solid foods?"

"You think her a doxy?" Burroun said the words quietly. Cairn smiled at the lack of tone.

"Maybe the two of you are spending your time in intellectual pursuits," he suggested.

"Leave the lass out of this," Burr suggested quietly. " 'Tis none of your concern."

"I'm the laird of the isle," Cairn said, and drank again. "Everything is my concern. Did you forget?"

"That you're the laird or that you're an ass?"

He made a sort of salute in Burr's direction with his mug. "Have you bedded her yet?"

The muscles in the Norseman's neck tightened, but he remained where he was. "I'd be tempted to beat you senseless, lad, but I see you've already achieved that state."

"They say it's best to teach them young."

The giant took a step forward. "Do you think your position will keep you from a thrashing?"

"Nay," Cairn said, and grinned. The devil churned in his belly. "I think your age will."

"'Tis too bad I didn't train your haughty lass the sooner," Burr said. "So she could have beaten some sense into you."

"Aye, but you've been too busy training young Gem, aye."

In retrospect, he realized he should have been better prepared. After all, one does not provoke a sleeping bear without expecting some repercussions. But he was half-drunk, and his thoughts were divided. And perhaps, even after all their years together, Cairn had believed his position would protect him from his best friend's tutelage. He was wrong, though not disappointed, and true to Burr's unpredictability, it was a bootheel and not a fist that caught Cairn in the shoulder. He spun off the throne like a top, tumbled off the raised platform, and struck the wall at an oblique angle. A candelabra crashed onto the floor, spewing hot wax in its wake.

The door flew open, and Peters leapt in.

"Get out!" they roared in unison.

Peters glanced from one to the other, nodded wide-eyed, and backed out, closing the door behind him.

Cairn returned his attention to his opponent. "Too weak to throw a decent punch, Burr?" he asked.

"Too proud to waste one on the likes of some pampered fool who doesn't know how to speak of his betters."

"Betters?" Cairn raised his brows and his fists in unison. But the truth was, he rarely used his fists. He'd learned to brawl from the dregs of society, and that meant using whatever lay at hand. Unfortunately, there was little in the way of ammunition in the throne room. The throne itself came to mind. "Do you think yourself my better, Burr?"

"Actually . . ." The old man moved like a castrato, light as a fighting cock on his feet. It would have been disconcerting had Cairn been sober. "I was talking about Gem."

"The thief?" He circled the giant, honestly surprised. He knew the man had formed a fondness for the girl, but perhaps it was deeper than he'd realized. He grinned. How amusing would it be if he were falling in love?

"Since when have you been one to look down on a bit of thievery?" Burr asked, and, moving in like a serpent, struck with the heel of his hand. Cairn leapt back, just avoiding contact and managing, by naught but pure luck, to land a brushing blow to his opponent's left cheek.

Burr nodded his admiration and circled lightly. "Perhaps your haughty lass has taught you a thing or two, aye?" Darting in, he planted a quick jab in Cairn's belly. It felt something like a volcanic explosion, but MacTavish managed to stay on his feet and stumble out of reach before he found himself dead. Burr grinned. "But then, she would be the one to do it, wouldn't she? What with a face like that, she's probably taught a good many men a host of lessons not soon to be—"

Cairn struck him square in the nose. Blood sprayed into the air, squirting like a geyser onto Cairn's loose-fitting tunic. The pattern of red on white distracted him for a moment, and in that second Burr darted in and landed twin punches to his gut.

Cairn refused to bend to the pain. Instead, he gritted his teeth into a smile and wondered if he would survive this archaic pleasure.

"You're out of your depth here, lad," Burroun said. "Why not admit it?"

Cairn laughed out loud, welcoming the challenge. "The day I can't best you, Norseman, is the day I happily lie down and die."

"And not a moment too soon," said Burr. "But I was saying you're out of depth with the haughty trollop."

Cairn charged. Like a callow youth, he lowered his head and ran at the mountain called Burroun. No one was more surprised than he when the other actually went down. Cairn stumbled back, trying to catch his balance, then fell like a downed tower atop him.

"Damn—" Cairn began, but in that instant, Burr bucked, tossing the other well over his head. He landed in a heap and rolled painfully to his side. Burroun was already up, half-bent, blood spattering onto his chest where the fur vest parted.

"I don't mind you swiving a few maids, lad, but it would be best if you kept yourself to the ones who weren't contagious."

"Aye well . . ." Cairn sat up slowly. Burr stood toward the end of the carpet Cairn had just rolled off of. " 'Tis obvious enough you wouldn't know an innocent if she bit you in the arse," he said, and, reaching out, yanked the carpet with all his might.

Burr teetered and toppled, landing hard enough to make the room quake. Cairn leapt to his feet, but by the time he had reached his fallen comrade, the other had already risen.

"What are you saying, boy?" he asked, and rumbled a laugh. "That you think Princess Rags is an innocent?"

Cairn came on, feinting with his right and striking with his left. Burr answered with a swing to his belly. He ducked and caught the blow on his chest. It felt like the kick of a loosed mainsail. But he stumbled back and managed to avoid the next blow.

"She *was* innocent, you harebrained ass."

Burr laughed. "Innocent my—" he began, then stumbled to a halt and narrowed his eyes. "*Was?*"

"Come on then," Cairn said, and motioned wildly toward the other.

"Was?" Burr repeated.

"Scared of me, old man?" he asked, and motioned again, though he felt a bit queasy.

"Aye, terrified," Burr said. "You're lying with her?"

Cairn felt the fight drain out of him like river water downhill. Raising his hand to his brow, he kneaded rhythmically. "No. I'm not."

"Then how do you know she was innocent?"

Cairn glanced toward the darkened window. Why wasn't he drunk yet? Or beaten senseless? "I'm not bedding her."

Burr straightened his mammoth back and narrowed his eyes. "But you did."

"I didn't know . . ." He ground his teeth. "How the hell was I to know she was untried?"

Burr's scowl deepened. He had no qualms about beating the hell out of most any man who walked the streets, but he had a strict policy against abusing women.

"You might have asked," he suggested, his voice low.

"You think I didn't ask?" Cairn said, and swore with dark vehemence before pacing to the window and back. "I asked everything. She lies at every turn."

"And so you thought she lied about this?"

Cairn said nothing, but winced. "She lied about everything else." He sounded like a mewling child, even to his own ears.

Burr was silent for a moment. And when he spoke, his words were deep and quiet. "Did you force her?"

Cairn's ire rose in an instant. And in that moment he was almost tempted to lie, to bring the other's wrath down on him like hell's brimstone. But in the end the truth was too vexing.

"Force her," he said, and shook his head. "Hell, man, I couldn't stop her."

Burr's brows had lowered all the more. He swiped a hairy wrist across his nose. It came away bloody, but he failed to notice. "I thought I taught you better than to boast, lad."

"Boast!" He barked a laugh. It sounded a bit hysterical. "I couldn't hold her off. You think I'm proud of that?"

The other's brows had risen. "I've seen some strides in her ability to defend herself. But it seems unlikely that she forced you, boy."

Cairn shook his head. "I didn't plan to . . . She's so . . ." He curled his empty hands like claws, trying to find the words. "She hasn't been touched."

"You're that sure she was innocent."

"Innocent! Aye. Aye." He shook his head. "She was that, but more. 'Tis as if she's never been touched in the entirety of her life. Not the simplest caress, not a stroke on her hair. 'Tis as if she's dying for the need of it. As if she can't get enough of it, and yet—"

"She's accepted none other."

He shook his head.

"So she gave herself to you because you're the laird."

Cairn remained silent for a moment, then, "You've talked to her, Burr, what do you think?"

"She doesn't seem to be overwhelmed by your title."

Cairn snorted a laugh at the understatement.

Burr shrugged, thinking. "I suspect there are those who find you somewhat appealing."

"You think she lay with me because of my features?"

The Norseman shrugged again. "As I've said a dozen times, I think you're plain as oatmeal, but the lassies sometimes have differing opinions. She may—"

"So she's aching for attention, and in all her years of men

slavering after her she's never found a single one to give her-self to?"

"You're sure she was untried?"

Cairn gave him a flat look, and Burroun sighed.

" 'Tis a strange thing," Burr said. " 'Tis not as if you can determine the truth when you lie with her again."

"Again!" Cairn scoffed. "Nay." He shook his head. "Not again. Not until . . ." He stopped, but he had already caught Burr's undivided attention.

"There's only been the once?"

"It's none of your concern, Norseman," Cairn said, and turned away.

"And she's eager for you?"

MacTavish turned in frustration. The fight had felt better. "She lies," he said flatly.

Burr's eyebrows had disappeared completely. "So you're punishing her by withholding your . . . favors?"

"Shut the hell up!" Cairn growled, and, grinding his hands to fists, roamed the chamber like a caged mountain cat.

"Is that your plan, lad?"

"She lies," he repeated, and turned toward Burr. "I don't know who she is. I don't know what she—"

But Burr was already laughing.

Cairn ground his teeth. "I'd hate to have to kill you, man."

"And I'd hate to see you try, lad." Never had there been more irritating laughter. " 'Twould be embarrassing after all me years of training you." He wiped his eyes. "Are you a complete dolt, MacTavish? How many times do I have to tell you? She's not Elizabeth."

"Isn't she?"

Burr sobered somewhat. "You said yourself she was un-tried. Elizabeth had more lovers than I have hairs on my arse."

"Maybe it was a hoax."

"Her virginity?"

Cairn nodded. If Burr laughed again, Cairn would personally cram the throne down his throat.

"Any idea how she'd manage that, lad?" he asked.

"Not offhand."

"I think we can assume she was an innocent."

"Then why did she give herself to me now?"

"Could be she feels the same about you as you do about her."

The world went silent. Cairn gritted his teeth. "I feel nothing for her."

Burr grinned. There were few things worse than seeing Burr grin, except to hear him laugh. "'Course not, laddie. You simply decided celibacy was the best course in this case." He sounded as though he would laugh again. "Cuz you're not interested anyway, swamped as you are with female companionship. And Princess Rags ... she's not hardly bonny atall. Repulsive, really, if you see her in the right light what with—"

"Shut up, Burr."

He laughed instead. "Wake up, laddie," he said, and sobering, thrust his oversized head toward him. "'Tis me you're talking to, not some scatterbrained nobleman. You say she's lying, but look at *yourself*."

"You're calling *me* a liar?" Cairn said, and drew himself up. Apparently their truncated battle had not gotten the bile out of his system.

"Aye, laddie, I am that. A liar and a coward if you can't even admit your feelings."

"I have no feelings, Burr. I would think that even someone of your limited intellect would know that."

"Care to step up closer and say that, boy?"

He took two strides nearer but a rap at the door interrupted his foolish intentions. Which may be for the best, considering he seemed particularly suicidal just then.

"Who is it?" rumbled Burr.

"'Tis Barton," said Peters from the far side. "Come with news."

Burr glanced at Cairn who nodded in return. "Let him in."

The door opened. Thomas Barton bowed, but Cairn had no time for formality.

"What is it?"

"'Tis news regarding Lord Paqual's man," he said. "He meets with a fellow called Stephen Bull. And there are rumors of an assassination."

Chapter 28

"The choice is the girl's," Burr said.

Cairn glowered. They were, once again, alone in the solar. "She's my prisoner."

"A prisoner you dare not risk?"

"She is my link to Wheaton."

"Ahh, so that's why you will not send her on another mission."

"Aye!" rasped Cairn, and, jerking to his feet, paced again.

"We are still talking about your prisoner, aye? The one you are certain has plotted against you and Teleere. The one you refuse to set free because of her treason."

Cairn ground his teeth. "She's a poor choice for this mission."

"Because she is coolheaded and bonny and gifted at languages?"

"Because she would just as soon escape as complete her task."

"Why didn't she do so last time then?"

"She had no opportunity."

"And neither will she this time."

"Can you be so certain?"

"Aye."

Cairn hesitated a moment, then shook his head. "Nay. 'Tis too dangerous."

"So you would trust me with *your* life," Burr mused, "but not with the life of your . . . prisoner. Interesting."

" 'Tis not her life that worries me but her presence. She is my only link to Wheaton."

"Wheaton," Burr scoffed and paced himself now. "Why not admit the truth, boy? You've fallen for her."

Cairn paused by the window, leaned one shoulder up against the wall with careful casualness, and glanced at the Norseman. "How many years have we been together, Burr?"

The big man shrugged but parried the change in conversation with his usual aplomb. "Since you were naught but a bawling brat."

"And in all that time I've not heard you say a more foolish thing."

"So she means naught to you."

"You begin to understand."

"Then there be no reason not to use her for the good of your country, lad," Burr said.

And though Cairn tried to think of an argument, he could not.

The situation was different now. Megs was not a barmaid. Indeed, she was dressed as a lady, for Martinez was not patronizing a wharfside dump, but a fashionable inn. And they had almost arrived at that destination.

She sat across from Cairn in the carriage. Her hair was upswept and embellished with striped blue ribbons and a single string of pearls, but it was mostly hidden now under the satin of a sapphire cloak. Beneath her wrap, her gown was of ivory and low enough to keep male patrons from delving too deeply into her personality. She looked entirely changed from her former role. In fact, she looked disturbingly right.

Cairn's jaw ached. "You've got the knife?" he asked.

She turned toward him. Her expression was absolutely serene beneath the shelter of her hood. He found he wanted to tear it off and rip away the subterfuge. But what was subterfuge and what was truth?

"Yes." The single word was perfectly enunciated.

He stared. Who the devil was she? Why had she lied? Was it too late to take her back to his bed? To hide her away? To take her into his arms and make love to her? She wouldn't resist. Indeed, she would welcome the contact. He knew it every time she looked at him, every time they inadvertently touched, though she had not mentioned it since he'd left the bedchamber naked and idiotic.

"Burr showed you how to use it?" he asked.

"Yes."

He nodded. "Carval will be there. He is a good man and will not be recognized, for he is rarely at Westheath. There is almost no risk."

It was true, in fact, and yet the thought of her there with those men . . . The memory of her at the last mission . . .

His teeth hurt. The carriage bumped over loose cobblestones. He glanced out the window, his mood as dark as the gathering clouds. "You don't have to do it."

"Burr said as much."

Silence settled in again, but it was not his friend. "And I'll not set you free," he said, turning abruptly back. "Not even for your help in this."

She stared at him. Her face was serene but there was something in her eyes, some fragment of emotion he would give his soul to delve. "Because of Wheaton?" she asked.

And the truth was right there, so close he could taste it. He wouldn't set her free because he couldn't bear to have her gone. To know that he would not see her again, would not possess her hot fire, not touch her satin-smooth skin.

"Aye," he said. "You are my only link to Wheaton."

She glanced out the window again. The beleaguered sun had nearly set, but an errant ray shone across the rain-washed landscape, illuminating her face. And in that moment she looked like nothing more than a freshly painted oil, a dreamy artist's rendition of a regal lady far above the concerns of the world. A princess.

"You don't have to do it," he repeated.

"Yes. I know."

Beside his hip, he crunched his hand into a fist. "Then why are you?"

"You said this meeting may adversely affect relations between Teleere and Sedonia. I would do my part to keep the peace."

Why? he wanted to ask, but just then the carriage jolted to a halt, and they had reached their destination. The footman exited his perch. His boots crunched against the gravel of the drive. From the window, Cairn watched Carval dismount. He wore strapped buff pantaloons and cutaway tails as if he were born to them.

When Cairn wore pantaloons and tails he looked like a painted penguin gone mad. In fact, he looked like a buffoon in anything more ostentatious than a plaid and a horsehair sporran.

But that didn't mean she was too good for him. He was laird here, sovereign ruler of all Teleere. And perhaps that title alone could win her affection. There was no reason to think she was another Elizabeth. Perhaps if he admitted his feelings for her, she would reveal her own. Perhaps it was time, he thought, but in that instant, the footman opened the door, and she exited without a backward glance.

* * *

Tatiana's heart stuttered in her chest. She laid her hand genteelly on Carval's arm and strolled toward the inn. Once inside, she nodded with regal disregard to the host and glanced with casual disdain at the patrons.

She saw him immediately. He was the same man as before. Her countryman, Black Martinez.

The host arrived, drawing her attention. He indicated a table with a sweep of her hand, but she declined immediately. Too close to the kitchens, she said. She preferred a spot by the window. She was ushered in. Martinez tried to catch her eye as she was seated, but she pointedly ignored him. It was easy. Simple. Things she had done a million times.

She ordered her meal, exchanged a few words with Carval, and sat quietly. Martinez was still alone, and finally he rose from his chair and made the short trip to her table. Once there, he bowed. The movement made him look even shorter than he was.

"Your pardon," he said, speaking directly to Carval. "But I believe we have met before. In Paris perhaps?"

He spoke in French. Carval looked at him blankly. Tatiana did the same, keeping her expression absolutely empty. It was so easy.

"I must be mistaken," Martinez said, now in Gaelic, and turned toward her momentarily to flash a smile. She supposed he was a handsome man. But it was difficult for her to say. "I am Lord Martin." He bowed again.

She didn't smile, didn't, in fact, respond in any way. There was great security in being wealthy and well-bred, and she used that security now.

His self-assurance faltered just a mite. "My apologies," he said. "You look so familiar. I thought I had met you once." He scowled slightly. "Perhaps it was in Bath."

She pursed her lips and watched him for a moment. He

fidgeted the slightest amount. "I have never been to Bath, sir."

"Ahh, and your . . ." He paused, not one to give up easily and glanced toward Carval. Boldness was in his veins. Or perhaps he had been drinking for some time before she'd arrived. "Father?" he guessed.

"I've not left Teleere for some years," said Carval. "And neither has my *wife*."

"Ahh, I see." Martin smiled again, but a bit less lustily. "Well, then, I am sorry to disturb your meal."

"You must be Martinez." The words were in French again, but came from another man. The Sedonian admitted as much, and in a moment they had taken their seats.

Tatiana's meal arrived, and she turned her gaze to it, though her attention was still fixed on the men. They sat nearly directly in front of her. She could watch them without raising her eyes.

"You're Bull?" Martinez asked.

"Yes."

"You're late."

"It looks like you've managed to entertain yourself." The newcomer's voice was blasé and quiet. He had dark, half-closed eyes, and though he was as short as Martinez, he carried himself as though he were much taller.

"I do what I can," Martinez admitted, as the server poured his wine.

Bull lifted his glass. "It's always nice to do so with big-chested women."

Martinez chuckled. Tatiana kept her gaze on her meal. Was this real life then? Was this how people talked about others? Was this how people talked about her?

She didn't blush. She never blushed. Except that once in MacTavish's arms. That once she refused to think about.

Bull ordered his meal, then settled back in his chair and drank. "You wished to meet with me," he said.

"Yes." Martinez drank again and fiddled with the stem of his glass. "I need a small task done. I was told you would be able to see it completed."

Bull shrugged, his demeanor casual. "That depends on the task."

"Murder."

Tatiana silently caught her breath, but not a soul turned toward the two.

"Murder is expensive," said Bull.

"Money is plentiful."

"Oh? And whose money would I be taking?"

Martinez smiled, drank, then lifted his chalice in a sort of offhand toast. "That is not for you to know just yet."

The other drank also, then settled his glass back on the table and rose slowly to his feet. "Good day then," he said and turned away, but he had not reached the next table before the Sedonian spoke again.

"It's the bastard's."

Bull swiveled around, retraced his steps, and sat again. "This bastard," he said. "Is he also a pirate?"

"Aye, some call him that."

Bull nodded and almost smiled. "And the victim?"

"I hope you have no special feelings for women."

The other sat, leaned back in his chair and studied the Sedonian narrowly. "They have their uses. Who is she?"

"No one of great consequence," said Martinez. "I believe her given name is Tatiana. We're planning a special event for her Midsummer's journey to Bartham."

Chapter 29

❦

Tatiana walked slowly back to the carriage, Carval at her side. She kept her strides carefully cadenced, her head high. She could feel her heart beating, slow and hard in her chest, keeping time with her footfalls. Her limbs felt strangely heavy, as if she were just waking from a deep dream.

A hand reached out of the darkness, snatching her arm, but she neither gasped nor spun about. Instead, she turned with slow deliberation, as if nothing held any more terror for her.

MacTavish stepped out of the darkness, his face shadowed. And in that dearth of light, she could barely recognize him. But really she had never known him.

"My lord," Carval said, and with a quick bow, he left them.

"Megs." MacTavish's voice was low. "Are you well?"

It seemed almost that she could feel the blood pumping steadily through her veins, as if she could track its winding course. It fascinated her, held her entranced inside herself. Perhaps she nodded.

From the left a couple strolled by. MacTavish glanced toward them, then tightened his grip on her arm and led her toward the carriage.

It rocked slightly as she mounted the single step. Inside, a small, ornate lantern illumined the scarlet upholstery.

MacTavish's face was sober, his blue eyes bright and intense. Gone was the laughter she usually found lurking in their depths. But then he could hardly afford to laugh. Unless he knew what she had just heard. Unless he knew all along, had set up this entire charade to teach her a lesson.

"What's wrong?"

Her mind was rolling placidly away, digesting, ruminating. It wasn't every day one was granted the opportunity to hear of her own assassination. And less likely still that she would then sit down beside the very man who had ordered her murder. What was the date? When was her Midsummer's Eve? A week's time perhaps? She'd lost track.

"Meg," he said. His voice was sharp.

She turned slowly toward him. The hood of her dark cloak shadowed her face from the sharp glare of the lantern.

"What did you learn?" he asked.

She studied him in the flickering light. "A good deal," she admitted quietly.

He frowned, his brows drawing downward slightly. "What was said?"

"You were right. There is to be an assassination."

"Whose?"

The carriage lurched into motion. She didn't respond immediately. "Tell me, MacTavish, what do you know of Princess Tatiana?"

"Tatiana?" His body was tense, his expression the same. "Of Sedonia? She's to be assassinated?"

She almost laughed at the surprise in his voice. "I believe that's what they said."

"Why?"

Because he had ordered it. The pirate bastard. At least that is what they had implied. But if he had given such an order, there was no need for her to learn of their plans. He would already know them.

"You did not answer my question," she said.

He studied her for a moment, then, "I know very little of her. She is young. Out of her depth, they say."

She glanced out the window. The landscape was dark now, rolling by in shades of deepening gray. "Did you order her death?"

He didn't answer immediately. Didn't deny nor object, nor speak at all. She turned back.

If the question shocked him, he didn't show it. "Do I seem that sort to you, Megs?"

"In truth . . ." She kept watching him, trying to see beneath the layers of pirate and lord to the man beyond. "Perhaps I do not know what sort you are."

"Don't you?"

"All I know with certainty is that you are the kind to hold an innocent against her will."

"An innocent?" She could feel his sudden anger. "And who might that be?"

"I've done nothing to harm you, MacTavish."

"Then tell me who you are."

She laughed, though she found nothing to amuse her. "And why would I do that?"

"So you admit you're not the good widow Linnet?"

For reasons unknown, the sound of that name sent memories swarming through her. The feel of his hands against her skin, the touch of his lips on hers. But she pulled herself back to reality, to the present, to the pain.

"Did you order her death?" she asked again.

"Why do you care?"

"Why?" She rasped the word and bent toward him, so that she leaned out of her seat into the narrow, swaying aisle. "There is to be a murder, and you think I would not care?"

"People die every day, Megs. Every minute most like. Why would this death concern you?"

"She is a princess."

Silence fell into the coach, accented only by the quick sound of hooves on cobblestones.

"And because her blood is royal, she is more valued, more important?" he asked.

She held his gaze for several seconds, then turned abruptly away, straightening as she did so. Where her heart had been slow and steady, it raced in her chest now. "I did not say that."

"You imply it, Megs. I but wonder why."

"If the princess falls, the entire country may fall."

"The country of Sedonia."

"Yes."

"Sedonia, filled with corruption and ill-gained wealth."

"What do you know of Sedonia?" Her tone was deep with passion.

"Tell me, lass, who sent you here?"

"Sent me?"

"Here. To me."

"What are you—"

"Are you a spy?" he asked, and grabbed her wrist.

"A—"

"Did they know I would be unable to resist you?" he snarled, and tightened his grip. "An unspoiled beauty with a lady's demeanor and a whore's passion."

She jerked at her arm, but he did not release it. "Did you order her death?"

He smiled, but the expression was grim. "Were I to execute someone, lass, it would surely be you."

She felt herself pale, for this was the first time the threat seemed real, close to the surface, truly possible.

He watched her eyes for a moment, then laughed. "And yet I have not. Did you not notice that, Megs? In fact, I have given you a score of opportunities to redeem yourself, to leave."

"Then let me go now," she whispered.

War raged in his soul. "I can't," he rasped.

It was her turn to laugh.

"Unless you tell me the truth. Who are you, Megs? Truly?" His grip was no longer tight, and his eyes were haunted, his voice low and deep.

There seemed to be no air in the coach, no room, nowhere to look.

"If I tell you . . ." She paused. Terror squeezed her lungs. He had ordered her death. But if such was the case, why did he need her to spy on his own man? It made no sense. Still, she could not trust him. He meant her harm. Maybe. But perhaps . . . She stared into his eyes, and for a moment it seemed almost as if she could see his very soul. Perhaps, it would be better to know the truth, better to take the chance of her own death than to live without knowing his heart. "If I share the truth, will you let me go?"

His expression didn't change, and yet it seemed for a moment that he fought a battle with himself. "Aye, lass. I will let you go."

"Do I have your word of honor. Your word as lord and—"

"You have me word as a man," he gritted.

She drew a deep careful breath, glanced out the window and closed her eyes for a moment. When she glanced back, his face was unchanged, his expression hard, his eyes brittle.

"I am Tatiana Octavia Linnet Rocheneau, princess of Sedonia."

He said nothing.

"I came here to . . ." She was sitting very straight, as if she were reciting poetry to a roomful of her noble cousins. "I came here on personal business."

"Alone."

"No. What I told you before was truth. I traveled with a single bodyguard. It was necessary for my disguise."

"And why the disguise?"

"As I said, I was on personal business. Business I did not want my advisors privy to."

"Surely there will be a panic at your disappearance."

"Nicol . . ." She paused, realizing the utter foolishness of the ploy she'd planned with the viscount. "I put another in my place."

"Another?"

"Someone who was trained to act the part, to pretend to be me until my return. The sojourn was to last only a few days. I was to arrive, meet an entourage told to await the arrival of an important lady, and conduct my business quickly and privately. But when we reached your shores, the wharves were chaotic. My guard left for a moment, and before he returned to my side my goods were stolen."

Hot wax spilled down the candle, hissing at the contact with the cool brass.

"The thief was young and small," she said. "Thus I gave chase. I realize the foolishness of that act now, but he had stolen all I had brought here. The crowd was thick and volatile. I was jostled about and finally, when I caught my wits, I was at the gallows." She was afraid, terrified really, and yet it felt good to spill the truth. At least she would know now, would be sure of his intent toward her.

"That was when I met you?"

"Yes."

"And why did you come here, princess?"

"I . . ." It felt almost as if her heart had stopped dead in her chest as she stared at him. His heaven blue eyes, his hard-bodied strength. "My reasons remain private."

He nodded, then glanced out the window. His eyes were thoughtful, his expression relaxed, but the cords in his neck stood out in sharp relief against his broad, sun-darkened throat. Finally, he turned back.

"I like the tale," he said, and nodded once. "But the story about the widow virgin is still my favorite."

Shock sluiced through her system. "You think I lie?"

He didn't bother to answer.

"I am Princess Tatiana," she said.

"And I am Father Christmas."

"Damn you," she said evenly.

"Harsh talk for a baby queen."

"Did you order my death?" she demanded, leaning into his space.

"If I had, lassie, you would already be in the ground."

She raised her chin a notch. "I will be leaving Teleere in the morn."

He stared at her for a moment, then laughed in her face.

She waited for him to finish, to look at her again, for the noise to seep from the coach. "You gave me your word."

He chuckled again. "I said you could go if you told me the truth, not if you spun yet another ridiculous tale for my entertainment."

"Because you choose not to believe does not make my words a lie, MacTavish. I am Princess Tatiana, and I will be returning to my homeland."

His face was absolutely sober. "Sedonia may be peopled with murderous diplomats and conniving counselors, but I hardly think they deserve to have you loosed on their hapless population."

The world was spinning slowly around her. "So you will not release me willingly?"

"I will not release you atall—"

And in that moment she pulled the blade from beneath her skirt. She did not raise it to his throat, but slipped it straight to his groin.

"I sail for Sedonia," she gritted, "and you will take me there, with or without your balls."

He raised his gaze from the knife to her eyes. His brows lifted slightly. "I know you too well to think you will drive that home, Megs."

"I am not Megs," she ground and pressed the blade easily through the fabric of his kilt. "And you do not know me at all."

He didn't even flinch. In fact, the crooked corner of a smile lifted his lips as he raised his hand slowly. She watched it, expecting him to take the knife from her and wondering madly if she would have the strength to make good her threat. But he only shifted his arm out the open window to rap the landau's hard veneer.

"Galen," he said. "Take us to the *Fat Molly*."

The journey seemed to last forever, but finally the carriage slowed and jarred to a halt. Tatiana's arm felt stiff, her fingers numb from her hard hold on the knife, so she slipped her other hand into her reticule and drew out the pistol he had supplied.

He raised his brows at her. "What now, princess?"

She glanced toward the window and back. "Now we set sail."

"Shouldn't we have a crew of some sort?"

"I am certain your *Fat Molly* has a crew."

"Mostly ashore and probably drunk."

Her heart was racing. "Then you'll have to use the men we have with us."

The smile broadened slightly. "There's a far cry between a soldier and a sailor. These men couldn't—"

She cocked back the pistol's hammer. "There's a far cry between a pirate and a lord, too," she said, "and yet you seem to make do."

The door swung open. "Why—" Burr began, but at first glance his eyes widened, and his words paused for a moment.

"The lass would like to go to Sedonia," MacTavish intoned, his gaze never leaving hers.

"Sedonia." There was a good deal of surprise in the Norseman's rumbled voice. "Whyever for?"

"I'm not sure."

"Is that why she's pointing a pistol at the royal jewels?"

"I believe so."

Burr's face split into a grin. "I've liked her from the start," he said. "Sedonia it is."

Chapter 30

The *Fat Molly* pitched sweetly beneath Cairn's feet. It felt lovely, like the gentle rocking of a babe's wee cradle, but not everyone, apparently, appreciated cradles.

"You look a mite flushed, Megs," he said.

Megs . . . He still called her that, for despite all, he had no more idea of her true identity than he had the day they'd first met. But whoever she was, she tightened her grip on the pistol and pursed her lips. Those bonny, luscious lips. The lips of a liar. The lips of a seductress. Not the lips of a runaway princess. Surely not. But something inside him cranked the screws on his conscience. Was he the liar? Had he been lying the whole time, lying to keep her at his side. But then, he wasn't the only one to blame. She could have been honest from the first, could have trusted him, instead of spewing outlandish tales of tailors and thieves and princesses. Damn, she made his head ache.

"Sit down," she ordered. She was braced against the wall of his quarters, looking too weak to stand against the delicate sway of his favorite vessel. He smiled.

"If you're planning to vomit, you'd best get topside, lass."

She pulled a sour face. "I am not about to vomit."

"Then you might as well relax." He sat on his berth and lifted a wooden bowl of fruit toward her. "Grapes?"

She glanced toward the bowl and swallowed once. The muscles in her jaws clenched, but she spoke articulately.

"Might you think this a lark, MacTavish?"

"Nay. You've a pistol pointed at my . . ." he began, then noted that her aim had wandered somewhat. "Wall," he said.

She rapidly corrected her aim, pointing somewhere between his navel and his left shoulder. And although that destination might be somewhat preferable to her earlier target, a bullet there would still be painful, if not fatal.

"Do you plan to hold me captive the entire voyage?" he asked.

"Yes," she said, and pursed her lips again. He watched them pucker.

" 'Tis a long journey."

She snorted. Her eyes were very wide, showing an immense amount of sclera around her expanded irises. "I thought you were a seaman, MacTavish. Surely a two-day voyage is no great feat for you."

He shrugged. "Aye, it might take two days, but it might well take a fortnight if we run off course."

Beneath them, the sea swelled merrily. He felt the tension build far before it should have been discernible. But it came, lifting them lovingly upward before letting them fall gently in its wake. Megs bumped against the wall, fumbled with the pistol, and brought it frantically back to bear. Maybe the swell wasn't quite as loving as it seemed to him.

"A fortnight!" she exclaimed. The flush on her cheeks had turned a strange shade. Something akin to the color of a Syrian olive.

He shrugged. "You did not give me time to gather me usual crew, lass."

"I cannot wait a fortnight."

"Why not?"

The *Molly* bucked and quieted again. Cairn waited expectantly, letting the silence grow around them. The girl remained as she was for a fraction of a second before her shoulders hunched and her cheeks swelled. Seeing the inevitable, he dumped the fruit onto the table and thrust the bowl toward her, but she had covered her mouth with her hand. He tore it away and shoved the bowl in its place. She tried to resist, to bring her weapon back to bear, but he grabbed the back of her head and pressed it downward. In a matter of seconds, she had emptied her stomach, shuddered, and vomited again.

"Sit down," he ordered.

"I'll—" she began, bringing the pistol up again. It wobbled like a cork float in her hand.

"Shut up and sit down," he said and shoved her toward the mattress. She struck it and tried to bounce back up. "Stay," he ordered, then bore the bowl to the door and yelled for Burr.

He was there in a moment, listened in silence, and strode away a second later, the bowl held in his gigantic hand.

Cairn turned back toward her. The pistol was trained on him once again. Her eyes were level, but her cheeks were notably paler.

"If you endeavor to take me back to Teleere, you have my vow to shoot you," she said.

He wondered if she would even manage to stand up. Still, he remained where he was, though he was tempted to push her back onto the mattress and feel her heat beneath him. He took a step toward her.

"You have my solemn vow," she said. The gun wobbled.

"And at this range, I or the door latch would surely be dead."

She corrected her aim shakily. "I'll not go back, Mac-Tavish." Her tone was steady, her huge eyes the same, but her baby lips quivered. His stomach twisted at the sight, but he pushed any asinine emotions to the rear and took another step toward her.

"Was it so terrible there, lass?"

"Do not come any closer," she warned. "Tell Burroun to maintain a course for Sedonia."

"Why?"

Her eyes were ungodly bright. She swallowed hard and raised her left hand to assist her right. "There's trouble there."

"What kind of trouble, lassie? Surely the princess cannot be shot if you are she and you are here."

He stepped toward her.

"Stay where you are." For the first time since their meeting, her voice sounded panicked.

"If you shoot me, Burr'll have no reason to obey your orders, lass. You'd be a fool to wound me. And though you may be many things, a fool you are not."

"Do not come any closer." She rose shakily to her feet, and in that moment he lunged.

The pistol fired. He grabbed it from sheer instinct, imprisoning her and the weapon in one swift movement.

"What's this then?" Burr asked from the doorway. His brows were raised, his hand wrapped about a wooden mug. He eyed Cairn up and down, apparently checking for blood in his nether regions, then raised his gaze to note their respective positions, inches apart with her hair wound about them like silken threads.

"Shall we keep hoping for a royal heir then, lad?" he asked.

"Not today, Burr."

The giant chuckled and set the mug on the table. "I brought the lassie's tonic."

Cairn nodded.

"So . . ." Burr drew himself up. "Where do we point our prow, laddie?"

Cairn felt the girl shiver against him, felt the heat of her body seep into his soul, felt her fear like a tangible force.

"She says there's trouble in Sedonia."

"Then Sedonia it is," rumbled the Norseman, and left the room.

Cairn tossed the pistol away and eased the girl onto the bed before retrieving the mug Burr had left.

"Drink this."

She stared at him. "You believe me?"

"That you're the princess of Sedonia?"

She nodded.

"Nay," he said, and tilted the smooth vessel up to her lips. "But whether you're royalty or riffraff, I don't want you soiling on me shoes. Drink this."

She did so finally, then made a face and pushed the mug aside. He pushed it back until she had finished it.

He settled onto the mattress and stared at her. Color had begun to return to her cheeks and her irises had returned to their normal size. "Better?" he asked.

She nodded once, then, "What are your plans for me?"

Her lips were calling to him. He didn't answer, but tightened his fist against the blankets and shored up his willpower, though his traitorous left hand seemed to have crept up to smooth a lost tendril of hair behind her ear. "The same as ever," he said. "To find out who you are."

She closed her eyes at his touch then opened them slowly. They were as round and soft as a doe's. "Wouldn't it be easier simply to believe me?"

His knuckles had strayed down her throat. Her skin was

ridiculously soft, at least for a thief's. Doubt cranked up in his stomach. He ignored it as best he could. "What did you hear in the meeting?"

Her expression was ungodly sober, making it all but impossible to resist leaning forward to kiss the corners of her plump mouth.

"That you had hired another to kill me."

His hand paused for a moment, before he slipped it behind her neck, feeling the incredible softness of her hair against his knuckles. "Me."

"Aye. But it will not work."

He nodded once. "Because there is another in your place."

"Yes."

He ceased kneading her neck and found her eyes. "Then you have nothing to fear."

She drew a deep breath. "Did you order my death, Mac-Tavish?"

He pressed the great weight of her hair over her far shoulder and caressed the kitten soft underside. "As I said before—"

"Martinez said the orders were yours." Her voice was a whisper.

"Martinez lied," he said.

Her lips trembled.

"Why did you come here, lass?" he asked, and leaned forward against his better judgment.

"I cannot tell you." Her words were a soft breath against his lips. "But I must return. I must."

"You are safe with me. You needn't worry."

"Needn't worry? Is that how I seem to you, MacTavish? As if I would put another in my place and not care if she died? Do I seem so cold?"

He watched her carefully. "Aye," he said softly, "sometimes you do."

Her cheeks went pale again, but it was not the *Molly*'s tossing now, but her own fractious thoughts. "Maybe I was," she whispered. "Maybe at one time, but no more. She will not die." Bringing her hand up, she crushed her lapel in her fist. "She must not die because of me. Do you hear me, MacTavish?"

He tried to hold firm to his jaded illusions. But her eyes were too large, her skin too soft, her lips too full. "When is the assassination to take place?"

"On Midsummer's Eve. Every year at that time the royal family rides to Bartham."

"Where is that?"

"It is a village. My people bring their best steeds there, and from that herd I choose the best. It is a great honor." He watched her throat convulse as she swallowed. "I am to be killed en route."

"You will not be."

"But the girl who sits on my throne—"

"She will not die either."

She raised her chin slightly. "Truly?"

"You have me word," he said. "As a man and a laird."

Her lips twitched. It was a rare visual of some internal turmoil. "And what then, MacTavish?"

"Then, when I save the princess, you will tell me the truth." She nodded slowly.

"Swear it," he said, "on your immortal soul."

"I swear," she whispered. "You shall know all." There was a sadness in her face suddenly. A loneliness. Fear curled in his stomach, tightening his senses. He skimmed his thumb across her cheek.

"And tell me, princess, after I know the truth, shall I see you again?"

She stared at him for an eternity, her eyes liquid and haunted. "Kiss me," she whispered.

He told himself he shouldn't. That it was a bad idea, that one kiss would never be enough, but there was no chance of him resisting. She opened her mouth to his, and he moaned as he pressed into her. Her hands were on his chest, pulling away his tunic and there was nothing he could do, no way to stop her. He was weak, after all. Only a man. Only a laird.

They were naked in a matter of seconds. She lay upon the mattress like a goddess, like a princess, awaiting him, welcoming him. There were no barriers, no words. He smoothed his palm down her breast and over her belly. She was beautiful, he thought. Beautiful and clever and none of the things she claimed to be. Most probably a spy, a spy for the very princess she was trying to save. But just now she was his. He slipped his hand lower. She moaned and arched up to meet him, rocking with the movement of the waves, and there were no more thoughts, not until she lay limp and sated in his arms, not until she was lulled by the sweet rhythm of the water.

He smoothed his hand down the length of her hair and wondered if he had lied. Perhaps he did not have the strength to let her go. Perhaps, even when he knew the truth, he would fail, but in that moment he felt a droplet of warmth against his arm. A tear had trickled from her eye and onto his biceps, and with that tiny tear, he knew that while it would be difficult to let her go, it was no longer possible to hold her against her will.

The wharves were busy. Tatiana stood at the prow, her heart leaping in her chest. The winds had not been favorable. The sea had been rough, the voyage long. She should have resented the delay, but she had been in MacTavish's arms, wrapped in his security. She closed her eyes, and fortified her strength. She could not turn back. It was over. They had arrived, and despite all Burr had done to hasten the trip, it was the day of her birth.

MacTavish strode up beside her. She didn't look up, but she could feel his presence.

"When will the princess make her ride?"

"After the noon feast."

"We have a few hours then."

"I hope so."

"You will remain on board," he said.

She skimmed the crowds. "No."

He scowled down at her. "Burr knows your country well. We will find our way to Bartham."

She didn't glance up. "Yes, we will."

He glared at her a moment, then cursed softly and called for Burr.

The Norseman appeared in a moment.

"Do you know what to do?" MacTavish asked.

"Keep the princess alive?"

"More specifically."

"I'll secure horses. We'll ride for the palace and warn her entourage."

MacTavish nodded, and in a moment they were off. But it was difficult to find enough horses. They hired a carriage instead and as many mounts as they could, piled inside, and galloped toward Skilan, the city of her birth, but once they reached the outskirts, the streets were flooded with people. Music played everywhere. Acrobats and jugglers plied their trade, and the smell of roasting foods permeated the air.

Their driver cracked his whip above the team's sweating croups, but their passage was jammed. And then they saw it—up ahead, a river of royalty moved down the streets like a slow-moving barge.

They'd left early. Tatiana pushed the door of the carriage open and jumped to the ground, trying to break through the crowd. They were almost there, but not close enough. She could not see Burr or the men who were mounted with him.

And then she saw her impostor, perched like a deity upon her favorite gray mare. For a moment she was stunned, caught in a strange netherworld where she was not who she was. Where she could be who she wanted. Not held by the bonds of blood, but free to love and be loved. To touch and be touched. But it was not to be. Duty was strong. She would do what she must. And yet she was trapped, blocked away from the royal entourage.

Nicol rode beside the impostor. His dark hair glistened in the sunlight. She screamed his name, but he didn't hear her. Soldiers crushed back the mob, and in that moment Mac-Tavish stepped from the carriage and onto the shoulders of the crowd. It was as if he were running on waves, skimming over heads and backs, coming ever closer to the winding stream of royalty. He was almost there. Almost—

A shot rang out. Tatiana screamed. The soldiers turned. The crowd shrieked, and MacTavish leapt. The gray mare bolted, and the girl fell. Another shot echoed in the milling streets. The crowd shrieked and scattered like chaff in the wind, trying to break free of the terror. But Tatiana raced ahead, pressing her way through the mob, straining to see what she could.

And then Nicol fell.

"No!" she screamed, and scrambled forward on her hands and knees. The viscount lay on the cobblestones, holding his arm. His face was pale, but he was alive. She breathed his name and he opened his eyes and smiled.

"Anna?" he said, seeing past her disheveled hair and shabby gown.

"Get off me!" a woman ordered.

Tatiana turned to the side. MacTavish lay sprawled across Birgit. She wriggled beneath him, and he rose slowly, pulling her up with him, still shielding her from the crowd behind.

Soldiers rushed in, better late than never perhaps, and the girl bent to retrieve her crown from the rough cobbles.

"Arrest him!" she said, pointing to MacTavish, but Tatiana found Nicol's eyes again.

"Hold," he said, and rising to his feet, bent to whisper in the girl's ear.

She turned her gaze toward Tatiana and raised one brow. Not a wrinkle showed on her forehead.

"We'll return to the castle," Nicol said, and hurried the girl toward the ornate coach. Tatiana and MacTavish followed.

Birgit ascended first. Nicol winced as he reached for the door.

"You're injured," Tatiana said, and touched his arm.

"Aye." His eyes were intense. "But you are not."

"I am well."

MacTavish stepped closer. "We'd best get out of sight," he rumbled.

Nicol mounted the carriage, but just as he stepped up, he cursed and leapt for the opposite door. It stood open to the dissipating crowds beyond. He stared at the backs of the surrounding guards, then scanned the mob for several seconds and fell into the seat, holding his arm. "She's gone."

"The princess?" MacTavish said, and scanned the crowds wildly.

Nicol seemed to notice MacTavish for the first time and raised his brows in question.

Tatiana remained silent, feeling breathless and chilled. She shivered once. A silken cape lay upon the seat. Nicol drew it carefully about her shoulders. The carriage lurched into motion.

MacTavish's gaze felt heavy and hard on her face. She avoided his eyes. Steadying her nerves, she spoke around the lump in her throat.

"Nicol," she said, "this is Cairn MacTavish, lord of Teleere. And this . . ." she began, turning her gaze to the Scotsman with an effort. "This is Viscount Nicol, my most trusted advisor."

Silence fell like the final note of a dirge into the carriage.

"And you?" MacTavish asked.

She dropped her gaze to her hands, then lifted it to the window. The crowds looked strangely blurry. Hoofbeats clattered along beside the carriage.

"Your Majesty!" Sir Combs leaned down from his galloping mount. She pulled the hood of the cape up to hide her wild hair. "You are well?"

She raised her head and caught his eye with an imperial stare. "Yes," she said. "I am safe."

She never heard his response, and though MacTavish said nothing, it seemed as if his silence drowned the chaotic noise of the entire universe.

"Stop the carriage," he said, his gaze hard on hers.

"What?" Nicol asked.

"What?" she breathed.

But he had already opened the carriage door. The ground whirred below his feet.

She lurched up beside him, grappling for his arm.

"Wait!" she demanded, but he did not.

Jerking from her grasp, he stepped out of the rumbling coach, caught his balance on the rushing street below, and disappeared.

There was nothing Tatiana could do. She was returned posthaste to Malkan Palace, where she was rushed to her chambers to be surrounded by her ladies-in-waiting.

Once there, explanations were simple. Birgit had remained isolated, and lies had become as much a part of Tatiana as her title. They accepted her explanations of a temporary impostor to replace her when she'd learned of an assassination attempt. What else could they do but accept? She was Tatiana Octavia Linnet Rocheneau. The princess.

Once in the bathing room, she was washed in scented waters, dressed in yards of silk and fussed over, but even before they'd laced on her slippers, Lady Evelyn rushed breathlessly into her sitting room.

"Your Majesty," she said, bowing low. She was no longer a young woman, but her face looked flushed with excitement. "Lord Paqual begs an audience."

Tatiana was weary. Weary as she'd never been weary before. So Paqual wished to speak to her. Was he a traitor? And what was she to do about it? Yes, she was the crown princess, but hardly did she have autocracity. Paqual had powerful friends. She wished she could say the same.

"Show him in," she said. Lady Mary rushed forward with her slippers, but she waved them aside. Being barefoot in the presence of her eldest counselor no longer seemed such a heinous crime.

The high, arched doors of the chamber opened. Paqual hurried forward and fell to his knees. Taking her hand in his, he kissed her knuckles.

"Your Majesty," he said, "I was so very worried. When I heard of the attack on your person, my heart stopped in my chest. I—"

"It stopped?" she asked. The world seemed strangely vague.

He paused in his soliloquy to glance up at her. "Nearly so, Your Majesty. I was that worried when—"

"But it did not stop."

He looked momentarily confused. "Mayhap for a moment, but all is well now that I see you are whole."

She stared at him. "Yes, all is well. Did you wish to speak to me about something of import?"

A frown momentarily marred his aged features, but he rallied. "The assassin is dead, Your Majesty."

Tatiana sat very still. Someone had died. The news affected her strangely, as if she were somehow far removed from this entire mess, far away from the horror of being royalty. And yet, because of her someone would never draw another breath. Would never laugh, would never cry. Her people believed he had almost killed her, but it was all a lie. All an outlandish twisted falsehood. "Who was he?" she asked, and felt that she cried inside, for him, for the unfairness, and maybe for herself.

"His name was Fitzgerald of Milton."

She watched him carefully. "You know already?"

"Your spies are many and range far, Your Majesty."

"Why did he do it?"

"He was a hired assassin. Of that much we are certain."

"Who hired him?"

He closed his eyes for a moment, as if immensely tired. "Sir Combs interrogated him before he died."

"And?"

"He was paid by MacTavish of Teleere, my lady."

She said nothing, but listened as the final pieces of a puzzle fell into place.

"Your enemies are strong, my dear," he said, and patted her hand. "But your allies are many, and eager to risk their lives for you."

She nodded. "And who was it who killed the would-be assassin?" she asked.

"That is the strangest truth yet," he assured her excitedly. "For it seems Prince Edward of Romnia was visiting our city when he saw the gunman in the tower. 'Twas the prince himself who fired the shot that killed the wretched traitor." He dropped his head and kissed her hand again. Tears? Were there tears in his eyes? "I owe him my very life."

"The prince saved my life?" she asked. It felt, almost, as if she were in a void, a deep chasm with steep walls and no air.

"Yes. I believe it was an act of God."

Pieces of a strange, abstract puzzle seemed to fall into place like pebbles in a stream. "Yes," she said. "Thank God and whatever unlikely coincidence brought him to that exact place at that exact moment."

"He is very concerned with your well-being, Your Majesty, and begs for an audience."

She glanced up at him. "And it would surely be rude to refuse him after all he has done."

"Shall I send him forth then, Your Majesty?"

"Certainly," she said.

He kissed her hand again, then backed away at a crouch. The prince of Romnia entered only minutes later.

He was as lanky and lackluster as she remembered from her childhood. She rose to her feet, extending her hand. "I am told I owe you my life, Prince Edward," she said.

He pursed his lips. They were very pale, but the bright circles of artificial color on his cheeks well made up for that lack. "You owe me nothing, Your Majesty," he said, and bowing over her hand, kissed her knuckles exactly as Paqual had. She drew away as quickly as she could. " 'Twas my duty and my honor as your ardent admirer."

She smiled. It seemed amazing that she could still do so on cue. "Tell me, Your Highness, what brought you to Sedonia?"

"I heard there was a carnival on your fair shores."

"Have you no carnivals in Romnia?"

His cheeks seemed to brighten under the ruse. "My ship needed to take on provisions."

She remained silent. He was a poor liar.

"And . . ." he added, "I had business here in Skilan."

She almost closed her eyes to the ridiculousness. "So threefold reasons then."

"Yes."

"And it was pure coincidence that put you at that exact spot at that exact moment?"

His lips opened and closed for the briefest moment. "I believe it was an act of God," he said.

"Yes." She glanced toward the window. "God must be very bored."

Nicol poured himself a bit of sherry with his left hand. His right arm was bound up against his chest. The bandage looked starkly white against the dark skin of his neck.

Tatiana watched him. "Does it hurt?" she asked.

He pulled his gaze from the window, saluted her with the glass and drank the contents. "Only when I'm not drunk." He sounded even more jaded than she remembered, and far more tired.

"Did you find the girl?"

"Birgit?"

Tatiana nodded.

"No," he said. His voice was slightly slurred. Perhaps he was already drunk. "I believe now that she did not disappear into the crowd as I suspected, but hid beneath the carriage." He chuckled a little, as if amused by some dark humor she did not understand and lifted his glass in a sort of salute. "I will not find her." He gazed out the window. "Not Megs."

She felt herself go cold. "Megs?" she said. "Her name was Megs?"

Nicol glanced up at her sharp tone, then shrugged his hale shoulder. "'Tis hard to say exactly. She seemed to have a host of names. The more I learned of her the less I knew."

"You said she was a barmaid. 'Tis what you told me."

"Aye, 'tis what she said at first—when I caught her nipping my pockets."

It seemed as if the world was spinning slowly off course. Her counterpart, the girl she had put on her throne, was a pickpocket, and not just any pickpocket, but the very lass who had stolen MacTavish's brooch. "She stole from you, Nicol? You put a thief on my throne?"

He glanced at her, and for a moment a fraction of his usual levity shone in his eyes. "A very clever thief, Anna. Not only could she steal a pocket watch in a moment's time, but she can deceive with the barest effort." A shadow crossed his features, but he shrugged it away. "And she was beaut . . ." He stopped himself, but his gaze remained on her face. "You must admit, she looked astoundingly like you. I can't help but believe that you would be much alike in the same situation. But I am sorry." He paused. "I should not have put you in such a situation, though I admit, I hoped you would learn the value of the common man."

"You are an amazing person, Nicol," she said. "A viscount who is also a champion of the people."

For a moment she thought he would argue, but he did not. Instead, he raised his glass in a sort of toast. "Aye," he said, "a viscount and a champion. What an unlikely combination."

She frowned at him, and he grinned.

"You would have liked her, Anna, had you known her. Whether she was a thief or a countess."

Perhaps Tatiana would have argued six months ago. But now . . . "So she is free," she said.

His mouth quirked slightly, as though he knew her meaning, but would not address it. "I won't find her," he said. "Not unless she wishes to be found." He filled his glass again. "And since she has your crown and half the royal jewels, there's little enough for her to return for."

Something about his tone caught her attention. Or was it the cast of his eyes? "Are you in love with her, Nicol?"

He raised his brows. "Since when did you begin wondering about others, Anna?"

The room went silent. "Have I been so selfish?"

He laughed, but the sound was empty. "Yes, you have."

She nodded, thinking far more than she cared to think. "I will be choosing a husband soon."

He was watching her carefully. She was just as careful to let nothing show on her face.

"What do you know of the prince of Romnia?" she asked.

"Ahh, Prince Edward." He drank again. "Let me think. He plays the lute like an angel, I am told. Oh, and I've heard he dances divinely."

She watched him for a moment. "And have I been *that* shallow?"

His dark eyes were somber, and maybe, behind the bored veneer, there was sadness, desperation even.

"No," he said, "you have not."

"Then tell me what you know of him."

He watched her for several seconds, and for that same span of time, it seemed he could read her thoughts, her doubts, her fears. "He couldn't shoot a pigeon out of his own ear without a cannon and a full battalion."

"Luck is a strange phenomenon at times," she said.

"And rarely seen in such astounding proportions."

"Then who shot the would-be assassin?"

"That I don't know."

"Can you find out?"

He nodded without hesitation.

"And can you learn who told the prince to be there at that precise moment?"

He settled himself into a chair. "Your time away has made you suspicious."

"As I said, I will be choosing a husband soon."

"And you would know whom to trust."

"Or at least whom to distrust the least."

He smiled a little, that roguish grin that was his alone. "MacTavish—" he began, but she cut him off in an instant.

"Not MacTavish."

The smile disappeared and his dark eyes narrowed slightly. "What did he do to you, Anna?"

She didn't answer immediately and he rose slowly, setting his drink aside. He was lean and handsome, dark of skin and hair, and as elegant as a Venetian waltz, but there was something in his eyes that made him seem suddenly dangerous. Her Nicol. Perhaps she didn't know him so well as she thought. Perhaps she didn't know anyone.

"Did he hurt you?" he asked.

"No," she said and turned abruptly away so she couldn't see the emotions she failed to control. "But he is not interested in . . ." She caught herself and straightened. "The match would not be in Sedonia's best interests."

"Sedonia's best interests."

"Yes."

"And what does Sedonia need, Anna? A king with half your wit and none of your strength."

"It needs a king who can better my people's lot."

He watched her carefully. "What did MacTavish—"

"I do not think it is your place to question me, Nicol."

"Nay, that would be a husband's place," he said. "If he had the nerve. MacTavish seems the type—"

She interrupted him quickly. "I am asking for your help," she said. "Will you give it?"

"Help." He watched her too closely. She held his gaze with some effort. "Aye," he said. "I will help you. I will always help you, whether you want it or not."

Chapter 31

❧❧

"**M**y lord." Peters bowed perfunctorily. His face was pale and solemn, his eyes wide. "It is good to have you home."

Cairn grunted as he pushed past his lieutenant. His mood was blacker than hell.

"What's wrong?" Burr's tone sounded no more congenial, and Peters stiffened even more.

"I fear we've had a bit of trouble here at Westheath, my lord."

"Trouble?" Burr rumbled.

Peters swallowed. "Some days past, Maid Carolyn thought she saw Wheaton in the village."

Cairn's spine stiffened. He waited.

"We tried to follow him, but he was gone. Like a shadow really."

"But all is well?" Burr asked. "No one was injured?"

"No . . ." Peters said, but the single word was uncertain. "No one was injured . . . so far as we know."

Burroun's scowl deepened. "What the devil does that mean?"

Cairn would not have thought the man could get paler. He would have been wrong again. Damn!

"The lass called Gem . . ." Peters paused. Silence fell like a cannonball into the room, and in that silence, Burr stepped forward and grasped the lieutenant by the front of his tunic.

"What about Gem?"

"She's gone, my lord."

"Gone!"

"Aye. One of the serving maids thought she heard something in your chambers, my lord. But when she checked, no one was there. Still . . ." He paused again.

Burr shook him like a rat. "Still, what?"

"She felt as if she were being watched."

"Watched?"

"Aye. Then later Cormick thought he saw the shadow of a man in the hallway near the girl's room. We kept a guard there all the while and one below the nearest window, but when we checked . . ." He swallowed again. "She was gone."

Burr let the man's feet settle onto the floor. A muscle ground in his jaw. "Was she forced? Or did she go of her own accord?"

"I do not know, my lord."

"When was this?" Cairn asked.

"Two days past."

"And you've searched for her?"

"Aye, my liege. We have searched diligently. But we've found no sign. Neither of her nor Wheaton."

Burr was atypically silent.

"But no one was hurt?" Cairn asked.

"No, my lord." There was another pause.

Burr reached for him again. Peters stepped back. "But Lord Burroun's stallion is gone."

The Norseman's eyes narrowed slightly, then he turned like a man of steel and left the room.

It was some days later that Cairn found Burr in the kitchen. The Norseman had been gone since the night of their return from Sedonia, but he had not found the girl called Gem. Nor had they seen any sign of Wheaton. Just now Burr was sitting alone on a stool near a thick slab table and didn't turn at the sound of his lord's approach.

Instead, he emptied his tankard and wiped the back of his hand across his mouth. In the giant hearth behind him, embers still glowed bright. A red-cored faggot popped and sizzled. The scent of cinnamon and cloves was heavy in the warm air.

"Burroun," Cairn said, and pulled up a stool next to his. "I've no wish to spoil your fun, but I have to tell you, you're not a drinking man."

Burr shrugged. "I believe you're wrong there, lad, but reality's a bit blurrier every minute." He refilled his tankard and drank again.

Cairn watched him a moment, then sat down. "Give me that," he said, and took the mug from the giant's hand. It was not Westheath's best brew, but he finished it in a moment and set the tankard aside. "Damn them," he said quietly.

Burr turned toward him with slow deliberation. "Them?" he asked.

"You think you're the only one who's been wronged, Norseman?"

A muscle worked in Burr's jaw. "She took me steed," he said, and nodded. "The one thing she knew I valued."

Cairn shrugged. "She wished to escape. It only makes sense. You'd do the same yourself."

Burr glowered into his empty mug. "She doesn't ride."

"Maybe Wheaton took the horse, forced her to go with him."

He paled for a moment and his fist tightened around the mug, but he shook his head finally. "More likely she told him just what steed was mine. More likely they're laughing over tales of an oversized Viking who—" He ground his teeth and filled the mug again. "I'd have thought I was too old to be made a fool by a scrap of a thing like her."

"Someone once told me that all men are fools where women are concerned."

Burr snorted a laugh. "He sounds like a fool."

"Better a fool than a liar," Cairn said, and, grabbing a new mug from the table, poured himself a full cup.

"Shut the hell up," Burr rumbled.

Cairn drank. "Some might think it unwise to speak like that to one's laird."

"And some would be an arse," Burr said. "And a dolt."

"Are you implying something in your own subtle way, Burr?"

"Aye," the Norseman growled, and leaned close. "I'm implying that you're an arse and a dolt."

Cairn drank thoughtfully. "Any particular reason?"

Burr rolled a jaundiced eye at him. "Because she's gone."

"And you blame her disappearance on me?"

"Who else? You're the damned laird."

"And you were in love with her."

"In love w—" Burr began, but he stopped himself immediately and paled just a little. "It could be that you are the stupidest creature ever to walk the face of the earth."

Cairn shrugged. It was possible. In the past few days he had come to a similar conclusion.

"The lass is gone, sent away by your own hand, and you don't even know who I'm talking about."

"Tatiana." He said the name slowly, trying it out on his tongue. It fit her so damnably well.

"Aye. Tatiana," Burr said. "The princess of Sedonia."

Cairn felt his muscles tighten up one by one. "She lied."

Silence fell softly into the room.

"Do you miss her, lad?"

"Miss her! 'Twas the same thing Lady Nedra asked. Nay, I don't miss her! She was—"

"And you do not lie," Burr interupted. "Is that your point?"

Cairn stared into his beer. There wasn't nearly enough. "A princess . . ." He choked a laugh. "Hardly do I need another fine lady to ruin me life."

"Clearly you can do the job well enough on your own," Burr said.

"Huh!" Cairn chortled. "Look at who's calling the donkey an arse."

Burr nodded rumatively. "Aye," he said. "You might well say so, lad, for I have made a host of mistakes. I left her alone here, and said she was safe in my—" He drank again. "I, too, visited Lady Nedra where she assists in the infirmary. But even she cannot guess where the lass has gone, though she has an uncanny way about her." He snorted a laugh. "The girl would have been better in the care of an old woman than in mine. She should not have come here. Should not have trusted . . ." He paused and emptied his tankard. "Aye, I made me own mistakes, but I would right them if I could."

"What are you saying, old man?"

Burr turned on him with a snarl. "I'm saying you're sitting here like a sack of moldy meal when you should be setting sail for Sedonia this very minute."

Cairn's throat tightened like a knot. The past three days were a blur of vague, unnamed agony. He could not seem to breathe properly, could not function. But she had lied from the start, and the truth had revealed a truth even worse than he had dreaded. She was not just some grand lady, capable of deception. She was a princess, bred to manipulate, born to betray. And yet . . . leaving her behind . . . watching her country fade into the mist had been . . . He winced. But perhaps Burr was right. Perhaps there was a way to right the wrongs, to fill the emptiness where his soul had been. Perhaps . . . Hope bloomed like wild orchids in his chest, but old wounds gnawed at him, crushing the blossoms.

"She's a liar and a noblewoman," he said. "Just like Eliz—"

Burr slammed down his mug. The table shook, but the Norseman failed to notice as he leaned toward his laird. "She's a fucking saint for not killing you when she had a chance, you lackwit. And you're too much the coward to admit it."

"I don't mind you calling me a lackwit," Cairn said. "But I don't care to be called a coward."

Burr straightened slowly. "Don't you now?"

"Nay."

"Then you can admit the truth?"

"And what truth is that, old man?"

"That she was naught but good for you."

"Good—"

"Aye. She opened your eyes, lad. You were all but dead before she came along."

"I had Wheaton in my grasp before she came along."

"Wheaton!" Burr scoffed. "Aye, he is a thorn in your side. But he is a small thorn. While you are the laird." He tightened his huge fist against the tabletop. "Chosen to lead, born to rule."

Cairn laughed. "Olaf Burroun, subscribing to Teleerian propaganda."

"Is that what she thought? Is that what she believed? Pro-

paganda? Aye, that was most probably it. She was too much
the fool to think on her own, so she believed what others told
her. She believed you were strong. That you were trustwor-
thy. That is why she came here at the outset, is that it?"

Cairn shrugged and Burr swore.

"Damn you!" he said, and smacked the table with his bare
hand. "She came to offer an alliance. She came because she
has a mind of her own. She came because, despite what she'd
heard—and she'd heard a good deal, lad, don't think she
didn't—she thought you were better than the average fool
who can prop a crown on his head. She believed you were
one to better the world. Not one to sit on his arse and do nothing." Burr shook his head. "It saddens me to see she was
wrong," he said, and rose to leave, but Cairn caught him by
the arm.

"I am laird," he said. "And I will rule as I see fit."

"As you see fit," Burr scoffed. "You don't even have the
courage to get her back, boy, when you know Teleere would
benefit from the alliance. When you know you are worthless
without her."

A dozen scenes flashed through Cairn's mind. She was in
each one, her face like a beacon, her voice like an incanta-
tion. She made him whole. She made him worthy, but he
would be damned before he would beg her to return.

Burr stared at him, then snorted as if he could read the
younger man's mind. "So Elizabeth has won. You are a
weakling, lad."

Anger seared Cairn, fueled by frustration, fanned by self-
doubt. But here was a course of action he could take. A
means of proving himself while admitting nothing. "I can
take you, old man," he said.

The giant grinned, showing the first sign of joy since their
return to Teleere. "I'll tell you what then, lad. We'll have a go
at it. Bare hands. No weapons. If you best me, you can sit on

your arse and pity yourself till you're rotting in the grave. But if I beat you . . ." His grin widened. "The lads should be able to wake you up before you reach her shores."

Cairn rose slowly to his feet. Hope had returned, making his heart feel too large for his chest, making his lungs feel tight. The floor tilted slightly beneath his unsteady stance, but he gave Burroun a smile and as he motioned for him to begin. He only prayed the Norseman wasn't too drunk to best him.

"So you are saying that Prince Edward did not shoot the assassin," Tatiana said.

Nicol shrugged. He looked tired, older. But maybe she did, too, for she felt weary.

"Edward fired a gun," he said. "But I believe it was one of his guards who killed Fitzgerald."

She glanced out the window. "Might the guard be in the market for a bride?"

Nicol smiled wryly. She could feel the expression, though she didn't turn toward him. "I haven't asked. But I hear Lord Malborg is."

"Lord Malborg?" She turned her gaze wearily back to the viscount. "Is he the suitor *du jour*?"

"He waits in the morning room as we speak."

"Well." She didn't sigh, didn't cry, merely gathered her skirts and hardened her heart. "I had best paint on my smile then," she said, and rose to return to her rooms, but Nicol stopped her.

"Tell me," he said, "if you weren't the princess of Sedonia, would you have remained in Teleere?"

And just like that, she weakened. Her mind drifted in an instant. She was in MacTavish's arms, feeling the strength of him surround her. Feeling the rightness of their union. But it was not to be. For a thousand reasons. "It matters little," she said, and straightened her back as she turned away. "For I *am* the princess."

Her ladies followed her silently back into her chambers, where she was coifed and powdered and primped, like a carriage horse on parade, with no more say, no more real value. Finally, unable to bear their attentions any longer, she sent them away and sat staring numbly at herself in the mirror.

There she was, Princess Tatiana. But who was she inside? Or did it matter? Nay, for she was Sedonia's sovereign head first and foremost. She would do what she must. She would marry whom she should. She—

"I liked you better as Megs."

She turned with a start, her heart racing. Gone for a moment was the cool princess, and in her place was a ragamuffin lass who hoped foolishly and loved wildly.

"MacTavish," she said. In her mind she wept his name, but despite her emotions, her tone sounded smooth, level. Lady training at its best. "What are you doing here?" There was calm reproach in her voice though her heart felt tight in her chest.

He stared at her, his eyes an intense blue. Her joints felt strangely loose. "I would give the same question to you, lass."

"These are my private chambers, MacTavish. Surely you do not resent my being here."

"Nay." He moved away from the wall like water, all long smooth motions. "'Tis what was in the morning room that I resent."

"Lord Mal—" she began, then, "*was*?"

"I fear he won't be able to consider a union with you after all, lass."

Her eyes widened despite herself. "What did you do to him?"

A muscle jumped in his jaw. It had been several days since

he'd shaved, and there was a purplish bruise on his cheek, making him look feral and dangerous. "I didn't kill him if that's your concern."

She relaxed with an effort and raised one brow. Perhaps she smiled a little, for in her soul there was a tiny flame of hope. "Nay," she said, and turned to open a window as she grappled for nonchalance. " 'Twas not my concern."

"He lisps."

She glanced over her shoulder to look at him. "I beg your pardon?"

"Lord Malborg. He lisps."

"Yes I know." She nodded. "And his country has three-score warships to protect his shores. I believe a bit of lisping can be overlooked in—"

"Teleere has twice that."

Her hands shook like windblown sails. She steadied them carefully. When had she begun thinking in nautical terms? she wondered. But the answer came immediately. Ever since she'd slept in his arms aboard the *Fat Molly*. She pushed the memories aside. "Malborg has a thriving timber industry," she said.

"Teleere has wool. Tons of it. The finest in all of Europe."

"Malborg has close ties to the Finnish throne. His diplomats are ever working to improve their relations with other countries. The possibilities are limitless."

He stared at her hard. She straightened her back. Like a mizzenmast, he would say.

"Teleere has me," he intoned.

Her chest literally ached, and it took every bit of her wavering control to keep herself from falling into his arms. "What are you suggesting, MacTavish?" She held his gaze hard and fast. It was his turn to glance toward the window, his turn to pace in that direction.

"My country is strong," he said, turning back. "Our resources are plentiful, our people are many and hardworking."

He paused. She waited, not urging, not assisting.

He scowled. "But we haven't the artisans Sedonia boasts. Nor the mines."

"I ask again, MacTavish, what are you suggesting?"

"I may not be polished, Megs, but I am strong and tempered, and I can stay the course."

She didn't respond.

"I . . ." He shifted his gaze rapidly to the window again. "I may not be refined, but I come from hardy stock and . . . dammit! I don't lisp."

She paced toward the east wall and ran her fingers lightly over a tapestry that hung there. "I know your fine attributes, MacTavish," she said. "Just as I know your faults."

The muscle in his jaw jumped again.

"What I am wondering is . . . why have you breached my private chambers to list them for me?"

He tightened his fists. Muscles clenched and danced up his forearms past his elbows. He had not changed from his favorite attire to come here. Nay, he wore naught but his plaid and a simple tunic rolled up at the sleeves and open at the neck to show the taut sinews of his sun-browned throat. She steadied herself.

"I think you know why I am come, lass," he murmured. There was a healing wound on his temple. She was tempted to kiss it away.

She shook her head instead. "No," she said. "I do not know why you have come, so you'd best tell me."

He glanced out the window again, but she doubted he saw past the heavy pane to the bailey below. Never had she seen him unable to meet her gaze. "I'm suggesting a union."

"A union?" She managed to sound baffled, but her heart was clanging in her chest.

"A union," he gritted, "between your country and mine."

"Ahh." She could not breathe, but she managed to give him a prim smile. "So you wish to trade with Sedonia."

His face reddened slightly, darkening his features. "You know what I wish for."

"Nay, I do not, for I distinctly remember you saying Sedonia had nothing to offer Teleere."

"I have been better educated since then," he said, and rubbed the knuckles on his left hand. She realized for the first time that they had been scraped raw.

"Have you?" she asked, and strode past, watching him from the corner of her eye. "By whom?"

"Lady Nedra had a few things to say to me. She is well and assisting the physicians," he said, then cleared his throat. "And Burr shared his knowledge."

"And pray, my lord, what is it you have learned?"

"That I can't live—" He stopped himself, but his body was tense, his teeth gritted. "Sedonia has much that is good about it."

She shrugged and raised her hands, palms up. Her throat felt tight. "Then we shall conduct trade," she said. "Have your chancellor contact mine. Now, if you will excuse me, I have a suitor to . . ." She brushed past him, but he caught her arm and pulled her toward him, stopping her words.

"Lass." The word was nothing more than a harsh whisper, but somehow that whisper echoed in her soul, raising goose-flesh in its wake. She stood frozen, mesmerized by his nearness, trapped by his touch. "Do you deny that want me?"

She couldn't speak, couldn't move. But finally she managed. "You?" she said. "I thought we were but discussing the good of our countries."

" 'Tis too late to act the fool with me, lass. For I know you too well."

Anger raged through her. She jerked her arm from his grasp. "You do not know me at all, MacTavish."

"And whose fault is that?" he asked, motioning wildly. "I have asked a host of questions, but you have lied at every turn."

"My country's security lay in another's hands, and you made no pretense about your disdain for Sedonia. Neither was I to believe that you were above ransoming me should you learn my true identity. I had no choice but to lie. My—"

"You have a choice now, princess," he said, and held her gaze like an iron vise. "Tell me true, do you want me or not?"

The horrid truth trembled on her lips, but she held it back and drew a careful breath. "Why are you here, MacTavish?"

He glanced toward the door and shuffled his feet like a lad caught pinching fresh scones. "Because I lost a battle."

She shook her head in bafflement, but he went on before she could question him.

"I have told you why I have come, lass. Don't—"

"You have told me naught except that our countries should ally. But in the past you swore Sedonia had nothing for you. Why now the change of heart?"

A tick danced in his jaw, but he didn't turn away. "I am a pirate, not a diplomat. I spoke in haste. My . . ." He clenched his fists again, as if they were sore. "My advisors have convinced me to see the wisdom in binding Teleere and—"

"*Convinced* you?" It was that one word that caught her attention, that one word that rang false. "No one convinces you of anything, MacTavish. You weigh the facts and you do as you will. And so I ask again, why are you here?"

"Tell me one truth, Megs," he said. "Why did you first come to Teleere?"

She considered lying, considered skirting the truth, but there had been enough of that. Too much in fact, and what had she gained from it? She raised her chin slightly and bore down on honesty. "I had learned a good deal about you," she said slowly. "Nicol visited your country many times and told me tales, and what I learned I—" She turned away, pulling her arm from his grasp, for she could no longer hold his gaze. "I knew you were rough and opinionated, but you reminded me of my uncle, the late king, and—"

"So Burr was right? You sought me for marriage?" The question spurted out like the gasp of an astonished lad. She turned slowly back to him, her hands gripping each other for support.

"Why have you come?"

He shook his head, obviously trying to clear it before speaking again. "Teleere—"

"Teleere is not the issue here. Neither is Burr, nor any of the score of men you could have sent in your stead. Why are *you* here?"

"Listen, lass, I am not on trial!"

"Aren't you?" She raised her chin and stared at him, wrapping herself in every thread of regal dignity she could find. Later, she would collapse. "You will tell me your feelings, MacTavish, the innermost thoughts of your heart, or you will leave, and I will marry another. Do you understand me?"

His mouth quirked. "My country—"

"Your country has not breached the sanctity of my chambers. You have. Why?"

"We can ship—"

"Damn you, MacTavish!" she swore and gripping his tunic in her fist, pulled herself up to his face. "Why have you come?"

They stood inches apart. Every fiber in her being thrummed with life. Every nerve ached for satisfaction. He made her daft, drove her past her reserves, and she hated him for that, for she could not even convince him to share a small bit of himself.

"Elizabeth's betrayal cut me deep, lass, I'll not deny it," he said, his voice quiet.

Someone knocked on the door. They ignored it.

"Revenge was everything," he admitted. "Revenge for my stolen brooch, revenge for her betrayal. I wasn't above using you to make Wheaton pay, but now . . . Now I see there is more to life than vengeance." He touched her face. "I swore I would never trust another noble lady. But you were not noble. Not when you were in my arms. You were Megs."

The knocking came again, louder now.

"Think of what we could achieve if we unite, lass. Your knowledge and my strength. Your courage and my skills. Your blood and my brawn. We could right the wrongs, strengthen the lower classes, temper the nobility. I will teach you the way of the sea and mayhap . . ." He winced as if pained. "You could instruct me in horsemanship. We would be all but invincible."

"I'll not marry you to become invincible, MacTavish. 'Tis not—"

"Then marry me because I cannot live without you."

She heard herself gasp, felt her knees weaken.

"Damn your title," he said. "Damn your heritage. Damn your whole country. I need you, whether your name is Megs or Tatiana or Captain Woodcock."

The pounding on the door became more insistent, but in that moment he pulled her into his arms and kissed her.

The door burst open.

A score of men rushed into her room, weapons at the ready.

"Stand back! Release her!" demanded the captain of the guard, but MacTavish turned slowly toward them, not retreating an inch.

"Shoot him!" Paqual shouted, striding into the chamber.

MacTavish turned his gaze slowly toward the counselor. "Lord Paqual," he said. "How was your visit with Martinez?"

The blood left Paqual's face in a rush. "If you will not shoot him, I will!" he hissed.

Tatiana stepped in front of MacTavish, her arms outstretched. "Shoot my betrothed, and I swear by all that is holy, I will see you hanged this very day if I have to tie the rope myself."

"Your . . ." Paqual stumbled back a pace. "Betrothed!"

"Aye," she said. "You have manipulated and murdered, but you have lost, and Sedonia has won. We will ally ourselves with a great force, with Teleere and her master."

"'Tis not for you to decide, girl," he hissed, stepping forward. "I have made you what you are, and you'll not ruin my plans by binding yourself to a bastard pirate."

"Better a pirate than a traitor," she said. "I know your plans, Paqual. You hoped to make me believe MacTavish had hired my assassin. You planned for me to fall into the arms of the prince of Romnia. But you are not so clever as you think, and you are naught but a murderer.

"Take him to the dungeon," she said to her guards. "And hold him there until his trial."

They did so, and he went, squawking all the way.

"Your Majesty." Lady Mary bowed nervously. "If Lord MacTavish will meet with your advisors, they could discuss the wedding plans."

"I will meet with them shortly," Cairn said.

"It is surely not proper—"

"Not proper." Tatiana smiled as she shook her head. "Nay, it is not. But it is what I want. He is what I want."

Cairn's gaze felt hot on her face.

"Your Majesty, you cannot—"

"I can and I shall."

"Get out," Cairn ordered, then he turned as if they were no longer there, and kissed her.

There were gasps and hisses, but in a moment the room was empty, for Nicol had arrived to usher them out. The door closed firmly behind them.

Tatiana reached up to softly touch Cairn's face. "You came."

"I may be a lackwit and a coward, but I'm not dead. You didn't think I'd let you marry another, did you?"

"Yes," she said. "I did."

"Then you don't know me very well, princess," he said, and, lifting her into his arms, carried her to their bed.

"Perhaps I do not," she agreed, and slipped her hand beneath his tunic, "but I intend to remedy that this very instant."

"You are everything I want," he murmured. "Lady, urchin, thief."

"I am not a thief, MacTavish," she reminded him.

"You stole me heart."

"But not your brooch."

"That I may yet retrieve, for I've a feeling we've not seen the last of Magical Megs. But this much I promise you, lass—my heart is forever yours," he said, and kissed her.

A romance from Avon Books is always a welcome addition at the
❧   beach, the park, the barbecue . . .   ❧

Look for these enchanting love stories in August.

TO LOVE A SCOTTISH LORD by Karen Ranney
An Avon Romantic Treasure

The proud and brooding Hamish MacRae has returned to his beloved Scotland wanting nothing more than to be left alone. But Mary Gilly has invaded his lonely castle, and while it's true that this pretty healer is beyond compare, it will take more than her miraculous potions to awaken his heart.

TALK OF THE TOWN by Suzanne Macpherson
An Avon Contemporary Romance

Nothing puts a damper on a wedding day quite like discovering your Mr. Right is *Mr. Totally Beyond Wrong*, which is why Kelly Atwood knocks him flat and boards a bus to tiny Paradise, Washington. One look at the gorgeous outsider and attorney Sam Grayson gets hot around his too-tight collar, because this runaway bride is definitely disturbing his peace.

ONCE A SCOUNDREL by Candice Hern
An Avon Romance

It was bad enough when Anthony Morehouse thought he had won a piece of furniture in a card game, but when he discovers that *The Ladies' Fashionable Cabinet* is actually a women's magazine, he can't wait to get rid of it. Then he sees beautiful Edwina Parrish behind the editor's desk, and Tony is about to make the biggest gamble of all.

ALL MEN ARE ROGUES, by Sari Robins
An Avon Romance

When Evelyn Amherst agrees to her father's dying request, she can scarcely imagine the world of danger she is about to enter — or that it will bring her tantalizingly close to Lord Justin Barclay. Here is a man to turn a young lady's head, but Evelyn refuses to be diverted from her mission, especially not by this passionate yearning for Justin's embrace.

REL 0703

Discover Contemporary Romances
at Their Sizzling Hot Best
from Avon Books

WHEN NIGHT FALLS   by Cait London
0-06-000180-1/$5.99 US/$7.99 Can

BREAKING ALL THE RULES   by Sue Civil-Brown
0-06-050231-2/$5.99 US/$7.99 Can

GETTING HER MAN   by Michele Albert
0-380-82053-6/$5.99 US/$7.99 Can

I'VE GOT YOU, BABE   by Karen Kendall
0-06-050232-0/$5.99 US/$7.99 Can

RISKY BUSINESS   by Suzanne Macpherson
0-380-82103-6/$5.99 US/$7.99 Can

THEN COMES MARRIAGE   by Christie Ridgway
0-380-81896-5/$5.99 US/$7.99 Can

STUCK ON YOU   by Patti Berg
0-380-82005-6/$5.99 US/$7.99 Can

THE WAY YOU LOOK TONIGHT by MacKenzie Taylor
0-380-81938-4/$5.99 US/$7.99 Can

INTO DANGER   by Gennita Low
0-06-052338-7/$5.99 US/$7.99 Can

IF THE SLIPPER FITS   by Elaine Fox
0-06-051721-2/$5.99 US/$7.99 Can

CRO 0203

Avon Romantic Treasures

*Unforgettable, enthralling love stories,
sparkling with passion and adventure
from Romance's bestselling authors*

Have you ever dreamed of writing a romance?

*And have you ever wanted
to get a romance published?*

Perhaps you have always wondered how to
become an Avon romance writer?
We are now seeking the best and brightest undiscovered
voices. We invite you to send us your query letter to
avonromance@harpercollins.com

What do you need to do?

Please send no more than two pages telling us
about your book. We'd like to know its setting—is it
contemporary or historical—and a bit about the hero,
heroine, and what happens to them.

Then, if it is right for Avon we'll ask to see part of the
manuscript. Remember, it's important that you have
material to send, in case we want to see your story quickly.

Of course, there are no guarantees of publication,
but you never know unless you try!

*We know there is new talent just waiting
to be found! Don't hesitate . . . send us
your query letter today.*

*The Editors
Avon Romance*